RICH GIRL, POOR GIRL

Val Wood

CORGI BOOKS

TRANSWORLD PUBLISHERS
61–63 Uxbridge Road, London W5 5SA
A Random House Group Company
www.rbooks.co.uk

RICH GIRL, POOR GIRL
A CORGI BOOK: 9780552156806

First published in Great Britain
in 2009 by Bantam Press
an imprint of Transworld Publishers
Corgi edition published 2010

Addresses for Random House Group Ltd companies outside
the UK can be found at: www.randomhouse.co.uk
The Random House Group Ltd Reg. No. 954009

Penguin Random House is committed to a sustainable future for
our business, our readers and our planet. This book is made from
Forest Stewardship Council® certified paper.

MIX
Paper from
responsible sources
FSC® C018179

Printed and bound in Great Britain by Clays Ltd, St Ives plc

Typeset in 11/13½pt New Baskerville by
Kestrel Data, Exeter, Devon.

10 9

For Peter

'It's not the falling down that counts;
it's the getting up again.'

ACKNOWLEDGEMENTS

With special thanks to my daughters, Ruth and Catherine, my grandson, Alex, my editor, Linda Evans, and the Transworld team who through their loving support have helped me through my dark times.

Books for general reading
History of the Town and Port of Hull, James Joseph Sheehan, John Green, Beverley, 1866
The Glorious Grouse, Brian P Martin, David & Charles, London, 1990
The Victorian House, Judith Flanders, HarperCollins, London, 2003

CHAPTER ONE

In the last few days of the year 1860 there was thick ice in the Humber, and for the following two weeks navigation was hazardous. The conditions were unprecedented, the locals said, and all agreed that the whole year had been an extremely difficult one.

There had been many fires in the old town of Hull that year, but the worst had been in March when at two o'clock one morning a raging fire tore through a wine merchant's warehouse near the ancient Holy Trinity church, completely destroying the building. Casks burned and bottles of fine wine shattered, and alcoholic vapours shrouded the street.

In October the steamer *Arctic* was wrecked with the loss of six lives, and it was the general opinion that it would be a relief to see the end of the year. Surely things could not get much worse.

*   *   *

On the evening of 23 December it was snowing in the poorer part of Hull. The pristine flakes settled as grey sludge across the dismal courts and alleyways, adding an austere and shadowy gloom to the misery within the dilapidated buildings, which housed the malnourished, the sick and the despairing.

'Fetch Granny Walters,' Polly's mother groaned. 'And tell her to be quick.'

Sixteen-year-old Polly stared wide-eyed at her mother. 'You're nivver up 'spout, Ma? You said there'd be no more after 'last time.'

'Never mind what I said,' her mother gasped. 'How to stop 'em, that'd be a fine thing. Now go . . . afore I bleed to death.'

'That Sonny Blake or whoever it was'll kill you,' Polly shouted as she grabbed a worn shawl and headed for the door. 'They'll be 'death o' you.'

'Tell me summat I don't know, girl,' her mother muttered. She staggered towards a metal pail and retched and retched until her insides felt as if they were on fire, her throat was raw and her eyes were burning hot slits in her pinched and pale face.

Across on the other side of town it was also snowing. The feather-like flakes drifted down and landed so gently that they piled in soft layers, until it seemed that a flimsy white blanket had transformed the elegant houses into a mystical fantasy scene.

'Mama!' Rosalie gazed out of the second-floor window on to the street below. 'It's still snowing! Perhaps we'll have a white Christmas like the ones on the Christmas cards.'

'Yes. Perhaps we will.' Behind her daughter's back her mother grimaced in pain. 'Rosalie dear, ring for Martha and ask her to send for Mrs Dawson.'

Rosalie turned to her mother and took an open-mouthed, shallow breath. Mrs Dawson had been coming regularly to see her mother. Rosalie knew perfectly well why she came, but was not expected to comment on the reason, and did not.

She pulled the bell rope and with gentle concern asked her mother if she wouldn't like to sit down as she looked a little tired.

Her mother shook her head. 'I'd rather walk about,' she murmured. 'I feel rather restless.'

Oh, Rosalie thought in some trepidation. An early sign: restlessness with an urge to nest-build. Some weeks before, whilst searching for a book to while away a wet afternoon, she had found on the top shelf in her father's study a volume packed with information which fully explained her mother's present indisposition. Rosalie's father was a military man and not due home for several months, so she had taken

11

the book to her room and completed her education regarding the mysteries of the human body and the union of a man and a woman, which had hitherto been an enigma cloaked in secrecy.

When Martha knocked, Rosalie met her at the door and asked her to fetch Mrs Dawson straight away. Fifteen minutes later Mrs Dawson was directing Mrs Kingston to retire to her room and telling Rosalie to ask Martha to bring up extra sheets and blankets and boil a pan of water.

'Mama!' Rosalie whispered. 'Is it not too early? I mean – for a child to be delivered?'

Her mother gasped and clutched her chest. 'Rosalie! What would you know? How can you speak so?'

'I know that you are expecting a child, Mama,' Rosalie said. 'Of course I do. I'm sixteen.' She didn't add that she had worked out how long it had been since her father's last leave, and knew that it wasn't yet time to be delivered of a full-term infant. But of course she couldn't say so, not without giving away the knowledge she had acquired from the book, which she knew her mother would be horrified to hear she had read.

'Tittle-tattling servants,' her mother groaned as she was led up the stairs. 'There can be no secrets from them.'

Rosalie nodded as if in agreement. They would know, of course, but not a word had been breathed in her presence. The servants in this house were very discreet. 'I wish Father were here,' she said as she and Mrs Dawson helped her mother out of her dress before drawing her nightgown over her head.

Both her mother and the midwife drew in a breath of censure.

'Don't be ridiculous, Rosalie.' Her mother clutched the bed rail. 'He's the last person I would want right now. Now please leave, there's a good girl. This is no place for you.'

In the sitting room, Rosalie looked out of the window again. The snow was falling steadily and she was barely able to see beyond the flakes in the dim and eerie gloom from the gas lamp outside the front door. There were a few people about, hurrying along the pavement with their heads down, the men with their coat collars turned up and the women shrugging down into their muffs and furs.

She sighed. It was going to be a long evening. According to the book she had read it could take until tomorrow morning or even the following night for her mother to deliver. But she was perturbed. Her father had returned to his regiment in the middle of July, and even taking into account that he had arrived home at the end of June . . . She flushed. Really! She

13

shouldn't be thinking of such things. But she also recalled that her mother had been ill only last year and Mrs Dawson had been sent for then as well.

Rosalie was an only child. She had had a brother, but he had succumbed to diphtheria and died at three years old some six years before. Had there been other pregnancies, she wondered. There was no way of telling. Her mother's constitution was delicate and the doctor often visited.

She went up to her room. A fire had been lit and the curtains drawn. The room was decorated in colours she had chosen herself: cream walls, pale green upholstery and rose-coloured cushions. She turned up the lamp and selected a book to read, but she couldn't settle and after a few minutes got up to open the door so that she could hear any sounds of activity from her mother's room along the landing. She picked up her book again and drew her chair nearer the fire, but presently the words began to blur and her eyes closed.

'Miss Rosalie! Miss Rosalie!' Martha was gently shaking her shoulder. 'Wake up, miss.'

'Oh!' Rosalie sat up with a start, rubbing her eyes. 'What time is it?'

'Half past nine,' Martha said. 'Mrs Dawson's sent for 'doctor, Miss Rosalie. Your mother miscarried. Do you know what that means, miss?'

'Yes,' Rosalie said. 'She's lost the baby.' She blinked up at the servant. 'Is she all right? Mother, I mean?'

'No, miss.' Martha looked anxious. 'That's why we've sent for 'doctor. Mrs Dawson can't stop 'bleeding.'

Polly had been sitting on the stairs outside their room when Mrs Walters came out. 'You'd better go in to your ma, Polly. She's right sick. I don't know what to do for 'best. We could do wi' doctor. He'd know.'

'Doctor! Where'd we get 'money for 'doctor?' Polly trembled. 'And it's snowing. He'd nivver come out on a night like this. Not to us.'

'He might.' The old woman lifted up her lamp as she looked at Polly. 'I'll send our Nellie's lad if you like. But you'll have to pay him a copper for going.'

Polly blew out a breath. 'Wait a bit. I'll talk to Ma. See what she thinks.'

The old woman shook her head. 'She's in no fit state to think about owt,' she said. 'You'll have to mek 'decision.'

Polly was scared. What if her ma died? Why hadn't she told her she was pregnant? Whose bairn was it? She'd suspected that Sonny Blake and her mother might have been lovers in the past, even though he was younger, but Ma had maintained he was just a good friend. This was his doing, Polly decided in her anguish. Rat bag! Lecherous cur!

'Ma!' she whispered as she went into the room. Her mother was lying under a thin blanket on the mattress in the corner. A stub of candle was burning in a saucer, but there was no other light. The putrid air stank of blood and vomit. She knelt on the floor beside her. 'Have you lost 'bairn?'

'Yes.' Her mother's voice was barely audible. 'Lost a lot o' blood.'

'Shall I run for 'doctor? Will he come, do you think?'

Her mother didn't answer, then began to weep. 'I'm bleeding, Polly. She can't stop it.'

'I'll run for Dr James. Mebbe he'll come.'

'No.' Her mother reached out and Polly took hold of her hand. 'Don't leave me, Poll. Ask . . . Mrs Walters . . .' Her voice was full of tears.

'Yes.' Polly scrambled to her feet. 'I'll ask her.' She ran out on to the landing. 'Fetch him,' she urged. 'Tell him to run. I'll pay him.'

'He'll want 'money first,' Mrs Walters told her.

Polly felt in her skirt pocket. Nothing. She dashed back into the room and ran her hand along the mantelshelf. A coin.

'A ha'penny,' she said to the old woman. 'I'll give him more when I've got it. Tell him to be quick.'

She went back in to her mother and knelt beside her again. 'I don't suppose he'll be long,' she said reassuringly. 'He'll have finished his supper. It's not that late, I don't think. I heard 'clock strike nine a bit ago. How're you feeling now? A bit weak? You rest, then. Shut your eyes and try to sleep.'

She was babbling, she knew, but she had to talk to stop herself from crying. 'I'm going to ban that Sonny Blake from 'house,' she said, only half joking. 'I'll tell him when I see him that he's not to come near.'

A breathy whisper came from the bed and Polly leaned closer. 'Not his,' she heard her mother say. 'I've not . . . seen him in . . .'

'Then who . . .' Polly began, and then her eyes opened wide. How gullible I've been! Or have I not wanted to know that Ma might have been trying to earn money from— She daren't put the thought into words.

Her mother was still weeping. 'Dear God, forgive me . . . my sins. I . . . needed money, Polly. To buy bread . . .'

As the boy reached the doctor's house the carriage was pulling away. He hammered on the door. 'Yes?' The housekeeper frowned down at the thinly clad caller. 'Stop that noise. What do you want?'

'Doctor. Can he come? Straight away? It's

urgent.' He tossed a coin up in the air amongst the falling snow and caught it. 'Woman's had a miscarry or summat.'

'The doctor's out. That was his carriage. Give me 'address and I'll tell him when he gets back. But I can't promise; he's got others waiting for him.'

The address was off the High Street and she frowned. 'I don't know if he'll want to go down there at this time of night, not in this weather.'

'It's all right.' The boy wiped his nose on the back of his hand. 'Nobody much about. I'll wait if you like and show him.'

'Come back in an hour,' she told him. 'He should be home by then and we can ask him.'

'All right,' he said nonchalantly. 'See you in a bit.'

'Miss Kingston.' The doctor came out of the bedroom, clasping his hands. 'I'm afraid it isn't good news. No use beating about the bush. Your mother has aborted a pregnancy and is bleeding heavily. I can't staunch it and I'm sorry to say that I have done all I can.' He shook his head. 'I fear she has lost too much blood to sustain life.'

Rosalie heard him as if from afar and she put her hand on the wall to steady herself.

'What are you saying?' she breathed. 'She's not going to die?'

Dr James nodded gravely. 'I'm afraid she is. Sit with her to give her comfort,' he said. 'You are young, but not too young to give her solace. Then you must get in touch with your father. He will be given compassionate leave, I'm sure. Unless he is abroad.'

I don't know where he is, was Rosalie's first thought, except that he's not here. He's never here! He's a soldier first and foremost. I've heard him say that so often. I daren't go in! What will I say to Mama? How can I comfort her when I'm so afraid?

'Mrs Dawson will sit with you, my dear,' the doctor said kindly. 'I'm so sorry to leave you, but I have many patients waiting for me tonight. I'll come again as soon as I can.'

Rosalie didn't answer but walked past him into the bedroom.

'Come, m'dear,' Mrs Dawson said from her mother's bedside. 'There's nothing to be afraid of. Just think of your mother going to another life.'

'I've to go back in an hour,' the boy said to his grandmother. 'I just missed him.'

'It'll be too late,' Mrs Walters muttered. She went into the room where Polly sat on the floor with her head bent to her knees. 'Doctor's been sent for, Polly,' she said softly. 'He'll be here as soon as he can. He'd just gone off on another case.'

'To somebody wi' money, I expect,' Polly muttered. She blinked and gazed at her mother, who was lying quite still. 'Well, he needn't bother,' she choked. 'We don't need him now.'

CHAPTER TWO

Polly paced the floor, weeping and shivering, unwilling to believe what had happened. Why hadn't her mother told her? They always shared everything. And why hadn't she noticed that her mother was pregnant? She was so thin, she thought, but then they ate so little, and if Ma was only a few weeks gone she wouldn't have been able to tell. She wondered who the father was. Had her mother really been with a man just so that they could eat?

She put an old shawl on the uncarpeted floor and lay down on it, putting her arms round her head, and as a thin sliver of dawn broke dimly through the uncurtained window she fell asleep. Mrs Walters woke her at nine o'clock.

'I've sent for 'doctor again,' she said. 'He'll have to issue a sustificate. Cause o' death 'n' that. It's what he has to do,' she added as Polly shuddered. 'And then I'll look after her.'

'But it's Christmas Eve,' Polly muttered. 'They won't bury her at Christmas.'

'No, they won't,' her neighbour agreed. 'But they might on Boxing Day or 'day after.'

'Where will I go?' Polly whispered. 'I can't stay here.'

The thought of staying any longer in the same room as her mother, who was lying there covered with a sheet, sickened her. She felt heavy with grief, and now that she could no longer blame Sonny Blake for killing her mother she felt impotent with rage and sorrow.

'Bless you, bairn, you can stay wi' us. There'll be no goose for Christmas dinner, onny a joint o' pork, but you're welcome to come 'n' share it.'

'I won't be hungry,' Polly muttered. 'I feel sick.'

'Ah! That's shock. You come back wi' me and I'll make a cup o' hot sweet tea. That'll do 'trick. We'll have it as soon as 'doctor's been and gone.'

But then what'll I do, Polly thought. I have to live somewhere. I can't afford 'rent on my own. My wage won't cover it. It had been a struggle to find enough money for food and rent even with two of them working, but now it would be impossible. The rent was due the following week, and after that she could only look forward to being given notice to quit.

Dr James came at midday. 'I'm sorry I was unable to come last night,' he told Polly. 'But I doubt that I could have saved your mother. Mrs Walters did what she could.'

'You'll have been to somebody wi' money,' Polly blurted out. 'They'd have come first!'

Dr James viewed her gravely. 'As a matter of fact yes,' he said softly. 'But they happened to send for me first.' He shook his head as Polly grunted. 'But I wasn't able to save that mother either. She had a daughter about your age who is grieving just as you are. There was a good deal of sickness and death in the town last night and Christmas will be an unhappy time for many people.'

Polly swallowed. She was awash with tears. 'Sorry,' she mumbled. 'But I can onny feel sorrow for myself.'

'I realize that,' Dr James said. 'And I wish I could help you. But I can't. Grief is not a sickness I can treat and there is no medication for it.' He picked up his top hat. 'I wish you good day, Polly. Be brave.'

Rosalie had sat by her mother's side and held her hand and wondered how she could give comfort as the doctor had said when she needed it so badly herself. 'Mama,' she whispered. 'Are you in pain?'

'No.' Her mother licked her dry lips. 'Not now. I was, but it's over now.'

'The child?' Rosalie asked. 'Was it—'

'There is no child,' her mother breathed. 'It was . . . too soon. Rosalie!' Her breathing was shallow and Rosalie had to bend her head to hear her. 'Send . . . for your father. You must send for your father. Tell him to come. Tell him I am very ill. Tell him – tell him . . .'

What else she should tell her father Rosalie never knew, for her mother closed her eyes, took a last breath and was gone, as Mrs Dawson said, to another life.

Rosalie stared at the midwife, who rose from the chair and looked down at her patient.

'She's gone, my dear,' she said in a sorrowing tone and placed her hand over Mrs Kingston's eyes. 'Gone to a better life.'

'How do you know?' Rosalie asked woodenly.

Mrs Dawson looked startled. 'Well of course she has! What's 'point of this life on earth if there isn't a better one waiting for us?'

'I don't know,' Rosalie murmured. She was dry-eyed. The evening's events had happened so swiftly that she hadn't taken them in. She glanced at the clock. It was ten minutes after midnight. 'It's Christmas Eve,' she said blankly. 'People will be preparing for Christmas.'

'Yes, well, there'll be no tree or celebration

for you this year, I'm afraid,' Mrs Dawson said rather sharply.

The tree was in the yard at the back of the house, Rosalie thought. It had been delivered only yesterday. I could dress it in black and purple, I suppose, she thought, and light just one candle in the window. But maybe that wouldn't be considered proper. And shall I have to wear black? I'm not a child, after all.

She was persuaded to go to bed. Martha brought her a cup of hot milk with a shot of brandy in it. 'It'll help you sleep, Miss Rosalie, and then tomorrow I'll bring you breakfast upstairs. There's no need to rise early.'

No, Rosalie thought, for what is there to get up for? No one here but me and no presents to put under the tree. Mama and I would have dressed it this evening if – if she hadn't . . . It was then that she began to weep.

Martha brought her porridge, tea and toast at nine o'clock on Christmas Eve morning. She set the tray on the bedside table and opened the curtains. 'It's still snowing,' she said. 'Looks ever so pretty.' She turned to Rosalie. 'How do you feel this morning, miss?'

'I don't know,' Rosalie answered, taking a sip from her cup. 'Numb. As if everything is unreal. As if I'm trapped in a bubble and things are happening outside the bubble and I can't control them.'

Martha looked at her oddly. 'You'll still be in shock, Miss Rosalie. It's a lot for you to cope with, you being so young.'

Downstairs in the kitchen Martha confided in Cook. 'Don't know how she'll manage. She's acting a bit strange, but then you would, wouldn't you? One minute you've got a mother and 'next you haven't.'

Cook sat down on a chair by the table and wiped her brow with a white cloth. 'What bothers me is what'll happen next. I reckon her father will take her with him to his regiment and find somebody to look after her. Then in a couple o' years he'll marry her off.'

'But where's that leave us?' Martha said in consternation. 'He'll sell 'house, won't he?'

'Aye, mebbe he will, but that'll be for 'best, won't it, cos he'll give us a reference and we'll be able to stay on wi' new owners.'

Cook's got it all worked out, Martha thought, but I'm not so sure. I think I might look for another position and ask 'master for a reference as soon as he comes home.

Dr James came to see Rosalie and said he would issue a death certificate. 'I'm so very sorry,' he said. 'Your mother was advised against another pregnancy. She was not strong.'

After his visit, Rosalie spent the rest of the morning composing a letter to her father. She found it difficult to write and tore up several sheets of writing paper.

Dearest Papa, she wrote, and then changed it to *Dear Father*. It was distressing to put into words that her mother had died in childbirth. It was as if she didn't want to admit it, and if she wrote it down it would become reality. Yet *I must*, she thought, *for how else will he know? Who else will tell him if I do not?* She sat back and chewed on the end of her pen. *What do I do next? Who will arrange the funeral? Who might I ask?*

Her mother had a friend, Lucinda Fellowes, who lived in Anlaby on the outskirts of Hull. Rosalie liked her. She was a very friendly person, although Rosalie's father thought her rather vulgar. It was true she had bizarre taste in clothing and a loud laugh, but nevertheless she sprang to mind as being someone who might help. Martha had asked her that morning what the staff should do about wearing mourning, and Mrs Dawson had returned to rearrange her mother's room and decorate it with flowers ready for any visitors who might want to come and pay their respects.

Rosalie finished the letter to her father with an urgent plea for him to come home as soon as possible, and an expression of her regret that the funeral would have to be held in his absence. *I must be advised of what I should do regarding this*, she wrote, *and have decided to ask Mrs Fellowes as I know of no one else apart from your lawyer who might guide me*. She ended by apologizing for being the bearer of such devastating news and added that she felt bereft and very alone.

She sealed the letter and addressed it to her father's headquarters in Aldershot. Then she asked Martha to order her a cab, and returned to her room to change into a dark skirt and bodice and her best wool coat, which was a deep burgundy with a beaver collar. She went into her mother's room and tiptoed past the bed as if afraid of waking her to open the wardrobe and choose one of her mother's hats. She decided on a grey felt with a black spotted veil and, glancing at the still form beneath the sheet, said tearfully, 'Sorry, Mama. I hope you don't mind.'

It was so cold that the cab driver was stamping his feet to keep warm as he waited for her and vapour was issuing from the horse's nostrils. She asked to be taken first to the post office, where she requested that the letter should be sent with all urgency.

'No post tomorrow, miss,' the counter clerk said. 'It won't get to the destination until after Boxing Day.'

She nodded and thanked him and thought that if her father was out of the country he might not receive the letter for weeks.

She settled back into the cab and asked the driver to take her to Mrs Fellowes' address in Anlaby.

'Do you want me to wait, miss?' he asked when they arrived. 'Weather's closing in and my missus likes me home early on Christmas Eve. I've to help hide 'presents from 'bairns. Not that there's many,' he added. 'Bin a bad year this year.'

'Do you have a Christmas tree?' she asked as she stepped out of the cab.

He gave a rueful grunt. 'Not us,' he said. 'No money for such nonsense.'

'If you'll wait for me and take me home, I'll give you a tree,' she said. 'I won't be wanting it.'

He expressed astonishment that she should be so generous.

'I've just lost my mother,' she told him. 'I'm in mourning.'

The cabby tipped his hat. 'Sorry, miss. I'll wait.'

Mrs Fellowes greeted her warmly. 'Well, my dear, how nice to see you. Have you brought news of your mother? She was in a fragile state when I last saw her but there will be a celebration soon, I do declare.'

'I'm afraid not, Mrs Fellowes,' Rosalie said, and then asked if she might sit down. She felt suddenly faint. 'I've brought bad news and have come to ask your advice. I don't know who else to ask.'

'Oh, dear. Of course, of course,' Mrs Fellowes fussed. 'Forgive me. Would you like a drop of brandy or sal volatile?'

'No, thank you. A glass of water.' She waited until Mrs Fellowes had rung the bell and then cleared her throat. 'Mrs Fellowes,' she said, 'my mother is dead. She had a miscarriage and died last night.'

Mrs Fellowes put one hand to her throat and with the other reached for the back of a chair. 'No,' she gasped. 'Surely not! I saw her only last week. She was a little unwell, as was to be expected, but oh dear! I cannot believe it.' She reached for the handbell again and rang it vigorously.

'Fetch brandy,' she told the startled maid who answered. 'And water. And ask Mr Fellowes to come immediately. This is a time when gentlemen have their uses,' she said to Rosalie. 'It just so happens that he is home today, since it is Christmas Eve. Oh, you poor child! We must write to inform your father, if you know where he is. Let us pray that he is in this country and has not gone gallivanting off to foreign fields.'

'I've just now posted a letter to his regimental headquarters and marked it urgent,' Rosalie said, and wondered if her hostess was going to

30

be of any help to her. 'But I don't know what to do about the funeral.'

'Goodness, neither do I,' Mrs Fellowes exclaimed. She reached for her fan, flipped it open and fanned herself furiously. 'Mr Fellowes will know. It isn't something a lady would deal with, is it?'

'But I will have to, Mrs Fellowes,' Rosalie said. 'For who else will?'

'The parson, my dear. I'm sure he'll be able to advise you.'

Mr Fellowes arrived and Rosalie heaved a sigh of relief. He was as calm as his wife was flustered, and after expressing his condolences he suggested that he go with her to the vicarage to make the funeral arrangements.

'I suppose that, erm . . . the doctor and so on . . .' He was obviously trying not to upset her, and she told him that Mrs Dawson had everything in hand and would arrange for someone to sit with her mother, and that Dr James would issue a death certificate.

'I will do all I can, Miss Kingston,' he said gently. 'This will be a very difficult time for you. Perhaps,' he glanced at his wife who was still briskly fanning herself, 'perhaps you'd care to stay with us over the Christmas holiday?'

'Yes, indeed you must!' Mrs Fellowes raised herself from her chair. 'You must not stay alone.

We shall be quite a jolly party. Our son and his wife and their three children, such dear little things though sometimes tiresomely noisy, will be with us, and my husband's maiden aunt and her friend. You will be very welcome. Very welcome indeed.'

'You are very kind to suggest it,' Rosalie responded. 'Thank you, but I think I had better be at home. There are letters to write and an announcement to prepare for the newspaper.'

'We understand,' Mr Fellowes replied before his wife could press her, 'but please remember to send for us if need be. Now, I'll just get my coat and hat. There's a cab waiting, I notice. Is it for you?'

'Yes,' Rosalie said. 'The driver agreed to take me home. Perhaps you would be kind enough to speak to the parson on my behalf? I don't want to keep the cab waiting any longer than I must.'

The cabby stood patiently whilst Martha unlocked the yard gate so he could collect the Christmas tree. 'We could've put it up in 'hall,' she grumbled, 'or in 'kitchen. It'll be a dowly Christmas without a tree.'

'Thought that young miss said she'd just lost her ma?' the cabby said.

'So she has.'

'Well for shame then, you thinking of

32

enjoying Christmas when she's in mourning.'
He hoisted the tree on to his shoulder. 'My
bairns'll be over 'moon. First time in their lives
that they've had a tree. God bless 'young lady,
that's what I say.'

CHAPTER THREE

'I'll get somebody to sit wi' your ma,' Mrs Walters said to Polly. 'It ain't decent to leave her alone.'

'Will it cost?' Polly asked. 'I've no money.'

'I'll see if I can get a whip-round wi' neighbours. She was a good sort was your ma, and folks'll be generous seeing as it's Christmas.'

'But who'll come to sit wi' a dead woman?' Polly wept. 'Especially at Christmas.'

'There'll be somebody so down on their luck that they'll be glad to earn a copper or two,' Mrs Walters said. 'Don't you worry.'

Polly went out after her neighbour had left, putting on her mother's shawl as well as her own. She couldn't stay in the room a minute longer. 'I'm sorry, Ma.' Hot tears ran down her cheeks as she glanced back. 'But I just can't bear it. It's not you under that sheet. You were allus singing and laughing, not lying so quiet and still.'

She snuffled into her shawl and went out into the court. The snow was wet and slushy underfoot, making walking precarious. She made her way down the High Street towards the seed mill. She should have been at work and knew that she would lose money by not being there. I'd best go and see 'foreman, she thought. He'll perhaps not dock my wages if I explain what's happened.

But the foreman was abrupt. 'You should have sent word,' he said. 'It's nearly eleven o'clock. You've lost nearly five hours.' Then he appeared to relent. 'All right. Get started now and you can have half a day's wages. Boss says we can finish at six seeing as it's Christmas Eve.'

Very generous I'm sure, Polly sneered beneath her breath. Bet he's not here working. He'll be packing up 'Christmas presents in fancy paper, or inspecting 'goose.

She thought of Mrs Walters' invitation to Christmas dinner. They were a big loud family with not much money and she knew that she would be welcome to join them. Indeed, they probably wouldn't even notice her. I'll go, I think, even though I'd rather be on my own. I can't possibly eat and sleep in that room with Ma lying there.

She had had no breakfast and by one o'clock she was faint with hunger. 'Have you got a bit o' bread to spare, Angie?' she asked one of the other girls. 'I'm famished.'

Angie shook her head. 'Eaten mine already. I hope Ma's got summat on 'stove when I get home.'

A tear trickled down Polly's cheek. The foreman was hovering near, so Angie lowered her voice to a whisper. 'What's up, Poll?'

Polly shook her head. 'My ma died during 'night.'

'You poor bairn.' Angie sounded shocked. 'Want to come home wi' me?'

'Thanks,' Polly said, 'but no. Somebody's already offered me a place to stop. I'll go there.' She couldn't stop the tears or the choked voice, and Angie frowned in consternation.

'You shouldn't be here,' she said. 'You should have asked for time off.'

'And then how do I pay 'rent?' Polly said. 'I've onny my wages now that . . . now that Ma's gone.'

Angie nodded, and then said, 'Cover for me, will you?' She glanced at the clock on the wall. 'Tell 'foreman I was caught short and've gone to 'privy.'

Polly nodded, and sighed. She'd have to get a grip on herself. No use crying and whining. Nobody could help her; she'd just have to help herself. But she was full of tears and sadness.

Her eyes and lips felt swollen and her face was sore with weeping.

Ten minutes later Angie came back, and the foreman hadn't noticed her absence. 'Here,' she whispered, pressing her hand into Polly's. It was full of coins. 'One and a tanner,' she said. 'Nearly everybody's tipped in a copper, whatever they could afford. I'll ask 'foreman at 'dinner break if he'll dib in.'

Polly began to cry again. 'Thank you,' she sobbed. 'I'm so grateful. I can't tell you how much.'

Although it was very cold, Polly sat outside at dinner time so that she couldn't see the other girls eating their food; one or two of them came across to her and said how sorry they were about her mother, and one of them gave her half an apple. Angie came back to her with sixpence. 'Foreman give it,' she said. 'He's not a bad sort if you treat him right.'

It was quite unexpected and far more than Polly could have hoped for. I'll give it to Mrs Walters, she thought. It'll go towards tomorrow's dinner. She counted up the money and separated the sixpence. I'll buy some bread and a bit o' cheese for tonight, and 'rest can go towards 'rent. It'll buy me time to look for somewhere cheaper. I just hope Ma wasn't in arrears.

She thanked the foreman at the end of the

day and he said gruffly that she should come to see him after the Christmas holiday and he would see about offering her extra work. Polly was grateful, but she did wonder how she could fit in any extra hours, unless she did a night shift.

'I'll have to tek time off for 'funeral,' she said. 'So if I don't turn up one day you'll know why,' she added, mindful that he'd previously said she should have sent word of her absence.

She walked slowly home, reluctant to return to the house. She was halfway down High Street when ahead of her she saw a familiar figure: tall, dark and with a recognizable confident posture. Suddenly she was full of anger where before she had been completely overcome by misery, and she began to run towards him.

'Sonny!' she shouted. 'Sonny Blake!'

He turned round. Recognizing her, he lifted his arm to greet her. 'How do, Polly.'

Unprepared, he was nearly knocked over as she launched herself at him, hammering her fists against his chest. 'You – you murderer,' she yelled. 'You and all men. Vile murderers.'

'Hey, hey!' He grabbed her wrists. 'Polly! Who have I murdered? Did I do it in my sleep? Cos I don't recall murdering anybody recently. Ow!' He jumped back as she kicked out at his shins. 'What's got into you?'

Polly sobbed. 'Don't reckon on that you don't

38

know.' She lashed out again with her boot. 'Lecher!'

'I've had enough of this,' Sonny snapped. 'Are you going to tell me what I've done or do I drag you home and complain to your ma?'

Polly began to wail. She snatched her hands away and covered her face. 'She's dead! Ma's dead.'

Sonny took a step back, his face draining of colour. 'What? How?' He shook his head in disbelief. 'No. No, she can't be. Not Ida. Not Ida! What happened?'

Polly swallowed and wiped her nose on her shawl. 'She had a miscarriage. I blamed you but she said it wasn't yours.'

He stared at her. 'It wasn't mine! Why did you think— I didn't know she was . . . I've not seen her in months. I've been away. I've been meaning to visit since I got back, but, well, you know how it is.'

'Yeh,' Polly snuffled. 'Other fish to fry, I expect.'

'In a manner of speaking, yes. I've been fishing. For cod,' he added as she cast him a look of disbelief. 'I had the chance of a job on a trawler so I took it.'

'Hard work for a change, was it?'

'Look, Poll,' he said softly. 'I'm really sorry about Ida, and I know how bad you must feel, but don't take your anger out on me. I'll do what I can to help if you'll let me. When did it happen?'

'Last night.'

'Last night! Oh,' he exhaled. His eyes flickered. 'It's Christmas. Where is she?'

'At home. I'm just going there now. But I daren't stop,' Polly choked. 'I'm that frightened. Mrs Walters said she'd try to get somebody to sit wi' her. And she said she'd mek 'arrangements for burial.'

Sonny pondered. 'I'll come and sit with you tonight,' he said quietly. 'I can't tomorrow as I've made other plans. But tonight, Polly, it's Christmas Eve. You should be there.'

'I know.' She wiped her eyes. 'That's why I feel so bad. I know I should be with her. She'd have been there for me.'

'All right. You go home now and I'll be along in half an hour. Trust me, Polly.' He gazed down at her. 'I'll be there.'

Her mouth trembled. 'Thanks. I'm – s-sorry that I blamed you, Sonny.'

He gave a ghost of a smile. 'You just needed somebody to blame and I happened to come along?'

'Yeh, that's right.' She made a brave attempt to smile back. 'I feel better now. I was full o' guilt at being so scared.' Tears rolled down her cheeks again. 'How could I be scared of my own ma?'

He gently patted her cheek. 'Shan't be long.'

Mrs Walters was sitting on the doorstep waiting for her. She had her shawl over her head and was chewing on an empty clay pipe. 'Guessed you'd gone to work,' she said. She screwed up her wrinkled face. 'Can't get anybody for tonight, Polly. Folks are a bit superstitious about spending 'night wi' – you know – on Christmas Eve. Tomorrow night'll be all right and Boxing Day night, and then I've booked 'burial for 'day after. Is that all right?' she added anxiously.

'I'm very grateful,' Polly said. 'And somebody said they'll sit wi' me tonight, so . . . so she won't be by herself.'

'Good.' Mrs Walters eased up off the step. 'So we'll see you tomorrow for Christmas dinner?'

Polly nodded. 'Yes. Thanks.' Impulsively she gave the old woman a kiss on her wrinkled cheek. 'Thank you.'

She took her place on the doorstep to wait for Sonny, but after ten minutes got up and went inside and slowly climbed the stairs to their room. She pushed the door open and stood looking. There was a calmness in the room which hadn't been there earlier. She stepped inside and went towards the mattress in the corner.

'I miss you, Ma,' she whispered. 'I never said afore what I felt and it's too late now. If I'd

41

known that you'd be gone so soon I would have told you what you meant to me. We had such laughs, didn't we, you and me? It was good wi' just 'two of us and no man to tell us what to do. You never told me about my da or who he was, and I was never bothered about knowing. I had you and that was what was important.'

She knelt down and took a breath and lifted the sheet to see her mother's face. She gave a little smile. 'You look beautiful, Ma.' Her eyes were awash. 'Really beautiful.'

She heard footsteps on the stairs and turned to see Sonny at the door. 'I was just telling Ma,' she whispered, 'I was just saying to her how beautiful she looks.'

He knelt down beside her and put his arm round her waist and she leaned her head against his chest as she wept. 'You're quite right, Polly,' he said in a choked voice. 'She does. More lovely than I've ever seen her.' Gently he put the sheet back over Ida's face. 'Let her rest now.' He swallowed hard and led Polly away. 'Look,' he said. 'I've brought us a treat.' He picked up a paper bag that he'd left by the door. 'Where can we sit? Here by the window?'

Polly nodded without speaking and pulled two wooden chairs towards the window. Sonny opened the bag. 'Got any plates?'

She nodded again, went to the cupboard and brought out two cracked plates. She felt unable to speak, she was so choked with emotion, but her eyes opened wide when he brought out a roast chicken, two hot potatoes and then a bottle of red wine. She had never drunk wine before.

'No glasses,' he said with forced cheer, 'but I thought you wouldn't mind sharing a bottle.'

He drew the cork and lifted the bottle in a toast towards the bed, saying softly, 'To you, Ida,' before handing it to Polly.

She hesitated a second, and then she took a deep gulp and then another, and gave it back to Sonny.

They devoured the chicken and the potatoes and Polly felt she hadn't eaten so well in her life. She began to feel warmer and more relaxed. Sonny handed the bottle to her again.

'Happy Christmas, Polly,' he said quietly. 'Finish it off. There's not much left.'

'Happy Christmas, Sonny.' She turned to where her mother lay. 'Happy Christmas in heaven, Ma,' she said. 'God bless.' She finished the bottle and put it down on the floor. 'I feel sleepy,' she confessed.

'Then close your eyes,' he said. 'I'll keep watch.'

She took a blanket from the back of a chair and curled up on the floor. Sonny waited until she had dropped off into a deep wine-induced slumber and then rose and went towards the bed. He lifted the sheet again and looked down at his former lover.

'God bless you, Ida,' he said softly. 'We had some good times together and you taught me to be a man; and, although we'd agreed to go our separate ways, I'm sorry I wasn't with you at the end.' He bent and kissed her cold cheek. 'But I'll keep a lookout for your Polly. And that's a promise.'

CHAPTER FOUR

Because of Mrs Kingston's prominence in the town a notice of her death was rushed through. Mr Fellowes had called at the local newspaper office and an obituary was to appear in the Hull *Advertiser* that very evening, though he deemed it insensitive to inform *The Times* before Rosalie's father received the news.

By early evening, Rosalie was seated in the drawing room, dressed in dark clothing, though not in black as she was only a minor, waiting for any callers who might wish to pay their respects and offer condolence. Mr and Mrs Fellowes sat behind her, ready to introduce her to friends and acquaintances of theirs and her mother's.

The first people to arrive were the vicar and his wife. Mr Fellowes had already been to see him in order to arrange a funeral service, and now he was here to offer Rosalie comfort. Unmoved, she listened to him as he droned on about being safe in the garden of heaven in the arms of Jesus, and heaved a sigh of relief when he went upstairs to pray at her mother's bedside, where Mrs Dawson was in attendance.

I'd rather Mama were here safe at home with me, she thought. Why did she have to die? She was not yet forty. Rosalie sighed again. Had her mother really wanted this baby, or had she had no choice in the matter?

Two ladies arrived together, both wearing black sashes over their cloaks and black spotted veils on their hats. One of them delicately placed a lace handkerchief to her nose and murmured, 'So sorry,' whilst the other patted Rosalie's hand and said softly, 'Too young to be taken; she was only a year older than I, and I am certainly not ready. You must come to me if there is anything I can do for you.' She leaned forward and whispered discreetly, 'Anything you might wish to ask. Anything at all; you must not be embarrassed. I recall how bewildered I was at your tender age. I will leave my card at the door.'

'So kind.' Rosalie, stony-faced, bobbed her knee, and considered that if the woman was referring to female bodily functions, then she probably knew as much as her visitor did about the subject. She had started her flux three years ago and had made it her business to find out what it was all about.

Neighbours, those who had heard of the death, also called. Few of them knew Mark Kingston as he was seldom at home, whereas Mrs Kingston had been born and brought up in Hull: her father had been a successful businessman in the town until his early death, which was followed by that of his wife a year later.

Rosalie's father had been born in North Yorkshire; he and his brother were brought up by elderly childless relatives whilst their parents were abroad. After leaving school Mark followed his father into the army whilst his brother Luke went back to run the family estate with his uncle.

Rosalie knew nothing of her paternal grand-parents. Her mother had never met them, or her husband's brother. 'Nor,' she had once said, when Rosalie had curiously asked if she had any relatives, 'do I wish to. Your father and his brother haven't met in years. I understand that they have nothing in common. And their parents did not come to our wedding, or even send greetings.'

By eight o'clock, Mr and Mrs Fellowes had decreed that no one else would come. 'It would not be proper to do so, so late in the evening,' Mrs Fellowes said. 'Even in the present circum-stances.' Again she urged Rosalie to accom-pany them home and spend Christmas Day with them. Rosalie graciously refused and thought she saw a hint of relief in both the Fellowes' expressions. It wouldn't be fair, she thought. My presence would only put a damper on the day. They would be conscious of sparing my feelings.

'You have been so very kind and thoughtful,' she said, and meant it. They had spent most of the afternoon with her, and Mr Fellowes in particular had been very considerate. 'But I would prefer to be at home where I can reflect on my position.'

After they had gone she called Martha upstairs. 'I'll be staying at home tomorrow,' she told her. 'I'll attend church in the morning so will have a light early breakfast. Was Cook planning to cook a goose for midday?'

'Yes, miss. It's been in 'cold larder since yesterday morning when 'butcher brought it, along wi' two pound o' sausages and a leg o' pork. She's got two lots o' stuffing prepared, forcemeat and chestnut, and 'plum pudding's been bubbling away all afternoon.'

What a great deal of food, Rosalie thought, and as far as I know Mama wasn't inviting anyone else.

'In that case I'll eat at one o'clock. But I won't need anything else until about six when I'll have a plate of cold pork and apple sauce.' She looked up at Martha. 'I shall pass the afternoon quietly so you and Cook may spend the day as you wish.'

'Yes, miss.' Martha dipped her knee. 'Thank you, miss. Is there anything I can get you now?'

'Just a hot posset and a slice of bread and butter, please, Martha.'

Martha smiled. 'Like you used to have when you were little and had a cold?'

'Yes.' Rosalie felt her eyes prickle. It was the remedy her mother had been given when she was a child, and she used to ask Cook to prepare it for Rosalie if she was unwell.

'Would you like it made with ale or brandy, miss?' Martha asked.

'Ale, please, and piping hot, and – and I'll have it in my room. I think I'll have an early night.'

'You do right, Miss Rosalie. You've had a hard day. I'll bring it up and I'll put a warm brick in 'bed as well.'

'Thank you. That will be lovely.' What Rosalie wanted most of all was some comfort. She wanted to feel warm and cared for, but there was no one to care for her now but the servants, and then only if she asked them.

She was woken the next morning by the sound of church bells heralding Christmas Day and for a second she was unaware of what had happened. Then, as she remembered, she felt a cold chill of unhappiness spreading over her. I'm alone, she thought. My first Christmas without any company. On other Christmases, neighbours had been invited in for glasses of sherry and mince pies. Her two best friends, who would have called after church to exchange small gifts, had both gone away for the Christmas holiday and were not due back until the end of January.

Martha tapped on the door and brought her a tray of tea and bread and butter and wished her the season's greetings. 'I won't say happy Christmas, Miss Rosalie,' she said, 'cos I know it won't be, but I hope you'll get through 'day as best you can.'

'Thank you, Martha. And I hope you and Cook will make the most of the day.'

Martha nodded. 'Cook's hopping mad cos scullery maid hasn't shown up again. She didn't come yesterday either. She must be sick,' she mused, 'cos she's not asked for her wages.'

'Oh,' Rosalie said, wondering if that meant she would have to hire someone else. I don't know how, she thought. Mama did all of that. She thought of how cosseted she had been; she had no conception of how to run a household. How could I? I don't know how to order groceries or what to tell Cook. How can I live alone? Papa! He'll have to come home. Will he want to stay here or will he shut up the house and take me back with him?

The enormity of her situation suddenly overwhelmed her. Up to now she had been numbed by the sudden and unforeseen death of her mother. Now she began to shake as she realized that the normality of her life was gone and from now on it was going to be quite different.

In church she sat and heard not a word of the vicar's sermon. She stood and mouthed the words of the hymns but no sound came out, and after the service, as she walked out of the doors, the vicar's wife stopped her and said gently, 'I'm so very pleased that you came this morning, Miss Kingston. It was very brave of you, and I do hope you found some solace in being in God's house.'

Rosalie shook her head. 'I did not,' she whispered. She glanced round at the congregation, who were standing chatting or calling out greetings to each other. They were a mixed bunch of people; some she knew by sight as regular worshippers but others were strangers who were there because it was Christmas Day. There were also people standing by the gate who, she thought, had probably not been inside for the service. They were poorly dressed, the women in worn shawls with children clinging to their dingy skirts and the men, caps in hand, tipping their foreheads when given a coin.

Rosalie dropped sixpence into someone's hat and wished them a happy Christmas and then watched as a group moved off together. An old woman hooked her arm into a girl's and they walked close together in what seemed like easy companionship. They have each other, she thought, and turned away to go home to dine alone.

Polly opened her eyes to see Sonny Blake asleep in the chair across from her, his head and shoulders lowered on to his chest. She shivered; her hands and feet were numb with cold and she wriggled her toes and shook her fingers to get the circulation moving. She glanced towards the bed and thought that she could not yet believe that it was her mother lying there.

'Morning!' Sonny's voice was husky with sleep. 'How are you this morning?'

'Don't know,' she muttered. 'I'm having difficulty in believing what's happened.'

He nodded and took a deep breath. 'Yes,' he said. 'So am I.'

'It's Christmas Day,' she said flatly. 'Do you go to church?'

'No,' he said. 'Well, sometimes. Do you want to go?'

'Don't know,' she said again. 'I might. I might ask Mrs Walters to go wi' me.'

He got up from the chair and stretched. 'I have to go, Polly.' He too glanced towards the bed. 'I'll come to the funeral. Do you want me to walk with you?'

Her eyes prickled. 'Yes please,' she said in a small, childish voice. 'It's at 'Northern General Cemetery, 'day after tomorrow.' She pressed her lips together. 'Paupers' corner.'

'I'll come early. It's a fair walk; I hope the snow keeps off.'

After he'd left, she wrapped her shawl round her head, closed the door behind her and went off to see Mrs Walters. She lived in another of the courts off High Street in a room which she shared with her daughter, her son-in-law and their four children, including the boy who had been sent to fetch the doctor.

'I was just coming for you,' she greeted Polly as she opened the door to her knock. 'Old Ginny is going to sit wi' your ma and I thought you could come wi' me to Holy Trinity. Service will have started and we might be able to pick up a copper or two when folks leave.'

Polly frowned. 'What do you mean?'

Mrs Walters grinned. 'It's Christmas! All 'nobs and swells'll be there this morning and

53

they'll be that pleased wi' themselves at being saintly that they'll give summat to 'poor. I go every Christmas.'

'Oh!' Polly said. 'But don't you go in?' She had thought that she would at least kneel down to say a prayer.

'Nah,' she said. 'No need. I can say my prayers anywhere and God'll listen to me wherever I am. He doesn't allus answer, though,' she added cynically. 'If He did I'd be handing out money 'stead o' beggin' for it.'

They waited at the gate along with several others who were on their uppers. The women huddled into threadbare shawls and the men turned up the collars of hand-me-down coats, most of which were green with age.

The bells started to ring and the waiting crowd shuffled forward in anticipation. 'Here they come,' Mrs Walters muttered. 'They'll shek hands and smile and wish everybody season's greetings an' then they'll all be off to an 'ot dinner and a glass o' sherry.' She gave a smirk. 'But they'll not enjoy it any more than us, them as are having an 'ot dinner, that is,' she added, looking round. 'There's some here who'll have nowt more than a bowl o' soup from 'soup kitchen.'

She moved forward with the crowd as the congregation began to walk down the path. 'Happy Christmas, ma'am,' she whined, holding out her hand. 'Season's greetings, sir. Thank you, sir. God bless you, lady.'

Polly followed her and held out her hand too, though she felt ashamed. Never in her life had she begged. Someone slipped a copper into her palm and she bobbed her knee. How humiliating. It wasn't right, she thought. Why should some have so much and others not enough?

'That's it. Come on,' Mrs Walters rattled the coins in her hand. She hooked her arm into Polly's. 'We've enough. There's others here who need it more'n we do. Let's go home and see how that leg o' pork's looking.'

CHAPTER FIVE

It was, as Polly had suspected it would be, a jolly noisy Christmas Day at the house of Mrs Walters and her family. The children were very excited, because someone had given their father a Christmas tree. 'I'm a cab driver,' Bob told Polly, 'and I took this young woman to Anlaby. She said she had a tree and would I like it cos she couldn't dress it or celebrate Christmas cos her ma had just died.'

Polly realized that he didn't know about her own mother or he probably wouldn't have mentioned it. She saw his wife nudge him sharply in the ribs and thought that he must have been at work when Mrs Walters told her daughter why she had invited Polly to share their Christmas dinner. For his sake, she decided not to say anything: he was a decent hardworking man and clearly delighted at his good fortune at being able to give his family an unexpected treat.

The children had cut up pieces of white paper to look like snowflakes and scattered them over the tree, which just touched the low ceiling. Their grandmother had found a piece of red flannel and they'd draped that round the zinc pail which held the trunk.

'It's better than a present,' one of the children said, ''cos we can all look at it, and we can sniff at it as well. It smells' – he wrinkled his nose – 'sort of like 'country, all fresh and clean.'

'It does,' Polly agreed. The pine scent was the first thing she had noticed when she came in. That and the mouth-watering aroma of the roasting pork. 'It's lovely. I've never seen one before. Not inside.'

The children's other grandmother, Granny Porter, arrived and was given the same story. 'Fancy giving away a tree,' she commented. 'We'll feel just like 'queen. She has one every year,' she said knowledgeably, accepting a glass of ale from her daughter-in-law. Three other relatives arrived, so there were twelve of them to share the pork. Each of them had brought something to add to the feast. One produced apples to make apple sauce, another a bag of chestnuts, and a fellow cab driver surreptitiously took a small bottle of rum out of his coat pocket. He winked as he handed it over. 'For 'plum pudding,' he said. 'It'll not be missed.'

'Don't tell me,' Bob said to him. 'I don't want

to know about ill-gotten gains. I'll have a little nip, though,' he added, grinning, 'just to mek sure it's palatable.'

There wasn't room for all of them round the table so the children sat on the floor with their plates on their knees and Polly said that she too would sit on the floor. She took the sixpence from her pocket, the one she was going to give to Mrs Walters, and handed it to her daughter Nellie. 'Will you put it in 'pudding?' she said quietly. 'I know you're supposed to mix it in when you mek it, but I don't think it matters and it might bring somebody luck.'

'Why, bless you, I will.' Nellie was red-faced and sweaty with cooking over the fire, but she beamed at Polly. 'I'll push it in afore I pour 'rum over. You just might win it back.'

Polly sat in a corner with her back to the wall to eat her dinner. She was rather overwhelmed by the noise and hilarity. She had never been part of a big family. It had always been just her and her mother, but now she could see that being amongst family could be a comfort in a time of sorrow. The pork was shared out between them so there wasn't a huge amount each, but the apple sauce and the huge mound of potatoes, carrots and turnip more than made up for the small portion of meat. Polly drooled. She had never eaten such a feast. The flesh was tender and succulent and they were all given a small piece of crisp crackling which they bit and sucked on, exclaiming at the flavour.

Then it was time for the plum pudding, which Nellie said had been steaming for three days. There were carrots and potato in the pudding to make up for the lack of fruit; there was also treacle and nutmeg and a good soaking of rum in the sauce and they all licked their lips in enjoyment. Then Polly put her spoon in her dish to scoop up the last mouthful and scraped up the sixpence. She gave a gasp and put her hand to her mouth.

'I've got 'sixpence!' she said in embarrassment. 'I should give it back.'

'No, it's yours, honey,' Mrs Walters told her. 'You were meant to have it. Any road, your need is greater than ours.' She gave her a lop-sided and gap-toothed smile. 'Mek a wish and spend it well.'

The noise grew greater and the children shouted and screamed as they chased each other round the room. The adults told them to shut up, but they too were laughing and joking and eventually Polly developed a headache and began to feel sick as the large amount of food she had consumed churned in her stomach.

'I'm going home,' she whispered to Mrs Walters, who was sipping her third gin. 'I need to be with my ma.'

The old lady nodded. 'You do what you must, m'dear. Your life is your own and you're behodden to nobody.' She lifted her glass to Polly. 'Good luck to you.'

Rosalie stood staring out of the sitting room window. She had only picked at her luncheon, though the goose was cooked to perfection and the accompaniments – the roast potatoes, the green peas, tender slivers of braised carrots, and sprouts tossed with butter and almonds – were beautifully served in her mother's best china. There had been potted chicken liver served with thin toast to start with, and Cook had baked a ham, studded it with cloves and glazed it with honey. Rosalie had sat and gazed at the table full of food in front of her and thought it quite excessive.

'Should I open a bottle of wine, Miss Rosalie?' Martha had asked. 'Just one glass would mebbe buck you up.'

Rosalie had considered. Normally she only drank water at mealtimes, though occasionally she would have half a glass of wine to keep her mother company. If she said yes, then Martha and Cook would enjoy finishing off the bottle.

'Just a small glass of claret,' she said. 'And you and Cook can have the rest with your luncheon, or use it for sauce.'

'Yes, miss,' Martha said. 'I think Cook's got some brandy for 'plum pudding.''

'Drink it then,' she said. 'Don't waste it.'

What shall I do now? she thought, looking down at the empty street. There was no one about; the museum opposite was shuttered, its doors firmly closed. Everyone will be home, I expect, finishing luncheon, opening presents or chatting to family and friends. Then she peered forward; there *was* someone, a girl, walking alone just below her, wrapped in a shawl and kicking at the heaps of snow which were piled at the side of the pavement.

Impulsively Rosalie knocked on the glass. The girl looked up. She was probably her own age, Rosalie thought, or maybe younger. She wasn't very tall and only slightly built. She put her head on one side as if asking why Rosalie had knocked. Why did I, Rosalie wondered. Am I so desperate for contact with another human being? She lifted her hand and waved.

The girl stopped for a moment, putting her hand hesitantly to her mouth, and then she waved back before continuing on her way. Rosalie turned away from the window and sat by the fire; she picked up a book but after a few minutes put it down again. She hadn't been upstairs to sit by her mother since breakfast and Mrs Dawson had been called away last evening to visit a new mother.

'She needs me more than you do, Miss Kingston,' she had said. 'I'm a midwife, after all. But I'll come to 'funeral.'

'I will quite understand if you can't come,' Rosalie had said dully. 'Please don't be concerned. You were here when you were needed.'

Reluctantly she climbed the stairs to her mother's room. 'Please come soon, Papa,' she breathed. 'I cannot manage this alone.' It was only two days since her mother's death; she had yet to attend the funeral but she felt that the world she had known was gone for ever. She was living in a vacuum, her life held by a restraining leash, the unknown future bleak and comfortless.

The day of the funerals was bitterly cold, an avenging biting chill that cut through to the marrow. 'Too cold for snow,' Mrs Fellowes said when, wrapped in furs, she arrived with her husband to accompany Rosalie from the house. 'You must wrap up warm, my dear. It will be very cold by the graveside.'

Rosalie felt faint. She had never been to a funeral before and was sick with apprehension. 'Must I go?' she whispered. 'Would it be wrong if I didn't?'

Mrs Fellowes drew in a breath. 'Of course you must! Whatever would people think if you did not?'

'She doesn't have to,' Mr Fellowes interrupted. 'What does it matter what people think? She's only young, and I can recall a time when women never went to funerals but always stayed at home.'

Mrs Fellowes was silenced for a moment and then reluctantly agreed that he was right. 'But it's different now,' she said, 'and it is her mother, after all. There should be a member of the family there.'

'Yes,' Rosalie said faintly. 'Of course. I'll get my coat.'

Martha was waiting in the hall with Rosalie's coat and wrap. 'Me and Cook'll be here when you get back, Miss Rosalie. We'll have a hot drink ready for you and we've prepared refreshments in case anybody else comes back.'

Rosalie nodded. She couldn't speak. She felt that her breath was gone from her and besides, she had nothing to say. She hoped that no one would come back to the house, for she couldn't possibly indulge in polite conversation. All she wanted to do was climb into bed and pull the covers over her head.

Polly was full of anger. Why, she kept thinking. 'Why? Why? Why?' Why should it happen to my ma? She's never done owt to harm anybody. She was allus full of life and merriment. And now she's gone. Gone and left me on my own.

She clasped her fingers together so tightly that they hurt. It's not fair.

She stifled a sob as Sonny took her arm and led her towards the funeral cart. There were no flowers, but Polly had laid her mother's one and only hat on top of the coffin. Her mother had bought it second hand from Rena's shop in the days when Rena sold used clothing, before she started to sell only the latest fashions. The hat was a riot of feathers, fruit and flowers, and Ida said it cheered her up whenever she brought it out of the cupboard.

'Nice touch, that,' Sonny said kindly. 'I remember Ida was wearing that hat the first time I met her.'

'When was that?' Polly could hardly recall a time when Sonny wasn't around.

'Eight years ago.' He smiled. 'Don't you remember? You were there; you'd be seven . . . eight? It was summer and I'd gone to Pearson Park with some friends. They'd taken me out to celebrate my birthday. I was eighteen. We'd had a few drinks and eyed up some ladies.' He paused for a moment. 'And then I saw Ida in that hat and made a comment about it. We sort of stayed together for the rest of the afternoon.'

'Yeh!' Polly said. 'I do remember now. You gave me a humbug and it stuck to my teeth.'

Mrs Walters had joined them and she bent to whisper in Polly's ear.

'Don't know if I'll mek it all 'way there,' she croaked. 'My rheumatics are playing me up today and this cold weather don't help, but I'll come as far as I can.'

They rattled up the High Street, the cart juddering on the cobbles. People in the street stopped as they went by; men doffed their caps and women stood silently, their gossip stilled until the small procession had passed. They crossed into Lowgate and then cut to Silver Street and Whitefriargate, and here again shoppers and business people paused in their rush and chatter until they had passed by. They continued over Monument Bridge, which Polly's mother had always called by its old name of Junction Bridge. Fortunately the swing bridge was closed to river traffic this morning; had it not been they would have had a long delay as the lock gates below them in Princes Dock allowed the waters of the Humber, and the many large vessels waiting on it, free passage to Queen's Dock, one of the largest docks in the country. Once across, they proceeded northwards along Prospect Street towards the edge of the town.

Polly glanced down Albion Street, where the elite of the town lived. She had walked along it after leaving Mrs Walters' house on Christmas Day, not wanting to go home immediately as she had known the night would drag, wandering aimlessly into areas that she didn't know. She had passed the Hull Royal Infirmary as they were doing now and had crossed over into Albion Street to see the fine houses and the Royal Institution and museum, which she had been told held a whale and a turtle that had been found alive on the banks of the Humber.

The snow here had been thick, she supposed because few people had walked on it, and she had kicked at it with her boots, annoyed because it hadn't turned to icy slush as it had in High Street. Someone knocked on a window and for a moment she thought they were admonishing her. Then she saw a fair-haired girl looking out of one of the houses. She stopped and stared; the girl was dressed sombrely in dark clothing, and Polly was mystified. If I lived here and had plenty of money I'd wear bright clothes, red or pink and blue. I wouldn't wear dark like she's doing.

The girl had waved, but she didn't smile, and Polly, after a momentary hesitation, had waved back before walking on. She'd turned back to look again, but the figure at the window had gone.

Now she glanced down the street as they passed and saw that there was a funeral carriage outside one of the houses. Two black horses were harnessed to it and they stamped their feet and snorted, tossing the black plumes attached to their headbands as they shook their heads.

Oh well, Polly sighed. Everybody has sorrow, even them wi' plenty of money, but at least they'll ride to 'cemetery and not have to walk.

'Can we leave now?' Rosalie said, coming back into the drawing room. She was dressed in her outdoor clothes and wanting to get the day over and done with. 'Is it time?'

'A few more minutes,' Mr Fellowes said. 'Not everyone is here. Dr James said he would come if he could. Your neighbours said they would follow us. Do they have their own carriage?'

'I don't believe they do,' Rosalie said vaguely. 'I have never seen one.'

'Mm.' Mr Fellowes gazed out of the window. 'There are two cabs waiting; hired, I think. Yes.' He peered closer to the glass. 'Your neighbours are coming out of the house. Ah! Here's Dr James arriving. Well.' He took his fob watch from his waistcoat pocket and examined it. 'Perhaps we could collect ourselves and go to the door.'

'Are you all right, my dear?' Mrs Fellowes asked Rosalie solicitously. 'If you should feel unwell at all just say. I have some sal volatile in my bag. It's very effective,' she added. 'I always carry it.'

Rosalie shook her head. 'I'm all right,' she

whispered. But she wasn't. She could feel her body starting to shake and her lips trembled when she spoke.

They climbed into the carriage and the horses skittered as the driver shook the reins. It had been snowing again, but now the snow was turning to icy sleet. Mr Fellowes had arranged for both the carriage and the service at the Northern General Cemetery and Rosalie was very grateful to him, for she wouldn't have known how to go about such things. I must send him a letter of thanks, she told herself, or perhaps Papa will do so when he comes home. Everything will be all right then. Oh, I know he can't bring Mama back, but he'll look after me. He'll tell me what is to be done.

They drove along Spring Bank towards the cemetery and Rosalie noticed that men in the streets paused as the carriage passed and doffed their hats or caps. The sight brought a painful, tearful lump to her throat. How considerate of them, she thought, and they don't even know Mama.

The horses, already travelling at a slow pace, slowed even more. 'What's happening?' Rosalie said. 'Why are we stopping?'

Mr Fellowes put down the window, letting in a blast of cold air, and Mrs Fellowes tutted and pulled her fur collar further up her neck. Her husband put his head out of the window.

'We're not stopping,' he called back to Rosalie. 'There's a funeral cart in front and we can't overtake it.'

'Surely you mean a carriage, Mr Fellowes?' Rosalie said. 'Not a cart.'

'No, m'dear.' He put up the window again and gave a little shudder before pulling the blanket which he was sharing with his wife over his knees. 'It's a funeral cart. Ah, there we are, they've pulled over to let us pass.'

Rosalie turned to the window as they drew level with the cart. The coffin was in the back but there were no flowers as on her mother's. Just a rather incongruous hat. An old woman hobbled along as if her feet ached, and immediately behind the cart was a young girl wearing a shabby shawl over her head, and a man walking beside her.

Who are they, I wonder, Rosalie thought. Could that be a son and daughter saying good-bye to their mother as I am doing? She turned her head discreetly as they passed and the man looked up. His hair was dark and long beneath his top hat. He gave a slight nod of his head in acknowledgement and she did the same.

Mrs Fellowes followed her gaze. 'Poor people,' she breathed in a morbid tone. 'Paupers. They'll be going to the paupers' corner.'

CHAPTER SIX

'I can't pay you all 'rent,' Polly told the rent collector. 'Have you a smaller room for less money?'

He was a middle-aged man with warts on his long nose and one eye that looked down on it. 'No,' he said decisively. 'Where's your ma? Skulking under 'bed?'

Polly glared at him, her mouth set. 'She's dead. Died last week. That's why I can't pay. I'm not earning enough.'

He sighed. 'How old are you?'

'Nearly seventeen. Why?'

'You'll have to leave.' He pulled a sheet of paper from his battered case and scribbled something on it, then handed it to Polly.

'What's this?' She looked down at his scrawl, so badly written she could hardly read it.

'Notice to quit. Mr Clowes won't rent to anybody under twenty.'

'Wh-what am I supposed to do?' Polly stared

at him. Could he just turn her out?

'I don't know. It's not my concern. I'm onny here to collect 'rent.' He shrugged. 'You'll have to get another job wi' better pay.' He turned his head to look at her with his good eye. 'You'll have to be out by next Sat'day.'

Polly stood watching him as he knocked on other doors. She'd had a miserable week since the funeral and at midnight on New Year's Eve she had sat by the window listening to the church bells ringing and revellers merry-making, and wept.

Mrs Walters hadn't made it as far as the cemetery. She'd called out to Polly that she'd have to turn back as her legs were killing her, so only she and Sonny stood by the graveside.

The parson was old and mumbled into his muffler and they couldn't hear what he was saying. The weather had worsened, the sleet falling like icy daggers which cut into her face and hands, and she felt the cleric was anxious to be off before he succumbed to pneumonia. He brought her no comfort at all.

When the man had finished and scurried away, she'd looked across to the other side of the cemetery. It would be lovely there in summer, she thought; the trees and shrubs were stark and leafless now but come spring would be covered in fresh green growth. Flowers, she had thought. I bet there'll be flowers growing there in summer. Here, in the corner where her mother now lay, was simply bare earth.

The carriage which had passed them on the road was on the other side. Polly had seen another clergyman come out of the chapel followed by a man and a woman and a girl, who seemed to be the chief mourners, although there were other people too. Then she saw Dr James. He stood for a moment and then glanced at his pocket watch. He bent his head to speak to the girl before touching his top hat and hurrying away to his waiting carriage.

'Going to see somebody else who's sick,' she'd murmured.

'What?' Sonny was preoccupied.

'Dr James.' She pointed to the departing brougham. 'That's him just leaving. He came to see my ma, but couldn't save her.' He said he couldn't help another woman either that night, she remembered, after I'd accused him of going to see somebody well off first. She looked more attentively towards the group of mourners. They were talking to the girl and she was nodding her head in response, but didn't appear to be speaking.

'I wonder who's died?' Polly murmured, half to herself.

Sonny hadn't answered, but had taken her arm. 'Come on,' he'd said. 'Let's be off. We're in for some more bad weather. I'll see you home.'

They'd walked in silence for most of the way until Sonny said, 'I've been thinking, Polly. Maybe you should try for live-in work. Laundry or scullery maid. The pay wouldn't be good but you wouldn't have to worry about the rent and you'd get regular meals.'

She'd looked up at him. 'Where? How do you know?'

He'd shrugged. 'Plenty of big houses in Hull, and some not so big who still want staff. Tradesmen's wives and so on.'

He'd put the thought into her head and it wasn't until after he'd left her at her door that she realized he hadn't said how he knew about such things. You're a dark horse, Sonny Blake, she'd thought. There's a lot you're not telling me.

She deliberated on his suggestion now as she stood in the court and wondered what she might do. The foreman's vague promise of extra work hadn't materialized and she was very short of money. How would I find a job like that? Do I knock on doors? It's true what Sonny said, there are some big houses in Hull, even some in High Street. Some belong to shipping merchants who haven't left to live in 'country. Then there's Parliament Street. She was thinking of the houses in the old town a stone's throw from her own room, where rich and poor lived cheek by jowl, although some of

73

the rich were moving out to splendid mansions in the country now, or so she'd heard. And not only the country: she recalled the houses they had passed on the way to the cemetery. More and more substantial properties were being built on the outskirts as the town expanded.

But why would they tek me? I've no experience. I've onny ever cleaned out this room, though Ma allus said I scrubbed 'floor better than she did. And that's what I'll have to do if I've to move out. She blinked hard. A week, I've got, and then 'home I've shared wi' Ma all this time won't be mine any more.

I almost gave the game away. Sonny heaved a breath as he left Polly at her door. He'd given her a kiss on her cheek and promised he would see her again soon. And he would. He meant to stay in Hull for a little while. He must buckle down to some work and earn his keep. Deep in thought, he headed towards Charlotte Street. It wasn't exactly home but it was the place where he lived and worked when he wasn't travelling.

He rented a loft above a stable which used to be home to a groom, for this was a mews area where the wealthy of Hull had once kept their horses and carriages. Since these worthy citizens had started to move out of town, not all the stables were required any longer and several of them were empty. Here in his loft, Sonny had a single bed, a comfy chair, a table where he could eat, and most important of all a large window overlooking a narrow courtyard, where he had set up his easel and another table to hold his paints and brushes. His canvases, some blank and some completed, were stacked against the wall.

It wasn't that he wanted his occupation to be kept secret, but he preferred not to be questioned by those who would not understand his need or desire to express himself in art. Only his fellow painters knew of his hidden lair and they respected his privacy as he did theirs. And Ida had known.

He had explained to Polly how he had met her mother at the park. He'd been slightly intoxicated as he and his friends had flitted between inn and hostelry in celebration of his birthday. The day had started well when his aunt Ettie, or Henrietta as he called her when he wanted to tease, had told him that from that day on she was halving his allowance.

'You must stand on your own feet now, dear boy,' she'd said. 'You have the talent to paint, though whether or not you will ever make a living from it remains to be seen. But the only way you will find out is to buckle down, and that begins today.' She'd reached across to a side table to pick up an envelope. 'Here are ten guineas. You may celebrate as you will, but out of it you'll pay the rent on a studio in Charlotte Street Mews in Hull. I've already reserved it for you and paid the first week's rent.'

She had smiled as he kissed the top of her head. 'But you must say whether or not it is suitable, the light and so on. I don't know about such things, but if it is, then you can buy whatever you need to furnish it and obtain your painting materials.' She'd given a big sigh. 'I hope I've done my best for you, Sebastian. I've done what I could, at any rate.'

He'd put his hand on her shoulder. 'No one could have done better,' he said. He was quite choked with emotion. He couldn't remember what his mother looked like, but he could clearly recall the day when she had brought him to the house in Hessle and said she was leaving him with her sister, his aunt Ettie.

Aunt Ettie had crooked her finger at this three-year-old and said, 'Come here, sonny. Let me take a look at you.'

He had tottered towards her and put up his arms. She had picked him up and put him on her lap. 'Go,' she had said to his mother. 'And don't come back until you've sorted out your life.'

His childhood was happy with Aunt Ettie which it hadn't been before. He had moved from place to place with his mother, and no

76

sooner were they settled than they would move on again. With Ettie he was secure and loved. She had never married but devoted her life to him and they had never seen his mother again.

Before he met his friends on that birthday he had gone to look at the mews studio. The sun was streaming through the window and the loft was full of light. He'd looked out from the top of the steps and seen that he was in the midst of real life. There were people living within walking distance who were poor but hard-working; there were churches where he could sketch, museums and reading rooms where he could study, theatres and music halls where he could be entertained. In short he was thrilled with the opportunity and his new-found freedom. This was the best day of his life, and then he'd met Ida.

She'd smiled at him and he'd smiled back and winked at the small girl by her side. They'd chatted and she'd told him their names. No, she'd said when he asked, she didn't have a husband and she didn't want one. She was several years older than him but he'd felt very grown up as they'd talked. He had told her that his name was Sonny Blake. They parted company but later that evening he'd met her again in one of the bars in town where she was working. He began to see her regularly and eventually he plucked up the courage to ask her if she'd sit for him.

'I can't afford to pay much,' he'd told her. 'I'm only a poor student.'

She'd shrugged. 'Pay as much as you can afford,' she'd said. 'I know what it's like to be poor.'

Ida had sat on his bed and looked over his shoulder, gazing into the distance, and he thought she was the loveliest woman he had ever seen. It was true that he hadn't met many up to now, but even when he had, later, he thought there were few who could match her natural unadorned beauty.

Inevitably they became lovers. She was the first for him and she calmed his youthful passion, curbing his eagerness and teaching him to give pleasure as well as take it.

He was always careful, as she had taught him to be, for she had told him that she mustn't get pregnant. After a few years, when they had outgrown their passion for each other, they remained good friends and she often sat for him. He sold some of his paintings, signing as *Sebastian*, and with the money decided to travel to improve his knowledge of art. He left for Paris and Florence and whilst he was away she sat for an artist friend Bertram, who was able to pay more than he could. And it was Bertram, he suspected, who might have been the father of her unborn child and therefore instrumental in her early death.

He did little work that week. The light wasn't good. The sky was heavy with snow and sleet, and besides he kept thinking of Ida in the cold earth and knew that if he did paint, it would be something dark. He thought too of Polly and wondered how he could help her. Somehow, he didn't think that she would knock on doors asking for work, but he was sure that living in somewhere would be the answer for her. On the Friday morning he put on his coat and went out.

He went first of all to call on Bertram, who had a room in Percy Street. He found him stretched out on his sofa. His room was very dark and lit by a dim oil lamp.

'Can't work, old chap,' Bertram greeted him. 'I keep thinking I'll up sticks and go abroad where the light is better. I've got to earn some money somehow.'

'Did you hear about Ida?' Sonny asked him.

Bertram rolled off the sofa. 'No. What's the darling girl been up to?'

'She died.' Sonny said flatly. 'She was pregnant, seemingly – and she died.'

'No!' Bertram breathed. 'Not the lovely Ida!'

'Was it yours?' Sonny asked abruptly. 'The child?'

'No.' Bertram shook his head. 'Haven't seen her in months. She stopped coming. Said she could earn more money working in inns than she could sitting for me. Poor Ida! What about her daughter? What's she going to do?'

'That's why I've come,' Sonny said. 'Do you know anybody who'd employ her?'

'As a model?'

'No. As a servant.'

But he didn't, and Sonny went on his way. He cut through into Albion Street intending to go to the museum. He wanted to take a closer look at the shark in the glass case. When he'd told Polly he had been fishing, it was partly true. He had been on a fishing expedition, but to paint and not to fish. A trawler owner had offered him the trip but he'd spent most of the time lying face down in his bunk trying to stave off waves of seasickness. By the time he had recovered they were heading back for the Humber. He had since decided that if he was going to paint the sea he would do it from imagination and memory rather than risk another voyage, but he was keen to look at the shark again to get the proportions right.

He walked down Albion Street, glancing up at the windows, for he was a keen observer, and then down into the basement area where the kitchens were. A woman dressed as a cook in a white apron and cap was giving instructions to another, who was wearing a grey dress and a white apron and a maid's cap on her head.

'No, put it higher,' he heard the cook say. 'Nobody'll see it there.'

The maid reached up on her toes and stuck a card at the top of the window, pushing it into a gap in the frame. 'There,' she puffed. 'Somebody'll see it there all right. I just hope we're doing right and don't get into bother.'

'Pah!' the cook said. 'It's me as has to manage, not her upstairs.'

Sonny paused curiously. He couldn't see what was written on the card, but was fairly sure it was a situation vacant sign. Mm, he thought. I'll have a look at that on my way back.

CHAPTER SEVEN

'I've got to have somebody,' Cook groused. 'It's no use Miss Rosalie saying we'll wait until her pa gets home. He might not come for weeks.'

Martha looked anxious. 'She's probably worried that she'll choose somebody unsuitable.'

'Tell her I'll interview 'em,' Cook said. 'I'm 'one who'll have to tell 'em what to do and when to do it. There's no need for her to even see 'scullery maid.'

But when Martha put it to Miss Rosalie again, she was told that she couldn't attend to the matter just now as she had more pressing things to do.

'We can see to it, miss,' Martha said. 'Cook knows who she wants.'

Rosalie took a breath. How very tiresome servants were sometimes. What was the point of hiring someone new if she were not staying here? Her father might want to pack up and leave. She was, though, becoming increasingly worried as she had still not heard from him. He must be abroad, she thought. How dreadful for him when he does return and learns the news of my mother's death.

A little later Martha again knocked on her door. 'Excuse me, Miss Rosalie. There's a gentleman enquiring . . .' Martha clasped her fingers tightly. 'That is, he just called on 'off chance . . .'

'Enquiring? About what?' Rosalie raised her eyebrows. 'I'm about to go out.'

'Yes, miss, I know. I told him that Cook'd see him but he insists on seeing you – that is, '"lady of the house" is what he said.'

'A gentleman? Well then, why would Cook see him?' Rosalie was flabbergasted and not a little annoyed. She felt that the staff were trying to take advantage of her.

'It's about 'scullery maid,' Martha said. 'Cook thought that . . . well, so as not to bother you, she – that is, we – would put a card in 'basement window.'

'For what purpose?'

'To get a scullery maid, miss.'

'You put a card in the window!' Rosalie thought how horrified her mother would have been. 'This is not a shop advertising its wares,' she said rather sharply.

'No, Miss Rosalie.' Martha was put out to be

on the receiving end of a rebuke. 'I said as how you wouldn't like it.'

'And this "gentleman"? What has he to do with it?'

'Well, we'd no sooner put 'card in 'window than he was knocking on 'door, miss. Said he knew somebody in dire need of such a position.'

Rosalie frowned. How bizarre. But Martha must be mistaken. No gentleman would make such an enquiry. 'I'm sorry,' she said. 'I can't possibly see anyone this morning. Ask him to leave his card,' she added as an afterthought. 'And I'll receive him tomorrow.'

Martha dipped her knee. 'Yes, Miss Rosalie.'

Her young mistress seemed to be taking to the running of the household with ease. 'Inbred, it is,' she told Cook when she went downstairs. 'She won't see him. I have to tell him to come back tomorrow.'

'Well I'll tell you this,' Cook retorted. 'I've washed 'kitchen floor for last time. I'll not do another and that's a fact. I'm a cook, not a skivvy!'

Sonny nodded gravely when given the news but declined to leave a card. He patted his pocket as if searching for one, but didn't actually possess any; it wasn't something he ever carried. His social circle didn't deem it necessary. If they wanted to call on someone they did just that. But he was curious. The two servants had appeared to be thrown into some confusion when he'd knocked on the basement door, which was why he had asked if he might speak to the mistress of the house.

He had also overheard some of the conversation between them as he had waited in the lobby. Who was this Miss Rosalie? Was she some eccentric old spinster who allowed her staff to place a card in the basement window and then refused to speak to the applicant?

He ran up the basement steps and was about to walk on when the front door of the house opened. He paused for a moment, curiosity getting the better of him, and was interested to see a young woman, in fact not much more than a girl, come down the steps. She was a member of the family, he concluded, for she was well dressed in good cloth with a hooped skirt, though in dark colours; and, he pondered, she seemed vaguely familiar. She wore a grey hat with a black veil; the design was far too old for her, for she couldn't have been more than sixteen. Was she bereaved, he wondered, to wear such sombre colours?

It was then that he recalled the funeral procession that had travelled behind Ida's burial cart. It had overtaken them and he had glanced inside the leading carriage. This was the same young woman. They had locked eyes for a second before the vehicle had driven on.

'Miss Rosalie?' He took a chance. 'Miss Rosalie!' He had no hat to lift, so he put his hand to his chest and gave a slight bow. 'I do beg your pardon for this intrusion.'

Rosalie turned in surprise and put her gloved hand to her mouth. 'Yes?' she whispered. 'Who are you?'

'Sonny Blake. We haven't met – at least, I saw you in a funeral carriage travelling to the Northern General Cemetery.'

'Yes? What of it?'

She was abrupt, and cautious as she should be, being approached by a stranger. 'I beg your pardon,' he said again. 'But I called on your servant after seeing the situation vacant card in the window.'

'It was put there without my permission,' she said haughtily.

Ah! A little smile hovered on his lips. So this is the eccentric spinster!

'When I saw the card, I was hoping that I might be granted an interview with the mistress of the house, in order to recommend a young woman for the position,' he explained. 'She's fallen on unfortunate times and sorely needs a live-in occupation.'

'I'm sorry, but I cannot discuss such matters out in the street.' Rosalie turned as if to walk away, but hesitated as he went on.

'I apologize yet again.' He put his hand to his chest once more. 'Do I take it that you are the mistress of the establishment?' Rosalie frowned and was about to retort when Sonny continued, 'I wouldn't normally be so crass as to presume to address you, but the young woman of whom I speak has recently lost her mother and is quite alone in the world. She presently works in a mill but doesn't earn enough to pay her rent.'

His eyes held hers and he knew he had her attention.

'Was she – did we pass her?' He saw her swallow and lick her lips. 'Was that when you saw me? On the way to the cemetery, I mean?'

'Yes,' he said softly. 'It was her mother's funeral. I was accompanying Polly. It has struck her very hard. So unexpected.'

Her mouth trembled and she turned her head away. 'Yes,' she whispered. 'Yes, indeed. I know how—' She stopped. She was obviously unused to discussing private matters. 'Ask her to call,' she said. 'Tell her to ask for Cook. We'll give her a month's trial. I cannot say longer,' she added. 'My future plans are unclear.'

'Thank you so much,' he said. 'She'll be very grateful.' He dropped his voice. 'May I ask – are you also recently bereaved?'

'Yes.' Rosalie took a breath. 'I am. My mother

also died. That was who – that was why we were travelling – when we passed—'

'I am so very sorry,' he said softly. 'Please accept my sincere condolences.'

'What relation to you is this young woman?' Rosalie was suddenly alert as to propriety.

'No relation.' He gave her a disarming smile. 'I've known the family for quite some time. Polly's mother was an honest hard-working woman who brought up her daughter alone for many years.' He somehow gave the impression that Ida was older than she had been and probably an impoverished widow.

'Very well.' Rosalie gave a dismissive nod. 'We'll try her out. Polly, you said?'

'That's right. Thank you again. Most commendable.' He gave another slight bow. 'May I ask to whom I am speaking?'

She lifted her chin and looked at him from clear blue eyes. 'Rosalie Kingston.'

'Thank you, Miss Kingston.' He stepped back. 'I won't detain you any longer. I wish you good day.'

Rosalie was strangely unnerved by the incident. How would my mother have reacted, she wondered. I don't think she would have spoken to him at all. She would have asked him to make an appointment, or perhaps Cook would have made the decision over hiring a scullery maid. I shouldn't have taken it upon myself. I made a mistake. There's so much to learn about running a household and Mama never got round to explaining it all to me.

She was on her way to visit the family lawyer, who had attended the funeral and requested that she drop by to see him whenever she felt up to it. She didn't feel up to it – in the week since the funeral she had kept mostly to her room – but now it was New Year she knew that she must make some effort towards normality.

Mr Benjamin's rooms were off High Street and she had only to wait a few minutes before she was called through to his poky office, which was filled with overflowing bookshelves and piles of paper in every corner.

Mr Benjamin swept aside a stack of files on his desk and invited her to sit down.

'I assume you have not yet received news of your father, Miss Kingston?'

Rosalie shook her head. 'I have not,' she said. 'I'm beginning to worry.'

'Far too early to start worrying,' he said kindly. 'Your father could well be abroad with his regiment, and if he is he might not receive any correspondence, although I imagine that you marked yours urgent.'

'Yes,' she said, slightly consoled by his benevolent attitude. 'I did.'

'Then I'm sure all will be well,' he said, but then gazed at her over the top of his tortoiseshell spectacles. 'However, we must be prepared. He is a soldier, after all, and military life is not without its dangers. I have to say that it concerns me somewhat that our Prime Minister, Palmerston, allows British soldiers to interfere in European affairs.' Almost as an afterthought, he asked, 'Was your mother in regular correspondence with your father?'

'Erm – yes, I believe so.' But not lately, she thought, so perhaps he really is abroad. 'My father was at home early in the summer and returned to his regiment in July.'

'Well, what I suggest is that we write to your uncle, your father's brother, to acquaint him with the news of your mother's death. I take it that you have not informed him?'

'Why, no!' Rosalie was flustered. 'I never thought to. I don't know where he lives. I don't think my mother had any contact with him.'

'Mm.' Mr Benjamin peered down his nose at some papers he had withdrawn from a folder. 'Well, I have here some instructions which your father left with me in case of any accident befalling him.' He raised his eyebrows and transferred his gaze to Rosalie. 'I do not think for a moment that anything has,' he explained. 'But it is my duty to be prepared.'

He thumbed through the sheaf of paper.

'Five years ago your father and his brother Luke met me to discuss various matters which affected them both. Most of it was relating to their father's estate, but one of the things that was arranged was that if anything should befall your father *and* your mother, then your uncle Luke would become your legal guardian until you came of age.'

Rosalie stared at him in astonishment. 'But . . . but I don't know him, nor does he know me. Was my mother aware of this?'

Mr Benjamin gave a little lift of his shoulders. 'Possibly. Or possibly not,' he murmured. 'Forgive me,' he said apologetically. 'But she didn't need to know. You would be how old, five years ago? Eleven? Twelve?'

'Yes,' she said. 'So could this have been arranged without my mother's knowledge?'

'Yes, indeed,' he said. 'But this action would only be put in place, as I say, if you were left without *both* parents. Someone had to be responsible for you, otherwise you would have been made a ward of court. But,' he said cheerfully, 'the question hasn't arisen. Your father I'm quite sure is fit and well and will be home before very long, but I felt that you should be apprised of the situation.'

'I see,' she said faintly. 'Well, thank you for the information. I know nothing of my uncle; I understood that my father and he didn't correspond, and that they hadn't been in touch for years.'

'I believe that was true until five years ago, when they realized that there would be a mutual advantage in making up their differences. Your uncle has two children, a son and a daughter who would have become wards of *your* father if anything had happened to theirs. Luke Kingston is a widower,' he added.

'Where do they live?'

'Oh!' He waved a hand. 'Somewhere up on the moors, miles from anywhere so I understand. Above Scarborough, anyway. Were you thinking of going to meet them?'

'Not at present,' Rosalie said, rising from the chair. 'But as you say, it is as well to be prepared.'

CHAPTER EIGHT

'Thank you so much, Sonny.' Polly flung her arms round Sonny's waist. 'Oh, thank you!'

He grinned and extricated himself from her grasp. 'You haven't got the job yet! You have to please the cook. Tell her that Miss Kingston suggested you ask her about the position. Kowtow to her a bit. Cooks like to think they own the kitchen and those who work in it.'

'How do you know that?' Polly asked curiously.

'Oh – a friend of mine had a relation who was a cook,' he lied, not wanting to tell her that as a child he was often in the kitchen being spoilt by Aunt Ettie's cook. 'She was the one who made the decisions about kitchen staff,' he added.

'Mebbe she was onny boasting,' Polly declared. 'I'd have thought that 'missus of 'house would have decided.'

'Mistress,' he laughed. 'Not missus!'

'Oh.' Polly was deflated. 'I don't know how I'll get on in a big house. I might not say or do 'right thing.'

'It's a scullery maid they want, Polly,' he told her. 'You're going to be scrubbing floors, not arranging flowers and chatting with Miss Rosalie.'

'Miss Rosalie? How do you know her name?' Polly gazed at him in awe.

'I made it my business to find out,' he said cheerfully. 'And' – his manner changed – 'I also discovered that she's just lost her mother, at the same time as you. You recall the carriage that passed us on the way to the cemetery? That was her.'

'Oh!' Polly breathed. 'So we've summat in common?'

His mouth turned down. 'Not much, but that at least, and she's about your age. But you're not likely to see her, Polly. I wouldn't think she spends any time in the kitchen.'

Polly nodded and sighed. 'I'll go now,' she said, 'and get it over with. Where did you say 'house was?'

'I didn't,' he said. 'But it's in Albion Street.'

Albion Street, she thought. That's where I saw that girl looking out of 'window. Could it be her? Is she living in that great house on her own? I wonder where her father is, or if, like me, she doesn't know.

She curled her toes against the cold as she trudged towards Albion Street. She'd scrubbed her hands and face and her skin had a rosy glow because of the icy water and the bitter air. I'm so cold, she thought, pulling her shawl closer over her head. How do I address 'cook? Do I dip my knee? I wonder how many other servants they've got.

It took her ten minutes to walk from High Street to Albion Street, but she didn't mind. It won't matter how long it takes me, cos if I get 'job then I'll live in and won't have to go back to High Street every night. I hope it's warm; I hope they have big fires. I shan't even mind cleaning them out as long as I can warm myself by them. She and her mother had a fireplace in their room, but only lit a fire when they could find kindling or beg some wood from the timber yards, for they had no money to buy coal.

After her mother died, Mrs Walters had advised Polly not to light a fire until after the funeral. She had stared uncomprehendingly for a second and then she wept. She hadn't lit a fire since.

She found the house number on the wrought iron gate which led to the basement area, and then looked up at the house. There were half a dozen steps leading up to the front door, which was painted black. She was fairly sure it was the house where she had seen the girl in the window. She'd waved, she recalled. I wonder if she was feeling as lonely as I was.

Polly knocked on the basement door. Sonny had told her not to go to the front door but the one down the area steps. Servants' quarters, he had said. The front door was only for family or friends.

A woman came to the door. She was wearing a grey dress with a white apron over it and a white cap on her head. Oh, Polly breathed. I hope I'll be able to wear a uniform like that.

'Yes?' The woman looked Polly up and down. 'What do you want?'

Polly licked her lips and bobbed her knee. 'Scuse me,' she said. 'I was told to ask for 'cook. Miss Kingston said I was to come.'

'She never did!' Martha was disbelieving. 'Did she tell you herself?'

Polly shook her head. 'No. She told a friend and said to be sure to ask for 'cook,' she repeated.

Martha grunted. 'You'd better come in then. But stop there in 'lobby. Don't come in 'kitchen wi' them dirty boots.'

Polly stepped inside. 'They're wet,' she explained. 'Snow's all slushy.'

'I can see that for myself,' Martha muttered. 'But Cook's washed 'floor 'n' she won't do it again.'

Cook called her in but told her to take her

96

boots off. Polly stood in front of her with cold bare red toes.

'Don't you possess any stockings?' The cook frowned.

'No, mum,' she said. 'We could never run to stockings.'

'So tell me about yourself.' Cook sat down in a wooden rocking chair and folded her arms. 'Where've you worked afore?'

'I'm Polly Parker, I'm seventeen in a few days and I'm a mill worker,' she said. 'I've allus worked but I don't earn much and my ma's just died and I can't afford to pay for a room wi' my wages.'

'What did your ma die of? Was it infectious?'

'No. She died of loss o' blood,' Polly said, unwilling to say her mother had died of a miscarriage.

'Loss o' blood?' Martha interrupted. 'How was that? Did she have an accident?'

Cook glared at Martha. 'Excuse me! I'm asking 'questions.'

'Sorry!' Martha shrugged.

The cook raised her eyebrows and Polly knew she would still have to answer the question even though Cook hadn't asked it.

'She – erm, she lost 'bairn she was carrying. Just afore Christmas.' Tears came unexpectedly and trickled down her cheek.

Cook lifted her head and her mouth turned down and Polly dreaded the next question, which she was sure would be where her father was. But she was mistaken. Cook simply said, 'I lost my ma when I was about your age. She'd been ill for some time, though, so it wasn't unexpected.'

'I didn't know that,' Martha said. 'You've never said.'

Cook shrugged. 'It's not summat you like to talk about,' she said. 'Besides, it was years ago, but you never forget it.' She straightened up in the chair. 'Let me tell you what'll be expected of you supposing I tek you on. You'll have to sleep down here in 'kitchen, cos you'll be 'first up to mend 'fire and get 'water on to boil. Then you'll wash 'kitchen floor and 'lobby. Windows need to be cleaned once a week and all 'pots and pans I use will want washing, and I like to see 'em sparkling,' she warned, lifting a finger. 'And it'll be you what scrubs 'vegetables for dinner.' She paused. 'But that's not all. You'll be at my beck 'n' call all day.' She looked hard at Polly. 'So what do you think? Are you capable of doing that?'

Polly nodded enthusiastically. 'Yes,' she said. 'I can manage all o' that. Will I get a uniform? My clothes are a bit shabby.' She looked down at her old skirt. She had two, one for wearing and one for washing. They were both thin and faded, as were her second-hand blouses. All she wore underneath was a cotton shift.

'Well, you could hardly be seen in them rags,' Martha commented. 'Not in this house. Mrs Kingston was allus most particular and I expect Miss Rosalie'll be 'same.'

Cook glared at her. 'I'm not finished,' she said. She turned to Polly. 'You'll get two wool skirts. They're not new but they're good enough. Two grey blouses and two pairs o' black stockings.' She looked down at Polly's bare feet. 'I don't know about boots. Do yours let 'wet in?' At Polly's nod, she muttered, 'I'll have to ask about them cos we don't have any spare.'

She perused Polly for a moment, and then, pursing her lips, said, 'Let's see how you shape up. Come and mek a pot o' tea.' She pointed to the range. 'Kettle's steaming, 'tea's in that caddy. That's our tea, not for upstairs, not that you'll be mekking that anyway.'

Polly looked at her anxiously. 'I've hardly ever made it,' she said. 'It's three and fourpence a pound; we could hardly ever afford it.'

'I'll show you,' Martha said. 'We can't afford to waste it either but we like a good cup, don't we, Cook?'

Cook agreed that they did and sat back as she waited for it. 'Put a bit extra in 'pot as there's three of us,' she instructed. 'We generally have two spoons.' Surprisingly she winked at Polly.

'But we'll give you a treat if you haven't had a cup for a bit.'

'I haven't,' Polly said, picking up the cloth to hold the kettle handle. 'Christmas Day it was, when I went to somebody's house for dinner. But there were that many of us and they'd added that much water to 'pot, when it came to my turn I couldn't taste 'tea.'

Martha had put the tea in the teapot and Polly poured the water on to the leaves and then stirred. 'We've to wait now till it's mashed, that's what my ma allus said. It brings out 'flavour.'

Cook nodded. 'She was quite right,' she said. Then she stroked her chin and pulled at a single protruding black hair. 'All right, Polly Parker,' she said. 'You seem willing enough. I think you'll be all right. We'll give you a month's trial. Can you start straight away?'

Rosalie was astonished by the news that the lawyer had given her. Surely my father would have discussed this with Mama, she thought as she walked home, or perhaps he did, but why did they not tell me?

She had almost reached her house when she was surprised to see a girl dash up the basement steps and run along the street, her skirts flying and her shawl slipping off her shoulders. She was shouting something and it sounded like *hurrah*. Rosalie sighed. How good it must be to be so free and unrestrained, to occasionally be capricious and not be concerned about other people's opinions. Not that I could be skittish just now, of course, not when Mama is not yet cold in her grave. But how invigorating it would be to taste such freedom and not always be so proper.

She didn't know why she suddenly thought of the man who had spoken to her earlier as she had come out of the house. He had been polite in the extreme, but as she remembered their conversation now she couldn't help but think that he might have been teasing her just a little and that he would have been more amiable and genial had she not been so formal. But there, she thought as she mounted the steps. It wouldn't do to be too friendly towards an unknown man who hadn't been introduced; and she became quite warm when she thought of it. I'm extremely vulnerable. Suppose he had heard that I am living alone! He knew about Mama and he'd seen me in the carriage. What if this business about a scullery maid was just a ploy, an excuse to speak to me, and he doesn't know a girl suitable for the position at all!

She rang the bell for Martha to come up when she had taken off her coat and hat.

'Martha,' she said, 'I hope you have taken the card out of the window. You may take it to the grocer's shop and ask if it could be placed in *his* window. We might get all kinds of odd people applying otherwise.'

Martha smiled. 'Don't you worry, Miss Rosalie. We've got it all arranged. Cook has took on a young girl who seems very suitable. We're giving her a month's trial. Her name's Polly Parker.'

CHAPTER NINE

A week later, the sky was grey and heavy with rain. Rosalie stood looking out of the window wondering what to do with her day. She saw the postman trudging down the street with his head bent and a heavy post bag over his arm. She had given up wishing that word would come from her father and was beginning to think that he had not yet received her letter. She heard the doorbell ring and waited for Martha to come up with whatever had been delivered.

Martha bobbed her knee. 'A letter, Miss Rosalie!' She sounded breathless. 'Mebbe it's news at last.'

'Yes,' she replied, turning it over in her hand. It was her father's handwriting. The servants, she realized, were probably as anxious over their fate as she was over hers. 'Thank you, Martha.'

The maid withdrew and Rosalie picked up a

paper knife from the escritoire by the window. She took a breath. She was nervous, full of unease over what decision her father would make about her future.

She sat down on a chair and inserted the knife into the envelope. It was thick and wouldn't slit easily and she had to tear at it before she could withdraw the pages.

My dearest daughter [it began],
    I cannot begin to tell you how distressed I am to hear of your mother's death. My own dear wife, who was in such excellent health when I saw her last. She had written to tell me that she was again with child and we both had great hopes that this time there would be a successful outcome. There is always a risk, of course. You must forgive me, Rosalie, for discussing such a delicate subject, but you are now fifteen or sixteen years of age, are you not, and I am sure that your mama acquainted you with these facts.

Goodness, Rosalie thought. Papa doesn't know how old I am! Mama always sent greetings from both of them on my birthday. It occurred to her that there would be no birthday card for her this year; and had her mother not told him that she had been advised by Dr James not to embark on another pregnancy?

However, you have, I gather, taken care of everything. I am sure Mrs Fellowes was more than happy to advise you on the funeral arrangements. In view of the fact that your conduct has been so exemplary under such harrowing circumstances, when it might have been assumed that a young lady so afflicted would take to her bed, I cannot but feel relieved to know that your good sense and ability will carry you through.

I have decided therefore that there is no advantage in travelling home at present, and as my regiment will shortly be returning to Ireland I have written to my brother Luke, who would be your legal guardian if anything untoward should happen to me [well I know *that* already, she thought], and I await his reply to say when it will be convenient for you to travel to his home.

'What!' she exclaimed aloud. 'But I don't know him!'

She continued to read, scanning the letter quickly as she sought enlightenment regarding her future.

The alternative would have been for you to come here to Aldershot and live

105

with the family of a fellow officer, who unfortunately was killed in action last year. I have tentatively broached the subject with his widow, as I felt that your kindness and understanding would help them over their bereavement. After some debate, however, I decided that it would be preferable if you lived with my brother until such time as you are of an age to consider marriage, and then you might come.

I will send funds to pay Cook and Mary for a month, which will be sufficient time for them to find alternative employment. If you ask them to close up the house they will know what to do, and when I return from duties I will decide what is to be done with it.

She dropped the letter on to her lap and didn't bother to read the final pleasantries or condolences. 'Shut up the house,' she muttered. 'And give Cook and Martha notice. He meant Martha, of course, not Mary. We've never had a Mary.' She began to cry. 'Why didn't he come? No advantage! Does he not realize that I'm living here alone?'

She wiped away the tears that were coursing down her cheeks. 'This comes of being capable,' she sniffed. 'If I'd behaved like a child he would have come instantly.' But then he might have taken me back with him, she thought, and foisted me on to this poor woman who has enough sorrow to deal with without taking in a bereaved stranger.

Polly was on her knees when Martha came down the stairs into the kitchen. She seemed to spend most of her time on her knees or else up to her elbows in greasy water. Cook was exacting, but she hadn't grumbled too much about her work. Polly quite enjoyed scrubbing the floor and seeing the rough tiles come up clean and shiny, although the shine disappeared once the floor was dry. She'd suggested that she might polish them but Cook was horrified. 'I'd slip,' she said. 'And what if I lost my balance when I was carrying a hot dish?'

Polly was amazed at the amount of food that was prepared every day for one person, although she'd noticed that Miss Rosalie didn't have a large appetite and usually sent most of it back. It wasn't often wasted, though, as she and Cook and Martha generally finished it off. She thought that had she been doing the cooking she would have rehashed the leftovers for the next meal, but when she mentioned it Cook insisted that fresh food had to be supplied for upstairs every single day.

'It's come at last,' she heard Martha say. 'I recognized his writing. Now we'll know what's going to happen; whether we'll keep our jobs or be given notice.'

Polly rocked back on her heels and picked up the bucket. She knew better than to ask a question, but had noticed that if she bided her time usually one or the other would impart some information.

'And you, young woman,' Martha addressed her. 'You might be out of work even afore your month's trial is up.'

'Oh,' Polly said. 'I'm sorry. Have I done summat I shouldn't?'

'No, not your fault,' Martha said hastily. 'It's just that we've been waiting on a letter from Master and it's just come in 'morning post.'

Polly chanced a question. 'Why? What's a letter to do wi' us?'

'Cos of Miss Rosalie,' Cook said. 'She can't stop here on her own. She's too young to run a household unless Master comes home, and I can't see him doing that, for why would he give up a career in 'army? So we could all be looking for work.'

Polly gazed at her. 'But – I gave up my job at 'mill to come here. Will you be able to give me a reference?'

Cook pursed her mouth as she considered. 'Well, probably, but don't let's cross that bridge till we get to it.'

'It's all very well for you, Cook,' Martha

grumbled. 'You can get work in a household or a bakery, but there's not allus a place for such as me. I'm thirty, past my prime, too old for a kitchen maid or even an upstairs maid in a new household.'

'You'll have to try for housekeeping,' Cook advised. 'Some old couple who want just one servant.'

Martha turned her nose up. 'Jill of all trades, you mean,' she groused. 'Aye, well, mebbe. Beggars can't be choosers.'

'But we don't know yet, do we?' Polly piped up. 'Mebbe it won't be as bad as it seems.'

Martha didn't answer but took her coat off the peg behind the door. 'I'm slipping out,' she said. 'Shan't be long. I'll not be wanted upstairs for a bit and I need some fresh air.'

Cook cocked her head towards the door as Martha went out. 'She's worried,' she said. 'I reckon she'll be putting 'word out that she's in 'market for a new position.'

'How do you mean?' Polly asked.

'She'll be calling on other maids that she knows in town. Asking them to let her know if anybody's in need of a servant. That way she doesn't have to go through an agency. Which nobody likes to do. It's a bit degrading waiting about for summat to turn up.'

'It's serious then?' Polly asked. 'You really think we'll have to leave?'

'Aye.' Cook nodded. 'I do. Now then, Poll. Go wash your hands and mek us a nice cup o' tea.'

Rosalie blew her nose and considered her situation. Although her father hadn't asked her opinion, he had at least considered two options for her welfare. I know nothing about my uncle except that he's a widower. Where does he live? Is it in the middle of nowhere, as Mr Benjamin implied? If I go to Aldershot I would be among strangers. I won't see my father, at least not very often, but perhaps more often than if I go to stay with his brother. Oh dear! Which would I prefer? Perhaps I should wait for the next letter. Uncle Luke might not want me there. He might only accept the commitment if Father dies. She gave a small gasp. Not that I would want him to, of course!

A headache began, probably because of her crying. She reached for the bell to summon Martha and order tea and toast, which her mother used to say was a comfort if you were feeling low. And an aspirin too, she thought, pressing her fingers to her temples. Poor Mama. Maybe she had often felt low, for she took aspirin quite often.

Martha was a long time answering the bell and Rosalie was about to ring again when there was a faint tapping on the door. 'Come in,' she called, frowning, for Martha generally knocked and then appeared a second later.

Slowly the door opened. 'Who is it?' she asked. 'Martha?'

A slightly built girl she did not recall having seen before stood hesitating in the doorway and holding the door with one hand as if she would fall over if she let go. Then awkwardly she bobbed her knee. 'Beg pardon, Miss Rosalie,' she croaked. 'Martha's had to go out so there's onny me and Cook.'

'And who are you?' Rosalie was astonished to find a stranger in front of her.

'Polly Parker, miss. I'm 'new scullery maid.'

CHAPTER TEN

'Please come in,' Rosalie said. 'Who recommended you?'

Polly came into the room and stood in front of Rosalie and bobbed her knee again as Cook had told her she should. 'Sonny Blake, miss. He said I should come and ask as I needed a live-in job o' work.'

Rosalie swallowed. The girl was about her age and she felt awkward asking questions as if she were her superior. 'I understand that you've just lost your mother?' she said.

Polly nodded. 'She died, miss. Christmas Eve.' She paused, wondering if there were boundaries she shouldn't cross. 'I think we buried her on 'same day as your ma . . .' Her voice trailed away as she saw her employer blink and press her lips together.

'Sorry, Miss Rosalie. I didn't mean to upset you.' She heaved a sigh. 'Sometimes, when I'm on my own, I want to cry, and I generally do, but not when there's other folk about. My ma used to say we should keep our troubles to ourselves, cos other folk have got enough of their own without hearing of anybody else's.'

'Yes, my mother would have said the same, I expect,' Rosalie answered hesitantly. 'Except – that it would help to be able to talk sometimes to someone who understood. So are you an orphan? Or is your father still alive?'

Polly shrugged. 'He might well be, but I don't know who he is, let alone where he is.'

She flushed when she saw Rosalie's startled expression and lowered her head, but she glanced at her from beneath her lashes. 'I don't mind,' she said. 'Ma and me were all right wi' just 'two of us. But now . . . well, now that she's gone, I do get sad and a bit lonely.'

'Yes,' Rosalie said softly. 'So do I.'

'Would you . . .' Polly faltered. 'I mean, it might not be right, but I was just mekking a pot o' tea and, well, mebbe you'd like to come down into 'kitchen and have a cup with us? There's just me and Cook, cos like I said Martha's gone out.' Polly chewed on her bottom lip. 'I mean, it might cheer you up a bit.'

'Well . . .' Rosalie wavered. 'I do need to talk things over with Cook and Martha as a matter of fact, so . . . I suppose I could.'

Polly beamed. 'That'd be grand. Shall I go and tell Cook?'

'No,' Rosalie decided. 'No, I'll come down with you now. If you told her I was coming she might get into a state and bring out the best china, and I don't want a fuss.'

Polly clattered down the basement stairs whilst Rosalie followed more slowly. She had been into the kitchen many times, but then she had been expected and both servants had been waiting for her. Now as she entered the kitchen Cook was sitting in her chair with her head back and her eyes closed. She sat up when she heard Polly.

'What did she want? Were you polite?'

Then she saw Rosalie standing in the doorway and hurriedly got to her feet and adjusted her cap.

'Oh, Miss Rosalie. I hope there's nothing amiss? I'm sorry that Polly had to come up, but Martha—'

'Yes, I know.' Rosalie smiled. 'She had to go out. It's quite all right, Cook. Polly said she'd just made tea so I've come down for a cup.'

'Oh, but Polly could have brought it up.' Cook was completely flustered.

Rosalie sat down at the scrubbed table. 'I need to talk to you, Cook. Please sit down.'

She did, slowly and reluctantly. It's odd, Rosalie thought. Cook is much older than me and yet she treats me with such deference. It's not just politeness – it's almost servility, and I don't think I like that.

'I received a letter from my father this morning,' Rosalie told her and watched as Polly poured three cups of strong brown tea. 'I've been waiting for a reply since I wrote to tell him of my mother's death.'

To her horror she felt her eyes prickle with tears. I mustn't cry, she thought. I mustn't cry in front of them. She swallowed hard and took a breath and saw both Cook and Polly watching her.

Polly sat down at the table beside her and placed a cup and saucer in front of her. 'Would you like a spoon of sugar in there, miss?' she asked, pushing a glass sugar bowl towards her.

'I don't know.' Rosalie looked down at the steaming tea.

'Miss Rosalie doesn't usually have this kind of tea,' Cook said. 'She might not like it.'

'Is there another kind of tea?' Polly asked.

Rosalie took a sip. 'I will have some sugar,' she said. 'It's stronger than I usually have, but very nice, very satisfying. Yes,' she said to Polly. 'There are different kinds of tea: Indian, China, tea made from herbs.' She took another sip. 'But I like this. Thank you, Polly, for asking me.'

Cook, open-mouthed, glared at Polly, and she knew she would be in hot water when

Miss Rosalie had gone back upstairs. Then the basement door crashed open and Martha burst in.

'Guess what,' she began, and drew in a breath when she saw Rosalie.

'Just in time, Martha,' Rosalie said. 'I was about to tell Cook about my father's letter.'

Martha glanced at Cook and then at Polly, both apparently entertaining the young mistress from upstairs. There was cake on the table and they were all drinking tea.

She sat down next to Cook and Polly got up again to pour her a cup. 'I had to go out,' she babbled. 'I didn't mean to tek so long.'

Rosalie disregarded her comment. 'My father isn't coming home as I expected he would,' she said. 'And although he hasn't made any final arrangements, I feel that it is only fair to tell you that he is going to close up the house.'

She waited a moment or two for this to sink in and then said, 'I am as upset about this decision as I'm sure you will be, especially as I'll have to leave and live elsewhere.'

Cook found her voice. 'We half expected it, Miss Rosalie. I was onny saying to Martha that I thought this might happen. You can't live alone, miss,' she added softly. 'It isn't right.'

'Will you be able to find other work?' Rosalie asked. 'I will ask my father to give you references, of course.'

'I've been offered an interview for second housemaid, Miss Rosalie,' Martha broke in. 'Whilst I was out today I met somebody I knew and she said that they were looking for extra help. I've to see 'housekeeper tomorrow if I can get 'time off.'

Cook glanced at Polly and raised her eyebrows with an *I told you so* expression.

'That will be all right, Martha,' Rosalie said. 'But we shall expect you to work your notice so you must make that clear if you are offered the position. And what about you, Cook? Will you be able to find other work?'

Cook nodded. 'I hope so, though plain cooks like me generally stay in one place if their employers are satisfied wi' them.'

'Well, I will tell my father that you must stay on until you find a new position, at least until I too have to leave.' Rosalie glanced at Polly, who was staring down into her cup. 'What will you do, Polly?'

Polly shook her head. 'Don't know, miss,' she said quietly. 'But I'll stay on and help until 'house is shut up.' She pressed her lips together and took a breath. 'And then I'll move on.'

Martha was offered the new position and worked two weeks' notice, but before she left she arranged for the regular washerwoman to wash the bedlinen, even though it took a lot of

117

drying in the cold damp weather. Then she and Polly folded the sheets neatly and put them in the cupboards in the ironing room and placed dried lavender between them. They sprinkled dry tea leaves on the carpets before brushing them vigorously, then polished the dining room furniture and covered it with fustian sheets; Rosalie had said that she would no longer use the room but would take breakfast in her own room and other meals on a small table in the morning room.

'Where will she go, do you think?' Polly asked Martha as they cleaned the windows. 'Who will she stay with?'

'Don't know.' Martha shrugged. 'Some relation. I don't suppose she'll have a choice; she'll have to go to whoever will have her.'

'I wouldn't like that,' Polly said. 'I'd like to be asked so I could say yes or no.'

Martha grunted. 'Well, those who are better off than us have to do what's expected of 'em, so in that sense they're worse off than us. I mean, Miss Rosalie will have a husband chosen for her; I bet her father's looking about for somebody right now and she'll not have any say in 'matter.'

Polly gazed at her. 'But that's not fair! Suppose it's somebody she doesn't like?'

'Oh, I don't suppose she'd be forced, but if there's somebody wi' money who's fairly presentable, well, she'd be hard pressed to find a reason why she shouldn't marry him.' Martha gave a sigh. 'I wouldn't mind if somebody'd find me a rich husband. I'd marry him like a shot and then I'd not have to work any more.'

Cook had put her name down at an employment agency. So far there had been no enquiries, but as there had been no letter yet from Miss Rosalie's father with instructions regarding the house she was not overly worried. She made sure that Polly scrubbed all the kitchen shelves, and then they listed everything in the store cupboard and cooked everything that was perishable. Preserves, pickles and bottled fruit were stacked in the limewashed cold larder, and she bought only enough from the fishmonger, butcher and baker to last a week at a time.

'We could put 'waste in a pig pail, couldn't we?' Polly suggested one day when Miss Rosalie sent back half of the food that had been cooked for her. 'There's too much for us to eat. We never had much left over but my ma allus used to send our scraps and peelings to 'pig man and earn a copper or two.'

'Nah!' Cook scoffed. 'In some houses them pittances are 'servants' perks, but when I first came here Mrs Kingston told me that I couldn't put food out for pigwash cos it encouraged vermin.'

'True, it does,' Polly agreed. 'I've seen many a rat jumping out of a pig pail.'

An interview for Cook came on the same day that Rosalie received another letter from her father and one from her uncle Luke.

'You must take the job if it's offered, Cook,' she told her after scanning both letters, 'and there will be no need to work your notice if they want you immediately. I shall be able to manage for the short time before I leave.'

'I'll stay and help you, Miss Rosalie,' Polly said. 'I'm in no hurry to go off anywhere.'

In truth Polly was dreading leaving the house. She had become accustomed to having regular meals every day, and even in the short time she had worked there she had put on some weight. She liked having her mattress by the warm range and she felt secure in the knowledge that there was no landlord to turn her out. Now she wondered what she would do next, but thought that if Miss Rosalie would give her a reference she would apply elsewhere for a similar job.

Cook had gone out for her interview in her black coat and hat and Polly thought how different she looked out of her white apron and cap, undistinguished and less authoritative. She was nervous, she said, for she hadn't been interviewed in over fifteen years. 'Miss Rosalie was just a toddler when I first came here. I used to make milk pobs for her cos she wasn't a good feeder.'

'It's a good recommendation if you've been in one job for such a long time,' Polly said. 'Somebody'll be glad to have you.'

When Cook came back an hour later she was beaming and her hat was askew. 'I can start tomorrow if Miss Rosalie agrees. 'Old cook at a house on Beverley Road has died and they're desperate for somebody to start straight away.'

'So there you are then,' Polly said. 'Isn't that what I said? I don't suppose they want a scullery maid as well, do they?'

'Shouldn't think so,' Cook said blithely. 'They've got a large staff, but I'll think on you, Polly if I should hear of owt,' she added. 'You're a good lass. You'll do all right.'

So I might, Polly thought, if I'm given 'opportunity. She heaved a breath. Mebbe I'll seek out Sonny Blake and see if he's got any other bright ideas.

CHAPTER ELEVEN

Rosalie sat down in a chair by the window and reread the letter from her uncle. Her father's letter had been brief, merely asking about her health and wellbeing and telling her that she should expect a letter from his brother fairly soon.

And here it was. She fingered the two pages. The writing was a scrawl as if the writer was in a hurry to rush off to do other things.

Dear Niece,

I am in receipt of your father's letter and am sorry to hear of the death of his wife, your mother. I too have suffered the affliction of losing a wife and therefore send my sincere condolences.

My brother has requested that I abide by our agreement to assume the guardianship of each other's children should anything untoward happen to either of us, and in

122

consideration of his request I hereby offer you a home until such time as you are of an age when you may wish to make some other arrangement.

It will be convenient for me to expect you here at the end of February. I cannot guarantee that travelling conditions will be ideal, and you must be prepared for harsh weather until the end of March. We live very quiet lives here and entertainment is non-existent. I will await news of the date of your arrival.

Yours sincerely,
Luke Kingston.

Goodness, Rosalie thought. How very welcoming! He's told me nothing of himself, or indeed of his children. Are they male or female? Will I have the company of a female cousin or will I be surrounded by males? Does he have a housekeeper? What kind of house does he live in, and where? All I have is an address – Nab Farm, near Kirk Moor. She threw the letter on the floor. He has told me *nothing*!

Polly knocked on the door and entered with a tray of tea and toast, which she placed on a table. 'Cook said you might like this, Miss Rosalie, and she said to tell you that she's been offered 'position and they'd like her to start straight away if you've no objection. Seemingly they knew about your ma – mother – and don't want to inconvenience you.'

Rosalie shook her head. 'Tell Cook it's quite all right. I'm sure I can manage. I'll speak to her later. Perhaps she'll prepare some ham or beef,' she murmured, almost to herself, 'to tide me over until I leave for my uncle's house.'

She frowned as she thought of the logistics of travelling so far in winter conditions. I must write to Mr Fellowes and ask him if he knows of a reliable driver who can convey me to North Yorkshire. To Polly she said, 'I'll be leaving at the end of February. There's quite a lot to be done before my departure; perhaps you could help me? There are clothes to be pressed and packed in the trunk, and I'd like to take some of my personal belongings with me. I don't know if I'll be coming back, you see.'

A tear trickled down her cheek. I weep so often, she thought, and yet I feel that I haven't yet cried enough.

Polly gazed at her. 'It must be difficult for you to leave 'home you've lived in all your life,' she said softly. 'Especially going on your own. I'll help you all I can.'

Rosalie took out a handkerchief and wiped her cheek. 'I'm sorry,' she whispered. 'It's no worse for me than it is for you, and at least I'm going to family, even though I don't know them.'

'I didn't have anything to leave behind, miss,' Polly said. 'Not a thing that I was bothered about, anyway. After my ma had gone there was nothing and nobody that mattered.'

Rosalie looked at her and blinked her wet lashes. 'You're very brave,' she said. 'I wonder where you get your strength from.'

'Don't know,' Polly murmured. 'But when you've never had much then you've no expectations of owt good ever happening.'

'But that's awful!' Rosalie exclaimed. 'You must surely have something in life to look forward to?'

Polly shrugged. 'Can't think of anything, Miss Rosalie. It's a question of tekking each day as it comes.' She gave a grin. 'Getting this job was 'best thing that ever happened to me.' She shrugged again. 'But I should've known that it wouldn't last.'

'I'm so sorry,' Rosalie said. 'So sorry to disappoint you.'

'Can't be helped,' Polly answered. 'It's not your fault.'

After Polly had left the room, Rosalie slowly sipped her tea and nibbled on the toast. I have so much more than she has and therefore more to lose. And yet she is more cheerful and accepting of her lot than I am. Is she not desperately unhappy without future plans? How could I live without expectations? And yet, she pondered, my life so far has been nothing out of the ordinary and perhaps I can only look forward to more of the same, though as a wife and mother rather than a daughter.

For a while she meditated on her probable future, and then she took out her writing materials and began a letter to Mr and Mrs Fellowes to enquire about transport to North Yorkshire. Pensively she bit on the end of her pen. I won't be happy about travelling alone, she considered, and they too will be concerned for my safety. Yet I can't expect them to travel with me. It would be stretching the bounds of kindness too far, I fear.

She gazed out of the window to the street below and remembered knocking on the glass to attract the attention of the girl below. It was Polly, she had since realized, who was alone, as she was. She turned from her desk and rang the bell.

Polly returned and went to pick up the tea tray. 'Beg pardon, Miss Rosalie,' she said. 'I didn't think you'd be finished yet.'

'Leave it for a moment,' she said. 'I want to talk to you,' and she stood up so that they were facing each other, head to head. 'Polly!' she said. 'Will you come with me?'

Polly stared at her. Miss Rosalie seemed animated and excited, and yet strangely nervous. 'Come with you, Miss Rosalie? Where to?'

Rosalie licked her lips. 'To my uncle's house. He lives in North Yorkshire. It's quite a long way from here – so maybe,' she hesitated, 'maybe you wouldn't want to come.' She heaved a breath. 'But if you felt that you could—'

'Oh! Miss!' Polly exhaled. 'Do you mean it? Do you mean . . . to stay wi' you – or just to travel with you?'

'Oh, but to stay, of course. My uncle will raise no objections, I'm sure. He wouldn't expect me to go alone.'

'Wouldn't he?' Polly thought that better-off folk had a funny way of going on when they could take other people along without asking and with no thought of the expense of feeding them. But who was she to object? 'Well then, yes please!' She grinned. 'That'd be summat I could really look forward to.'

Rosalie put her hand across her face as emotion threatened to envelop her. 'Good,' she managed to stammer, and then burst into tears.

Polly put her hand on Rosalie's arm and led her back to her chair, murmuring, 'You've not had a proper cry yet, have you? Come on. Let it all out. Better out than in, my ma used to say.'

She too felt a prickle of tears as Rosalie sobbed, but hers were tears of happiness and expectation. Hope you're watching me, Ma, she thought. I think things might be coming right after all.

After Cook had left, Polly was in charge of the kitchen, a chore she revelled in. 'I'm no great shakes at cooking, Miss Rosalie,' she told her, 'but I can cook shin o' beef and mek a stew. I watched Cook do that and it's easy enough. And I know a good baker where we can get fresh bread every day, and cakes too if you've a fancy for 'em.'

Rosalie smiled. It was such a relief not to have to plan meals every day and tell Cook what she should do. Now they could eat whatever they wanted whenever they felt like it. She looked round the kitchen, at the well-scrubbed table, the cooking range Polly cleaned out every morning, the clock ticking steadily on the wall.

'Shall we live in here, Polly?' she said.

Polly put her head on one side. What did Miss Rosalie mean? Polly already lived in the kitchen, and slept here too, although she could have had either Martha's or Cook's vacated room if she'd wanted to.

'How do you mean, miss?'

'Well, it's so cosy and warm and there's really no point in lighting a fire upstairs just for me. I don't mean I should sleep here,' she added hastily. 'I know that you sleep down here, and besides, my own bed is very comfortable, but I thought that we could bring down two easy chairs and one or two more lamps for reading; the light isn't very good for that,' she said, glancing round. 'It would save a lot of work, wouldn't it?'

'It's true, it would.' Polly nodded. It would mean one fire fewer to clean and light every day, and save hauling a bucket of coal upstairs. Not that she minded doing that. She liked to see a fire blazing merrily in the cleanly swept hearth and she liked to look round the sitting room with its patterned wallpaper and large gilt mirror over the fireplace and big windows overlooking the street.

'Would I be in the way?' Rosalie asked anxiously. 'Because if you'd rather not . . .'

'Oh, no,' Polly assured her. 'But it's a bit unusual isn't it? I mean, suppose somebody calls to see you? Like 'parson or somebody.'

'Well, if they did,' Rosalie declared, 'we would answer the door as usual and explain that as we were busy packing to leave I was unable to receive visitors, except in the drawing room. They wouldn't stay long,' she said with some satisfaction, 'if there wasn't a fire. I am, however, expecting a visit from Mr and Mrs Fellowes, for I've written to them regarding transport and will of course receive them.' She frowned. She had sent the letter two days ago but there had been no response as yet.

'It's your house, miss,' Polly said. 'You must do what you think best.' She wondered what Martha or Cook would have thought. They would have been horrified, she was sure, if their employer had suggested she come to live downstairs with them. Not at all the thing to do, they would have said. Upstairs and downstairs shouldn't mix. But Polly didn't mind. She liked Miss Rosalie, and the crying session she had had upstairs seemed to have eased her tension. She was much more cheerful and positive now with regard to travelling to her uncle's house.

Rosalie went through her wardrobe choosing clothing she thought would be suitable for life in the country. 'My uncle said they lived very quietly and that there was no entertainment, so we'd better pack only plain gowns.'

'And warm ones, Miss Rosalie,' Polly said. 'It's bound to be cold in 'country.'

'Yes,' Rosalie said thoughtfully. 'I've looked on a map of my father's, and it seems to me that it is in the middle of nowhere. Uncle Luke only told me the names of the house and the moor. I found a place with the same name on the map, but I've written back to him and asked for more details.'

She selected some of her clothes, two grey

gowns and one in blue, and a wool coat, and put them on the bed.

'Why don't you try these on, Polly?' she said. 'They're a little too tight for me, but you're thinner than I am and I think they'll fit you.' She sank down on the bed and sighed. 'I don't really know how to go about things, you know. I suppose Mama ordered clothes for Martha and Cook but I don't ever recall her mentioning it, though I'm sure she would have taught me eventually; to prepare me for running my own household,' she added.

Polly nodded, fingering the soft wool of the dresses. Ordering clothing for the staff seemed an odd thing to teach a young girl, she thought, but if that young girl was destined to be the mistress of a house she would have to learn everything about housekeeping and what to tell the servants to do, she supposed, otherwise everyone would live in a muddle.

'These are lovely, miss. Can I try them now?'

'Yes,' Rosalie said. 'Why not? And then you can pack your trunk as well.'

'I don't have one, miss.' Polly slipped off her cap and apron and unfastened the ties of her skirt. 'I wore one skirt and carried 'other one under my arm.'

'Oh!' Rosalie exclaimed. 'Then in that case we must fully kit you out. You can have those three gowns and the coat; you'll need stock-ings and new boots, four nightgowns and a dressing robe, slippers, a shawl . . . I'm sure I can find several that I no longer wear.' She pondered, her hand on her chin. 'What else? A bonnet – two bonnets, one for weekdays and one for Sunday.'

Polly stared at her. 'I've never had so much. And you're forgetting, beggin' your pardon, Miss Rosalie, that I'm onny a scullery maid.'

Rosalie blinked. She had indeed forgotten Polly's role. They had spent so much time in each other's company since the other servants had left that she had treated her as a friend, a confidante. But she was suddenly aware that Polly hadn't forgotten her place. She always treated her, Rosalie, with respect and never overstepped the line between mistress and servant.

'But you won't be a scullery maid in my uncle's house,' she quavered. 'I didn't mean you to think that. He will have his own servants.'

Polly licked her lips. 'So what, then, Miss Rosalie? What will I be?' She clung tightly to the blue gown. She so badly wanted to wear it; it was such a beautiful blue, the colour of a summer sky.

Rosalie put her hand on Polly's. 'Will you not be my companion?' she asked diffidently. 'It doesn't matter to me that we've had a different

132

upbringing – that I have had so much and you so little. It seems to me that we've travelled on the same sad and stony path in order to meet.' She swallowed hard. 'I do not enter friendships lightly, Polly, but I would like you to be my friend, if you think you could.'

CHAPTER TWELVE

Polly gave a wide smile. 'I'd like that, miss. I think we'd get on ever so well and we'd be sort of allies, wouldn't we, up in that place where we don't know anybody.'

'Yes, we would,' Rosalie agreed excitedly. 'And you're so much more sensible than I am. I'm far too sensitive. That's the result of a sheltered upbringing. Oh, I'm so eager to be off now that I know you're coming with me as a friend. It will be quite an adventure into the unknown.'

'Yes!' Polly said. 'It will. It'll be different from anything I've ever known, anyway.' She pulled the blue gown over her shift. 'Would you mind, miss, if I told a friend I'm going away? He might worry if he finds me gone.'

'Of course you must, Polly. Would you like me to come with you so that he knows who you're with? Oh, Polly! That suits you so well. I must find you a hoop to go underneath it, or some extra petticoats. But the colour is perfect. I have always loved that blue. Take a peek in the looking glass.'

Rosalie took Polly's arm and led her to the full-length mirror. Polly stared at her reflection. That was never her!

'Are you sure I should have it, miss?' she said. 'It's – it's too good for me.'

'Nonsense,' Rosalie said. 'Of course it's not,' she added generously, for in truth she had always loved the gown. 'I have a bonnet which matches and we'll buy a blue ribbon for your hair.' She fingered Polly's fair hair. 'And shall we wash it so that the colour is brighter?'

Polly let out a sigh. She hadn't washed her hair in months. She never did in winter. In the summer months she would put her head under the pump, but in the winter the pump was often frozen up. 'I'll heat some water,' she said. 'I've had a bath since I came, in 'tin bath when Martha and Cook had gone to bed, but I'll have another and wash my hair so that I'm sparkling when we leave.'

Rosalie laughed. 'We're not going yet. You'll need another one before then.'

Polly gasped. 'Too much washing is bad for you. That's what my ma used to say.'

'Well this time I think your ma was wrong.' Rosalie giggled. 'You go and heat the water and I'll find some nice soap and powders for you.'

Polly reluctantly took off the blue gown. 'I'll keep that one for best,' she said. 'And wear a grey one to look for Sonny Blake.'

'Sonny Blake? You've mentioned him before. Is he the man who . . .'

'Yes,' Polly said. 'He's the one who spoke to you about me. He said he did, anyway.'

'Yes,' Rosalie said softly and idly twisted a lock of hair round her finger. 'He did.'

The following day they set out together to look for Sonny Blake. It was bitterly cold and Polly decided that she would wear the blue dress after all, with the warm wool coat. Rosalie had found her a matching velvet bonnet and she exclaimed as she put it on that Mr Blake wouldn't recognize her.

Rosalie too had washed her hair and the two of them could have been mistaken for sisters, being of a similar height and both fair, though Polly's hair was thick and strong while Rosalie's was soft and fine.

'You might not like where I'm tekking you, Miss Rosalie,' Polly told her as they walked towards High Street. 'It's a bit rough down here, but I want to ask Granny Walters if she's seen Sonny.'

'Your granny?' Rosalie said. 'I thought you said you hadn't any relations?'

'Nor have I, but everybody calls 'old lass – I mean, 'old woman – Granny Walters. She's a sort of midwife and nurse. She's allus there if anybody's sick or pregnant.'

Polly fell silent, thinking of her mother and about how the old lady wasn't able to help her. The memory of that awful day and night came rushing back and she stifled a sob. If she went away with Miss Rosalie she would be leaving behind all those she knew, and the memories too. Or would she think of her mother as she once was, beautiful, caring and loving, once she had left these streets and courts behind?

'It's not all rough,' Rosalie said as they entered High Street. 'There are some fine houses. My mother knew several people who lived here, although quite a few of them have moved to the country now.' She put a handkerchief to her nose. 'What's that smell?'

Polly put her nose in the air and sniffed, and then laughed. 'That's 'reason they've moved, miss. Cos of 'smell! It's seed oil, fish oil, and 'stench from other industries.' She refrained from mentioning the charnel house, although she could see smoke coming from the tall chimney. 'And not everybody wants to live amongst 'poor.

'We go down here,' she said, cutting through an alleyway. 'Mind where you're treading. Some folks are not too particular where they throw their rubbish.'

Rosalie held her breath. There really was a most awful stench. Drains, she decided, though on looking round she didn't see any. Then she spotted the pump at the bottom of the court and next to it a privy with its door wide open. She put her hand to her nose and wilted.

'I don't think I can bear this, Polly,' she faltered. 'I think I'm going to be sick.'

'Oh, it's not that bad.' Polly turned to look at Rosalie, and saw that her face had drained of colour. 'You should be here in 'summer. Even 'locals are ill wi' stink. Are you really going to be sick? Cos if you are—' She stopped as Rosalie turned and ran. 'You stop up there, miss,' she called after her. 'I'll not be a minute.'

Mrs Walters wasn't there, but Polly left a message with one of her granddaughters to say that she was going away. 'Be sure to tell her,' she said. 'I'm going away to a new life in 'country.'

Rosalie was leaning against a wall in High Street. 'I'm sorry, miss,' Polly said. 'I never thought . . . I mean, I'm used to it.' She heaved a breath. 'There's nobody about, anyway. I'll have to come back tonight.'

'Not in the dark!' Rosalie objected. 'It won't be safe.'

'Yes it will,' Polly said cheerfully. 'I lived here,

don't forget. But I won't come in this frock,' she added thoughtfully. 'I don't want folks to think I've come into money.'

Money! 'Polly!' Rosalie exclaimed. 'I haven't given you any wages. What did Cook say when she interviewed you?'

'She said five pounds a year,' Polly said, 'and all found. She give me a shilling at 'end of first week and said I'd get another shilling in spring and then 'rest next November if I was still here. Riches!' she crowed.

Rosalie made a mental note to give Polly some money before they left. She would need to see Mr Benjamin again too, to arrange for her allowance to be sent on to her uncle's house.

They crossed over Lowgate to make their way back home and Polly suggested they cut down Charlotte Street and round the edge of the town dock as it would be quicker. The sky was dark and ominous and more snow threatened. People were scurrying for shelter and a familiar figure was hurrying towards them with his head and shoulders shrugged down into his overcoat.

'Sonny?' Polly called to him. 'Is that you?'

He looked up. 'Polly!' He grinned. 'It's never Polly Parker all dressed up and nowhere to go!'

Polly stuck her chin in the air. 'It is me,' she said pertly. 'And I have got somewhere to go. We were coming to look for you to tell you.'

Sonny glanced at Rosalie. 'Miss Kingston. How do you do.' He smiled. 'How very nice that we should meet again.'

Rosalie dipped her knee. 'Polly was coming to look for you,' she said awkwardly. 'And – and I came along to confirm where she was going.'

'Oh?' He looked from one to the other. 'And where are you going?'

'Somewhere above Scarborough,' Rosalie said and wondered why she felt so dumbstruck with this man when Polly was so free and easy. But she knows him, she excused herself. He said he was a friend of the family. 'I'm awaiting further details from my uncle.'

'Above Scarborough?' He frowned. 'How far above Scarborough? Not the moors?'

'Yes,' Rosalie said hesitantly. 'But I've not been given full instructions.'

'I hope you're not contemplating travelling just yet,' Sonny said briskly. 'There's still thick snow up there. The roads will be impassable.'

Rosalie swallowed. 'At the end of February. That is the suggestion.'

'What nonsense!' he exclaimed. 'How do you propose to travel? Is someone travelling with you?'

'Just 'two of us,' Polly said.

'I've written to friends of my mother,'

Rosalie added, 'to ask if they know of a reliable driver.'

'No,' he said. 'You can't. Come with me.' He took Polly's arm and would have taken Rosalie's but she drew away, and steered them both back the way they had come and into an inn.

'A pot of coffee for the ladies,' he called to the landlord as he led them to a table in the corner away from the drinkers at the bar. 'And a pint of your best ale.' He seated himself opposite them. 'Now. What's this all about?'

Polly unbuttoned her coat, pushing open the collar to show off the blue gown, and sat back with a sigh of satisfaction as Rosalie began to explain.

She began hesitantly at first, and in a low voice, for she didn't know this man and the thought ran through her head that it might not be wise to tell him that the house in Albion Street would be empty once they had left. She was reassured when one of the first things he said was that if they were going to shut up the house they must inform the police.

'You should travel by train to Scarborough,' he went on, 'and ask your uncle to arrange transport from there. A local driver who knows the route, if the house is indeed on the moors. But perhaps it is not,' he added thoughtfully. 'It could be that it is only at Scalby or Hackness.'

'He said they lived very quietly and that

141

there was no entertainment,' Rosalie said. 'And the house is called Nab Farm. I believe it is a very isolated place.'

'Ah!' he said. Suddenly he smiled. 'Well, if it is on those glorious moors, then perhaps I could visit you in the spring? You must write to me, Polly, and tell me for sure. Send a card care of Charlotte Street Mews. The postie will find me.'

Rosalie drew herself up. 'I'm not sure if my uncle would allow – followers,' she faltered. 'We must first discover his feelings regarding visitors.'

Sonny laughed irrepressibly. 'Follower!' he hooted. 'I'm no follower.' He gazed at Rosalie from his dark eyes and she felt herself blush. 'I promised Polly's mother that I would look out for her,' he said in a softer tone, 'and I will, even if it means going to God knows where.'

'Did you, Sonny? Really?' Polly's mouth trembled. 'I didn't know that. Thank you.'

Sonny nodded. No need to tell her that Ida was already dead when he made the promise. He intended to keep it anyway.

'I – I'm sorry,' Rosalie stammered. 'I didn't mean – I didn't mean to be offensive, Mr Blake.'

'No offence taken,' he said solemnly, but she felt once again that he was teasing her. 'Of course you must be careful. It wouldn't do to invite all and sundry to your relative's home. But I assure you' – he smiled at her – 'I shall bring impeccable credentials!'

Before they left the inn, he remarked on how well Polly looked. 'Miss Kingston is treating you very well. May I ask what role you will play when you leave town?' He glanced at Polly but his gaze lingered on Rosalie.

Polly didn't reply. The agreement to be friends had been solely between themselves. She was still a servant as far as anyone else was concerned. What would Miss Rosalie say to Sonny?

'Polly is to be my companion,' Rosalie said firmly. 'That is . . . *we* will be companions, although Polly will receive a salary, which is her due.' She raised her eyebrows quizzically at Sonny Blake. 'I trust that will meet with your approval, Mr Blake?'

He held back a grin. It couldn't be better. Polly would teach this correct and formal young lady how to unwind, and she in turn would teach Polly manners and how to behave.

'Admirable, Miss Kingston.' Sonny held her gaze. What fine features she has: beautiful skin, high classical cheekbones, azure eyes as wide and blue as a cloudless sky. He felt his senses quicken. I'd like to paint her. He smiled at Polly. Her gaze was eager and alert, her

143

features sharper than Rosalie's but attractive nevertheless. 'I most heartily applaud you.'

He gave a short bow as he left them. 'I hope to hear from you when you receive more details from your uncle and I'm at your service at any time. I'll escort you to the station, if you will permit me, and help you with your trunks.'

'Goodness!' Polly exclaimed, watching him as he walked away down the street. 'What's got into him? He seems so different. He's quite a gent, isn't he?'

Rosalie also watched him until he turned a corner. 'Yes, I think you're right, Polly,' she said abstractedly. 'Mr Blake is more than he appears to be, or at least more than he would like us to think he is.'

Polly frowned. 'I'm not sure what you mean, Miss Rosalie. He's just Sonny Blake that I've allus known. But he's acting sort of different from usual.' She gave a grin. 'I think I know what it is,' she said. 'Beggin' your pardon, miss. But I think he's tekken a shine to you.'

'Don't be ridiculous, Polly!' Rosalie responded, but her eyes creased and she couldn't help but smile. She nudged Polly with her elbow. 'How silly you are.' She tucked her arm into Polly's. 'Come on,' she said. 'Let's go home.'

CHAPTER THIRTEEN

A few days later a letter came from Luke Kingston with abject apologies for omissions in his previous correspondence.

My daughter Clementina normally handles domestic affairs [he wrote], but she is presently away and staying with her grandmother until spring. You will travel by train to Scarboro'. You must let me know the date and time of arrival a week before, and Amos will collect you and bring you to Nab Farm. Strangers don't know the way. The boys will be here if I'm not.
Your uncle,
Luke Kingston.

'Well, we have an address to give Mr Blake, but I'm none the wiser as to where it is; and who is Amos and who are the boys?' Rosalie took out her father's map again and laid it out on the kitchen table. 'What do you think, Polly?'

Polly gazed at the map. 'I don't understand it,' she said. 'I've never seen one before.'

'Well, these lines here are roads.' Rosalie pointed. 'And look, this sign shows a castle, or the site of a castle.'

'Oh,' Polly said. 'I've never seen a castle. Would we be able to go in it, do you think?'

'It might be a ruin,' Rosalie told her, 'but we might be able to see some of the stones or walls. There's a castle in Scarborough,' she added. 'Perhaps we'll see that.'

Their preparations were complete and Rosalie wrote to her father informing him that she would be travelling to her uncle's very soon. Then she called on Mr Benjamin to ask him about her allowance and to tell him when she was leaving.

The weather had been improving slightly, but a week before the end of February it snowed again and they wondered whether or not to travel.

'It might be milder in a week's time,' Polly said. 'We could chance it.' She was eager to be off, to find out what was in front of her.

'On the other hand, it might be worse,' Rosalie dithered. 'February is such a difficult month. Oh, dear. I don't know what to do for the best.'

'I'll ask Sonny, shall I?' Polly said. 'Perhaps he would know what it's like up there.'

She went in search of him, wearing her warm coat and huddled under a gamp. This time she went straight to Charlotte Street and walked up and down, wondering which door to knock on. But he must have seen her from a window for he suddenly appeared with a coat thrown casually over his shoulders and a scarf flung round his neck.

'Where did you come from?' Polly asked. 'You've got paint on your face and on your hands!'

'Oh, so I have!' He spread out his long fingers. 'I've just been – erm – painting an old chair.'

'Mm!' she said. 'Wouldn't have thought you'd choose that shade of blue. It'll show up every grease mark.'

'Hark at the housewife!' he grinned. 'Is this the Polly I once knew? But no, it isn't,' he went on. 'I meant to say when I saw you last how very becoming that dress is. And you've done something with your hair.'

'Washed it,' she said. 'Miss Rosalie's got all kinds of soaps 'n' stuff which she lets me use.' She took hold of a strand of hair and held it to her nose. 'Smells nice; just you smell it.'

Dutifully, he put his nose close to her hair and sniffed. He laughed and patted her cheek.

147

'So it does.' He looked seriously at her. 'I'm really pleased that things are going well for you, Polly. I think Miss Rosalie is genuinely pleased with you.'

'She is!' Polly looked eagerly up at him. 'That's why she asked me to be her companion. It's a sort of friend, you know,' she added in case he didn't know.

'Good,' he said. 'So what are you doing round here? It's freezing cold, even though you've got a lovely warm coat on.'

'I've come looking for you,' she said. 'We don't know what to do. Weather's bad and we're supposed to be travelling next week. Should we go or not? Miss Rosalie's got to write and tell her uncle which day we're coming.'

'No!' he said emphatically. 'The roads will be bad, if not impassable. Put it off for a little longer.'

Polly sighed despondently. 'I wanted to go. I can't wait to set off.'

'You'll probably be there for a long time if you like it,' he said. 'Another week or so won't make any difference.'

'All right,' she agreed. 'I'll tell Miss Rosalie. We decided we'd ask you as you might know what it's like up on 'moors. How *do* you know?' she asked. 'Have you been?'

'Yes, often, especially when I was young,' he told her, omitting to say that he was there the previous autumn. He loved to see the changing colours of the moors, the gorse and the heather. He took a canvas tent, a blanket and his painting equipment and sometimes lived rough for a few days; he had been doing that for many years.

'Is it nice?' she asked eagerly. 'Did you see any castles?'

'Only old ruins.' He smiled. 'But it's beautiful, Polly. You'll love it. You won't ever want to come back to the town.'

She left him then with the assurance that she would let him know their travel arrangements so that he could help them to the station, but when she returned to Albion Street to tell Rosalie what he'd said Rosalie was as disappointed as she was.

'Of course we don't have to take his advice,' Rosalie said petulantly. 'We're quite ready to go. I could write to my uncle and tell him that we shall be a little later than planned. We could travel on the first of March. The weather will surely have improved by then!'

Polly took off her wet coat and bonnet and picked up a towel to dry her hair. There had been quite a blizzard as she'd returned; the gamp had blown inside out and her bonnet was soaking. 'I hope so,' she sniffed. 'Cos it's really, really cold.'

The following week they went looking for

Sonny, but there was no sign of him in the mews or in the town. Then Polly saw Mrs Walters shopping in Whitefriargate and hailed her. The old lady was surprised to see her. 'I thought you'd left,' she said.

'Not yet,' Polly said, 'but we're going soon. You know Sonny Blake, don't you? If you see him about will you tell him that we're leaving on Friday on 'ten thirty train?'

'Aye, I will.' Mrs Walters looked quizzically at Rosalie. 'How de do, miss,' she said. 'Polly's a good lass.' She nodded her head emphatically. 'Very reliable. We'll miss her round our way.'

'I'm sure you will,' Rosalie murmured. 'Your loss is my gain.'

On the Friday morning the sky was black and sleeting rain as sharp as needles was bouncing off the road. Polly had looked for Sonny again but couldn't find him.

'Mebbe Mrs Walters hasn't seen him,' she said. 'He wouldn't let us down, I know. It's half past nine. Shall I run and find a lad to fetch us a cab, Miss Rosalie?'

Rosalie took a breath. She was exceedingly anxious. She had never travelled alone before and as she knew Polly hadn't either and would have no idea what to expect, the responsibility was hers alone. She had written to her uncle again but hadn't received a reply.

'We'll wait just a little longer,' she said tightly, 'and if he hasn't come by ten we will just have to manage on our own.'

At five minutes to the hour a furious Sonny Blake turned up in a hansom cab. He hammered on the front door and stormed in when Polly opened it.

'This is madness!' he bellowed. 'You should have waited until the weather cleared. I've only this morning heard from Mrs Walters that you're going today.'

'Shh!' Polly put her finger to her lips. 'Miss Rosalie will hear you.'

'I don't care if she does! It's not fit weather for you to travel.'

'If it's inconvenient, Mr Blake,' Rosalie's cool voice came from the top of the basement steps, 'I'm sure we can manage. We did not have your address,' she added cuttingly, 'otherwise we would have informed you earlier.'

He turned a furious face to her. 'As a matter of fact it is not convenient, and I had great difficulty in hiring a cab at such short notice. Every man and his wife need a cab in this downpour. But I'm not talking about that! It's madness that you attempt to travel to the moors at this time of year.'

Rosalie lifted her chin and looked down her nose. 'It was my decision, Mr Blake, right or wrong. I can't change our plans now as I have written to my uncle telling him to expect us at Scarborough railway station.'

'Well let's hope he can get there,' he muttered. 'Where are your trunks?'

Three of Rosalie's trunks and a portmanteau and one trunk for Polly were stacked haphazardly in Rosalie's father's study.

'Good heavens!' he said bluntly. 'Are you planning on going to balls every night or have you got a suite of furniture in here?'

Rosalie crimped her lips and didn't answer him, but Polly attempted to explain that as Miss Rosalie didn't know if or when she was coming back they had packed most of her winter wardrobe.

Sonny grunted. 'Have you no idea when you'll return?'

'None,' Rosalie said flatly. 'It depends on my father and what plans he has for me.' She swallowed and gazed stonily at him as he straightened up from lifting a trunk into the hall. 'I am not a man, Mr Blake, who can decide his own future.'

He sighed. 'Your life is your own, Miss Kingston. We have only one. Don't allow anyone else to dictate to you what you should do with yours.'

She blinked and frowned as if she didn't understand what he meant.

'It's yours,' he advised softly. 'Don't waste

it on petty conventions or conformity. Swim against the tide if you want to.'

He heaved a trunk out of the door and on to the top step, and whistled to the cab driver. 'Come and give me a hand,' he called. 'Otherwise we'll miss the train.'

'Hello,' Polly said brightly, as the driver came up the steps. 'I know you. You're Bob, married to Mrs Walters' daughter.'

'I am,' he said. 'Hello, Polly. And I know you, miss.' He touched his cap at Rosalie, who was hovering inside the doorway. 'You give us your Christmas tree.'

'I did,' she said. 'I hope you enjoyed having it.'

'That we did, miss,' he said. 'It was a really nice thing to do.'

Sonny glanced at her and nodded. 'So it was.'

It was a cold, miserable journey and there were few passengers brave enough to venture on it. Sonny had collared a porter to help put the trunks in the luggage van and had then seen the two young travellers into a ladies only compartment. Polly had had the foresight to pack two blankets in her portmanteau and they huddled under them.

'You'll go through Beverley and Driffield and then Bridlington, Hunmanby and Filey;

Scarborough's the end of the line.' Sonny frowned, worried that the line might be blocked with snow or ice. 'I trust all will go well for you.' He handed Polly a slip of paper with his address. 'Write if you have any difficulties.'

'Thank you very much for your kindness, Mr Blake,' Rosalie murmured. 'I'm sorry if we've caused you any inconvenience.'

'That's all right,' he said. 'But do remember what I told you.'

Rosalie looked puzzled and tilted her head enquiringly. She was wearing a fur bonnet and a coat with a deep fur collar. Beneath it he saw a glimpse of dark blue cloth.

'About life,' he reminded her.

'Oh yes,' she said, and sighed. 'I'll try.'

'Don't just try,' he responded. 'Do it!'

The engine got up a head of steam and the train juddered as brakes were released and wheels began to turn.

'Goodbye,' Polly said excitedly as Sonny slammed the door and they began to jolt forward. 'I'll write and tell you what it's like.' She jumped up from her seat and went to the window, frantically waving as the train gathered speed. 'Goodbye! Of course,' she admitted as she sat down again, 'I don't write very well. I didn't have much schooling.'

Rosalie was pondering on Sonny Blake's last words to her. 'I'll help you, Polly,' she said vaguely. 'Reading and writing might be the only thing we can do up on the moors.'

'Oh!' Polly exclaimed. 'Will you, Miss Rosalie?'

'Yes,' Rosalie said. 'And Polly! Will you call me Rosalie, and not *Miss*, please?'

Polly gazed at her, her lips parted. 'Oh!' she said. 'Yes, Miss Rosalie, I'd be glad to. Thank you.' She shrugged and smiled and drew next to Rosalie. 'If we sit up close we'll keep warmer,' she said, adding, 'Don't you think that Sonny Blake is the nicest man you've ever met, and very handsome?'

Rosalie's cheeks flushed. 'Yes,' she admitted. 'I think he probably is.'

CHAPTER FOURTEEN

Polly rubbed the steamed-up window and then pulled it halfway down, letting in a blast of cold air. She leaned out. 'This must be Bridlington,' she gasped as the wind tore at her face. 'But I can't see 'sea.'

'Close the window,' Rosalie complained. 'You're letting the cold in. The railway station won't be near the sea, will it? It will be in the middle of the town, I expect.'

'Sorry.' Polly heaved the window up again. 'Mebbe we'll see it when we get further on. See the sea,' she giggled. 'I've never been to 'seaside. Ma used to say we'd go to Withernsea when we had some spare money. But we never had.'

She sighed and sat down again. 'Have you been to 'seaside, Miss Ros— er, Rosalie?'

Rosalie laughed. Polly was trying so hard to remember to drop the Miss, but she kept forgetting. 'Yes, often,' she said. 'But not recently. My nanny took me to Withernsea several times and once my parents took me to Bournemouth. I only remember that it was a long way from home. But my mother disliked the seaside; she always preferred towns, like York or Bath, so that's where we went.'

Polly gazed at her wide-eyed. 'And did you ever go to London?'

'Yes,' Rosalie said. 'And I expect we would have gone more often if Mama . . .' She heaved a breath. 'If Mama hadn't died. I would have gone for the Season, you know.'

Polly shook her head. She didn't know. She jerked forward as the train began to rumble on with a screech of steam.

'It's a sort of hunting ground to find a husband or a wife,' Rosalie explained. 'My mother used to say that we would go when I was eighteen. There are balls and dances and dinners where you meet people who would be suitable.' She shrugged. 'But I won't go now. There's no one to chaperon me.'

'I could chaperon you,' Polly said eagerly. 'I'd look after you.'

Rosalie gave a hoot of laughter. 'It's not like that, Polly! You have to go with someone who will introduce you to all the best people and they introduce you to others.'

'Why are they 'best?' Polly asked curiously. 'Who says they are?'

'I don't know,' Rosalie answered. 'And I don't know if they are. It's a matter of birth, and a matter of money,' she added.

'Oh!' Polly said, slightly deflated. 'That lets me out on both counts then.' Then she shrugged her shoulders up to her ears and looked smug. 'But I'm going to Scarborough and up to 'moors, so what could be better than that?'

Rosalie smiled back at her. 'I'm so pleased that you are with me, Polly. You lift my spirits.'

The sky became darker and the rain turned to snow, obliterating any view from the window. Both girls began to shiver with cold, despite their blankets. The train was travelling slowly and occasionally stopped, but they didn't open the window again to find out what was happening. At Hunmanby, a woman dressed in a thick coat and covered in several shawls came out of the station master's house with a tray of tea for the ladies' compartment. 'The station master sends his apologies for the delay,' she told them as they eagerly took the hot tea from her. 'You'll be on your way in about fifteen minutes.'

They thanked her and looked about them as they drank their tea. At the side of the track were large grain warehouses and alongside them were stacks of bricks, waiting to be transported.

They handed back the empty cups with effusive thanks. Rosalie gave the woman sixpence for her trouble, and a few minutes later they were off again. At Filey, a porter opened the door of the carriage to let in an elderly woman.

'At last!' she gasped as she plonked down in the seat opposite. 'I hope we get through to Scarborough; the snow's getting thicker by the minute and they're saying a blizzard is on its way. I've waited nearly an hour for this train. Why is it so late?'

'It kept stopping,' Polly said. 'But we don't know why.'

'They'd be brushing the lines probably,' the woman said. 'It was freezing this morning, and then the snow came. I hope they're wrong about a blizzard; I've a three-mile walk when I get off the train. I've been visiting my sister, but when I saw the weather closing in I thought I'd better head for home.'

Rosalie and Polly glanced at each other. Maybe we should have waited after all, Rosalie worried. I'm afraid Sonny Blake was probably right.

How daring we are, Polly thought. What if our transport gets stuck on 'moors and somebody has to rescue us? What if it's a wealthy farmer who rides up on his horse and plucks us out of 'snow and falls in love with Miss Rosalie?

159

And then I can be her attendant and wear a lovely gown and flowers in my hair.

The train stopped and started and they could hear the shouts of the railway men, the driver, the fireman and the guard, as they attempted to clear the line. Eventually they reached Scarborough. It was three o'clock in the afternoon, and the station was as dark and gloomy as night.

Polly ran off to fetch a porter, but found one already in the luggage van heaving the heavy trunks on to the platform, where another porter was loading them on to a wooden hand-cart.

The woman who had joined them at Filey gave them a wave. 'Weather'll get worse,' she called out as she hurried off. 'Mark my words!'

'Someone is collecting us,' Rosalie told the porters. 'Has anyone enquired?'

They both shook their heads. 'No, miss,' one of them said. 'We hardly expected any passengers on a day like this. You'll be best going to the ladies' waiting room and sitting there till they come.'

They waited over half an hour in the cold and draughty room, which had a low coal fire burning in the grate, but they were grateful for the facilities: a privy and a tap where they could wash their sooty hands.

Polly groaned as she huddled over the fire. 'I'm so hungry!' She had packed bread and cheese and an apple each, but those had been eaten before they had reached Filey. 'Shall I try to find a baker or a pie shop?'

'Oh, what a good idea,' Rosalie said, and fished about in her purse for money. 'We don't know how long it will take to get to my uncle's house. We could be hours.'

Polly dashed off and Rosalie once more was thankful that she had asked Polly to travel with her. She was so eager, so willing to please, whilst I, Rosalie thought, wouldn't have dared move from here in case I missed Uncle Luke's driver. And I would have hated travelling alone.

Ten minutes passed and Rosalie grew anxious, wondering where Polly had got to. Then a porter and a tall man with a thick beard and a shock of grey hair, wearing a grey wool cape-coat and a large-brimmed hat, came down the platform towards the waiting room.

'Here we are, miss,' the porter said. 'I think this is who you're waiting for.'

Rosalie rose unsteadily to her feet. She felt very shaky, from either lack of food or the effect of the train travel. 'Who are you?' she asked the man, who took off his hat.

'Amos. I've come from Mr Kingston,' he said gruffly. 'Are you Miss Kingston? We need to be off. Weather's bad up yonder. Madness to travel if you ask me.'

'We must wait a few moments for my companion,' Rosalie said. 'She's gone to find refreshments for us. We've been travelling since this morning.'

'Well, as long as her baint too long. Weather's bad up there,' he repeated. 'Don't want to get stuck in a snowdrift.'

'I hear you,' Rosalie said pertly. 'I'm sure she will be as swift as possible.'

Another ten minutes passed. The men took the trunks outside to the carriage and then Amos came back and paced up and down the platform, before Polly appeared clutching two paper bags. She was out of breath. 'All 'bakers are closing early,' she puffed. 'But I managed to find a grocer still open. I got two pork pies and an apple pie. Is that our carriage outside?'

'I expect so,' Rosalie said. 'And that wild man striding about is Amos, our driver.' She pursed her lips. 'I can't think it will be a comfortable ride.'

Polly was thrilled to be riding in a carriage but Rosalie looked at it in dismay. It was an ancient brougham which had seen better days. The upholstery was torn and dusty and there was no lantern inside. The two greys pulling it stamped and snorted impatiently.

'Your uncle must be rich,' Polly said as they stepped in. 'To own a carriage like this!'

'More likely he can't afford another one,' Rosalie muttered. 'But yes, he must have been rich enough to own a carriage and pair at one time. People in towns rarely own their own carriage and generally hire one, but I suppose he needs one if the farm is isolated.' She heaved a sigh and wondered if she had made the right choice. Perhaps she should have joined her father after all.

Polly leaned out of the window to speak to Amos before he climbed on to his seat. 'Will we be able to see Scarborough castle?'

He stared at her. 'No. We don't go on that road. Besides, it's only a ruin.' Then he appeared to relent. 'Mebbe in summer Maister'll let me bring you, but there's nowt there for young ladies. Now for young lads it's a different matter. I spent many a happy hour climbing up the cliffs to get to it when I was a nipper.'

'Goodness,' Rosalie murmured as Polly closed the window. 'A speech! You must have charmed him, Polly.'

The carriage moved off, swiftly turning its back on the town; snow was falling fast, not yet covering the ground but turning into wet slush. There were few people about and shopkeepers were putting up shutters outside their premises and closing the doors.

'I wish I'd asked Amos how long it will take to get there,' Rosalie said. 'Perhaps he'll stop en route to allow us to eat and rest.'

Polly was doubtful. Amos seemed anxious to get home as soon as possible. But they had only been travelling ten minutes or so when the carriage slowed at the top of a rise and Amos appeared and opened their door.

'Don't tek long now,' he said. 'But if you look back towards town you can just see the castle.' He pointed back the way they had travelled.

They both stepped down and looked in the direction he indicated. 'Oh, yes!' Polly exclaimed as behind the curtain of snow she saw the turreted outline faintly etched against the brooding skyline, its open windows like unseeing eyes. 'Oh, we must come and see it again in daylight, Rosalie. It's so romantic!'

Amos humphed at her comment and muttered that they'd have to be off, because the light was almost gone and they had a long journey ahead of them.

'How long?' Rosalie asked.

'As long as it teks.' His reply was surly and he held the door for them to board again.

'What a miserable fellow he is,' Rosalie said. 'Does he never smile?'

'We'll see if we can make him,' Polly grinned,

and then the carriage jerked as the horses pulled away and she was almost thrown to the floor.

They took the Scalby road, and although it was getting very dark Polly peered eagerly out of the window to catch a glimpse of the receding town.

'It's ever so hilly,' she commented. 'Not like Hull at all. You'd be all right walking down to town but you'd need a deal o' breath for 'pull back up.'

They drove along the road for about two miles before turning off on to a narrower one. The snow was coming down faster now, and as they travelled further away from the sea it began to settle, covering the rough road with a soft white carpet. The air was sharp and both girls drew their blankets closer round them.

'I'm worried,' Rosalie said, a few miles further on. 'I wish I knew how far we were going.'

'It wouldn't make any difference,' Polly said wisely. 'It'll tek 'same length of time whether we know or not.'

Rosalie giggled in spite of her anxiety. 'You are so funny, Polly,' she said. 'But I wish we could stop somewhere and finish the journey in the morning.'

'So do I,' Polly said, 'but I don't think old Amos would hear of it. *It'll tek as long as it teks*,' she mimicked in a gruff voice, making Rosalie laugh again.

'Let's try to guess what your uncle will be like,' she suggested. 'And the boys. It might help to pass 'time.'

'Well,' Rosalie said. 'I think he'll be an absent-minded country gentleman. Fairly tall like my father, but heavier built because of living in the country, and not as upright as a military man like my father.'

'And the boys? Are they young, do you think? Or your age?'

'I'm not sure.' Rosalie pondered. 'I don't know if Uncle Luke is younger or older than my father, but I'm going to guess that they will be about – erm, twelve or thirteen. Oh, but then why are they not away at school? So, don't know! Give in.'

The carriage slowed and rocked, throwing the girls about. Polly rose unsteadily to her feet and clung to the window frame to look out.

'It's thick snow and I can't see any houses or shops! Nothing!' she exclaimed. Never had she been anywhere where there was space which hadn't been filled by buildings.

'There must be some.' Rosalie joined her and peered out. 'We can't have left civilization behind yet, surely?'

The carriage rocked again and they fell

back into their seats; the horses appeared to be going at walking pace, as if they were picking their way. Then Polly saw a yellow light, and then another. 'We've passed two cottages. Oh,' she breathed. 'This is so exciting!'

The carriage drew to a halt and they waited expectantly. Amos opened the door. His coat, hat and beard were covered in snow. 'We'll have to stop,' he said. 'One of the hosses has gone lame. There's a tavern up yonder that I'll tek you to and you can stop there till I get back. You'll have to walk; I can't get the carriage up the hill. Snow's too thick.'

'But where will you go?' Rosalie said.

'Back to the Hackness road. There's an inn and a blacksmith there, but up yonder's not much more than an alehouse. It's respectable,' he added. 'You'll be quite safe.'

They both stepped down into deep snow. 'My boots!' Polly wailed. She was very proud of her new boots. She'd never had such a pair and now they would be ruined.

Rosalie lifted the hem of her coat. She was relieved to be stopping. At least they would be able to have a hot drink and rest for a while. 'Come on, Polly.' She put out her hand. 'They'll clean up, don't worry.'

Polly snorted. She had cleaned and polished Cook's and Martha's and Miss Rosalie's shoes and boots whilst working as a scullery maid.

Rosalie didn't know, of course. Probably never gave a thought as to who did jobs like that. She sighed. Well, some things don't change. I expect I'll have to do them again. She reached for Rosalie's hand and took a long stride and fell headlong into a snow-filled ditch.

CHAPTER FIFTEEN

Rosalie screeched 'Get her out! Get her out!' as Polly disappeared into the ditch. Amos hauled her out and Polly spluttered and then roared with laughter. Her eyes, mouth and hair were full of snow and she shook herself and looked up at Amos, who was having difficulty keeping a straight face. His shoulders were shaking.

As she brushed herself down Polly said gleefully, 'I haven't done that since I was a bairn and some lads held me down in a snowdrift.' She sniffed. 'Oh, come on Amos. Lead on. I'm wet through.'

'You'll catch a chill,' Rosalie fussed. 'I do hope there's a good fire at the hostelry.'

'There will be, miss.' Amos reverted to his glum self but his mouth twitched as he glanced at Polly. 'They'll put on supper as well, shouldn't wonder.'

They tramped up the hill, lifting their feet high and keeping to the middle path so there was no more fear of falling into a ditch. It was a long way up and the girls panted with the exertion. At the top of the hill was a terrace of four cottages, one of them being the alehouse. Amos pushed open the door and the smell of beer, tobacco and a smoky fire gushed out. Three elderly men sat at a table with a jug of ale in front of them; the landlord leaned with his elbows on the small counter.

'How do, Amos.' He straightened up. 'What brings you up here this time o' night?'

'On an errand for Maister,' Amos grunted. 'But I've got a lame hoss who'll never mek it home. Can you look after these young ladies till I get back from the blacksmith? They'll want a hot drink and a warm by yon fire.'

'And a little supper, if you please,' Rosalie said. 'We've been travelling all day.'

'You've got a bit wet, miss,' the landlord said to Polly, who was shivering in her wet clothes. 'What happened? Amos make you walk?'

Polly sneezed and shook her head. 'I fell in a ditch,' she snuffled. 'Should've watched where I was going.'

'You going to Nab Farm?' he asked, raising a hand to Amos as he went out of the door. 'That's a fair way to go at this time o' night, specially in this weather. Move over, lads,' he called to the men at the table near the fire. 'Let the fox see the rabbit.'

Polly and Rosalie looked at each other and then thanked the old men, who got up and shuffled the table and chairs to make room for them.

The landlord called for his wife, who took one look at Rosalie and Polly and went immediately to fetch blankets and towels. She helped them off with their coats and suggested they take off their boots and dry their feet by the fire.

'I'll get chilblains,' Polly said. 'I allus do if I put my feet by 'fire.'

'Rub them briskly with the towel,' Rosalie suggested. 'It'll get the blood moving.'

The landlady took away their wet coats and a few minutes later came in with a bowl of luke-warm water. 'Here, miss. Dip your feet in here; you'll soon get the feeling back.'

Polly did as she was bid and within a second felt her toes tingling as if pierced with red hot needles. 'Ow, ow!' she complained, looking so pathetic with the blanket draped over her shoulders and a towel over her wet hair that Rosalie put her hand over her mouth to stifle a giggle.

'I'm sorry,' she chortled. 'But you always make me laugh, Polly.'

'I'm so glad, Miss Rosalie,' Polly mumbled. 'So pleased to be of service.' Then she grinned. 'What a lark, eh? And this is onny 'start.'

They were brought hot soup and bread,

which warmed them up, and then prepared for a long wait for Amos to return. The landlord had told them that it might be an hour or more before he came back.

'That's if he doesn't finish up in a ditch,' he added lugubriously.

They both dozed by the fire, warm now with the blankets round them. Polly opened her eyes to see the old men preparing to go home, wrapping mufflers round their necks and pulling up their coat collars.

'G'night,' the landlord called after them. 'Mind how you go now. See you tomorrow, all being well.'

'I hope they'll be all right,' Polly murmured. 'Do they have far to travel?'

The landlord rubbed his chin. 'Just next door,' he said. 'Oxtoby brothers in the first cottage, Jack in the next. Reckon they'll mek it home if they watch where they put their feet.'

It was close on two hours before the door blew open to admit a flurry of snow and cold air and Amos, once more covered in snow and looking, Polly thought, like a giant snowman.

'By, what a night,' he panted. 'Give us a hot toddy, Bill and charge it up to Maister.' He glanced towards the fire and nodded to the two young women. 'I took both hosses out of the traces, rode the good 'un and led the lame,' he told Bill. 'I'd have been out there yet if I'd tried to tek 'carriage. As it is, I don't know how we'll get home.'

'Can't we stay until the morning?' A dull headache made Rosalie unwilling to move from the fireside, and she was about to say more when the door crashed open again and a young man almost fell inside.

Amos turned. 'Mr Howard, sir! What 'you doing out tonight?'

The stranger took off his hat and dashed the snow off it. He was tall and lean with thick fair hair and an inch-long scar across his left cheek.

'You might well ask, Amos. That tom-fool of a cousin of mine sent me on a wild goose chase. Pour me a glass of your ale, landlord, and put a hot poker in it, if you please, and then I'll get off home.'

He caught sight of Rosalie and Polly and gave a slight bow. 'Beg your pardon, ladies. Good evening.'

'Are you on foot, sir, or horseback?' Amos asked him.

'Why, on horseback, of course. What fool would be walking on such a night? You could die of exposure out there if you fell into a ditch.'

He quaffed his ale and rubbed his gloved hands together and then glanced over towards the fire again. 'I trust you are staying the night, ladies, and not venturing further?'

Amos interjected before Rosalie could speak. 'The young ladies are on their way to Nab Farm, sir,' he said. 'We were in the carriage, but one of hosses went lame.'

Mr Howard gave Amos a questioning glance. 'There's no one at home,' he said. 'Were you expected?' His question was addressed to Rosalie and Polly. Rosalie looked dismayed.

'They *are* expected, sir,' Amos interrupted again. 'I set off this morning on Maister's instructions to collect 'em from Scarborough railway station. Mrs Moody knows.'

'Really? She didn't tell me.' The young man shrugged. 'But nothing new there! Does Edwin know?'

'That I don't know, sir,' Amos said grimly.

Mr Howard came towards the fire. 'Please excuse me,' he said to them. 'We live in rather a disorganized household where the right hand rarely knows what the left hand is doing. My name is Howard Carleton.'

Not Uncle Luke's son, then, Rosalie thought. Is he one of 'the boys'?

'I'm Rosalie Kingston,' she said. 'And this is Miss Parker. We have travelled from Hull and are coming to stay with my uncle Luke Kingston. At his invitation,' she added.

He seemed astonished. 'I didn't know Uncle

174

Luke had any nieces. You're not sisters, then? You're very alike.'

Rosalie gave a slight frown. 'We are not sisters,' she said. 'We are companions. So Luke is your uncle too?'

'Mm.' He nodded. 'His wife and my father were sister and brother. He and Aunt Jane brought me up when my parents died.'

'I see,' Rosalie murmured and sat back in the chair. Luke Kingston must be a remarkable kind of man to take in his relatives' children. Perhaps that is why Papa asked if he would look after me. He must have known that he had already taken someone else's child into his protection. 'And who is Edwin?' she asked.

'Luke's son. My cousin . . . and seemingly yours. Then there's Clementina, Edwin's sister. She's away at present.' He gazed quizzically from one to the other. 'I hope you know how to entertain yourselves,' he said. 'There's absolutely nothing to do; not for ladies. That's why Clemmie goes away in the winter.'

'And what do you do, Mr Carleton?' Rosalie asked. 'Do you have an occupation or are you a gentleman who doesn't need to work?'

Polly looked astonished at Rosalie's question. Not work? Surely all men had to work? How did they keep body and soul together otherwise? She gazed expectantly at Howard Carleton, waiting for his answer. He seemed amused, she thought.

'I work on the farm,' he said. 'I'm a farmer, a shepherd.' There was a glimmer of a smile. He cast a glance at Amos who was fidgeting, wanting to be on his way. 'It's some small repayment for Luke's care of me during my childhood.'

'Excuse me, Mr Howard,' Amos said. 'But I want to get these young ladies home. Can you assist me?'

'Of course, but how? You said you had the carriage.'

'Carriage is down at the bottom of the hill. It'll be nigh on impossible to get up Harwood Dale. I've now got two well-shod hosses. If you would travel with us, I'd ride one, young ladies would ride the other, and you could bring up the rear. That way we'd get home in one piece. I'd rather not risk it on my own.'

'But I can barely ride!' Rosalie objected, and Polly added, 'And I've onny ever been on 'coal hoss's back!'

Howard Carleton laughed. He looked from one to the other. 'Well, this is going to be very interesting!' He thought for a moment. 'We can't risk them coming off, Amos. I suggest that we each take a young lady behind us and I'll lead the spare mount.'

Amos looked dubious, but then reluctantly

agreed. 'If the young ladies are happy with that?'

'Yes,' Rosalie said. 'I would prefer it. I feel very nervous about riding under these winter conditions. Polly?'

Polly shrugged, and then nodded. Either way she felt it would be a thrill of a lifetime. She felt as if she was entering another world, a world about which she knew nothing.

Their dry coats were brought and they put on warm, though rather damp, boots. The landlady also brought them a warm shawl each. 'Amos can bring these back when he's next down this way,' she said.

Rosalie thanked her. Polly put the shawl over her head and tucked it into her coat. 'That's grand,' she said. 'We'll be as warm as toast now.'

But it was still snowing and an icy wind blew, quickly chilling them. A stool was brought for them to stand on and the landlord helped them to mount. Rosalie sat in a side-saddle position behind Amos, which pleased her. Someone so solid, she surmised, must be very dependable. Polly, who hadn't been given a choice, sat astride behind Mr Carleton. Or Mr Howard, she thought, or whatever name he gives himself. Amos calls him Mr Howard, but he introduced himself as Howard Carleton. What a funny way of going on, not knowing what to call yourself.

'Hold on to my belt if you wish, Miss Parker.' Howard Carleton turned his head as they moved off. She heard the amusement in his voice as he asked, 'What did you hold on to when you rode the coal hoss?'

Huh, she thought. I suppose you think that's hilarious. 'I held on to his mane,' she said, adding caustically, 'but I don't suppose you'd want me to hold on to yours?'

He chuckled and urged on his steed. 'No. I have a feeling you might tug it if I misbehaved. Where was this coal hoss, Miss Parker?'

'It was in Hull, where I lived. And I'm Polly,' she said, grabbing hold of his belt as they moved forward.

'Polly Parker,' he murmured. 'Well, I hope you'll like it up here. We're midway between Fylingdale Moor and Howdale Moor, the middle of nowhere really. It will be quite different from what you are used to. No shops, no theatres, only miles and miles of moor, rocks, wild flowers, heather – and sheep, of course. And if I might speak confidentially' – they'd moved well in front of Amos and Rosalie, but even so he lowered his voice – 'when you meet Edwin Kingston, make sure you are introduced as Miss Parker, otherwise he will look down on you. He tends to stand on ceremony; likes to know that people fit into their natural order or place. Do you know what I mean, Polly Parker?'

'Oh, yes,' she said in a small voice. 'I do. You don't have to explain, Mr Carleton. But I know my position. I'm here as Miss Rosalie's companion. She pays my wages.'

'Good,' he said cheerfully. 'Then you don't take orders from anyone else. Is that clear?'

'Yes, sir,' she said.

'And my name is Howard,' he said. 'Only old Amos and the housekeeper call me Mr Howard. According to my cousins I'm only a hanger-on.' A note of bitterness had crept into his voice. 'But I work for my keep just as you do.'

'Honest work, then,' Polly said. 'Nobody need be ashamed o' that.' She was about to say more when a screech went up from Rosalie and a shout from Amos.

Howard wheeled their horse round, almost unseating Polly, and they saw that Rosalie was lying in a heap on the snowy ground.

CHAPTER SIXTEEN

'Rosalie! Miss Rosalie. Are you hurt?'

Polly stumbled towards the crumpled heap. Amos had dismounted too and they both bent over her. Howard Carleton looked down at Rosalie from his cob and gave a deep sigh.

'I'm all right,' Rosalie said crossly. 'Just very wet, and I've bruised my elbow.'

'I said you should have sat astride, miss,' Amos grunted. 'This ain't a saddle for sitting ladylike.'

They pulled Rosalie to her feet and Polly brushed her down.

'I'm all right, Polly,' Rosalie repeated. 'Please don't fuss!'

'Would you care to swap over, Miss Kingston?' Howard asked. 'You could come up in front of me and Pol— Miss Parker can go behind Amos. She's got the hang of hanging on!'

'No, thank you.' Rosalie took exception to

the humour in his voice. 'I'll sit astride behind Amos.'

Howard Carleton dismounted to help her up behind Amos again. The carriage horse, a Cleveland Bay with powerful shoulders and wide body, was too big for this slight young woman.

Polly looked up at Howard Carleton as Amos and Rosalie began to move off. 'So how will I get up?'

He grinned. 'I'll mount and put out my hand, and you'll put your foot in the stirrup iron and jump!'

Polly let out a breath. 'You don't ask much, do you?' she said sarcastically.

'Well, it's that or walk.' He took a leap and was astride. 'Like that,' he said. 'Easy!'

'What were you?' she jeered. 'A fairground rider?'

After two failed attempts to mount he found a low ridge of snow-covered rock abutting the track. Balancing on this, she tucked her foot into the iron and launched herself towards his outstretched hand.

'Good girl! We'll make a rider out of you yet,' he exclaimed and she felt a sense of pride and achievement.

'I haven't got a hoss,' she said.

He laughed and dug in his heels. 'I'm sure we can find a retired coal hoss or small hack for you to ride.'

'You're not going to forget that, are you?' she muttered into his ear. 'You'll have a great laugh over this town girl with your gen'lemen friends.'

'No,' he said sharply. 'That I won't. And I'm no gentleman and nor are my friends, the few that I have,' he added.

'What are you, then?'

'I told you. I'm a farmer and work for my uncle. A hired hand,' he added. 'No more, no less.'

They travelled on in silence. Amos and Rosalie were a short distance in front and Polly could just make out their outline through the falling snow, which was rapidly becoming a blizzard. She saw nothing of the terrain, for there was a complete white-out; most of the time she kept her head down with her forehead against Howard Carleton's back.

After a while she heard him curse. 'Madness,' he muttered. 'Absolute madness! We could get stuck in a drift and be here all night. Amos!' he shouted. 'Are you sure we're on the right track?'

Amos halted until they caught up. 'No, I'm not, but the hosses seem to know. Bonny here is leading and I'm putting my trust in her. She'll be after her supper and some warm straw and will know where to find it.'

'It's our fault,' Polly murmured. 'We should have waited another week or two.'

'Did Luke suggest you come?' Howard turned his head to speak to her and she caught a close-up of his right profile and thought how handsome he was with his straight nose and generous mouth. The only other attractive man she knew was Sonny Blake, but he was dark and foreign-looking.

'He wrote to Miss Rosalie,' she said. 'He said 'end of February, so we decided to come in spite of 'weather, but a friend told us it was madness, just like you said. He used to come here when he was a boy.' She paused. Sonny had seemed as sure about the weather conditions as if he came often. He was a mystery man, she decided, realizing that really she knew very little about him, or what he did for a living.

'How much further?' she asked after what seemed an interminable time.

'I don't know,' Howard muttered. 'I can't tell where we are. We might even have gone past the road to Nab Farm, except the horses would know. They have a homing instinct like all animals. But we're climbing again and coming out of a valley bottom.'

They made slow progress. Amos kept calling back to make sure they were still following. At one point he halted for them to catch up. 'Best stick together,' he grunted. 'But I don't think we're far off. I'm going to ride t'other hoss for a bit. Give Dancer a break from carrying us both. Missy here says she'll be able to manage.'

'I was thinking the same thing,' Howard said. 'I'm wearing stout boots, so I'll walk and lead Kasper.'

He told Polly to duck whilst he dismounted. 'Take hold of the reins,' he said. 'It's all right, don't worry. I have tight hold of his nose band, not that he's likely to bolt. He loves me.' He laughed. 'He won't leave me.'

Polly felt insecure to begin with, but after a while she began to enjoy the sensation of being astride the horse. Better than walking, anyway, she thought. She called out to Rosalie and asked if she was all right.

'Y-yes,' Rosalie said. 'But a little scared. If only we could see where we're going! It's like riding into a white wall, and I'm so cold.'

It was cold, Polly agreed, and they were very wet. But no wetter than the two men, she thought, although they were better prepared than the girls were, with heavy footwear and thick coats.

After about another half-hour or so, the track became very steep and Howard couldn't keep up with Amos and Rosalie. 'You keep going,' he shouted to Amos. 'I think we'll reach the turn soon. Call out when you get there.'

Shortly after, Amos shouted, 'Here we are, sir. Here's the turning for Nab. Nearly home.'

'Thank God,' Howard muttered. 'I'm just about beat.' They reached a gate, just visible against the snow, and Kasper turned towards it. 'Good lad.' Howard patted the horse on the nose. 'Soon have you in a warm bed.'

Kasper snickered and increased his pace. 'Whoa, boy.' Howard hauled him back. 'I'll have to ride this last mile,' he said to Polly. 'The track is too steep and the snow's too deep for me to walk. So shift forward, Polly Parker, and I'll come up.'

She took her feet out of the stirrups and with one swift movement he was behind her with his arms round her waist, taking the reins from her hands.

'Very cosy,' he murmured into her ear. 'Bet you've not done this before?'

She heard the smile in his voice and guessed he was as relieved as she was that the journey was almost at an end. She felt secure now and warmer with him behind her. 'I might have done,' she retaliated. 'But I'm not going to tell you!'

'Quite right,' he laughed. 'Everybody should have some secrets.'

'Have you any?' she asked.

'Might have,' he said. 'Or more like secret thoughts and wishes.'

'I've never gone in for them,' she said. 'Never thought owt nice would ever happen.' She paused and took a deep breath. 'But it has, and I'm very, very lucky.'

He gave a chuckle. 'What a strange girl you are, Polly Parker. Here you are in cold bleak surroundings; you don't know where you're going, you're wet through, and you consider yourself lucky!'

'You haven't seen where I come from, Mr Carleton,' she said. 'If it hadn't been for Sonny Blake finding me work with Miss Rosalie I might be spending my time on 'streets of Hull rather than looking forward to a warm fire and a bed for 'night.'

'Sonny Blake!'

'Yes. He's 'one I was telling you about, that said we shouldn't travel yet.'

'Is he, by Jove? Well, well. And – erm, how do you know this admirable fellow?'

She gave a little shrug. 'Known him for years. He was a friend of my ma's. But he's a lot younger than her – than she was, I mean.' Her words trailed away. Polly hadn't thought of her mother at all today. Usually she thought of her often, but today had been full of adventure and incidents. I'm inhabiting a different world now, Ma, and you're not in it, she thought, and suddenly she felt sad and missed her terribly.

Rosalie felt like weeping as she rode alone. She had started her flux that evening as they waited at the inn, which was why she was so uncomfortable riding. She had a blinding headache and a griping ache inside as well as a tender elbow from her fall. But worse, she felt really miserable. I don't know where I am or what I am doing. I'm not in charge of my life; but then, she considered, I never really have been. How good it would be to make my own decisions; if only I knew how to.

They were now on the last lap to what Amos called home. The horses had turned in at a gate and increased their pace up a hill or rutted track. She still couldn't see a hand in front of her, but Amos had assured her that it wouldn't be long before they were inside in front of a good fire.

'Mrs Moody'll have some hot soup waiting, I expect,' he called to her from his position in front. 'And a warm bed with a hot brick in it. Dunno about t'other young lady,' he'd added. 'Can't say if she's expected or not.'

'Is Mrs Moody the housekeeper?' Rosalie asked, ignoring his comment about Polly.

'Aye, she is. Been there for years. She looked after Mr Edwin and Miss Clementina after their mother died. They can do no wrong in her eyes,' he added, and Rosalie thought she detected a note of disapproval.

Presently she called to him, 'Can you see a light? Will that be the house?'

'Yes, miss. That's Nab Farm. There's nowt else it can be. No other dwellings for miles.'

The comment didn't hearten her at all, rather the opposite. Whatever are we going to do in this isolated place? Oh, I'm so pleased that I asked Polly to come with me, she thought for the hundredth time.

The blizzard began to ease and through the thinning curtain of snow she saw two and then three lights, and the blurred outline of a large square house. One flickering light – firelight, she hoped – was in a downstairs window, one showed from an upstairs room, and the third came from a sconce set on the wall beside the door, up to which led a short flight of steps.

'Here we are, miss.' Amos dismounted and came to help her down. 'This is Nab Farm.'

She couldn't move; she felt as if she had seized up completely.

'Put your arm round my shoulder, miss,' Amos said. 'That's it. Now lean on me; let me tek your weight. I'll not let you drop.'

Rosalie did as she was bid and let herself topple off the horse into Amos's arms. 'I'm very sorry,' she apologized as he placed her on the ground. 'I'm so stiff.'

'Aye, well, it's been a long hard journey,' he agreed. 'I'll be glad to get to my bed tonight.'

'Yes. You must be very tired too,' she said, realizing that Amos had also been out all day on his mission to collect them from Scarborough.

Polly and Howard Carleton rode up. Polly was gazing open-mouthed at the house. 'Is this it?' she said breathlessly. 'Is this where we're staying?'

'Yes,' Howard said. 'This is Nab Farm, your new abode, Miss Parker. I trust you will be very happy here.' He dismounted and held out his hand, but she slid off on her own, landing with a bump.

'Oh,' she gasped. 'Isn't it magnificent? So huge! I've never seen such a grand place before.'

He smiled. 'There's more,' he said. 'This is only the front. I reckon we shall lose you in the first few days and have to send out a search party.'

Polly grinned back at him. Her eyelashes were tipped with glistening snow and her nose was red. 'I shall enjoy exploring,' she said. 'If I'm allowed to,' she added, and then called to Rosalie, who appeared to be leaning heavily on Amos. 'Rosalie! Isn't it exciting?'

'Yes,' Rosalie said half-heartedly. 'Very!'

The door opened and several dogs bounded towards them, hurtling towards Howard Carleton and Amos, their tails wagging, and then rushing to sniff at Rosalie and Polly. Rosalie stepped back in alarm. She wasn't used to dogs, but Polly bent to pat them and received exuberant licks on her face.

'Down!' Howard shouted. 'Inside!'

The dogs obeyed immediately and raced back to the house, where a woman in a woollen dressing robe and a night cap was now standing by the door.

'The dogs woke me,' she said to Howard as he escorted the two girls up the steps. 'I never thought you'd get home tonight, nor Amos either.' She looked curiously at Rosalie and Polly. 'Have you travelled together?'

'We have,' Howard said. 'But quite by chance.' He turned to Rosalie. 'This is Mrs Moody, Uncle Luke's housekeeper. Mrs Moody,' he said, 'here at last, after a long and arduous journey, are Rosalie Kingston and her companion Miss Parker.'

Mrs Moody gave them a cursory nod. 'You'd better come in. The fire's gone down; I kept it in till an hour ago but then give up. I nivver reckoned anybody'd be foolish enough to travel in such weather. Madness, I'd say!'

Rosalie and Polly exchanged po-faced glances. Everyone seemed to agree it was madness. Well, maybe it was, but they were here at last.

Dominating the hall was an immense carved wood inglenook. Comfortable chairs were placed on each side of the hearth, where a low fire still burned and the dogs had settled themselves on a rag rug. To one side of the hearth was a bookcase, each shelf packed with books, and to the other a gun cupboard. Large paintings and tapestries hung on the walls, which were painted dark red, and the wood floor was scattered with carpets and rugs. Several doors led off to other realms.

'How do you do, Mrs Moody?' Rosalie was determined to assert herself from the start. 'We are both very tired indeed. I expect it is late for you to be up, but if we might have a hot drink before retiring we should be most grateful.'

Mrs Moody looked at her and then at Polly. It was hard to tell the difference between them. Both were wet through and each had a bedraggled shawl draped round her shoulders. 'Which of you is Maister's niece? I was expecting onny one young lady.'

'Really?' Rosalie said. 'I am Rosalie Kingston.' She gave a perplexed frown. 'My uncle has surely not forgotten that Miss Parker was coming also?'

'Well, happen he did,' the housekeeper grunted. 'But it wouldn't be the first time he's forgotten to tell me who's coming and who isn't. You'd best go and warm yourselves in front of 'embers. Mr Howard, if you'll shift the dogs, please, I'll go and boil the kettle yet again. There's soup and some cold chicken,' she added, 'and a piece of pie. Would that be sufficient?'

This time Polly answered. 'That would be very nice, Mrs Moody, thank you. Are there fires lit upstairs?'

Mrs Moody frowned. 'Onny in one room. Like I said, I was onny expecting one guest, but the bed will take onny a minute to make up and I'll slide the warming pan over it.'

Rosalie smiled. 'Not guests, Mrs Moody,' she said sweetly. 'Family. Just treat us as you do our cousins.'

'Yes, miss.' The housekeeper glanced at Howard, who kept a perfectly straight face as he nodded in agreement. 'Of course.'

'Thank you so much,' Rosalie and Polly chorused. 'So kind!'

CHAPTER SEVENTEEN

'There's only Mr Edwin home at present.' Mrs Moody clutched a burning candle as she led Rosalie and Polly upstairs. 'And he'll be in bed. Master's not got home.' They were warmer now after hot soup and several slices of chicken and bread and butter. Howard Carleton had stirred the fire, put on more wood and then wished them good night.

'I hope you sleep well,' he had said. 'The beds are very comfortable, that's one thing my uncle insists on. I shall see you sometime tomorrow, perhaps at midday when I come in for my dinner. We tend to eat at midday.' He smiled. 'A good dinner keeps us going for the rest of the day.'

'Thank you for your assistance, Mr Carleton,' Rosalie said. 'You've been most kind.'

He'd tipped his head to one side. 'If you are coming to live here, Miss Kingston,' he said. 'I think we should at least address each other by our first names. We are *almost* related.'

Rosalie blushed. 'Yes, I'm sorry. Of course. Howard.'

He gave a small bow. Then, turning to Polly, he put his hand to his chest, bowed again, and winked. 'Miss Parker!'

'Mr Howard!' she answered cheekily. 'Good night.'

Rosalie's room was very cosy with the fire and a lamp turned low. A soft rose pink eider-down lay on the high bed with several pillows. A communicating door led to Polly's smaller room. There was a lamp lit at the bedside here too but no fire in the grate; Polly put her hand between the sheets and found that Mrs Moody had swept the warming pan over the bottom one. A hot brick wrapped in a piece of flannel was in the middle of the bed.

'It's lovely,' she told Rosalie, when the latter commented on the smallness of the room. She took a breath. A room of her own. What luxury.

'Will you be warm enough?' Rosalie asked. She turned to Mrs Moody, who was hovering in the doorway, obviously anxious to return to her bed. 'Mrs Moody, you will be sure to have a fire lit in here tomorrow? Miss Parker is susceptible to the cold.'

'Then this baint the place for her to live,'

the housekeeper replied sourly. 'We get a lot o' weather up here.'

'I'm sure I'll be fine.' Polly gave a sudden sneeze. 'I'm quite hardy. You mustn't worry about me.'

'I'll bring another blanket,' Mrs Moody conceded. 'And I'll tell the maid to light a fire first thing.'

'I'll come to fetch 'blanket,' Polly said. 'Show me where they're kept and then you can get off to bed.' She smiled at her, thinking that she should keep her sweet. 'You must be tired. It's very late.'

She followed the housekeeper along the wide landing until she opened a door to what Polly thought would be a cupboard. Instead, a low step led them into another narrower landing with doors along one side. Mrs Moody opened one of them, lifting the candle to reveal a large room with sheets suspended from a drying rack. From a cupboard she brought out a thick blanket which she handed to Polly. She then picked up a saucer with a stub of candle from the top of a chest of drawers, lit it from her own and gave it to Polly.

'There you are miss,' she said. 'Will you be able to find your own way back?'

'I'm sure I will,' Polly said. 'Thank you.'

'I'll wish you good night then,' Mrs Moody said. 'I can go this way to my room.' She nodded towards the other end of the narrow landing. 'Saves traipsing through the house. Close the door after you if you please, miss.'

Polly put the candle down on the chest and wrapped the blanket round her shoulders. It smelled of lavender. She looked round the ironing room. Two walls were fitted with high cupboards, and on opening one she found it full of neatly folded sheets. An ironing table stood in the middle of the room. A fire was laid ready for lighting and in the hearth stood several irons and a small metal pail filled with water which would be used to test the heat of the irons. Bet everybody fights to do 'ironing in winter, she thought. It'll be 'warmest spot in the house.

She picked up the flickering candle and carefully closing the door behind her made her way back to the main landing and her room. The adjoining door was ajar and she saw that Rosalie was already undressed and in her night shift and dressing robe.

'I'm so cold,' Rosalie said. 'I'm going to sleep in my robe. I'd sleep in my stockings too except that they are damp.'

'Mine are too,' Polly said. 'But we'll soon get warm. This is an amazing house,' she went on enthusiastically. 'There's a hidden landing where there's an ironing room and it leads to another part of 'house. I think mebbe where 'maids sleep.'

'Oh?' Rosalie shivered and climbed into her bed.

'G'night then,' Polly said reluctantly. She would have liked to chat more about the possibility of exploring the inner workings of the house, but Rosalie obviously wasn't interested. I suppose it doesn't mean so much to her, Polly thought as she undressed. She's used to better things. Not like me.

She pulled on her new flannel nightdress and jumped into bed. This to me is like being a princess in a palace. She blew out the candle and turned down the lamp until it popped and there was instant darkness. She gave a deep satisfied sigh, put her head on the pillow and was asleep at once.

Rosalie shifted and shuffled in the unfamiliar bed. It was comfortable, as Howard Carleton had said. The feather mattress was deep, the pillows were soft and the eiderdown was cosy. But she was too tired to sleep. She ached from sitting astride the horse and her elbow was very painful. She turned the lamp low but not off.

Polly is so lucky, she thought. She has a happy nature and can adapt to different situations. Whereas I – I'm entrenched in rules and aware of what society demands of me as a woman, and I must discover what is required of me here in my uncle's house. Must I be passive, virtuous and disciplined and never self-indulgent, as was expected of me in my father's house? For it was always my father's house, even though he was rarely there, and it was my mother who took care of the household management.

She turned over in bed but that made her elbow even more painful so she sat up, propped herself on her pillows, pulled the covers up to her chin and resigned herself to a long sleepless night.

For some reason Sonny Blake came into her mind. He'd been angry with them for setting out when they did. And of course he was right, she admitted. The weather had been appalling and they could so easily have been marooned. *Madness*, he'd said. She gave a little laugh. That's what they'd all said. Amos, Mrs Moody, Howard Carleton; she still couldn't bring herself to call him by his first name, nor Sonny Blake either. But what was it that Sonny Blake had said to her? 'Your life is your own. We have only one. Swim against the tide if you want to.'

'But I don't know how,' she murmured. 'I need someone to teach me.'

It seemed like hours and she was still awake and cold. From somewhere in the house she heard the distant chimes of a clock. Two o'clock! The lamp spluttered and went out and darkness overwhelmed her. At home there had always been some light from a street lamp seeping into her bedroom, but here was total blackness.

She threw the covers back, searched for her slippers and crept towards where she thought the window would be. She felt about, her arms outstretched, and finding the curtains she pulled them back and peered out through the glass. Nothing! No moon, nothing but a snow-covered window sill and white ground below her. Then she looked up and saw a thousand brilliant stars in the sky.

Rosalie turned about and with her arms in front of her explored the wall in search of the door leading to Polly's room. She found the knob. The door was still open, and she went through.

'Polly,' she whispered. 'Are you awake?'

There was no answer and she made her way towards the bed; she stubbed her toes against the iron bed rail. 'Polly!' she breathed again and there was an answering grunt.

'I'm sorry, Polly,' Rosalie said. 'I can't sleep. I'm so cold and anxious.'

Polly sat up. 'Miss Rosalie?' she said in a thick, sleep-sodden voice. 'What's up?'

'I'm sorry to wake you, Polly,' Rosalie said again. 'I'm really cold and very restless; apprehensive, I suppose, about what's in store for us.'

Polly drew back the covers. 'Get in,' she mumbled. 'It's warm in here. Come on,' she coaxed when Rosalie hesitated. 'Be quick or we'll lose all 'heat.'

Rosalie took off her slippers and crept in beside Polly, who was as warm as toast. 'I'm sorry,' she repeated.

'It's all right.' Polly yawned. 'Ma and me allus shared a bed. Top to toe usually, but when it was really cold we allus cuddled up. Come on.' She put her arm round Rosalie. 'Snuggle up and you'll soon be asleep. It's a lovely bed.'

Polly's voice trailed away and Rosalie knew she had dropped off to sleep again.

It was very comforting, Rosalie thought. It was the first time she had ever shared a bed with anyone. She could recall her cot where as a small child she was tightly wrapped and then left alone. A night light burned, and every evening before the grown-ups retired someone, whether her mother or Nanny she knew not, opened the door a crack and looked in, but didn't enter. When she was older and in a proper bed, she said good night downstairs and then stayed in her bedroom until morning.

She moved closer, stealing the warmth from Polly's body in its flannel nightdress, and put her cold toes against Polly's warm ones. 'Thank you, Polly,' she murmured, and in a few minutes Rosalie too was fast asleep.

Polly woke to a bright light seeping through a gap in the curtains. For a moment she didn't know where she was or who it was beside her. She blinked when she saw Rosalie and then recalled being woken during the night. Poor girl, she thought. She was really cold; caught a chill I shouldn't wonder.

She slipped quietly out of bed, padded towards the window and opened the curtains. 'Oh!' she breathed. 'Oh, how wonderful!'

The view was spectacular. The house stood midway up a hill and below it for as far as she could see were acres of rolling moorland covered in glistening pristine snow. In the far distance was a jagged peak with patches of brown where the snow had slid away. Immediately below the track which led to the house she saw a stone wall and the road they had ridden on.

As she gazed in awe and wonder she heard a familiar sound out in the corridor. The rattle of cups on a tea tray. She turned away from the window and glanced at Rosalie, still soundly sleeping. Oh! The maid with a breakfast tray! There came a soft knock, not on her door but on Rosalie's.

With only a second's hesitation she flew into Rosalie's room and took up a place by the window. Another knock, firmer this time. 'Miss Kingston,' a voice said. 'I've brought tea.'

'Come in,' Polly said, turning to face the door.

The young maid murmured 'Good morning' and put the tray on a small table. She dipped her knee. 'Is there anything else required, Miss Kingston?'

Polly looked at the tray, nicely set out with teapot, milk jug and sugar bowl, but only one cup and saucer.

'Thank you,' she said. 'Have you prepared a tray for Miss Parker?'

The maid looked at her blankly.

'Next door?' Polly pointed to the adjoining room. 'She's still sleeping but I'm sure she'd love a cup of tea when she wakes.'

'Beg pardon, miss.' The girl bobbed again. 'I didn't know there was anybody else. I'll see to it right away.'

'If you would.' Polly smiled benignly. 'Thank you.'

Polly put her hand to her mouth and suppressed a giggle as the girl left the room. She sat down at the table and poured a cup of tea, then added a drop of milk and a large teaspoon of sugar. 'Ah!' she sighed, sitting back and taking a sip. 'This is 'life for me.'

CHAPTER EIGHTEEN

'Tea, Miss Parker.'

Rosalie woke to an unfamiliar voice and the brilliance of the day as the maid opened the curtains letting in a stream of light.

'It's a lovely morning,' she said, turning from the window. 'But no sign of a thaw.'

Rosalie sat up feeling refreshed but slightly dozy. 'Th-thank you,' she said huskily and gazed round the room. 'So it is, erm . . .'

'Dora, miss. Miss Kingston's up already and had her tea. I didn't know there was anybody in this room,' she said. 'Mrs Moody didn't say.'

'There was a mix-up with the arrangements,' Rosalie said. 'And we were late arriving. We had a very long journey.'

The girl looked warily at Rosalie, perhaps unnerved by her manner and voice. 'Begging your pardon, miss, but are you Miss Kingston's lady's maid, or . . . It's just that nobody has told me owt so how am I supposed to know?'

From over the maid's shoulder Rosalie saw Polly negatively gesticulating from the inner doorway. She hid a smile. Whatever had she been up to?

'No.' Rosalie tried to keep a straight face. 'I'm her friend. She's quite alone, an orphan, which is why I am accompanying her.'

'Oh, sorry, miss.' The girl seemed embarrassed. 'I hope I haven't spoken out o' turn?'

'It's quite all right.'

Dora blushed. 'Is there's anything else, miss?'

Rosalie thanked her. 'Nothing else for the moment. But perhaps you'd bring up hot water?'

'We've a separate room with a bath and pan closet, Miss Parker. Maister went to the Great Exhibition, so Mrs Moody said, and had one fitted straight after. He's going to get one of the new ones from Mr Crapper as soon as he can. I wish he would.' She wrinkled her nose. 'I'd rather use 'outside privy.'

'Yes, well, thank you, Dora,' Rosalie said hastily, thinking that her uncle was a forward-looking man. She and Polly burst into laughter as soon as Dora had gone. 'Polly!' Rosalie admonished her. 'You naughty girl.'

Polly giggled. 'What a lark! I didn't know what she might think, finding us in 'same bed. She might have thought us a pair o' jades; as it is she's just a country girl who's probably used to sharing a bed, like me.'

Rosalie nodded vaguely. 'Jades! What are they?'

Polly stared and regretted her big mouth. 'Erm, not a polite word, Rosalie. Sorry. I shouldn't have said it.'

'But what does it mean?' Rosalie persisted. 'I've never heard it before and I thought I was well read.'

Polly swallowed. 'Too embarrassed to say,' she muttered. 'Come on, drink your tea. We've a whole new world to explore.'

By the time they had bathed, donned clean clothes and brushed their tangled hair it was ten o'clock. Rosalie was wearing a blue gown and Polly a grey with a paisley shawl which Rosalie had loaned her, and both had dressed their hair in a similar style.

'I hope we haven't missed breakfast,' Rosalie said as they made their way down. 'I must ask the housekeeper when we are expected for meals.'

'You're a member of 'family now,' Polly said. 'Find out what 'others do. Don't let her dictate to you. She's a servant, after all.'

'Yes,' Rosalie whispered. 'But it's often the servants who run the household. They have to be kept sweet.'

Polly sighed. 'You worry too much. It's them

205

who'll lose their jobs if they don't do things right.'

Dora was crossing the hall carrying a tray laden with a jug of hot water and fresh bread. She balanced the tray with one hand and opened a door with the other. She glanced at both girls and then her eyes swept from one to the other.

'After you, Miss Kingston,' she said to Polly. 'Miss Parker,' she added, looking at Rosalie.

'No, I'm Miss Parker,' Polly said.

'And I'm Miss Kingston,' Rosalie added. 'We're alike, are we not? People are often confused.'

Dora opened her mouth to say something but seemed to think better of it and followed them into the dining room where a large table was covered in a white cloth. She put the tray down on a side dresser among several covered dishes and tea and coffee pots.

'Begging your pardon,' she said. 'I thought—'

'I'm really hungry this morning,' Polly interrupted, 'after that long journey yesterday.'

'So am I,' Rosalie agreed. 'I'd like coffee, please, Dora.'

'And I'll have tea. There,' Polly said. 'Now you'll be able to tell 'difference between us.'

Dora dipped her knee. 'Yes, miss. And would you like a cooked breakfast? Cook's just frying some more bacon. Mr Howard's been and gone,' she informed them. 'Mr Edwin's not arrived home yet, nor has Maister.'

'No, here I am, Dora.' A man in his mid-twenties came through the door. 'And starving for eggs, bacon, sausage, black pudding, toast and coffee. Look sharp, there's a good girl.'

As Dora scurried out, he smacked her rump and turned to Rosalie and Polly. 'Ladies.' He gave a swift nod. 'Edwin Kingston. One of you I believe is a cousin?'

Polly took a small step back. This was a man to be wary of, she thought. Foxy! He was dark-haired and thin-cheeked, with a long nose and an arrogant manner.

'I am Rosalie Kingston.' Rosalie was un-nerved by him. 'I'm pleased to meet you, Cousin Edwin.'

He came towards her and she felt his eyes sweep over her. 'Likewise, Rosalie, though I must say it came as a surprise to find I had a cousin. Father obviously forgot to mention it, as he frequently does with other matters.' He turned and glanced at Polly. 'And are you a cousin too?'

'This is my good friend and companion, Miss Parker,' Rosalie said nervously. 'Polly, may I introduce my cousin Edwin Kingston?'

'How do you do?' Polly said boldly and inclined her head as he had done. 'Delighted to meet you,' she added, making Rosalie smile.

'Have you had breakfast?' Edwin began to help himself to coffee from the jug. 'It's a free-for-all in the morning. Father insists that we wait upon ourselves, which is a terrible bore.'

'We've onn— only just come down,' Polly told him. 'We were very late arriving last night.'

'And very tired,' Rosalie added. 'But we would have been much later if it had not been for your cousin Howard's assistance.'

'Oh, really?' Edwin looked at her over the rim of his cup. He took a sip of coffee. 'And why was he so late, I wonder.' He gave a scornful grunt. 'Did he get bogged down in the snow?'

'No, but we almost did,' Polly said. 'And one of Amos's hosses went lame.'

'Hah, you've picked up the local lingo already,' he said derisively. 'That didn't take long!'

'We say hosses in Hull where I come from.' Polly lifted a defiant chin. Although she knew she had to be polite because she was a guest, she wasn't going to accept any unnecessary criticism from Edwin Kingston. Howard Carleton had given her a timely warning.

'Of course we do!' Rosalie gave a nervous laugh. 'Don't you, Edwin?'

'Certainly not. I don't wish to speak with the rustics' vocabulary.' He put down his cup and marched to the door. 'Dora!' he shouted. 'Hurry up with that breakfast, girl.'

Polly saw that Rosalie was trembling and pulled out a dining chair for her. 'Would you like coffee, Rosalie? Sugar?'

'Please,' Rosalie nodded. 'One lump.'

Polly poured the coffee, and tea for herself. It came out rich and strong. 'Are you a farmer like your cousin Howard, Mr Edwin?' she asked. He had placed himself at the table opposite Rosalie. 'It must be very hard work.'

He stared at her as if she was insane. 'What? Howard farms in order to earn his keep. He's lived here since his parents died, or lived off us I ought to say. He was left without a penny.'

'Poor man,' Rosalie murmured. 'And how very good of your father to oblige him; as he has me also.' She paused. 'Although I expect my father will have agreed some recompense.'

Edwin Kingston had the grace to look embarrassed. 'Oh, I'm sure it will be of no consequence to my father. You are a woman after all, and hardly expected to earn a living.'

Some of us are, Polly thought. But I suppose Mr Edwin would consider me to be of no significance if he knew I was just a poor girl from the back streets of Hull.

'When is your father expected home?' Rosalie ventured, hoping with all her heart that he wasn't anything like his son.

'No idea,' he said abruptly. The door opened again and Dora came in with another loaded tray. 'At last!' he said. 'About time. Serve me first, Dora. I haven't got all day to waste. Excuse me, ladies.' He glanced at them. 'I'm sure you are happy to linger over breakfast, but I am not.'

As Dora stood next to Edwin to serve him, he put his hand on her thigh. Rosalie and Polly saw the gesture and both stared at him. He shifted in his chair but his lip curled in a disdainful smirk.

Dora's cheeks flushed as she piled his plate with everything he had asked for, and then in a low voice she asked if she could serve the ladies.

'No, thank you, Dora,' Polly answered for them both. 'We can help ourselves. We are women, after all, and quite capable of doing so.'

Edwin looked up, unsure if there was sarcasm in her tone, but Polly had turned her back on him as she went to the dresser. 'Bacon, Rosalie? Scrambled eggs?'

When Dora left the room, Edwin glanced at Rosalie. 'I hope you're not a bluestocking, Cousin?' He indicated casually towards the door. 'I was merely jesting.'

'I might be,' Rosalie answered coldly, though nervously. 'But what I am isn't an issue. What I can't tolerate is intimidation, particularly if someone isn't in a position to answer back.'

Polly served Rosalie and herself and sat down next to her. She said nothing to Edwin; not my place, she thought, but she looked him challengingly in the eye.

Rosalie heaved a great sigh when Edwin left the room after wolfing his breakfast and curtly wishing them good day. 'Thank goodness he's gone,' she whispered. 'I could hardly eat a thing while he was here. What an insufferable man.'

Polly nodded; she'd just taken a bite of toast. She licked her lips. 'Glad he's not my cousin. I wonder where he's off to in such a hurry if he's not going to work.'

Dora had come in as she finished speaking. 'Excuse me, miss, but Mr Edwin always goes to his room to read the newspapers after breakfast. He likes to read 'em first, afore Mr Kingston comes back in.' Then she added tremulously, but as if she was trying to make light of the situation, 'Then we have to iron 'em again cos he leaves 'em in such a state.'

So he does have all day to waste after all, Polly thought. And that's what he is, a wastrel. I wonder if Dora feels threatened by him.

'Where will it be safe to walk, Dora?' she asked. 'We need some fresh air but don't want to stumble into a snowdrift.'

'Oh, I'm not sure,' the girl said. 'Miss

Clementina hardly ever goes out if the weather's bad and then onny on horseback. I suppose you could go up the hill behind the house. There's a track there but it might be covered over. Have you got galoshes?'

'I have,' Rosalie said. 'They're in my trunk. If I'd been sensible I would have travelled in them.'

'I haven't any,' Polly said. 'I'll have to walk in my boots and they're still damp.'

'There's a spare pair of Miss Clementina's downstairs,' Dora said. 'You could borrow those, miss, and I'll unpack the trunk to find yours, Miss Kingston,' she said. 'Just as soon as I've cleared away.'

'Rosalie,' Rosalie explained. 'Miss Rosalie. Miss Clementina will prefer to be called Miss Kingston, I expect.'

Dora gave a little shrug. 'She might,' she said. 'It'll depend.'

'And I'm Polly,' Polly said. 'What will it depend on?' she asked.

'On her mood, Miss Polly,' Dora mumbled. 'On how she is when she gets up of a morning.'

Rosalie and Polly sighed. Polly pulled a face when Dora had gone. 'Do you think Clementina will be like her brother?' she whispered.

'Yes,' Rosalie said. 'I rather fear she might be.'

When they had finished breakfast and Dora had cleared the dishes, Polly went down the steps to the kitchen and knocked on the door. She knew better than to barge in without invitation, knowing how the cook at the Kingstons' house would have been offended had anyone done so in her domain.

'Galoshes, Dora.' Polly peered over her shoulder when the housemaid opened the door. The kitchen was huge; tall cupboards ran along one wall and a massive inglenook fireplace containing an iron range took up most of another. It had several fire-bars and side-plates; a roasting spit was holding a joint of pork which was sizzling and crackling and dropping juices into a metal tray.

Polly licked her lips. The aroma was tantalizing. Pork dripping and bread with a touch of salt, she drooled. Heaven!

The cook was rolling pastry on a large table in the middle of the room. She looked up, and seeing Polly waiting in the doorway she nodded her head and murmured, 'Good morning, miss.' A girl, younger than Dora, was standing at a sink up to her elbows in soapy water. She glanced at Polly, but when she saw she was observed she bent her head back to her task.

There were several other doors in the kitchen and Polly wondered where they led. One's 'back

door, she thought, but what's behind 'others?
Then Dora came out from one of them holding
a pair of galoshes.

Ah, Polly thought. Boot and shoe room. And
mebbe laundry room through the other. She
was intrigued. Never had she been in such a
large establishment. Another maid came down
the basement steps carrying towels and excused herself as Polly made room for her. Mr
Kingston must be very rich, she thought, to
employ so many servants.

'Here you are, Miss Polly.' Dora handed the
galoshes to her. 'I hope they fit. Miss Clemmie's
bigger than you so you might need an extra
pair of stockings on. Miss Clementina, I mean,'
she said hastily.

Polly grinned. They'll have pet names for
everybody, I should think. I'd like to know
what mine will be, she thought.

Upstairs she and Rosalie dressed in their
warmest clothes, adding extra layers of petticoats and wool stockings.

'You do know that I wouldn't venture out in
this snow on my own,' Rosalie said. 'It's only
because you want to go that I'm coming too.
It's *madness*,' she laughed.

'It'll do you good,' Polly told her. 'Bring
some roses to your cheeks. Besides, you have to
find out what kind of place you're living in. Do
you know, there's a huge kitchen downstairs

with four servants that I saw; yet there'd onny be four people living here if we hadn't come. There's Mrs Moody, Dora, Cook . . .' she started to tick them off on her fingers.

'That's the way it is,' Rosalie interrupted. 'Come on, Polly; let's be going if we must. It will be almost dinner time by the time we get out.'

They crossed the hall and two young dogs rose from the fireplace wagging their tails.

'Are you coming?' Polly said in a bright voice and they bounded eagerly towards the door.

'Will it be all right for them to come?' Rosalie said.

'Course it will,' Polly said airily. 'All dogs like to have a run in 'snow. Come on, boys,' she said, opening the door, and the dogs raced down the steps.

The icy air almost took their breath away. Polly took great gulps of it but Rosalie put her shawl over her nose and mouth.

'I'm not going,' she said. 'It's too cold.'

Polly looked at her. Rosalie still looked pale and tired. Yesterday's journey had knocked her back.

'You go in then,' she said. 'Go and sit by 'fire and I'll just take a ten-minute hike. I'll have 'dogs for company.'

'You don't mind?' Rosalie said meekly.

Polly laughed. 'Course I don't, Miss Rosalie. But do you mind if I leave you alone?'

Rosalie shook her head. 'No, Miss Polly, I don't.'

Polly whistled the dogs and strode off round to the back of the house where she thought she would find the track up the hill. There was a pig pen where the swine snuffled and snorted, and a wide-aisled cattle shed housing four or five cows; a man was halfway up a wooden ladder which led to the floor above them where straw was stacked up to the roof. Hens scratched about in the cleared yard and alongside the stables and tack rooms, where a stable lad looked up as she went by. He touched his cap as she called good morning. Then there's Amos, she thought. How many more servants are there? Fancy owning all of this.

She opened a gate leading out of the yard and turned to look down at the moors beyond. To her right at the side of the house was a snow-covered field where pregnant ewes bleated at her from low stone housing. What must it be like to live here for always, she thought. To be able to look at this view every day. The sun was so blisteringly bright on the snow that she had to narrow her eyes to see into the distance. The dogs snuffled round her feet and she leaned down to pat them.

'What's your name then?' she said. One of the dogs was a wiry terrier, the other a mix of Labrador and sheepdog.

'Caesar and Brutus.' A voice came from behind her. 'And what do you mean by stealing my dogs?'

CHAPTER NINETEEN

'Mr Howard!' The relief on Polly's face was evident. 'I'm sorry. Are they yours? I asked them if they wanted to come out and they said yes.'

He grinned. 'They would, of course. They were not well pleased to be left behind this morning.'

He was wearing a greatcoat with the top buttons undone and beneath it held something close to his chest. He was carrying a shepherd's crook. Another dog was by his feet.

'I can't stop to talk,' he said, opening his coat to show a newly born lamb. 'I've got to get this baby somewhere warm.'

'Oh,' she breathed. 'Where's its mother?'

'Dead,' he said grimly. 'Along with another lamb. If it hadn't been for Shep this one would have died too. Are you going walking?'

'Just to 'top of 'hill,' she said. 'Can I take 'dogs?'

'Yes, but be careful.' He started to walk away. 'The snow's very deep. Keep to the middle of the track.'

She watched him hurry towards the stables and then continued her walk. Poor little lamb. I hope it lives. I wish I could have it. She felt a sudden lurch of emotion. I might have had a brother or sister if Ma had carried 'child through to birth. But what a big gap there'd have been between us. I'd have been too old to play with it, but I could have looked after it. That would have been nice, she thought. Somebody to love. A tear trickled down her cold cheek. Ma! I wonder what you'd think if you could see me now. Here I am living in a grand house with servants and a lady as a best friend.

But what if Mr Kingston doesn't want me to stay? Why would he feed me and give me a home? He doesn't even know me. Her spirits drooped. I expect I'll have to go back.

At the top of the rise, she saw a figure with a dog at his heel leading a horse towards her. She puffed onward and Howard's dogs ran ahead, their tails wagging furiously.

'Good day to you,' the man said as they met, touching his leather hat. 'Lovely day.'

'It's beautiful,' she said fervently. 'Best day I've ever seen in my life.'

He smiled. He had a weather-beaten face

with a generous mouth. He was muffled up to his chin with a thick scarf and wore a heavy long coat and sturdy boots. He had a dark short beard streaked with grey. 'And how many have you seen, young lady. Not so many?'

'Well, I'm seventeen so I've seen a few, but never one like this.' Polly spread her arms to encompass the landscape. 'Just look. You can see for miles. I wonder what it's like in spring or summer?' she said pensively. 'I hope I'm here to see it.'

'Surely,' he said sombrely, 'at such a young age you will see many springs and summers, and autumns and winters too, I should hope.'

'Oh, I didn't mean *that*,' she said. 'I just hope that I don't have to leave.'

'Well, if you should be so unfortunate,' he said, 'I can tell you that spring is lovely; the moors start to show their freshness and the young lambs are frisky. In summer there's the scent of heather and the sound of birdsong, but I love the autumn most of all, when the colour of the moors starts to change, the heather is purple and the gorse golden yellow.' He looked down at her and she thought he seemed a giant of a man. 'Why do you think you won't be here?'

'I've come without being invited,' she said. 'And when Mr Kingston, who's my friend's uncle, comes back, he might ask me to leave.'

She took a deep breath. 'And I just love it. It's so beautiful.'

'Some people consider it desolate and lonely,' he murmured. 'They don't have a feel for it at all.'

'I could stay here for ever,' she said fervently.

'Well, let's hope that this fellow keeps an open house and asks you to stay,' he said.

Polly pulled a wry expression. 'If he's anything like his son he'll send me packing.' She put her hand to her mouth and looked up at him. 'Beg pardon, sir, I'm speaking out o' turn. Perhaps 'Kingstons are friends of yours?'

'Everybody knows everybody else round here. There are so few of us. But don't worry,' he said, tapping his nose. 'I'm very discreet.'

Polly nodded. 'I'd best be off. I'm going to 'top of hill and then down again, like 'grand old Duke of York,' she added. 'I don't want to be late for dinner. It's at twelve and I expect 'cook'll be mad if folks are late.'

He pulled a timepiece out of his pocket and glanced at it. 'Plenty of time,' he said. 'I'm sure they'll wait for you.' He touched his hat. 'Good day to you. No doubt we'll meet again.'

'I hope so,' she said. 'Goodbye.'

She reached the summit and looked down the other side of the hill. The moor stretched for as far as she could see. She felt dizzy with the hugeness of it. 'I'm on top of 'world,' she murmured, 'surrounded by whiteness. Is this the view you'd get from heaven? Can you see it, Ma? Can you see its brightness from where you are?'

Communing with her mother seemed a perfectly natural thing to do up here in this solitary isolation. That she was in heaven Polly had no doubt whatever, and up here so high she felt nearer to her even though she knew her mother had never stepped out of the flat-land of Hull.

I wish Rosalie were here to share this with me, she thought as she retraced her steps. Down below she could see the full extent of the Kingston house and outbuildings. In the stable yard figures were moving about. Someone with a horse; the stable lad, she thought. I must ask his name. Several dogs were running around, their excited yapping and barking carried clearly on the sharp air. Caesar and Brutus looked up at her, obviously anxious to be off to join them, but they stayed with her.

I wish I had a dog. But I was wishing for a lamb before, she chided herself. She heaved a breath, filling her lungs with invigorating cleanliness. This is – this is – she cast around to find a word to describe in some small measure the sensation within her – this is *joy*. This must be contentment, or it would be if I didn't have this niggling feeling that it won't last. Cos nothing ever does.

She was quite out of breath by the time she reached the yard. The stable lad was rubbing down one of the horses. Polly went towards him.

'Good morning again,' she smiled. 'Is it still morning?'

'Don't know, miss.' He looked up at the sky where a pale sun shone. 'I reckon it's on dinner time.' He was a fresh-faced lad, and gave a shy grin. 'My belly tells me it is, anyway.'

'What's your name?' she said.

'Sam, miss. Sam Little.'

'Is that Mr Howard's hoss?'

'No, miss, this is Maister's. He's just got in.'

Polly gaped. What a fool I am! That was him! The gentleman I met with his horse and dogs. What must he think? And I said that about Edwin! I might as well go and start packing right now.

'You all right, miss?' Sam asked curiously.

She nodded. 'Yeh,' she breathed. 'I think so.'

Polly took off the galoshes in the hall and ran upstairs to take off her coat. She could hear voices coming from behind one of the doors and then heard Rosalie laugh. She won't laugh when she knows what I said to her uncle, she thought. Or mebbe he's telling her what I said, how I put my big foot in my mouth, and they're laughing about that. But she'll plead my case, I'm sure she will.

She pulled off her coat and grabbed a brush for her hair. At least I hope she will, she thought as she pulled at the tangles. She swallowed hard. But Rosalie'll feel safe now that she's here wi' family, and he, Mr Kingston, if it is him, seems like a caring sort o' man, someone who'll look after her. She mebbe won't need me any more.

Polly was close to tears as she went down the stairs. I was so happy, she thought. It just goes to show you shouldn't ever be too happy because it's worse when everything falls apart.

Dora came up the kitchen stairs carrying a tray of glasses. 'Everybody's in the drawing room, Miss Polly,' she said. 'Mr Kingston has put lunch back for half an hour cos he wanted to change after his journey.'

Polly nodded and took a breath. Had he really done that for himself, or was it for her? She'd told him that she didn't want to be late. Hope fluttered inside her, but then it died again. Why should he? She had been rude about his son and she'd told him that she was uninvited.

Dora opened the door and motioned her to go inside ahead of her. Polly took a deep breath. This is it, then. Will he ask me to leave in front of everybody or will he take me on one side after dinner and tell me to pack my bag? Will he ask Amos to take me back to Scarborough or will I have to walk?

All eyes turned towards her as she entered the room. Rosalie was sitting in an elegant gilt chair by the fireplace and opposite her in a deep cushioned one was Howard. Edwin was by the window and Mr Kingston, the very man she had met on the hillside, was standing with his back to the fire looking straight at her.

CHAPTER TWENTY

Polly dipped a wobbly knee to the assembled company. She pressed her lips together and glanced at everyone.

'Polly.' Rosalie stood up. 'Please come and meet my uncle, Luke Kingston. Uncle Luke, this is my friend Miss Parker, of whom I have been speaking.'

Luke Kingston moved forward as Polly dipped her knee again. 'Why, Miss Parker,' he said jovially. 'I do believe we've met! Was that not you admiring our wonderful scenery from the top of the hill?'

'Yes, sir,' Polly said. 'It was.' She opened her mouth to apologize, then closed it again. What was the use, she thought. The damage is done. He'll think me a fool.

'I'm delighted to meet you.' Luke Kingston gave a small bow and she saw that his eyes were merry. 'I understand from my niece that you are inseparable, so may we expect to enjoy your company as well as Rosalie's?'

Polly licked her lips and scanned Rosalie's face, but she was smiling and nodding. 'If – if that's all right, sir,' she said in a low voice. 'If it's – erm, convenient to you.'

She glanced at Howard, who had risen and now gave her a sly wink, and then at Edwin, whose expression was stony.

'We'll enjoy having you here, Miss Parker,' Luke said. 'You'll be a welcome addition to our family. Isn't that so, boys?'

Edwin said nothing but Howard grinned. 'Indeed she will, as long as she doesn't keep stealing my dogs.'

'Oh?' Luke enquired. 'Do you like dogs?'

Polly breathed out as she felt a huge wave of relief. 'I do. I've never had one of my own. I onn— only ever fed strays.'

'Well,' Luke mused. 'We'll have to see what we can do about that. Do we have a bitch in pup?' he asked Howard.

'Yes. I believe Floss is expecting a happy event at any time,' Howard said. 'But I don't know the sire.'

Polly stared at him and then said, 'Let's hope she was particular about his character and temperament then, Mr Howard, and didn't choose him only for his charm.'

Rosalie went pink, but both men burst out laughing. Edwin turned to the window muttering something about mongrels.

'I'm truly grateful to you, Mr Kingston,' Polly said, feeling much more at ease. 'For letting me stay, I mean. I'll try not to be a bother.'

'I'm sure you won't be,' he said warmly. 'This is an open house to all of our friends, though regrettably they don't come so often in winter.' He beckoned her to the chair that Howard had vacated. 'And yet the moors are at their most beautiful, as you so rightly observed when we spoke earlier,' he continued. 'But they can be dangerous nevertheless. I understand from Amos that you had a difficult journey here.' He turned to Rosalie. 'Why did you choose to come when you did?' He put his finger to his chin and pondered, and before she could answer said, 'Don't tell me that I advised it. Did I? What month are we in?'

He asked the question of no one in particular, but Edwin answered. 'March. The second. A ridiculous time to travel anywhere in this weather. Unless it's to somewhere abroad,' he added.

'You'd like that, wouldn't you, Edwin?' his father said sharply. 'But I'm afraid we're not made of money. Not enough for you to take a continental tour, at any rate. Besides, you know

228

very well that there's plenty of work to be done in winter as well as at other times of the year. By the way, did you look at the old fencing as I asked you to?'

'No.' Edwin's reply was brief and direct. 'I haven't had time.'

Polly saw Howard give him a swift penetrating glance. 'It's fallen,' he said. 'The weight of the snow must have brought it down. I saw it when I was digging the lamb out.'

'Tomorrow then,' Luke said tetchily. 'We must crack on whilst we can. There'll be a thaw soon and we'll need to get our coats off and into our spring jobs. Will the lamb recover?' he asked Howard.

'Perhaps,' Howard said. 'I'll go back in an hour and give it another feed.'

'Oh!' Polly said instinctively. 'Can I help?'

'Yes,' Howard said. 'You can. He needs to be kept warm and fed every hour. He's in one of the stables. I'll show you after dinner.'

The midday meal was plentiful and after their late breakfast Polly and Rosalie were not able to eat all that was put before them. Mrs Moody, dressed in black with a white cap, supervised the silver platter bearing the joint of roast pork, which was served with Yorkshire pudding. A sauce boat held puréed apple and a dish of strong mustard made Rosalie cough and Polly's eyes water. Two more dishes contained buttered carrots and floury potatoes and there was a large jug of thick onion gravy.

'This will fatten you up, young ladies,' Luke Kingston commented as he carved a second helping of meat. 'You need flesh on your bones to survive out here.'

'No more for me, thank you,' Rosalie said. 'We ate very well at breakfast. Much more than I usually have.'

He lifted a slice and beckoned to Polly to pass her plate, which she did even though she knew she had eaten more than enough already. I'll be as fat as this pig must have been, she thought. She had eaten well since going to work at Rosalie's house, although once Cook and Martha had left she had prepared less food than Cook had deemed necessary for the two of them. But even so she had put on weight; she felt fit and well and her flux, which had been spasmodic, was now regular.

She gave a small hiccup; the pork was delicious, tender and tasty, but she put down her cutlery and blew out her cheeks. Luke Kingston saw her and laughed. 'Old Henry's too much for you, is he?'

Polly raised her eyebrows. 'Henry?'

He pointed to the meat on her plate. 'That was Henry,' he said. 'A good fat pig. He's served us well. But you'll have to do better than that, m'dear,' he said. 'Cook won't like it if you leave food on your plate.'

Rosalie had turned pale and clutched her throat. She turned to look at Polly and then at her uncle.

'Are you saying that you *knew* this . . . pig?' she asked in a low voice.

'Why yes, of course.' Luke Kingston took another generous mouthful. 'One of ours. We'd hardly eat anyone else's, would we?'

Polly hiccuped again. 'No,' she said bravely. 'Of course you wouldn't. But where I lived, folks'd keep a pig, but they never gave it a name; they never got too familiar with it.'

Howard grinned. 'We like our animals to feel wanted, Polly. Henry liked nothing better than to have his ears scratched. He was very friendly.'

Rosalie gazed at him and then at her uncle. Edwin wasn't joining in the conversation. 'But how can you bring yourself to eat something whose ears you've scratched, or talked to? It doesn't seem right.'

'Where did you buy your meat, Rosalie?' Luke Kingston asked mildly.

'Cook bought it,' she said. 'Oh, I'm not denying where the meat came from, but it's the fact that you knew the animal!'

Edwin got up abruptly and flung down his

napkin. 'Excuse me,' he said. 'What a puerile conversation.'

'Edwin!' his father roared. 'Come back here at once!'

But Edwin had slammed out of the door and his father, his face florid, took a deep breath and said, 'I must apologize for my son's rudeness, young ladies. I shall speak to him privately over his lack of manners.'

Rosalie murmured something conciliatory but Polly was stunned. What a loathsome man he was, she thought. It was just a conversation. How could anyone get so angry over a piece of pork? But then I don't think it was just that. He was obviously simmering over something else. The fencing, perhaps? He didn't like it when Howard said it had fallen.

After they had finished eating, Howard excused himself and asked Polly if she'd like to give the lamb its feed. 'Would you like to come too, Rosalie?'

She hesitated for a moment and then said she would and went off to get coats for herself and Polly. Polly went down to the kitchen again to borrow Clementina's galoshes.

Dora opened the door to her. She seemed agitated but stammered that she would bring the galoshes to the front door.

What's wrong wi' her, Polly wondered. Bet Cook has been getting at her over something.

The two girls, well wrapped up in scarves and shawls, followed Howard round to the stable block. 'I've put him in an empty stall,' he said. 'Don't want him to get trampled on.'

'Won't he be lonely?' Rosalie said. 'He'll be missing his mother. Can't one of the other sheep be put with him?'

'Not now,' Howard said. 'Had he been born in the spring and lost his mother then we could, but he's a couple of days old and been buried in the snow, so the other ewes will reject him.'

'Poor little thing,' Polly said when the lamb bleated at their approach. 'Can I feed him?' She took the bottle from Howard and knelt down next to the lamb.

'Put him between your knees,' Howard said, 'then he'll feel more secure.'

Polly sat down on the straw and stretched out her legs, then drew up her knees to enclose the lamb. She asked Rosalie to pass her shawl to put over him. 'There,' she said with satisfaction, 'he's starting to suckle.'

Rosalie knelt down too and gently put her shawl over him. Howard smiled and said, 'I'll leave you to it, ladies. You've got the mothering touch.'

'What shall we call him?' Rosalie whispered as Howard left. 'If they can call a pig Henry, we'll have to give this little fellow a name. What about Louis?'

Polly laughed. The lamb was sucking hard at the teat. 'Louis the lamb! Yes, that's a good one.' Then she sighed and added soberly, 'But we mustn't get too attached to it, Rosalie. What if it doesn't survive? And if it does, what is its future? We're on a working farm, remember. They're not at all sentimental.'

'Oh,' Rosalie said. 'Of course. We'll have to hold back, then.'

'Too late,' Polly said. 'I love it already.'

The thaw began two weeks later. The snow melted, showing patches of brown moorland which grew larger each day. Snow on the sandstone slate roof of the farmhouse slipped in great chunks on to the ground below, catching out those who were foolish enough to walk too close to the building. The gutters ran freely and streams began to rush faster, and the trickle and gurgle of water was constant.

The sheep were back on the moor. Rosalie asked her uncle how they knew which were their sheep and which weren't, as the moor was unfenced.

'Well, they're what we call hefted sheep,' he said. 'They know their own area. These flocks have been grazing here for generation after generation. They're hard work,' he added. 'Shepherding might seem to be a peaceful occupation but we're forever running about after them. Lambing, dipping, shearing; there's always a job to be done. There's been pastoral agriculture on this land since medieval times, you know. Cattle husbandry as well as wool production. Now, though, some of the land is used for grouse shooting which brings us in another income.'

Rosalie looked out of the window. They were in the dining room waiting for the midday meal to be served. The view of rolling moorland was lit by the soft light of a mist-shrouded sun. Grazing sheep dotted the hillside, which had prompted her question. 'It's beautiful,' she murmured. 'And yes, it does look peaceful. No wonder you decided to stay here rather than join the army as my father did.'

He nodded. 'I loved the country life,' he said. 'And I was very fond of Uncle Josh and Aunt Emily who gave us a home. But your father and I were as different as chalk and cheese, even from our school days. I was the one who didn't conform. I refused to take up a career in the army as our father had done and as we were both expected to do.'

He gave a little smile and Rosalie thought there was perhaps some regret. 'And so,' he went on, 'Mark and I didn't so much fall out as agree to go our separate ways. He was intent on making his way in the army, whereas I abhor war and all it stands for; and after our parents died, we had no real desire to keep in touch. But there was another reason for my staying here. I fell in love with a farmer's daughter, my late wife, and I knew she would never move away.'

'How long have you been widowed, Uncle?' she asked softly, for it seemed to her that he looked wistful when he spoke of his wife.

He considered. 'Must be all of ten years. I'm not much good with dates. Edwin would have been about twelve, Howard perhaps fourteen and Clemmie only a child of eight or nine. They were spoilt, of course, even by the servants, trying to make up for the loss of their mother. A double loss for Howard, as he'd already lost his own parents when he was very young. He's made of strong stuff, though, is Howard. Not like Edwin,' he added almost as an afterthought.

'Have you never considered remarrying?' she asked. The door opened as she spoke and the others trooped in. He didn't answer, but Rosalie thought a fleeting expression crossed his face as if he would have revealed a confidence.

Mrs Moody again brought in the roast. This time it was shoulder of mutton. Rosalie and Polly glanced at each other and Polly murmured that at least they knew it wasn't Louis, who was doing well and tottering about in his stable. Sam Little was keeping an eye on him and had remarked the day before that he would soon be able to go outside. Rosalie and Polly had expressed doubts about this but they were proved wrong, for that afternoon after taking the bottle he escaped from the stall and, bleating plaintively, followed them back to the house.

Laughing, they turned about to take him back and were surprised to see Dora coming from the stables towards the kitchen door. She blushed scarlet on seeing them and begged them not to tell Mrs Moody.

'I'll be in hot water,' she said fearfully. 'I've onny been to talk to Sam and we're not allowed to have male friends.'

'You don't have to worry about us,' Polly said. 'We won't tell.'

'Of course we won't,' Rosalie agreed. 'But you must be careful, Dora, or otherwise you might both be dismissed.'

'Not Sam!' Dora snivelled. 'He wouldn't be. But when can I ever go out to talk to anybody? I'm stuck indoors all winter and don't go out till Mothering Sunday, 'n' by the time I've walked over the moor to see my ma it's time to come back again.'

'Why don't you ask Sam to walk with you next time?' Polly suggested. 'Take him to meet your ma.'

Dora looked alarmed. 'Can't do that, miss!

He'll think he's committed and Ma'll think there're going to be wedding bells.'

Rosalie and Polly both shook their heads. Polly thought she would hate to be so restricted; she had always had friends of both sexes since she was a child. As for Rosalie, it wasn't anything she had considered before. Perhaps Mother laid down directions for the servants regarding followers, but if she did I didn't know of them, she thought. There had to be rules, of course; the household wouldn't run smoothly otherwise. It wouldn't do, she supposed, for servant girls to be slipping out to meet young men whenever they wanted to. They're vulnerable, and an employer should be responsible for protecting them.

She wondered what Luke's reaction would have been had he seen his son's behaviour towards Dora. He would have been angry, she was sure. And she wondered at Dora's seeking out Sam. How did he behave towards her, and had she told him about Edwin? It was not a subject for discussion, she thought. Dora would surely have kept it to herself. She would be too frightened and too ashamed to tell.

She sighed. Life is full of constraints for women, she thought. We don't have the freedom that men have. She linked arms with Polly. At least, most of us don't.

CHAPTER TWENTY-ONE

The next two weeks saw the weather improve. The sun became warmer and the snow all but disappeared; pockets of cowslips appeared in ditches, and primroses raised their faces in sheltered corners and under hedges around the farm.

Rosalie and Polly roamed the surrounding area, sometimes staying out all afternoon, revelling in the wild beauty of the moor. Polly in particular took in great gulps of air as if she couldn't get enough of it.

Howard said one evening that if they were up early enough the following morning they could go with him up the moor towards the village of Littlebeck. They were more than eager to go further than they could explore on foot.

'If you could ride then you could each take a horse and go wherever you wanted,' he said as they jogged along in the trap. 'Clemmie rides. Would you like me to teach you?'

Polly was enthusiastic, Rosalie less so, remembering the uncomfortable journey to the farm in the snow.

'You should try something new, Rosalie,' Howard teased. 'Where's your sense of adventure? You have a freedom here that you'd never get in the town. You'd have to be a very proper lady there.'

Rosalie pondered. He was quite right. His attitude reminded her of Sonny Blake, who had said something similar. And both seemed to regard men and women as equals. They were forthright in their opinions, something she found intriguing and exhilarating not having come across it before. When she had previously discussed the subject with Polly, Polly had replied that she didn't know what she meant.

'Amongst folk I know, we *are* equal,' Polly had commented. 'It's onny when we're among toffs that we're not and that's because we haven't been educated.'

Rosalie had considered this, and said, 'But I know girls with brothers, and the boys go away to school to be educated, whilst the girls stay at home and learn things like sewing and music; they have a smattering of education which is not for their own sake but to enable them to understand their future husbands' business activities.'

'Pah!' Polly exclaimed. 'You don't think like that, do you, Rosalie?'

'No,' Rosalie had told her. 'I don't. I've often read my father's books in order to improve my mind.' She'd sighed. 'But I'm not sure that it will make any difference to my life.'

Howard looked round at them in the back of the trap, waiting for an answer. 'So which do you prefer?' he asked. 'Freedom to behave as you wish, up to a point that is, or to behave as is expected of you?'

Polly just laughed. 'I'd choose freedom every time,' she said. 'As long as I could have a good meal every day; and a roof over my head,' she added.

Rosalie wondered why it was that Polly didn't have a problem in answering a direct question from a man, as she did. Am I always searching for an answer that I think will please them, as is expected of me? Which I suppose is exactly what he is saying!

'I don't know,' she confessed. 'Never having had that freedom I can't say or even know what it is I really want.'

'Oh, come!' Howard said. 'You must have some heart's desire, some longing that you'd like to fulfil!'

Rosalie took a deep breath. 'Well, I've never

really allowed myself to consider concepts that were out of my reach, but—'

'Yes?' he encouraged. 'What is it that is out of reach?'

She paused. It was such an unlikely eventuality that it seemed ridiculous to mention it. She gazed out at the passing scenery as they bowled along, the dip and rise of the rolling hills, the wide valleys lush and green after the snow, the roe deer which she had seen on the skyline that morning moving towards the distant dark woods.

'Well,' she murmured again. 'This is so beautiful and dramatic; it has awakened my . . . my *long* desire to travel abroad. In my father's study at home there are many books describing the countries he has been to; and others also where he has not been. Some of the books have line drawings and coloured lithographs. There was one about Ireland, which I believe is very green, and another about India where it is very hot.' She paused as she recollected. 'Another one was about Egypt, with pictures showing the pyramids. Perhaps I'd never go there, but to be able to visit the Italian lakes, or even Spain, would be wonderful.' She sighed. 'But unlikely!'

'Good heavens!' Polly declared. 'You'd have to marry a very, very rich man to do all of that.' She smiled. 'I'd be happy just to stay here for 'rest of my life!'

'What, and not visit your old friends back home in Hull?' Howard asked.

Polly was silenced. 'There's nobody,' she said softly. 'Not since my ma died.' She cast a glance at him and he turned his head and smiled at her as she said, 'I'll just have to mek new ones.'

'What about me?' Rosalie said plaintively. 'I thought we were friends?'

'So we are,' Polly said. 'But you're planning on travelling abroad and leaving me behind!'

They drove along narrow roads and crossed stone bridges over swiftly running streams to reach the village of Littlebeck, which nestled at the bottom of a steep wooded valley. Howard dropped them off to stretch their legs whilst he made his calls. He told them that he wanted to look at a cow and calf, with the intention of buying them, for himself, he said, not for his uncle. 'I'd like to start breeding,' he told them. 'Luke has some cattle, but he prefers to concentrate on his sheep.'

He was also going to order a quantity of wood and nails, and pick up some supplies that Mrs Moody had requested. He told them he would meet them in half an hour.

Littlebeck was a very pretty village, greener and softer than the high moor of Fylingdale. They climbed a hill and sat down on a rock to look down at the cottages nestling below with their neat gardens; the air was full of birdsong and they breathed in the scents of newly mown grass and wood smoke and chatted about how their lives had changed since they had met.

'Never did I think I'd come somewhere like this,' Polly said. 'I didn't even know such a place existed, and yet we are still in Yorkshire.'

A fresh wind got up and they started to feel the chill and so made their way back down the hill to where they could see Howard talking to someone. Their cheeks were glowing with the exertion, but they were both exhilarated.

'It's lovely here,' Polly said. 'So pretty. Much greener and softer than up on our moor.'

Howard laughed. 'Claiming it as your own, Polly?'

'Yes.' She breathed out. 'I am. And if Rosalie decides to go on her travels or doesn't stay for any reason, then I shall try for work on a farm or in an inn.'

'Or marry a farmer,' Rosalie suggested.

'Or that,' she said. 'If anybody'd have me. Howard, why do you come on these errands? Don't you have a lad who could do them, like Sam?'

'I'm quite sure that Sam would be glad to come on a jaunt rather than be in the stables, but I like to keep my ear to the ground and find out what's happening in the district: keep up with the price of wool, who's selling what, and so on. But also,' he hesitated, 'I like to earn my keep, to keep busy. I'd like to think I'd be missed if I ever moved on.'

'But you won't, will you?' Polly asked.

Howard shook his head. 'Who knows? If Luke ever gave up farming and Edwin took over, then I might.'

'But surely Uncle Luke won't?' Rosalie said. 'He's rooted here.'

'So he is,' he said, but he raised his eyebrows as if he had reservations about his answer.

Before turning for home, he took them to see the Falling Foss waterfall, cascading and glinting like silver as it fell. The flow was swift after the winter snow and it frothed and gurgled over the rocks below.

When they arrived back in the yard, Edwin came out of one of the stables. On seeing them he carefully closed the door behind him and stood with his back to it, folding his arms in front of him.

'Been out, Edwin?' Howard asked.

'No,' he said abruptly. 'Just checking round, making sure everything is all right.'

Howard frowned. 'Why wouldn't it be?'

'Oh, Sam's out. I sent him on an errand and Amos has gone to Scarborough to fetch Clemmie.'

'Oh! Does she know?'

Edwin gave a thin smile. 'She'll know when he turns up at the door.'

Howard shrugged as if to say that it was nothing to do with him, but Polly and Rosalie noticed the frown as he turned away and both saw how the scar on his cheek had reddened.

When they had changed from their outdoor clothes they came down to sit by the fire in the drawing room. It was an hour before midday and they were both ready for a hot drink after their outing. Rosalie rang the bell and Mrs Moody came in answer to it. She folded her hands in front of her and said, 'Yes, miss. What can I get for you?'

'Coffee, please, Mrs Moody,' Rosalie said. 'Isn't Dora here?'

'I've sent her upstairs to change before dinner,' she said sharply. 'Mr Edwin asked her to go and tell Sam he wanted him and she came back ages later, looking an absolute disgrace.'

Polly heaved a breath as the housekeeper went out of the room. 'Hope she wasn't caught rolling in the hay with Sam,' she whispered.

'Polly!' Rosalie was scandalized. 'Don't think such a thing. You know what Dora said – she'd be sent packing if she was found out.'

'Mm,' Polly said. 'But Edwin told us that he'd sent Sam out on an errand, so why did he ask Dora to go and look for him?'

Rosalie lifted her shoulders resignedly and whispered, 'Who knows why Cousin Edwin does what he does? He's a law unto himself, I should say.' She lowered her voice even further. 'I can't imagine that I would ever become fond of him.'

Luke came into the room and Rosalie rang the bell again for more coffee for him. Dora answered the call. She was red-faced and anxious and glanced nervously at Mr Kingston when he asked her to tell Amos to saddle up a horse as he had to go out.

'Amos has gone to Scarborough, sir. To fetch Miss Clementina.'

'Fetch her?' He looked puzzled. 'Isn't she here?' He looked blankly at Rosalie and Polly. 'Oh! Of course she isn't. Did someone write to her?'

They both shook their heads. How could they? They didn't know where she was.

'Very remiss of me,' he muttered when Dora went out. 'I'm so forgetful sometimes. Having two young ladies here made me forget about my own daughter. But who told Amos to fetch her?'

'I believe that Edwin might have done, Uncle Luke,' Rosalie ventured. 'We saw him earlier and he mentioned where Amos had gone.'

Luke drew in a breath. 'Clemmie will not be pleased. I should have written. She likes at least

247

a week to prepare, and Amos will not like to wait!' He sighed. 'I wish that Edwin wouldn't— never mind. I can saddle up my own horse.' He glanced at them. 'I'm going out now and might not be back until the morning. Would you tell Mrs Moody I won't wait for dinner?'

'Of course,' Rosalie said. 'And when Clementina comes home?'

'Ah!' He seemed to reconsider. 'Well, erm, give her my apologies and tell her I'll be back tomorrow. Would you, erm, would you also tell Mrs Moody that I will be bringing a guest home with me, so would she please prepare a room.'

'Odd,' Polly said after he had gone. Through the window, they saw him ride away. 'If it wasn't that he was too old, I'd have said he had an engagement – with a lady!'

'He's not too old,' Rosalie said. 'He can't be more than late forties, and men can marry quite late in life. And he's still handsome, don't you think?'

Polly agreed that he was. 'And a good catch for some lucky lady,' she added. 'I don't mean for his wealth, if he has any, but because he's very agreeable. So, I wonder who it might be, and if he has told his son and daughter?'

Rosalie laughed. 'We now know how people up here spend their long winters: they speculate on romance and who is doing what!'

'Mm,' Polly said. 'And I'm going to speculate that when you tell dear Mrs Moody that Mr Kingston is bringing a guest home, she will not be pleased!'

CHAPTER TWENTY-TWO

As Polly had predicted, the housekeeper was not pleased to hear that Mr Kingston would not be in for his midday meal or that a guest would be arriving the next day. She humped disgruntledly and muttered that 'Maister should have informed her himself'.

Rosalie merely raised her eyebrows in her direction and said nothing, and Polly pondered that here was the difference in breeding between herself and Rosalie. I'd have told her it was nowt to do wi' her, she thought. Just because she's been here for ever doesn't mean she has to know all that's going on in 'household.

'Did Maister say the name of the gentleman he's bringing?' Mrs Moody asked. 'If it's one of his shooting friends I know where to put 'em.'

Rosalie drew herself up and looked askance at her. 'I am not privy to Mr Kingston's affairs, Mrs Moody,' she answered coldly, 'so I cannot say. Perhaps Miss Clementina will be able to tell you when she arrives home.'

Mrs Moody stared open-mouthed. 'Miss Clementina's coming home as well? In time for dinner? Or supper?' She heaved a breath when Rosalie shook her head and answered that she didn't know. 'Well I never! Scuse me, miss.' She gave a cursory nod of her head as she departed. 'It seems like I'll have all on to get the rooms ready.'

Rosalie tapped her fingers to her mouth and murmured, 'It seems like the cat's amongst the pigeons.'

'I hope she doesn't take it out on Dora or 'other maids,' Polly said. 'But I bet she does.'

Rosalie, Polly, Howard and Edwin were finishing supper when they heard the wheels of the carriage on the drive. Edwin got up and went into the hall and Howard rose from his chair and stood with one hand on the mantelpiece. He glanced at the girls and gave a wry smile.

'Now for it,' he said in a low voice. 'You are about to meet your other cousin.'

Rosalie and Polly rose from the table as the door opened and a tall, broad-shouldered and handsome young woman entered. Clementina was dark-haired like Edwin, but whereas he was pale and thin-faced, she was chubby-cheeked and had a rosy complexion. She looked from the two young ladies to Howard and then over her shoulder at Edwin.

Rosalie and Polly both dipped their knee but Clementina just gazed blankly at them. Behind her Edwin grinned. 'Told you there was a surprise waiting for you, didn't I, Clem?'

'Don't call me Clem,' she snapped. 'You know I don't like it.' She undid the cord which fastened her cloak and threw the garment on to the sofa, from where it slid on to the floor. 'Where's Papa?'

Howard stepped forward. 'Clementina, may I present your cousin, Rosalie Kingston, and her friend Miss Parker? I'm not sure if your father told you that they were coming!'

Clementina gave a perfunctory dip. 'No, he did not. How do you do? Have you been here long?' She threw herself into a chair, her voluminous green gown billowing about her. Rosalie and Polly sat down too. 'I didn't know I had any more cousins. Did you, Edwin?'

'Father told me the day before they arrived,' Edwin drawled. 'Whilst you were away,' he added.

'Papa is hopeless!' she sighed. 'Nor did he write to say that I was to come home today. I was quite prepared to stay at least another week. I couldn't believe it when Amos turned up at dinner time and the maid had to start packing my things.'

Rosalie and Polly cast a glance at each other and waited for Edwin to say that he had sent Amos. But he did not.

'Forgetfulness seems to be a trait which runs in families,' Rosalie murmured. 'I did not even know that I had cousins until *my* father informed me that arrangements had been made for me to come here to live.'

Clementina looked astonished. 'To live? Why – where is your mother?'

Rosalie's eyes filled with tears. 'She died at Christmas.'

'Oh. Sorry,' Clementina said, and it seemed that she was, for her harsh expression softened. Then she said. 'But to live? You mean for good?'

Rosalie pressed her lips together. 'I believe that was my father's intention.' But he was rather vague about it, she thought, and he hasn't written to ask how I'm settling in or if I'm happy here.

Clementina's gaze went to Polly. 'And – Miss Parkin, is it? Have you come to live with us too?'

'Parker,' Polly corrected her. 'Polly Parker. I'm an orphan and am Rosalie's friend. Your father has kindly invited me to stay.'

'Has he?' Clementina pursed her mouth. 'I wish he'd told us. I wonder if he told Moody! I would think he probably forgot. Where is he, by the way?'

Rosalie hesitated, waiting to see if Edwin or Howard would offer any information, but neither did and she surmised that perhaps they didn't know that Luke Kingston had gone out.

'He went out this morning,' she told Clementina. 'And said that he wouldn't be home until the morning. He also said to tell you that he's sorry not to be here when you returned. I don't think he realized that you'd be home today,' she added rather slyly.

'Not know! How could he not know?' Clementina remonstrated. 'What's the matter with him? He must have known if he sent Amos!'

'Ah! Well, that was me,' Edwin admitted. 'I thought you'd wish to be here to entertain your cousin.'

Clementina shot a look of pure loathing at her brother but he seemed unperturbed.

'Your father also said that he would be bringing a guest home,' Rosalie added to fill the silence.

'Who?' Clementina and Edwin asked, whilst Howard walked across to the window and Polly thought she saw a smile play about his mouth as he crossed in front of her.

'That I don't know,' Rosalie said, adding, 'Will you excuse me? I've rather a headache and would like to lie down for half an hour.'

254

Polly rose too, saying, 'And I must go and tuck Louis up for the night.'

'Louis?' Clementina said peevishly. 'Not another guest?'

Polly smiled sweetly. 'A lamb; one that Howard rescued from a snowdrift. I've been feeding him. He likes to see me before he goes to sleep!'

She was gratified to see Clementina's non-plussed expression and Howard's grin as she followed Rosalie out of the room.

'I'll come with you,' Rosalie whispered to Polly out in the hall. 'I haven't really got a headache. I just wanted to get out of there.'

Polly pulled a face. It wasn't her place to comment on Rosalie's relations, but she was pleased that they were not hers. She pulled on the galoshes. 'Do you think Clementina will mind my using her rubber boots?' she said.

'She might.' Rosalie followed her down the steps, and they ducked down as they passed the dining room window so as not to be seen. 'We'll have to get you some of your own. Maybe Howard would know where to buy them. It seems strange not to have any shops nearby.'

When they asked him, Howard told them that now the weather was improving the packman would be arriving soon, though he doubted if he would carry galoshes. 'Scarborough's the place,' he said. 'Lots of shops there. Ask

Clemmie; I'm sure she'd relish going back, but she'll have to persuade her father to let Amos take you.'

Neither of them knew what a packman was and he explained that it was a traveller in goods; a pedlar or hawker, who visited country districts carrying silks and cottons and household items, the sort of thing a housewife might need.

'A travelling shop?' Polly said. 'So they don't have to go out to the nearest town?'

'That's it,' he said. 'There are times when we can't get out, as you saw when you came, but the weather then was changing for the better. Sometimes we are locked in for weeks on end.'

'So the cook or housekeeper or farmer's wife has to be prepared?' Polly said thoughtfully. Being a town girl she was used to having butchers, bakers and haberdashers on her doorstep.

'Yes,' Howard told her. 'And they have to be very thrifty, so there's rarely anything wasted.' He looked at them sideways, 'For instance, if they kill a pig every single part of it is used – even its squeal!'

'Goodness!' said gullible Rosalie, but Polly raised her eyebrows and heaved a shrewd sigh.

They didn't see Clementina again until the

following day when they met for the midday meal. Luke had not yet returned.

Clementina was quite chatty to Rosalie, asking her whether there were theatres and balls in Hull and if she had a good social life. She studiously ignored Polly, not speaking to her or asking her anything about herself. Polly was quite relieved that she wasn't expected to answer questions about her life, but felt that Clementina had guessed that she had been Rosalie's servant before she became her friend.

After they had eaten, Polly excused herself. Howard seemed preoccupied and wasn't joining in the conversation and Clementina was monopolizing Rosalie while Edwin sat picking at his nails, and she felt neglected and of no account. Outside the dining room door she bent down to fasten a shoelace that had come undone and heard Clementina's voice quite clearly.

'What a very odd young woman Polly Parker is, Rosalie. I warrant she hasn't always been your companion. She was your maidservant, wasn't she?'

Polly heard the sneer in her tone and gasped. How would Rosalie answer?

'Polly is my best friend,' she heard her say. 'What she was before is unimportant. We have much in common, having both lost our mothers on the same day.'

257

'Well, so you might have,' Clementina answered. 'And I'm sure it's very noble of you to treat her so well, but you don't need her now. I suggest you dismiss her; she will find other work, especially if you give her a reference.' Polly reeled. She heard Clementina laugh as she said, 'I can be your best friend now, Rosalie. We can have such fun together.'

Polly fled out of the hall and down the steps towards the back of the house and the stables. How could she, she thought tearfully. How could anyone be so cruel? Suppose Rosalie is persuaded? What will I do?

She went into the stable and leaned against the wall and the lamb came towards her, nudging her knees. Howard had said that soon he would be able to go out on to the moors with the other sheep. Polly had resisted, saying he wasn't ready; now tears trickled down her cheeks as she realized that she would lose him altogether if she had to go away.

The stable door swung open and Edwin looked in. 'I thought I might find you here,' he said. 'Did you hear what Clemmie said? She's hardly the soul of discretion.'

His voice was soft and she thought he was being sympathetic. She brushed away her tears. 'I didn't mean to listen,' she said. 'But the door was open.'

'Oh, it was quite deliberate,' he said, coming closer. 'She intended you to hear.'

'Why?' she asked. 'Why would she?'

He reached out a hand and touched her cheek. 'Because she's a spoiled brat. Poor little Polly,' he murmured. 'If you're nice to me I'll make sure that you're able to stay.'

She took a breath as he put both hands on the wall behind her, effectively trapping her within his arms. She put up her hand to push him away. 'Please don't do that,' she said.

He bent his head towards hers. 'That's what I like about you,' he whispered. 'Such an independent spirit. I'd think you are a very fiery young lady.'

'I am,' she said, giving him a shove. 'Please get away from me.'

He laughed and put his face against hers. 'Don't want to. Not without a kiss first, and then maybe something more after.'

Polly turned her head away as he searched for her mouth. 'Get off me,' she said angrily.

'As I thought,' he murmured. 'A lady of passion.' He put his hands on her waist and ran them up to her breasts. 'And how lovely you are, Polly, hiding your curves beneath your gown!'

She punched his chest. He was so close, his body pressing her to the wall so that she couldn't move. 'Get off me,' she repeated. 'I'm a guest in your house! How dare you treat me like this?'

With his knee pressed against her and one hand holding her fast, he lifted her skirt with the other. 'You're not a guest,' he smiled. 'You're a servant girl, like Clemmie said.'

With a mighty effort she forced him off her and with her fist swinging she hit him across his face, making him stagger. She hit him again and headed for the door.

'If you dare to touch me again,' she shrieked, 'I'll tell your father.'

Edwin stroked his reddened cheek. 'Just you try,' he snarled. 'I'd tell him that you led me on with your promises.'

Polly kept her hand on the door ready for escape and looked at him. 'He wouldn't believe you,' she whispered, but she felt sick. Why would Luke Kingston listen to her, a stranger, rather than his own son?

She heard someone whistling and she stepped outside into the yard and safety. Howard came round the corner. 'There you are, Polly,' he said. 'We wondered where you'd got to.'

'Why?' she said, feeling agitated and as if she couldn't trust anyone. 'Who's looking for me?'

He frowned. 'Well, Rosalie for one, but I'm going up the moor to check on the sheep. I wondered if you'd like to come.'

'No, thank you,' she said. 'I'm going in-doors.'

'Is Louis all right?' He continued to gaze at her.

She swallowed. 'I think so.'

'There are some lambs due. I'm going to bring the ewes down. Are you sure you don't want to come?'

She shook her head, hardly daring to speak. 'No,' she said. 'I don't feel well.'

Howard raised his eyebrows. 'You too? I just met Rosalie in the hall and she excused herself to go to her room.' He smiled. 'I hope it's nothing catching.'

'It isn't,' she muttered. 'Nowt that men can catch, anyway.'

'Ah!' He glanced towards the stable, where the top door was swinging. 'Is someone in there?' he asked. 'The door needs fastening back or the hinge will break.'

Polly licked her lips and glanced nervously at him. 'There might be,' she said.

'What's the matter, Polly? Has something happened?'

She didn't answer and he frowned. Then he strode to the stable and looked in. 'Edwin!' he barked. 'Come on out. What the hell are you playing at?'

CHAPTER TWENTY-THREE

Polly watched the two men confront each other.

'Get out of my way,' Edwin snarled. 'Get back to work.'

'What are you doing skulking in there? Have you upset Polly?' Howard's voice was tense and he seemed barely able to contain his temper, which surprised Polly as he usually seemed so calm and self-controlled.

'It's nothing to do with you what I'm doing.' Edwin put his face close up to Howard's. 'So keep your nose out of it.' He stalked away, back towards the house.

'What did he do, Polly?' Howard came back to her. 'Did he try to compromise you?'

'Erm.' Compromise me? Is that 'same as molest me? She blinked. 'He was after a kiss,' she said. 'And summat more if he could get it.'

Howard swore. 'Try not to be alone with him,' he said. 'He's a rake, I know that for sure.'

'He – he came into 'stable,' she told him, hoping he didn't think that she had encouraged Edwin. 'He must have followed me after what Clementina said.'

He looked startled. 'Did you hear what she said, or did Edwin tell you?'

'I heard,' she said in a low voice. 'Edwin said that she intended me to hear. That it was deliberate.'

'I'm sorry, Polly.' He put his hand on her arm but she flinched and he drew it away. 'They are not nice people.'

'Why do you stay?' she asked. 'Why do you live with them?'

He gave a little shrug. 'It's my home. And because of Luke. He doesn't know half of what goes on; and if I left the farm would go to rack and ruin. He can't farm it alone and Edwin does nothing. But . . .' He hesitated. 'One day I might.'

Polly left him and went back to the house and he turned to go down the track, whistling for his dogs who went bounding after him towards the moor.

When she went inside, Clementina was sitting in the hall by the fire. 'There you are, Polly,' she said sweetly. 'We were wondering where you'd got to. Rosalie was quite anxious. I said you'd turn up sooner or later.'

'Like a bad penny?' Polly said. 'Yes, course

I would. I've been having a chat with your brother, as a matter of fact.' She stared right at her. 'He's very fond of you, isn't he? He's got such a good opinion of you.'

Clementina looked at her warily and her cheeks flushed. 'Why, what did he say?'

Polly laughed and it sounded forced even to her. 'I couldn't possibly tell you, Miss Clementina. That'd be breaking a confidence. But he described you very well.'

She turned away and went upstairs to look for Rosalie. She found her sitting on her bed and weeping with anger.

'I'm so sorry, Polly,' she said. 'Clementina is a beast! I knew that you would have heard what she said.' She wiped her eyes. 'Are you very upset? You know that I would hate it if you left; in fact I wouldn't stay. I'd go back home even, to an empty house.'

'I was upset,' Polly stood beside her. 'I don't mind admitting it. But I can put up with those two if you can. I just love this place. It's so wild and untamed and there's so much space. I don't want to go back to 'life I had before.'

Rosalie heaved a deep breath. 'Well then, we'll stay.' She blew her nose. 'Those two? Do you mean Edwin? He's very arrogant, but he's not as bad as Clementina. Oh, how nice it was before she came back!'

'It's her home, Rosalie. We're the outsiders,'

Polly said, deciding not to go into the subject of Edwin's behaviour. 'Mebbe she resents us, or me anyway; she's probably quite pleased to have you here. She must get very bored with her own company. I don't think she even likes Howard very much.'

'No, I don't think she does,' Rosalie agreed. 'And he's so very nice.'

Polly looked at her. Did Rosalie find Howard attractive? She was surprised to feel a sudden spasm of jealousy, but it swiftly went away. It would make sense for them to be attracted to each other, she thought; and there was I thinking he was my friend.

Polly looked out of the window and saw Clementina striding round the corner of the house as if towards the stables. She hadn't changed into her riding costume but had draped a shawl over her shoulders. She wondered if she had gone in search of her brother to find out what he had said about her.

'Shall we go for a walk?' she asked. Rosalie agreed and they put on their outdoor clothes. Polly felt guilty at spurning Howard's invitation to go on to the moor with him and suggested they might try to follow him. But as they came to the top of the stairs the front door was being opened by Dora, Mrs Moody was hurrying up the kitchen stairs and Luke Kingston was calling out something to Sam Little who was outside on the front drive, holding the reins of two horses.

Luke was taking the arm of the woman by his side and ushering her into the hall. She was of medium height, slim and elegant and dressed in a dark red riding costume. On her fair head was a jaunty hat with a frivolous feather.

'Mrs Moody,' he said, 'will you send up tea and a plate of Cook's scones with jam and cream? This is Mrs Radcliffe. She has come to stay. I trust you have a room prepared for her?'

At the top of the stairs Rosalie and Polly stared at each other, their mouths in a round and delighted *Oh*.

The housekeeper bobbed her knee. 'Yes, sir. It's all prepared. Perhaps you'd like to take tea first and rest yourself before you go up to change, ma'am?'

'She means so that she can swap rooms,' Rosalie whispered. 'She was expecting a gentleman.'

They heard Mrs Radcliffe murmur something and Luke nodded. 'Shall we go down?' Rosalie urged mischievously. 'Meet her before Clementina does?'

Polly nodded, her eyes sparkling. She had been right. Here was a romance, she decided, and Luke Kingston was clearly not too old; it was quite obvious by the way he gently led his companion into the drawing room.

They ran down the stairs, holding up their skirts, and knocked on the door before entering. 'Uncle Luke,' Rosalie began. 'We heard you arrive and – *oh*, I do beg your pardon.' She dipped her knee and Polly did the same. 'We wanted to tell you we were going walking.'

'Come in! Come in!' he said. He seemed very animated but in an anxious way. 'I thought it might be Clemmie come to chastise me for not being here when she arrived. She did come back from Scarborough, I suppose?'

Before they could answer, Mrs Radcliffe, who was standing by the window, said, 'My dear!'

'Oh! Sorry, yes. Anna, I'd like you to meet my nieces; erm . . .'

Rosalie came forward and put out her hand. 'Rosalie Kingston,' she smiled.

Polly too came towards her and, dipping her knee again, said, 'Polly Parker, ma'am.' She dropped her voice and whispered, 'I'm not a niece. I'm a friend of Rosalie's.'

Anna Radcliffe laughed. It was a happy sound, Polly thought, as if she laughed often.

'I'm very pleased to meet you,' she said. 'I'm an old friend of Luke's, who was a dear friend of my late husband. Do you have to dash away now? Do stay and talk for five minutes.' She took a seat near the fire. 'Luke has told me so little about his family. I knew he had a son and daughter and a nephew, of course, and I've been looking forward to meeting them, but I can't recall you saying anything about your beautiful nieces, Luke.'

She shook her head at him in mild reproof and Rosalie and Polly both smiled. She was a breath of fresh air, Rosalie thought, whilst Polly prayed that Anna Radcliffe was going to be a permanent addition to the family.

'Perhaps that's because we haven't been here very long,' Rosalie explained. 'We arrived just a few weeks ago and as a matter of fact we only met Clementina yesterday when she arrived home.'

'I'm longing to meet her, and Edwin and Howard. Are they nice?' she asked conspiratorially. 'Do you all get on well? I have a son and daughter,' she said, before they could answer. 'Jonathan is sixteen and still away at school, and Elizabeth is fourteen. Ah! Tea.' Mrs Moody, in a clean white apron and cap and carrying a china teapot, came in behind Dora, who was carrying a laden tray.

Dora placed the tray on a low table and Mrs Radcliffe thanked her. Dora flushed and bobbed and backed out of the room, unused, it seemed to Polly, to receiving such gracious thanks.

'I'll pour, Mrs Moody,' Mrs Radcliffe said.

'Oh, there are only two cups! Are you not staying for tea?' she asked Rosalie and Polly.

'Dora'll bring more cups, ma'am,' Mrs Moody said quickly. 'I didn't realize the young ladies were here.'

'Thank you,' Rosalie said. 'That would be nice.'

Luke Kingston sat down opposite his guest and, giving a deep sigh, stretched out his legs. It was almost as if he had cleared a hurdle. 'Where is Clemmie?' he asked. 'Is she out riding?'

'I saw her going towards 'stables,' Polly said, 'but she wasn't dressed for riding. I'm sure she'll be back in a minute. She must have heard 'hosses come.'

'I recognize that accent,' Mrs Radcliffe said. 'You're from Hull!'

'I am, ma'am,' Polly told her. 'Born and bred.'

'My late husband was born in Hull,' Mrs Radcliffe said, 'and although he came to North Yorkshire when he was very young, we used to go back there from time to time to visit his relatives.' She looked sad for a moment. 'I haven't been for many years,' she said. 'Not since his death. There never seemed to be enough time; the farm and the children took up most of it.'

'Do you farm yourself, Mrs Radcliffe?'

Rosalie said in astonishment. This lady was immaculate, a fair skin which wasn't pale but had a golden glow, as if she spent some time outdoors, yet didn't look as if she ever got her hands dirty.

Anna Radcliffe smiled. 'Well, not exactly. I have an excellent foreman and staff, but I look after the books and I'm always aware of what is happening on the farm.'

Dora brought more cups and another pot of tea and they were indulging in quiet conversation when they heard quarrelsome voices in the hall.

'That'll be Clementina.' Luke sighed and rose to his feet. 'And Edwin too, I should think.'

Clementina burst through the door. 'Papa! Why were you not here to meet me?'

She stopped in her tracks and gazed open-mouthed as Anna Radcliffe rose from her chair to greet her.

'Clemmie, my dear,' Luke said, 'I want you to meet a very good friend of mine, Mrs Radcliffe. Anna, this is my daughter Clementina, and here, skulking in the doorway, is Edwin. Come in, Edwin, and be introduced.'

Anna was extremely gracious in her greeting and clasped Clementina's hand. 'I've been looking forward to meeting you, Clementina,' she smiled. 'Your father has told me so much about you that I feel I know you already.'

Polly and Rosalie exchanged glances, and watched with interest as Edwin gave Anna Radcliffe a formal bow.

'Now I just have to meet Howard, Luke,' Anna sat down again, 'and then I think I have met all of your family.'

'Have you known Father long?' Edwin asked abruptly. 'I don't recall him mentioning your name.'

'Yes,' Luke butted in. 'You must have heard me speak of Jim Radcliffe, Anna's late husband. We used to go shooting together.'

Edwin shrugged. 'Can't recall.'

'Well, it's some years ago, of course,' his father admitted. 'How long is it since Jim died, Anna?'

'Close on twelve years,' she said. 'Elizabeth was only a toddler; she doesn't remember her father at all, which is very sad.'

Polly was keeping a close eye on the reactions of Edwin and Clementina, and both, she thought, seemed very uneasy with the present situation. Clementina won't like her father's attention being diverted away from her. Bad enough to have Rosalie and me in the house, but an attractive, marriageable widow! And I can almost hear Edwin's mind going tick, tick, tick, she thought. Mr Kingston would hardly have brought Mrs Radcliffe here without some intention. If his father should marry a woman with a son, there are endless possibilities for Edwin to have his nose put out of joint.

'Ring for Mrs Moody again, will you, Clemmie,' her father said. 'Tell her we'll have an early supper, say at seven. And ask her to tell Cook we'll have one of her meat pies with thick onion gravy.'

Mrs Moody came in to take Mrs Radcliffe upstairs to her room. Rosalie and Polly excused themselves and went out, as had been their intention, leaving their uncle with his son and daughter.

'Let's try and find Howard,' Polly said as they trekked down the track to the moor. 'I can't wait to tell him the news!'

They saw him some way off and trudged up towards him. Beyond him, standing on a high ridge, was what looked like a house or farm. It was a square building, outlined against the skyline. 'I haven't noticed that before,' Polly said breathlessly. 'Why haven't I?'

She asked the same question of Howard when they eventually caught up with him.

'You've come up at a different angle,' he said. 'From some parts of the moor the house is unseen. It's hidden by various ridges, crags and valleys. But the view from it is spectacular – the moors, the valleys and the becks and streams.'

'I'd like to see it,' Polly said eagerly. 'Could we walk there?'

'Yes,' he smiled. 'I'll take you, but not today. And it would be quicker on horseback – if you dare!'

'Well of course we dare,' Rosalie said boldly. 'We're intrepid, aren't we, Polly? But we came to tell you something, Howard. There's a visitor and she wants to meet you.'

'And we're having an early supper,' Polly told him. 'So you'd better come home and get smartened up.'

'What?' he said mockingly. 'Am I not smart enough? I'm wearing my best working clothes.' He was clad in a pair of corduroy breeches, an old tweed jacket and a battered hat. 'Good enough to meet anybody!'

Rosalie looked at Polly. *Home*, she had said, and as if she meant it. She belongs here, she thought. It's as if she really has come home; Howard too seems to blend into the landscape. They would be right for each other, she mused thoughtfully.

Polly put her head on one side as she scrutinized him. 'I think for this lady you probably would be smart enough,' she said. 'But *we* want you to make a good impression.'

273

CHAPTER TWENTY-FOUR

When they assembled in the drawing room before supper Rosalie and Polly were wearing their prettiest gowns, Polly in her favourite blue and Rosalie in primrose yellow muslin with a sprig pattern. They had both pinned up their hair. Polly wore a blue ribbon and Rosalie a lace cap.

Clementina wore white satin and Edwin and his father wore dark frock coats with stiff starched neckcloths. Howard had not yet come down but as Rosalie and Polly chatted to Mrs Radcliffe, and Clementina and Edwin remained silent, the door opened and he came in.

'There you are, my boy,' Luke greeted him. 'Come along and meet Mrs Radcliffe. This is Howard, my dear.'

Howard had indeed smartened up; his fair hair was still wet from washing and he wore a pair of light-coloured trousers, a white shirt with a cravat, and a dark blue waistcoat under a short velvet jacket.

'I'm very pleased to meet you, Howard,' Mrs Radcliffe said. 'And how very modish you are. We don't often see such style on the moor.'

Howard gave her a courtly bow. 'I understood we had a special visitor,' he said, giving her a quick disarming smile. 'And I wanted to make a good impression this time. Alas, you may never see me looking like this again!'

Anna Radcliffe laughed. 'Oh, I do hope so. But have we met before?'

'We have, ma'am,' he said. 'When I was a boy. My friend and I came with Uncle Luke to your home during the school holidays, and we went grouse shooting with your husband.'

She raised a finger. 'You did! I remember. Well, how nice to meet you again after all these years.'

'Indeed the pleasure is mine, Mrs Radcliffe,' he said. 'You had a young son, and a little girl, I think.'

She was about to answer when Mrs Moody knocked on the door to announce that supper was served and they rose from their seats. Luke took Anna's arm; Clementina and Edwin went next. Edwin muttered, 'Fop,' as he passed Howard, but Howard was quite unfazed and merely winked at Polly and Rosalie and held out both elbows akimbo.

Cook had surpassed herself with her beef and ale pie. The meat was tender and succulent and the pastry rich and crumbling. Carrots, leeks and roast potatoes accompanied it, and there was thick onion gravy as the master had requested. When the maids had cleared away, Luke asked that the dessert might be delayed for ten minutes.

He opened a bottle of sparkling wine, filled Anna's, Edwin's and Howard's glasses to the brim, and gave half a glass each to the three young ladies. Then he stood at the head of the table with Anna at his right hand and carefully poured his own. He took a breath and surveyed them all, his gaze lingering on Edwin and Clementina before coming to rest on Anna, who smiled.

'My dears,' he said, 'I have something to say before dessert is brought in. I – we' – he glanced at Anna – 'have an announcement to make.'

Clementina gave a breathy gasp and clutched her fingers together and Edwin lifted his lip in a sneer. Polly and Rosalie glanced at each other and raised their eyebrows expectantly.

Luke took another breath and continued. 'I have asked Mrs Radcliffe to do me the honour of becoming my wife, and she has consented. We are to be married at the end of April.' He broke into a wide grin as he spoke, and reaching for Anna's hand he tenderly kissed it. 'I am very, very happy!' he said joyously.

Rosalie and Polly clapped their hands, and after a quick glance at Edwin, who seemed rooted to his chair, Howard rose to his feet.

'Very many congratulations, sir. May I say that I think you a very fortunate man?' He raised his glass and looked round at the assembled company. 'May I propose a toast?'

Edwin clumsily pushed back his chair and stood up. 'I rather think that it's my place to do that,' he said grudgingly. '*I* am my father's son, after all.'

Howard nodded in acquiescence and sat down again.

It was a short toast, to the effect that the announcement was quite unexpected but they were both old enough to know what was in front of them and wishing them health and happiness together.

It was put so plainly and baldly that Rosalie thought that perhaps Edwin's heart wasn't in it. He seemed totally unprepared and none too pleased. Does he still think of his mother, I wonder, she thought. Is he hurt that his father is taking another wife? But Edwin is a grown man; surely he must want his father to rediscover the joy of love and companionship with someone else? But then she wondered how she would feel if her father took another wife. It is too soon for that, she thought. Far too soon, and once more she puzzled over why he hadn't yet written to her.

As Polly ate the dessert of apple sponge pudding, and sipped at her first glass of sparkling wine, she listened to the conversation around her. Clementina and Edwin said little, but that made Polly feel easier, for she was very aware of her lowly status and didn't want to speak unless spoken to. She felt rather out of place, as if she were an outsider, an interloper who really should have been waiting on table or else down in the kitchen washing up at the sink.

'You're very quiet, Polly,' Anna Radcliffe said. 'Are you quite well?'

'Oh, yes, thank you, ma'am.' Polly blushed. 'I'm just enjoying listening to everybody.'

'What do you think of our wedding plans? The weather will be settled and our guests will be able to travel more easily.'

'I've never been to a wedding,' Polly confessed.

'No?' Mrs Radcliffe was astonished. 'Would you like to be an attendant? Let me see,' she went on. 'One, two, three, four with Elizabeth. What do you think, Luke? Would four attendants be all right? How lovely they'll all look, three fair angels and one exotic brunette.' She smiled at Clementina as she spoke.

How kind she is, Polly thought, she's including us all and yet Clementina is glowering at her. I wonder if she's thinking that she's losing her father.

It was still dark the next morning when Howard saddled his horse and rode up the moor. There had been lambs born during the night in the lower field but no more were due for a few days so he took the opportunity to visit High Ridge House, the building that Polly and Rosalie had seen the previous day. It was his favourite place, even though it was in a state of dilapidation.

He had first seen it as a boy when he came to live with his uncle and aunt; it was a place he came to when he wanted to think or to escape from his hated cousin Edwin, who did his best to make his life a misery. In the distant past it had been built as a field house with a byre and a barn. Howard hadn't known then that the building was on his uncle's land and that Luke's own uncle and aunt had lived in the front, close by their animals, when they were first married.

It was a good pull up the moor and when he reached the house the wind was whistling round it. It needs a shelter belt, he thought. At least it would if anyone lived here. It was built of sandstone and blended in well with the rocky outcrop at the top of the moor. In the late summer and early autumn it stood out proud against the purple heather.

He tethered his horse and sat down in the lee of a wall to eat his breakfast of bread and beef. The sun was rising, lifting the darkness into a suffusion of blue, gold and silver, with apricot-coloured clouds racing across the sky.

He watched as the view of steep wooded valleys and spreading moorland came out of the shadows, and the streams and rivulets ran like silver down the hillside. Sheep were cropping the young heather and here and there were patches of scorched earth where the farmers had burned the invasive ling and bracken.

Should I ask Luke to let me have it, he thought. I could rebuild the broken walls. The roof is fairly sound, for the moment anyway, and I could repair the windows and doors. I could work for him just as easily from here as I do below, and Mrs Radcliffe might be glad to have some extra space. She's stuck with Edwin, but Clementina, I guess, might, just might, want to go back to Scarborough to our grandmother.

His grandmother was also Clemmie's and Edwin's. Howard was very fond of her, even though he didn't see her as often as he would have liked. She was a very merry and sociable woman who had taken him into her care when his parents had died, until Luke said he and his wife would gladly bring him up with their own children.

When he was growing up their grandmother had told him that she would one day find a suitable husband for Clementina, and with a twinkle in her eye had added that she would search out a wife for him when he was old enough.

He'd shaken his head at her and begged her not to. 'I'll need a hardy country girl,' he'd said. 'Not one who likes to go to balls or be seen at the theatre.'

He put his hand to his forehead to shade his eyes and gazed down the valley. There was someone far below on horseback; a rider wearing a wide-brimmed hat and a red scarf round his neck. His mount was carrying saddlebags. Howard smiled. He watched for a while and saw the rider cross the valley floor and turn in the direction of High Ridge House. This was a very welcome visitor.

The rider was halfway up the moor when Howard put his fingers to his lips and gave a shrill whistle. The man looked up and waved. It was twenty minutes more before he reached the summit. Howard went to meet him and as the newcomer dismounted he put out his hand.

'Good to see you, my friend. Were you expecting me?'

'I'd a feeling that when the weather began to improve you'd be here before long,' Howard said. 'It's good to see you too, Sonny. Or are you Sebastian now?'

Sonny Blake lifted his shoulders. 'I can be whoever you want me to be. How are your visitors? Are they settling in or anxious to get back to civilization?'

'I gathered that you knew them.' Howard laughed. 'Taken to it like ducks to water. Although they are having a little difficulty with the residents.'

'Not your uncle?' Sonny asked anxiously.

'No. With Clemmie and *young maister,*' Howard said ironically. 'Anyway, I have news for you. Your timing is perfect. Let me tell you about a wedding!'

'Not yours?' Sonny said in astonishment. 'Surely not. The confirmed bachelor!'

'No! What bosh! Of course not – yet. But do you remember how we fell in love for the first time and with the same woman?'

Sonny opened his mouth in astonishment. 'Not the lovely Mrs Radcliffe?'

'The very one.' Howard grinned.

'Who?' Sonny asked. 'Who would dare to steal her from us?'

'Luke,' Howard said. 'Stolen her from

282

beneath our very noses. They're to be married in April. It has come as a complete surprise to the family,' he added. 'At least to some of us.'

'But not you?' Sonny asked sagely.

'No.' Howard gave a wry grin. 'I'd seen him in Harwood Dale on more than one occasion, heading towards the Radcliffes' farm, and at first I thought nothing of it, but then he began disappearing from time to time and was vague about where he'd been. I just began to suspect. He seemed to me to be like a dog with two tails.'

'And he never said?'

'Well, would you?' Howard asked. 'How could he possibly say anything to Edwin and Clemmie until he was sure of the lovely lady?'

'Ah!' Sonny exclaimed. 'And then fait accompli! Lucky fellow. I'm green with envy – although . . .'

'What? Who?'

'Can't tell,' Sonny said. 'But I've met a fair and lovely woman to die for. But you?' He gave a puzzled frown. 'You said *yet*! What does that mean?'

'Nothing.' Howard grinned, and wouldn't be drawn further.

They sat in silent companionship, and Howard offered Sonny a slice of bread and beef, which he took.

'You know, life's a funny thing,' Sonny said,

with his mouth half full. 'We both fell in love with the unattainable Mrs Radcliffe, who treated us gauche youths with such graciousness and gave us an understanding of the type of woman we'd be happy with.' He sighed deeply. 'It was only a few years later that I met the woman who would teach me all the things I needed to know about my manhood. She was very poor but very beautiful and she always reminded me of Anna Radcliffe. Our relationship ended but we remained friends, and when she died – I was devastated.'

'She died? This was Ida? I recall you telling me about her. I'm so sorry,' Howard said.

Sonny nodded. 'I promised her on her death-bed that I would look after her daughter, who promises to be just as lovely as her mother was.' He paused and then shook his head, adding, 'But Polly is a different personality entirely from Ida. So vivacious, so resolute—'

'Polly!' Howard turned in astonishment to his friend. 'You mean—'

Sonny raised his eyebrows. 'Yes. The one and only Polly Parker. Ida is, or was, her mother.'

Howard swallowed. 'I'd no idea,' he said quietly. 'But then why would I know? So, you promised – that you'd always take care of her?'

'Yes. I did. And I will.' Sonny gazed out at the landscape. 'Always.'

CHAPTER TWENTY-FIVE

Howard watched silently as Sonny was greeted rapturously by Polly, who then berated him for not confessing that he knew Rosalie's uncle as soon as he heard they were coming to Nab Farm. He saw how Rosalie received him graciously and how Sonny treated her differently from Polly. He was all charm as he inclined his head at her dipped knee, whereas he had joked and laughed with Polly.

Mrs Radcliffe remembered him and said that they were gathering together all their old friends for the wedding and that he must come too.

He accepted, but said that he must first go back home and would return on the appointed date. 'Is there anything I can bring you from Hull, Miss Kingston?' he asked Rosalie. 'Any messages I can deliver for you?'

Rosalie smiled. 'How formal you still are, Mr Blake. Please call me Rosalie. I don't think there is anything we need, but perhaps if you are passing Albion Street you might look up at the house and see if all is well there.' She paused for a moment. 'Perhaps I should go back and check for myself.'

'Perhaps you'd permit me to escort you?' Sonny said. 'I shall be travelling back by train in a few days' time.'

'That would be very kind of you,' she said. 'I must admit that I left in rather a hurry . . . against advice,' she added teasingly, remembering how cross he had been. 'And it would be wise if I went back just to be sure.'

Clementina was pleased to see Sonny again, Howard noted, and she primped her hair as he came towards her.

'How very nice to see you again, Clemmie,' he said. 'You grow lovelier each time I set eyes on you.'

Clementina blushed and Howard thought that Sonny was playing a dangerous game. She responds to kindness and compliments and yet is so naïve that she'll think he's making advances.

'I must write to your father and tell him about our wedding,' Luke said to Rosalie. 'He'll surely want to come.'

'He must be abroad, Uncle Luke, for I've heard nothing from him and we've been here almost a month.'

The very next morning a letter arrived for Rosalie and she opened it with relief. 'Father says he has been in Ireland,' she told Polly, 'and that he has only just arrived back. He's coming to see me,' she said excitedly, 'and has some news.' She scanned the rest of the letter. 'Oh, and then he's away on another tour of duty and so must speak to me about my future.' She gazed at Polly. 'I hope he doesn't want me to leave here and live in Aldershot. He suggested it previously and I do *not* want to go,' she said firmly.

'But you're not old enough to decide for yourself,' Polly pointed out. 'What can we do if he suggests it?'

Rosalie shook her head. 'I don't know,' she said miserably. 'I just don't know.'

Polly looked out of the window. Sonny was strolling in the garden. 'I'll ask Sonny's advice,' she said. 'And you tell your uncle what your father says. Maybe he can persuade him that you should stay here.'

Luke was out somewhere, and as Rosalie stood pondering in the drawing room Howard put his head round the door. 'Have you seen Luke about?'

'No,' she said. 'I need to speak to him too.'

'Oh? What's up?' He came into the room. 'You look sad.'

'Oh . . .' She hesitated. 'Things. I'm not sad,

287

but worried. I've heard from my father and I'm anxious that he might want me to leave here and go and live in Aldershot to be nearer him.'

She gazed out of the window and saw Polly walking alongside Sonny in animated conversation. Howard saw them too and pressed his lips together.

Rosalie gave a deep sigh. 'And I don't want to. And neither do I want to lose Polly.'

Howard saw Sonny put his hand on Polly's arm. 'And do you think that you might?' he murmured.

'Yes,' she nodded, also noticing the gesture. 'Almost sure to,' she said softly. 'And she's such a splendid friend, the best possible.'

When Rosalie told Luke about the letter from her father, he said he had had one too. 'He says he'll be here at the end of April,' Luke said, 'so hopefully he'll arrive in time for the wedding.'

Rosalie was surprised. Her father hadn't mentioned to her when he would come, only that he would.

'My father thinks I'm still a child,' she said pettishly to Polly later, as they changed for supper. 'And I'm not.'

'When I asked Sonny what he thought you should do, he seemed bewildered,' Polly said. 'Which isn't like him at all. He's usually so positive. Anyway, he said that you must explain very firmly your reasons for staying in order to convince your father. In any case, if he's going to be away such a lot, you're going to be stuck wi' somebody you don't know and might not even like,' she added. 'Though I dare say there'll be lots of sodgers after marrying you, Rosalie. That's what I said to Sonny, and he got quite heated and said you must definitely onny do what you want to do and not agree to marry anybody just because they're wearing a fancy uniform.'

Sonny sought out Rosalie before he returned to Hull and she told him she had decided not to go back with him at present. 'It's nothing to do with me, Rosalie,' he said quietly, 'but if your father wants you to leave here, think very carefully about it. You are old enough to have views on what you want to do with your life, even if society decrees otherwise, and you should explain them to him.'

He had said his farewells, and his manner had puzzled her. It's very kind of him to show such concern, she thought, especially when he has no reason to trouble over my dilemma. He'll be worried about Polly's future, of course, so perhaps that is why he is anxious.

Fittings were arranged for the making of the attendants' gowns, and Clementina drove Rosalie and Polly in the trap to Lower Farm, Mrs Radcliffe's home in Harwood Dale, where the dressmaker was waiting for them with Anna's daughter Elizabeth. She was a sweet shy girl, still being taught by a governess, and both Rosalie and Polly took to her at once.

'Isn't she lovely, Clementina?' Rosalie said as they drove back. 'How lucky you are to be having her as your sister.'

Clementina turned her head sharply to look over her shoulder at Rosalie. 'What do you mean?'

'Well, she'll be your sister, won't she?' Rosalie said. 'And once your parents are married she'll be coming to live with you.'

'I suppose so,' Clementina said sullenly. 'But we've got a houseful already. And then there's her brother!'

'Oh, but he's away at school,' Rosalie reminded her. 'He'll only be home for the holidays.'

Her cousin made no answer, but raised her whip to urge the pony to go faster until Rosalie and Polly had to hold on to their bonnets.

Polly shrugged and made a *moue* when Rosalie looked quizzically at her. There was no point in her getting involved in the discussion. For the most part, Clementina ignored her altogether. It was almost as if she were invisible. But she didn't care. She was having a most wonderful time and knew that it was here that she wanted to stay. The only cloud on the

290

horizon was the possibility that Mrs Radcliffe would want her to leave once she was married to Luke. She was always kind to her, but Polly was aware that as she wasn't a relation she had no rightful place here.

The marriage ceremony was to be witnessed by the immediate family; all the attendants would be wearing crinolines in sprigged muslin in shades of spring flowers. Anna's son Jonathan was to give her away and Edwin would be his father's best man. The reception was to be held at Nab Farm and a hundred guests were expected, including Luke's mother-in-law from Scarborough, his first wife's mother.

The April day dawned cloudy with a mist hovering over the moor but by ten o'clock it was bright and sunny. Extra serving maids and kitchen staff had been brought in from nearby villages and it was expected that there would be a great gathering outside the church, for both Luke and his bride were very popular.

'I'm so excited,' Polly said. 'I don't know what to do. Do you know what to do, Rosalie? Do we have to say anything?'

Rosalie laughed. She was excited too but wished that her father had come in time. 'We don't have to do anything,' she told Polly. 'We just have to stand behind the bride and look pretty. And we shall have our photographs taken later, I expect.'

'Oh, goodness,' Polly said. 'I hope I can sit still for long enough.'

Luke, Edwin, Howard and Sonny set off on horseback to the church in Harwood Dale with all the dogs following behind. The three young ladies were driven by Amos, in a new green caped coat and top hat, to Mrs Radcliffe's house in order to accompany her, Elizabeth and Jonathan to church. Anna looked serene and lovely in grey silk over a large hoop which swayed as she moved, with white lace gloves and a grey and white hat edged with lace. She was a picture of elegance and Rosalie and Polly gazed at her in admiration.

'I'd love to look like you one day, Mrs Radcliffe,' Rosalie murmured. 'You are so beautiful.' Polly nodded in agreement but Clementina looked away.

'But you are all beautiful now.' Anna smiled. 'It's just that you are too young to realize it.'

Anna took Clementina to one side; she had noticed how downcast the girl was. She sat her down beside her. 'Clementina,' she said softly, 'I don't want you to think that I'm stealing your father from you or that I'm trying to take the place of your mother, for I know I could never do that, nor would I want to. It's different for Elizabeth, I know, for she doesn't remember her father, but she is also apprehensive about our marriage. She wonders what it will be like

292

to have a man in the house, when all of her life she has only had her mother and brother.'

Clementina began to cry. 'Nobody wants me,' she wept. 'I've tried to replace Mama, but Papa doesn't even notice me. And he notices me even less since Rosalie and Polly have come to live with us. It's not fair!'

'Oh, my dear,' Anna said gently, 'that's men all over: they never notice. But they don't mean anything by it, and sometimes' – she smiled – 'we can use it to our advantage. Come now, wipe your eyes. We don't want you to be red-eyed on such a splendid day, especially when you look so lovely.'

Clemmie perked up at this and managed a smile and looked into the mirror. She saw her shiny dark hair and rosy cheeks and became aware that she was a complete contrast to all the other, fair-haired bridesmaids.

The church door creaked slightly as it was opened during the ceremony and again as it was closed. Polly couldn't resist a peep over her shoulder and saw a tall man in military uniform take a seat at the back. Rosalie was sitting next to her in the pew and so she gave her a nudge and indicated by a shift of her head that she should take a look behind her.

Rosalie beamed and mouthed *Papa*.

Polly smiled back at her. She'd thought so. She was pleased for her friend, but now she was anxious. Her own life was tied up with Rosalie's and she wondered what was in front of her.

When they came out of church, Rosalie's father was waiting to greet her. 'My dear,' he said, and kissed her cheek. 'How lovely you look. So grown up – and so like your mother.'

'It's good to see you, Papa,' she said, unable to help being tearful. 'I hoped you'd come in time for the wedding.'

Mark Kingston looked over to where his brother was chatting to his guests, his new bride on his arm and the dogs milling round their feet. 'It was a close thing,' he said. 'I went up to Nab Farm but everyone had left, even the dogs. That's just like Luke, to take the dogs to his wedding. He seems very happy. And his bride is lovely.'

'She is,' Rosalie agreed. 'And so kind and agreeable too. It will be a pleasure to live with her and Uncle Luke.'

'Ah!' he said. 'We must discuss that, Rosalie, only not today.'

'No,' Rosalie said meekly, 'not today. Papa, I'd like you to meet my very best friend.' She signalled to Polly, who was standing alone, to come over. 'Polly,' she said, 'this is my father. Papa, this is my friend Polly Parker.'

Polly dipped her knee to the officer. 'Pleased to meet you, sir,' she said and thought how majestic he was in his red frock coat trimmed with gold braid. He's quite different from his brother. Luke Kingston looked very smart today in his grey morning suit, but he was usually very casual in his dress and preferred to wear an old flannel shirt and cord breeches which had seen better days.

'I'm very pleased to meet you too, Miss Parker,' Mark Kingston said, gazing at her. 'So delighted that Rosalie has found a friend so quickly. Do you live here on the moor?'

Before Polly could answer, Rosalie said, 'Oh, no, Father. Polly and I have known each other for some time. We met in Hull – oh,' she waved her hand distractedly, 'ages ago.'

'I see,' he said thoughtfully. 'Good. Good.' He smiled. 'Would you excuse me for a moment whilst I offer my brother congratulations? We can catch up with all our news later in the day, Rosalie. After the reception, perhaps? I'm staying for a few days so we've plenty of time.'

Rosalie nodded and Polly dipped her knee. 'Phew!' she said. 'Your father's rumbled me, Rosalie.' She watched him as he walked straight-backed towards his brother. 'In spite of my fine clothes, he knew as soon as I opened my mouth that I wasn't what I seemed.'

'Nonsense!' Rosalie said, but she was nervous. She knew that Polly was right. I have to stand up for myself, she thought. Polly is my friend no matter what her background.

Howard and Sonny came over to speak to them. They both bowed deeply. 'Ladies,' they chorused. 'Would you do us the honour of speaking to us?' Sonny added, and Howard interjected, 'We would be so grateful.'

'Idiots!' Polly grinned. Then she spun round, her skirts rustling and showing her layers of lace petticoats and ankle-length drawers. 'Don't you think we look splendid?'

She preened as Sonny flamboyantly took her hand and lifted it to his lips. 'A picture of elegance and grace,' he agreed.

'You look pretty good yourselves,' she said. 'We almost didn't recognize you in your fine clothes. And you haven't got paint on your hands today!'

'No,' he said. 'No more chairs to paint!'

Howard gave a great guffaw. 'Chairs!' he laughed. 'Don't tell me you've been wasting your time painting chairs!'

Sonny turned to him and gave him a warning glance. 'I'll paint anything that stands still long enough,' he said. Then he looked over Rosalie's shoulder. 'I would guess that is your father, Rosalie?'

When she said yes, it was, he looked thoughtful. 'Has he come to claim you?' he murmured.

Rosalie swallowed. 'I don't know,' she said in a small voice. 'I hope not.'

CHAPTER TWENTY-SIX

They returned to Nab Farm in procession, Luke and Anna in her carriage, the bride's attendants and Clementina's grandmother in the Kingstons' carriage, and the four men on horseback, with young Jonathan riding Luke's horse.

'We must learn to ride, Polly.' Rosalie gazed out at the men as they passed them by. 'How splendid they all look.'

The men, apart from Rosalie's father, were wearing morning coats in shades of grey: silver, slate and pearl. All were laughing and joking and lifted their top hats in salute to them.

'Couldn't you just fall in love with them all?' Polly said. 'Would we look so good on horseback? I don't think we would; not if we kept falling off like we did before.'

'Mm,' Clementina said. 'I'd offer to teach you but I haven't the patience. Ask Howard. He's not got a bad seat.'

'I'd say he'd a nice one,' Polly giggled and Rosalie clapped her hand over her mouth and glanced at Clemmie's grandmother, who seemed to be wool-gathering and didn't hear. Perhaps she's thinking of her daughter, the first Mrs Kingston, Rosalie thought. How sad for her today.

Back at the farm the other guests had gathered outside the house waiting for the bridal pair's return. A great cheer rang out as the first carriage rolled up and then another as the second appeared. The riders were not far behind and everyone milled about chatting and laughing before going inside.

The hall had been cleared of the old rugs by the fire, the floor had been polished and a great wooden table had been set in the centre. The drawing room and dining room doors were open and tables set for the wedding breakfast had been put in both rooms. There were flowers and silver candlesticks with glowing candles on every table and fires in each room.

'Mrs Moody has excelled herself,' Rosalie murmured to Polly. 'She must have been driving the servants hard to achieve all this.'

Howard appeared at Rosalie's side. 'Sonny and I would like to sit with you and Polly, if we may,' he said. 'Apparently the reception is quite informal and we can sit wherever we please. Some of the guests are even out in the garden. Tables have been put in the orchard.'

Rosalie hesitated. She should really join her father, she supposed. But he was talking earnestly to an elderly gentleman and she quickly took her seat in the dining room with the others.

'Are there to be speeches?' she asked.

Howard told her that there would be later. 'Luke doesn't want a fuss,' he said. 'Though Edwin ought to say something, if he will,' he added grimly.

Polly looked about her. Edwin had barely spoken to anyone since they'd arrived back at the house. There he was, with a glass of wine in his hand, the first to be served it seemed for the maids were only just circulating with trays of wine glasses. He's been down in 'cellar and helped himself to a bottle, I bet, she thought. He seemed to be weighing everybody up. Perhaps he's thinking of what to say in his speech, though he seems more interested in watching the maids than anything else. Just hope he keeps away from me, she thought. He had hardly spoken to her since the incident in the stables.

For the wedding breakfast they were served with chicken in aspic, cold meat, and poacher's soup, which contained venison, game, celery and wine; baked carp with orange sauce, lemon sorbet, and a main course of braised venison with claret, loin of pork with sage and onion stuffing, and spit-roasted wild duck. There were crisp roast potatoes and parsnips, carrots sautéed in butter and braised cabbage; for the dessert a selection of rich syllabubs and flummery, fruit fools and chocolate puddings, jellies, and by special request from the groom a jam roly-poly served with hot custard.

Phew! I'm stuffed, Polly thought as she shook her head at the offer of dessert. Never in my life have I eaten so much. She felt slightly guilty as she thought of how her mother had scrimped and saved to afford even the most basic of meals. It's only a few months since I was wondering how I'd survive, and now I'm refusing food.

Luke stood up to welcome everyone and to thank them for coming to join in the celebration of the marriage.

'I have known Anna for very many years,' he said. 'Her husband and I were good friends and I was devastated when he was taken from us at such an early age. My wife Jane, whom many of you knew, also died whilst still young.'

He looked at Clementina who sat very still, but with a tear trickling down her cheek; at Edwin, who stared stonily back at him. And then at Jonathan and Elizabeth who were watching and listening intently.

'It has not been easy for our children to lose their parents, and in this I include my nephew Howard who has been like another son to me. And it has been difficult for Anna and me to bring up our families without the help of a loving partner by our side. But' – he smiled down at Anna – 'it did not occur to either of us to consider marriage to anyone else. And then' – he smiled broadly – 'after all the dark years, I saw the light. I saw Anna as a loving, faithful wife and mother and I knew that I could love her, and thankfully, for better or worse, she found she could love me.'

He swallowed hard and said in a voice which occasionally cracked with emotion, 'I want to explain to our children that it doesn't mean that we love their mother or father any less. We have those fond memories to keep for ever, and now we have the chance to make some more together.'

He raised his glass and everyone stood up, many of them wiping away tears. 'I give you a toast,' he said. 'To love.'

Rosalie couldn't stop the tears from flowing. Luke had waited a long time for his second chance of happiness. Would her father take the same path and marry again? I wouldn't blame him if he did, she thought. If at some future time he should find someone to love, I wouldn't object. But he has his career to sustain him, and I don't really think that he is a family man.

Howard sat quietly next to Polly and she glanced at him, seeing that he had been affected by his inclusion in Luke's speech. She slipped her hand into his and he turned to her and with a wistful smile he gently squeezed it.

'What a tear-jerker, eh?' he whispered.

'Yes,' she said huskily. 'And haven't we been lucky? You to have had your uncle and me to find Rosalie.'

He nodded. 'What a courageous girl you are, Polly. You find good fortune in everything.'

She looked at him and smiled. 'No point in looking on 'black side. When you've been at 'bottom of 'heap like I have, there's onny one way to go and that's up.'

'You're a tonic, Polly,' he said. 'I wish—' He stopped and smiled back at her.

'What?'

He shook his head. 'Nothing.' His eyes swept over her. 'How old are you, Polly?'

'Seventeen. I had my birthday in January same as Rosalie, 'cept that she's a few days older. Why?'

'Just wondered,' he said, and then stopped as Luke stood up once more to ask if Cook and Mrs Moody would come in. When they did, he thanked them both for the tremendous effort they had made to put on such a sumptuous meal and reception. Then several other people stood up to say a piece and no one seemed to notice that Edwin had left the room. As Polly looked round, she saw that so had Dora.

Edwin had held on to Dora's elbow as she'd leaned over to clear away the dessert dishes to make room for champagne glasses.

'Meet me in the usual place in half an hour, Dora,' he muttered.

She gasped. 'I can't, Mr Edwin,' she said. 'I'll get found out.'

'Half an hour,' he said firmly. 'Nobody'll miss you. There's too much going on. Mrs Moody will think you're clearing dishes. Do you hear?'

She bit her lip. 'I'll lose my job.'

He patted her thigh and then bent as if to pick something up from under the table and grasped her ankle. 'No you won't. I'll make sure of it. Thick stockings, Dora,' he murmured. 'Have to do something about those.'

Dora's eyes filled with tears. She didn't know who she was more afraid of, Mrs Moody or Mr Edwin. But she would have to do as he said. He'd be angry if she didn't. Once before she had refused and he'd threatened that he would tell Sam and Mrs Moody. Today Sam would be with Amos, busy looking after all the horses. They would also be very merry because Mr

Kingston had arranged for a barrel of ale to be given to all the workers and a table had been set up in the stable yard with enormous platters of meat and steak and apple pies.

Edwin had taken her to the potting shed, which was set beyond the orchard and behind the stable. This, he said, was to be their special place, for the old gardener only came to it in the early morning to collect his tools. She'd shaken with fright and shame, but that only seemed to excite him all the more and she hardly dared refuse his demands on her.

She slipped out of the side door of the kitchen as Cook and Mrs Moody and some of the hired menservants were sitting at the table eating and drinking. Mrs Moody was quite merry and unlike her usual dour self since the public compliments from Mr Kingston, and failed to notice Dora's departure.

'What can I do?' Dora whimpered. What if Sam finds out or even catches us? He'll not believe that Mr Edwin's forcing me, she thought. I'm afraid of losing my job, but if I don't go with Mr Edwin he'll make it so difficult for me that Mrs Moody will sack me anyway.

She was breathing heavily when she reached the shed. She opened the door and for a moment she thought it was empty and that Edwin hadn't come. She was about to back out when he suddenly jumped out from behind the door and grabbed her. She almost screamed, she was so surprised, but Edwin pulled her inside.

'Ha! Got you! You were going to run away, weren't you?' He started to unfasten her apron strings. 'Why on earth have you come out in your apron? Anybody can see you in this starched white. Besides,' he yanked it off roughly, 'you should have come prepared. I hope you've taken off those awful stockings.'

She began to cry. 'Please, Mr Edwin. I don't want you to do those things to me. I'm afraid. I don't like it.'

'Yes, you do.' He put his face close to hers and she could smell the alcohol on his breath. 'You love it! This is what you'll do if you ever marry Sam!' He gave a coarse laugh. 'That is *if* he'll marry you when he finds out I've been here first.'

He lifted her skirts and ripped down her stocking tops and on discovering that she wasn't wearing any under drawers he closed his eyes and gasped. 'Oh, Dora! What a lovely girl you are,' he muttered. 'You're just what every man wants.'

'I'm not, sir. Please, Mr Edwin, I'm not. I don't want—'

'Turn round,' he ordered brusquely. 'And shut up!'

He pushed her roughly against the bench,

forcing her down amongst the clay pots and trowels so that her cheek was resting against the scratchy splintered wood.

'This is what I'm going to do, Dora,' he whispered in her ear, 'and then,' he whispered again, '*this* is what you're going to do!'

She moaned. 'Please! Please don't.' She sobbed, but he laughed when she did, and then he seemed to get angry for he grabbed her thighs so hard she was sure they would be bruised.

'A toast,' he muttered scathingly as he pushed into her. 'To love! What rot! This is what it's all about, isn't it, Dora? Don't you love it? Isn't this what life's about? And you're going to get such a rollicking, such a trouncing, that you'll never forget it!'

She wanted to scream with the pain, but he put his hand over her mouth; she thought she would choke, and gasped and retched, her saliva wetting his hand as her body took his battering; there was nothing she could say and nothing she could do to stop him. It was no use appealing to his better nature for he didn't have one. He was beyond restraint, determined to master her, to control her with his body, his power. I'll leave, she thought as she fought to keep back her tears. But where will I go?

When he had finished with her he gazed at her, his mouth twitching, and picking up her apron he threw it at her. 'Bitch!' he said. 'Slut! If you so much as breathe a word of this I shall deny it and you'll be out on your ear.'

Then he grabbed her by the shoulders and pulled her towards him. 'And I'll see you again soon, Dora.' He jerked his body towards her and she was afraid he would start again, but he was spent, no energy left. He patted her cheek and smiled. 'Don't forget,' he murmured. 'Our little secret.'

He went out first, leaving her to put her apron and cap on and calm her throbbing body. She opened the door and looked out. There was no one about, although she could hear the sound of laughter and merrymaking.

Everybody's happy but me, she thought. This is a day that everybody's enjoying, even the servants. She felt a sob rising in her chest and felt sick at what he had forced her to do, but she took a deep breath and stepped out and walked towards the house.

CHAPTER TWENTY-SEVEN

Anna moved into Nab Farm after the wedding and left her own farm in the capable hands of her foreman. Elizabeth came with her and her governess too, and Jonathan went back to school.

Clementina seemed more settled but told Rosalie that she would go to Scarborough in the summer. 'You may come if you wish,' she said generously, to which Rosalie replied that she would love to, providing that Polly could come too. Clementina shrugged and said no more about it.

Sonny had stayed on for a few more days after the wedding and then left, saying he would be back in the autumn.

'Won't you come for the grouse?' Luke had asked him. 'I can lend you a gun.'

Sonny had smiled. 'I'll come, if I may, sir, but not for the shooting. There are other things I'd rather do.'

'As you wish,' Luke said amiably. 'You're very welcome anyway.'

He welcomed everybody. Anyone could stay and so the house was often full to overflowing with friends and visitors, but none expected to be entertained for Luke went about his daily business and so did Howard, although Edwin was often in the house rather than on the moor or the farm.

Rosalie's father took his leave of her two days after the wedding, telling her that he must return to his regiment. 'I promise that I'll come back before I go abroad,' he'd said. 'But now I must return.'

'But it's a long way, Papa, for such a short visit, and you said you had some news to discuss with me.'

'So I did,' he said. 'But it will keep until next time.' He looked at her. 'I can see you have settled here, Rosalie, but do not get too comfortable. Next time I come I want to discuss your future. It will be more convenient, I feel, if you come to live in Aldershot, where I will see more of you.' He bent and pecked her cheek. 'There are people there whom I feel you could become fond of; but it is too soon.' He turned and gazed out of the window and Rosalie felt that he was avoiding her eye. 'I'll discuss it another time.'

'There are people *here* that I am fond of,

Papa,' she'd replied firmly. 'I like it here. I'm not saying that I don't want to visit other places, I do, but for the moment I'm happy here.'

He turned back and gazed at her. 'Your friend Miss Parker. Where did you say you'd met her? Not socially, I think?'

'I – we met in Hull. She's a good friend. We have much in common. She lost her mother at the same time as I, and was left alone as I was.'

'Ah, yes,' he murmured. 'I should have come, but everything had been done by the time I received the news.'

Rosalie said nothing in response. Yes, he should have come to give her support and a shoulder to cry on if nothing else, she thought.

'Have you been to see Mama's grave?'

'N-no. Not yet,' he answered. 'But I will as I pass through Hull, and I'll also call at the house to make sure all is well there. And as I was saying, Miss Parker? She's from the servant class, I think, Rosalie. What was she? A domestic? Kitchen maid?'

'What she was doesn't matter,' Rosalie said. She felt like crying. How hard he was. How unfeeling. He had not given her the comfort she needed when her mother died and now he was questioning her friendship with the one person who had helped her through that difficult time. 'What matters is that she's my friend now.'

'You have changed, Rosalie,' her father said bleakly. 'You have become – bold. You're not the sweet demure child you once were. But it is my fault perhaps,' he admitted. 'I should have come earlier and taken you back with me.'

Rosalie faced him. 'I'm no longer a child, Father. I've had much to contend with, and that is why I have changed.'

'True,' he acknowledged. 'And I must make reparation. You are still young and in need of the guidance of someone who is able to advise you, as your mother did. Someone who can introduce you into society.'

She was astonished at his words, but he had left then and she couldn't help but think that there was more to be said, and her father had deliberately avoided saying whatever it was that he had originally intended.

It was a warm sunny day, the primroses were in flower on the banks of the streams, the trees were in full leaf, the air was ringing with birdsong and there was a constant sound of rushing water from the becks and the bleat of new lambs as they hopped, skipped and jumped round their mothers.

Howard put his head round the dining room door. 'When you've finished breakfast will you come out to the stables? I've got something to show you.'

Anna and Elizabeth had breakfasted early. Anna had brought her grey Connemara horse with her to the farm. She had great riding ability and managed not only to handle her mount well, but to look elegant and confident too. Her daughter Elizabeth rode a sturdy Welsh cob and she too was a competent horsewoman. Both had gone off this morning to exercise their horses on the moor so there were just Rosalie, Polly and Clementina at the table. Clementina looked up from her plate and looked at him questioningly, but he indicated with his thumbs that he meant Rosalie and Polly.

Clemmie nodded conspiratorially and said, 'I'll come too, shall I?'

Rosalie and Polly glanced at each other. 'What?' they both said. 'Has Floss had her pups?' Polly squealed.

'She has,' Howard said. 'But it's not just that. Something else too.'

Polly hastily pushed her chair back. 'She's never had kittens as well!'

Howard grinned. 'No, just six pups, all healthy. You can have your pick, but come on; I want to show you something.'

They hurried outside, not stopping to pick up shawls which were in any case unnecessary on such a beautiful day.

The pups were adorable and Polly longed to pick one up, but Howard advised her not to. 'The mother will reject them if they are handled so soon,' he said. 'Wait a few days more and then she won't mind.'

Polly sighed. 'Oh, I want the little black and white,' she said. 'See, the one with white tips to her ears and on her paws. I'll call her Tippy.'

Rosalie laughed. 'I don't know. I've never had a dog. Which shall I have? That one, with the brown marking. Is it a male or a female?'

Howard confessed he didn't know yet. 'We'll have to wait a bit. Now come on,' he said again. 'There's a present waiting for you both.'

'A present? What do you mean?' Polly was flabbergasted. She'd never had a present, or at least only from her mother at Christmas and then perhaps only a ribbon.

Howard led them round the corner of the coach house block to the loose boxes where Sam was grooming one of the horses, a dark brown with a shiny coat and a long thick tail. Inside one of the stalls was another horse with an even darker coat.

'Are they new?' Rosalie asked. 'I don't recall seeing them before.'

'Bought last week at Egton Bridge,' Howard said. 'They arrived first thing this morning. What do you think? Clementina chose them.'

'Oh, how handsome.' Polly ran her hand

over the horse's neck. 'What kind of horse is this?'

'He's a Fell pony,' Clementina said. 'And this one,' she opened the stable door and led the other horse out, 'is a Dales pony. They're very similar, probably a related breed.'

Rosalie came forward and tentatively stroked it. 'Such a lovely coat.'

'Don't be nervous,' Clementina said. 'He's very good-natured. This is Damon. He's a bit bigger than Hero but very docile and a steady ride. You'll be perfectly safe on him, Rosalie.'

'For me?' Rosalie was astonished.

Her cousin nodded. 'And Hero is for Polly.' She gave Polly a swift glance. 'Papa said you must both learn to ride and I agreed to teach you.'

'*Oh!*' Polly breathed. 'Thank you, Clementina. *Thank you!* I'll take great care of him.'

Clementina shrugged. 'He's not mine; I suppose he's a house pony if anyone else should want to borrow him. I've got my own mount,' she added superciliously.

Polly couldn't believe her good fortune. She had been given a puppy and a pony. Her cup of happiness overflowed. If you could onny see me, Ma, she thought, and a lump came into her throat. Did you have to die to allow me all this? She put her hand to her face and still the tears flowed down her cheeks.

Clementina saw them and her face softened. 'I felt the same when I was given my first pony,' she said. 'But I was only seven.'

Rosalie saw and understood. For her it was different. It was an adventure and not one she would have enjoyed if she had stayed in Hull.

'Can we try now, Clementina?' she asked. 'No time like the present.'

'Mm. Not sure if I can teach you both at the same time,' she said.

'I've got half an hour,' Howard said. 'What if you lead Rosalie, Clemmie, and I'll take Polly?'

'Yes, all right; although they're not dressed for riding. You'll need a proper riding habit, Rosalie. I'll show you a catalogue later and you can choose something suitable. And we only have one pommel saddle, so—' She glanced at Polly. 'You'll have to manage on an ordinary one and use longer stirrups.'

The horses were led to a mounting block and they were helped to mount. They were led round and round the yard to get the feel and motion of the ponies and both took deep exhilarated breaths.

'Well done, ladies,' Luke called to them, coming into the yard. 'You're doing well.'

'Take me to him,' Polly said to Howard.

'Take him yourself,' Howard said, and

unfastened the leading rein. 'Walk him over, nice and steady.'

Polly did so and pulled on the reins as she drew up next to Luke. Hero stopped and nuzzled into Luke's outstretched hand.

'I don't know how to thank you, Mr Kingston,' she said unsteadily. 'I'm so grateful.'

He smiled up at her. 'Not at all,' he said. 'If you're going to be a country girl you must learn to ride. It was Anna who suggested that you both should have a horse, and' – he leaned across to whisper – 'she thought it would give Clemmie an interest teaching you both to ride.'

I don't think she wants to teach me, Polly thought, but she nodded and expressed her thanks again. Then she dug in one heel and clicked her tongue, and to her delight and amazement Hero wheeled round and moved towards Howard.

'Well done!' he laughed. 'You'll be riding on the moor before the week's out.'

Howard was right. Very soon they were out on the moor, Polly riding with abandon, exhibiting no finesse but possessing a surety which came naturally. Even Clemmie admitted that she was a natural and unafraid. Rosalie on the other hand carefully developed a sure seat, a straight back and an elegant posture.

They chose their puppies, which soon began

to know them and greeted them with high-pitched yapping whenever they approached. Anna said that once they were house trained they would be allowed in the house, but not in the bedrooms, she emphasized, much to Polly's disappointment.

They began to explore the moors, each day riding out a little further. They rode north to the top of Fylingdale Moor, on one occasion making a detour to visit the standing stone, Old Wife's Neck, which Polly said she just had to see, even though Clementina said it was only a bit of old stone.

The early summer was warm and dry and occasionally they took food with them and stayed out all day, on one occasion going as far as Burndale before riding towards the village of Grosmont; then they turned about to ride back to Nab Farm with Howard's warning that they must be home in time for supper ringing in their ears. He had written out details of places of interest for them, but told them how quickly the weather could change on the moor, the mist coming down so swiftly they could lose their bearings.

'The moor might seem tranquil,' he said, 'but it can also be threatening and dangerous. Never take it for granted.'

Sometimes Clemmie would go with them, but once she had taught them the essentials of horsemanship and shown them the best views and the best rides she soon became bored, and as she had no conversation to speak of they became bored with her too.

Then one day Clementina announced that she was going to Scarborough to stay with her grandmother. When her father asked why now, she said airily, 'There's more to do there in the summer. Lots of visitors come to the Spa.'

She pronounced it *Spaw*. Polly wondered what she meant and later had to ask Rosalie.

'It's a place for taking the waters,' Rosalie said. 'Special mineral water which is supposed to be health-giving. I've never tried it. I wonder—'

'What?' Polly asked.

'Well, should we go too, to Scarborough, and then return to Hull for a few days? I need to see if all is well with the house. Papa said he would go, but he hasn't written to say if he did; and besides, we could do with some summer clothes. We only brought winter things.'

Polly gave a wry smile. Until she had been lucky enough to meet Rosalie, she had only ever had one set of clothing and it had to do for summer and winter. Two skirts and two bodices, one shift and a shawl. She and her mother took turn and turn about whenever any item of clothing wanted washing, and that was done in the summer, not the winter, for how would they ever get them dry?

'It would be lovely to go and see 'castle at Scarborough,' she agreed. 'In daylight this time, and mebbe we could look at 'sea! But,' she added anxiously, 'will we come back here after you've been home?'

'Of course!' Rosalie gazed at Polly. 'That's what you want, isn't it?'

'Oh, yes. Please! I do.'

'But you'd like to see Hull again? I don't want to return alone.'

'No, I'd like to go back,' Polly said. 'Mebbe I could go and see Mrs Walters. Or Sonny. We could visit him. Wouldn't he be surprised!'

'Ye-es,' Rosalie was hesitant. 'I'm not sure if that would be the proper thing to do, Polly. You know. He's a single man, after all.'

Polly laughed. 'Yes, I do know; but what difference does that make? He's a friend, isn't he?'

CHAPTER TWENTY-EIGHT

Polly said the same thing to Howard when they told him they were considering going back to Hull, and hoped to see Sonny.

'I'm sure Sonny will be pleased to see you again,' he said. 'He'll be the envy of his friends having two beautiful ladies visiting him.'

His tone was jocular, but Rosalie thought there was a hint of concern, and then she was sure of it when he added, 'But you will come back? You won't desert us?'

He suggested that he should drive them to Scarborough with Clemmie and put them on the Hull train and that they could stay with his grandmother for a few days on their return. 'She'd welcome your visit,' he said. 'She loves to have young people round her.'

They had met her at the wedding and found her charming. Rosalie said that would be most agreeable if Clemmie didn't object.

'Grandmother is my grandmother as well as

Clemmie's and Edwin's,' Howard said rather testily, which was quite unlike him. 'She's always pleased to see my friends.'

And so she was, when the following week they travelled to Scarborough in the carriage. Clementina took a large trunk with her, indicating that she was probably going to stay all the summer.

'Members of the aristocracy visit Scarborough,' she said loftily. 'And some ladies come to catch a husband. I go to hear the concerts at the Spa,' she said. 'Grandmama goes with me and we meet up with her friends and their grandchildren. Of course,' she added, 'their mothers are there too, but we generally manage to escape and go shopping on our own, or else we take our swimming costumes and bathe in the sea – in a bathing machine, of course. And then there are the Pierrot shows which are such fun.' She gave a little smirk which Polly was sure was for her benefit. 'We have a lovely time; you just don't know what you're missing, Rosalie.'

Mrs Carleton was delighted to see them and disappointed that they were not staying that evening. 'You must have some lunch,' she insisted, and assured them that they would not miss their train.

Her house was situated high up on Nicholas Cliff looking over the sea.

Polly gazed out of the window and was over-whelmed. 'How wonderful,' she said. 'I'd no idea it would be like this. Look, Rosalie, there's a lighthouse – and look, look over there on top of that hill. There's 'castle!'

'It's a Norman castle.' Mrs Carleton came up behind them. 'Over the centuries there have been many attempts to destroy it.' She smiled fondly. 'But still it stands guard over this lovely old town. You must visit the Spa when you return and perhaps take the waters. Clementina likes to hear the concerts and I suppose it is a very romantic place to be when you're young and the sea is sighing or frolicking and the moon shines upon it.'

Polly turned an enraptured face towards her. 'Oh,' she breathed. 'I would love to see that, wouldn't you, Rosalie?'

Rosalie agreed that she would, but she was becoming anxious that they might miss their train and so lunch was brought forward and Howard hurried them off as soon as it was polite to do so.

He helped them on to the train. 'It will be a more pleasant journey than you endured when you came in February,' he said. 'But we'll look forward to your return.' He paused and then said, 'Will you stay in Scarborough for the rest of the summer or will you write for me to come and collect you?'

'Oh, we'll write,' Rosalie said. 'I wouldn't want to impose on your grandmother for so long.'

'And besides,' Polly said, 'Hero and Damon and the puppies'll miss us. We'll have to get back for them.'

He smiled, his eyes crinkling at the corners. 'Of course they'll miss you,' he said, 'and I'm sure everyone else will too.'

'Thank you, Howard,' Rosalie gave him her hand. 'You're very kind.'

'Yes, you are,' Polly said, impulsively giving him a kiss on his cheek. 'Thank you.'

He touched his cheek. 'I shan't ever wash my face again,' he said jovially.

'Idiot!' Polly laughed, and as the whistle sounded she shouted 'Goodbye' over the top of it.

'Polly!' Rosalie admonished her. 'You might be giving Howard encouragement without meaning to.'

'He knows I'm joking,' Polly answered. 'It was only fun!'

Rosalie shook her head. Polly was incorrigible and she wished that she could be so relaxed. It's my upbringing, she thought. I have been taught to be always a lady and to act with decorum. I could never kiss a man in public as Polly just did, and I think Polly is wrong. I think Howard did take it seriously, in spite of his joking about never washing his face again. I think that Howard has a fondness for her. Or as Polly would say, 'tekken a shine to her'!

It was raining hard when they arrived at Hull railway station and Rosalie insisted that they take a horse cab.

'It isn't far to walk,' Polly said, 'and we've hardly any luggage.'

'No, we must take a cab. We shall get wet and cold and the house will be freezing. There'll be no fire to welcome us, remember!'

Polly hid a smile. Rosalie didn't know what it was like to endure life without the luxury of a fire or a hot meal cooked by servants. How would she ever have managed if she'd lived 'same life as I have? But she would have, she thought. It's a matter of what you don't have you don't miss, and she admitted to herself that during the few months at Nab Farm she too had become used to the bliss of life with servants, when food miraculously appeared on the table, and clothes were washed without your lifting a finger, and you knew that some-one would make your comfortable bed ready for the next time you got into it.

But it's a drone's life, she thought. I'm getting fat and lazy. Oh, I'm enjoying myself with 'horse and 'puppy and 'company, but where's 'incentive to get up in a morning when I don't have a job of work to go to, for I can't by any means call being Rosalie's companion, work!

The house was cold. A window on the top floor had been left open and the wind whistled through it and down the stairs, chilling all the rooms.

'I'll soon get a fire going,' Polly said. 'There's plenty of wood and kindling. Shall I light it in 'kitchen, Miss Rosalie?'

She clapped her hand over her mouth and they stared at each other. Polly hadn't called Rosalie *Miss* for months.

'It's cos we're here,' Polly said. 'It just slipped out. It seemed 'natural thing to say.'

'Then stop it at once,' Rosalie said in a feigned harsh tone. 'Or I'll have to give you notice.'

'Oh, please, miss.' Polly clasped her hands together and fawned. 'Please don't do that. I'll never get another job o' work like this!'

They both laughed and Rosalie gave Polly a hug. 'Oh, Polly,' she said. 'My life has changed so much since I met you. And all because of Sonny. I should thank him.'

'We'll seek him out tomorrow,' Polly said. 'But it's getting late so let's just get 'range going and 'kettle on for a cup o' tea, and then shall I go out and buy a pie or something for supper?'

She had to consult Rosalie over such matters for she hadn't any money of her own; she had refused the salary Rosalie wanted to pay her, saying she had no desire to buy anything for she had all she could possibly want: food, clothing and a warm bed. As far as Polly was concerned, those were the essential substances of life and she had them in abundance.

The next morning Rosalie said she would visit Mr Benjamin to find out if her father had made any decision about the house. She still hadn't heard from him and had written again to remind him of his promise that he would come to see her before he travelled abroad with his regiment.

Polly said she would go shopping and buy enough food for the next few days, for they didn't intend staying any longer than that. Both in their own way were missing the moor and the horses and the dogs.

'I don't miss Clemmie or Edwin,' Rosalie said. 'But I miss Uncle Luke and Anna. They are such kind people.'

'And Howard,' Polly declared. 'You must miss Howard. I do already and we onny left yesterday.'

'Really?' Rosalie gave her a knowing look and a wry smile.

'Oh, *very* funny!' Polly exclaimed. 'He wouldn't look at *me*. Though he might at you.'

Rosalie laughed. What fun it was to discuss the possibilities of a romance with a friend.

She couldn't imagine ever having such a conversation with her former friends, without them taking it very seriously indeed.

Polly shopped for food at a grocery shop in Savile Street and bought chops from the butcher. It didn't take her long, so she decided to continue on to High Street and see if there was anyone about that she knew. She walked with a jaunty step; she felt fit and well and full of energy, the result she knew of eating well and getting plenty of fresh air. But as she neared her old home area, she felt a despondency creeping over her.

Children were playing in the dirt-strewn courts and alleys behind High Street just as she had done and she wondered how she had ever survived. Just a few short months, she thought, and I, and my life, have changed completely.

She felt choked with emotion as she turned into the court and saw the dilapidated house where she and her mother had shared a room. She saw the uncurtained window and the dirty doorstep which they had always kept clean in spite of their privations, and stood looking with a sob in her throat and tears in her eyes.

Polly turned about, making a decision not to call on Mrs Walters, and headed for the main thoroughfare. The old lady had been kind towards her when her mother was dying, but, she thought, how would she feel if she saw me now, dressed in decent clothes, a shopping basket full of food over my arm? Would she be envious of my good fortune, scathing at the sight of me looking plump and healthy?

'Polly! Is that you?'

It was an old quavery voice that hailed her and she turned reluctantly. Mrs Walters was waving a walking stick at her.

'Yes, it's me,' Polly said and walked towards her. 'How are you, Mrs Walters?'

'All 'better for seeing you, Poll,' the old lady said. 'I bet you just knocked on my door and found nobody in?'

Before Polly could answer she went on, 'Everybody's in work, 'Lord be praised. And look at you! Dressed to 'nines and looking very perky. I'm glad you came to see us. Not forgotten your old pals, then, have you?'

Polly heaved a breath. 'No, I haven't, Mrs Walters. I'd never do that. You were very good to me.'

'Ah, well! You were one of us, you and your ma, and we miss seeing you. Bet you wouldn't come back though, would you? Still working for that nice young lady, are you?'

'Yes,' Polly said. 'But not in Hull. She went to live in 'country and took me with her.'

'Aye, I remember. That's why you're look-ing as plump as a chicken.' Mrs Walters gave a grin, showing a mouth completely devoid of teeth. 'I'm pleased to see it. Will you come in for a dish o' tea?'

'I can't. I have to get back with 'shopping. Miss Rosalie'll be expecting me,' she said. 'We're not staying for more'n a day or two and then we're catching 'train back.'

'My, my,' the old lady said. 'What a treat. Well, good luck to you, lass. Don't forget us, will you? And come back again some time.'

'I will, Mrs Walters.' Polly had a lump in her throat when she thought of how she had misjudged her old friend. 'And I won't ever forget you or how you looked after my ma. I'll remember that to my dying day.'

'A long time, then,' Mrs Walters cackled. 'Be seeing you, then, Poll.' She waved her stick and turned into a nearby court and was gone.

Polly sniffed and felt for a handkerchief in her pocket and blew her nose. She took a breath. I shan't ever worry about coming again, she thought. I should have known that decent folk are always pleased to hear of other people's good fortune.

She cut across Lowgate and headed towards Charlotte Street Mews, intending to seek out Sonny. A man and woman were crossing the street and Polly approached them and asked if they knew where he lived.

'I've seen him going up there,' the man said,

pointing towards some wooden steps. 'I think he lives above 'stables.'

Above 'stables? How peculiar, Polly thought. He's not a stable lad. Sam Little lived above the stables at Nab Farm; she couldn't imagine Sonny doing the same. She climbed the steps and knocked on the door. There was no response and she knocked again and tried the sneck. The door yielded and she pushed it open a little.

'Sonny!' she called. 'Are you there?'

It was quite a large room and she glanced about it. It was a living area; there was a chair and a table, a bed and a chest of drawers, but there was also an easel with a cloth over it, and a stack of blank canvases propped against one wall. Against the other wall were more canvases, but with landscapes painted on them. Many of them looked familiar to her: they were of the moors in all seasons, in deep midwinter with snow-covered stone walls and cottage roofs; in the lush green of spring and early summer, as now, with waterfalls and sheep grazing; and also with the heather in full bloom, which she had yet to see. But there were others of different landscapes: lakes and rivers, places with brilliant hues.

Polly stepped inside. She was curious. Is this what Sonny did? Was he the painter? She bent to look at one of the paintings. The name

Sebastian was written at the bottom. Not Sonny then, she thought. But if not his, why are they here?

The easel was placed against the window with enough room for the artist to stand with his back to the light. Under the cover she saw the bottom edge of a canvas and on it was painted something, like material, in a shade of blue.

I've seen that blue before, she thought. What does it remind me of? Then she recalled the day when she had come looking for Sonny once before. Yes, she thought. He had blue paint on his fingers. He said he had been painting a chair.

But what else, she asked herself. What else is that colour?

Gently, with just her fingertips, she lifted the cover from the bottom of the canvas and slowly the picture was revealed. A woman's feet clad in dainty shoes, a skirt in the blue which teased her memory, a ruched bodice and leg o' mutton sleeves, a pale and creamy neck—

'What are you doing?'

The harsh voice startled her and she dropped the cover and turned to find Sonny standing in the doorway.

'D-door was open,' she stammered. 'I thought you were in and couldn't hear.'

He put down the leather bag he was carrying.

'Well, as you see, I was not. What are you doing here, Polly?'

'I'm sorry,' she said miserably. 'We've come to Hull for a day or two and I thought I'd come and see you. I didn't mean to pry.'

Sonny shrugged. 'It doesn't matter, I suppose.' He gave a laconic grin. 'It's no secret really.'

'Are these yours?' Polly indicated the paintings against the walls.

He nodded. 'Yes. That's what I do. How I earn my living.'

'It says *Sebastian*.'

'That's my real name,' he said. 'My aunt who brought me up always called me Sonny.'

Polly turned back to the easel. 'Can I look at this? I thought I recognized 'colour.'

Sonny hesitated. 'I suppose so. It's not finished.'

She picked up the cover again and lifted it completely to reveal the painting of a young woman in a blue gown. She caught her breath. For a second she thought it was a portrait of her. The skin was as fair as hers, the eyes as blue, but the hair was more golden than her own and the lovely face had a sad and wistful expression. It was Rosalie.

CHAPTER TWENTY-NINE

'Don't read anything into it that isn't there, Polly,' Sonny said hastily. 'It's just a portrait of a girl on the threshold of womanhood.'

Yes, I can see that, Polly thought. But I can see something else as well. There's a glow about the sitter that I've never noticed, but the artist has – or hopes to. He's painted it with love!

'It's beautiful,' she murmured. 'I never thought that a likeness could be caught so well in a painting. But then, I've never really seen any paintings of anyone I know.'

Sonny smiled. How well Polly was learning to express herself. After such a short time under Rosalie's influence, she had achieved that fluency. And had Polly's easy-going amiability rubbed off on Rosalie?

'You won't tell?' he asked. 'I'd rather you didn't.'

Polly turned to face him. Her eyes sparkled.

'Not if you don't want me to. But I won't anyway,' she said. 'It might embarrass her. Or frighten her away,' she added slyly.

He caught hold of her hand. 'You little madam! I said don't read anything—'

'I know, I know,' she laughed. 'And I won't. I won't breathe a word.'

'How is Miss Kingston, anyway?' he asked stiffly. 'And what are you doing in Hull?'

'Miss Kingston! *Rosalie* has come to make sure 'house is all right and has gone to see her lawyer. She's not heard from her father yet. But she's also come for some more clothes.'

'I'm coming up to Nab Farm in a couple of weeks,' he told her. 'But only for a few days, then I'm going abroad. I won't be back until next year.'

'Next year!' she exclaimed. 'Why so long?'

'I hope to go to Italy to paint,' he said, 'and then I'll go walking in the Dolomites. Then . . .' He paused. 'I'm not sure after that. Wherever my spirit takes me.'

'Will you come to supper tonight?' Polly asked. 'I've bought food and there's plenty of it. You could tell us about your travel plans. Would it be proper for you to come?' she added, frowning a little.

'As if you cared about convention,' he teased.

'I don't,' she said. 'But Rosalie might.'

He nodded. 'She might. If I turn up on the doorstep will she turn me away?'

Polly smiled. 'I'll make sure she doesn't.'

She hurried back to the house, made sure the range was burning well and prepared some lunch for her and Rosalie, then turned thoughtfully to plans for supper. She had bought mutton chops from the butcher, and to eke them out for three she scrubbed potatoes and beat up a batter for Yorkshire pudding and set it aside to rest. She had never made it before but had seen Cook prepare it often enough.

Rosalie came in as Polly was on her hands and knees, halfway inside a cupboard, searching for a suitable meat tin.

'Whatever are you doing?'

'Trying my hand at cooking,' Polly said. 'It might come in useful one day. Perhaps I might marry a poor farmer,' she appeared, dishevelled, from the cupboard with a large meat tin in her hand, 'and not be able to afford a cook.'

Rosalie sighed. 'You're incorrigible,' she said. Then she asked, 'Can I help? I've never cooked either.'

'It's as well to be prepared,' Polly agreed. 'You might fall in love with a poor man too and not live the life you've been used to.'

'It would be nice to meet someone, wouldn't

it?' Rosalie said dreamily. 'But then would my father agree? He wouldn't agree to a poor man, that I do know.'

Polly cleaned the meat tin. 'You'd have to run away. Oh, by the way,' she said nonchalantly. 'I bumped into Sonny while I was out. I invited him to supper. Is that all right?'

Rosalie gazed at her. 'That's what all this is about, isn't it? Nothing to do with learning to cook. It's for Sonny.'

'No,' Polly declared. 'I *am* learning to cook. I'm just practising on Sonny, that's all. If you don't want him to come . . .'

Rosalie blushed. 'But it's just the two of us,' she said. 'I'm not sure it's the right thing to do. Suppose someone calls whilst he's here?'

'And?' Polly stared back. 'What then? You can say he's a friend o' mine, can't you? Which he is,' she said adamantly. 'And I thought he was one of yours too.'

'So he is,' Rosalie replied. 'Oh, heavens. Of course it doesn't matter!'

Between them they prepared the supper and set the kitchen table with a white cloth, for Rosalie decided that the dining room would be too cold even if they lit a fire. The range was belting out heat and the kitchen was very cosy. Then they both dashed upstairs to wash and change, and Rosalie was persuaded by Polly to wear blue.

'Colour suits you so well,' she told her.

Sonny arrived at six o'clock bearing bon-bons and flowers. 'I decided against bringing wine,' he said. 'I didn't want you to think I had unscrupulous intentions.'

'We would never think that,' Rosalie murmured. 'You seem like an honourable man.'

'Ah, but how can one tell?' He looked down at her and smiled. Then he looked round the kitchen. 'This is lovely,' he said. 'Very snug. So much more comfortable than dining in state.'

'That's what we thought,' Rosalie said, relaxing a little. 'Polly and I lived in here before we went to the farm. It seemed silly to use the whole house when there were just the two of us.'

'So you are not conventional after all.' His eyebrows rose. 'You don't mind stepping out of line sometimes?'

She gave a shy smile, shaking her head, and invited him to sit down. It had been decided between her and Polly that she would entertain Sonny whilst Polly would dish up the food. At least, Polly had decided.

'I find that I don't,' she said, answering his question. 'Sometimes formality seems like a straitjacket and often quite unnecessary.' She looked across at Polly, who was taking a dish out of the oven. 'That's Polly's influence, of course. She's taught me such a lot.'

'Well, can somebody teach me to get this on to 'table without dropping it,' Polly said through gritted teeth as she balanced the meat tin on the top of the range, 'and before 'Yorkshires start to go flat.'

Sonny and Rosalie both rose to their feet but Sonny got there first. He picked up a cloth, took the tin from Polly and placed it on the table.

'Just look at that!' he said admiringly. 'I've not seen Yorkshire pudding like that in a long time.'

Rosalie had given the batter an extra beating and they'd poured it over the chops, which they'd cooked with onions. Now it was risen and golden.

'We didn't know if this was the usual way to cook them,' Rosalie began, and Polly finished for her: 'But we wanted to save on washing up seeing as it's 'scullery maid's day off.'

Sonny laughed and took off his jacket. 'Well done, ladies,' he said. 'Will you allow me to serve?'

The evening passed very pleasantly, the food was delicious and pronounced a great success and both girls felt very self-satisfied.

'I never thought that I could enjoy myself so much,' Rosalie said.

'But you wouldn't want to do it for a living?' Sonny asked.

'No,' Rosalie said. His eyes had lingered on her as he spoke and she felt her cheeks flushing. 'But now I know I could.'

He told them some of his travel plans, and that before he went away he would visit the moors. 'I'm a painter,' he said, catching Polly's eye and being assured that she hadn't told Rosalie of his secret. 'Not a very good one,' he said modestly, 'but I manage to sell some of my work. I like to see the moors at all times of the year and just now the heather is coming into bloom. I shall commit something to canvas, and then set off on my travels. I'm heading to Florence first, and then I shall go to the mountains. I'll avoid Austria if possible as there is still much unease and Bismarck is playing a game I wouldn't want to become involved in.'

'Will there be danger?' Rosalie asked tremulously.

'Not for me,' he assured her. 'I shall avoid it at all costs.'

He left at nine, for in spite of what he had said to Rosalie about convention, he didn't want to give the neighbours any reason to gossip. He kissed their hands in turn and thanked them for inviting him and said he would see them at Nab Farm within the next few weeks.

'He's different from how he used to be,' Polly said as she closed the basement door and locked it.

'Different how?' Rosalie asked, peering through the window and waving her hand as Sonny turned at the top of the steps.

'Sort of – more like a proper gent, which I never thought of before. He was just Sonny when I was little.'

'Mm.' Rosalie turned to go into the kitchen. 'It's probably you that's different,' she said. 'You're seeing him through grown-up eyes instead of a child's. Do you like him more?'

'Oh, yes!' Polly teased. 'I do!'

After a few more days they decided to return to Scarborough and make the visit to Mrs Carleton. They caught the train and took a cab to her house. Both felt elated at accomplishing the journey alone without any assistance from anyone.

Rosalie had had a long discussion with Mr Benjamin regarding the house in Albion Street and he had suggested that he should write to her father proposing that he employ a temporary housekeeper until a decision was made on whether to rent or sell the house. Rosalie had agreed with this for, as she told him, another winter without fires would render the house very damp.

She was disappointed that he hadn't heard from her father either and they concluded that he had been called away on military duties.

But she mused that her mother couldn't have had a very satisfactory married life if this was the pattern that it had always taken.

Mrs Carleton was delighted to see them, Clementina less so, though at her grandmother's suggestion she reluctantly agreed that they should join them for a concert at the Spa that evening.

Polly was overcome with emotion as she listened to the orchestra. Never had she been so enthralled as the sound drifted over her; nor could she imagine how such sweet music could spring forth from the piano, violins and other stringed instruments she was listening to. At the end of the concert she sat wordless and didn't even applaud, being unwilling to break the spell.

'Polly!' Rosalie said for the second time, and gently shook her arm. 'Shall we go outside and join the others?'

'If you like.' Polly cleared her throat; she felt as if she couldn't speak.

'Are you all right, Polly?'

'Yes,' she said huskily. 'I'm fine, thank you.' She followed Rosalie through the doors to where the sea was rushing and tumbling and breaking against the wall below. The sun had not yet set, but was slowly sinking and casting its dying colours of gold upon the waters.

It's beautiful, she thought, and felt as if she wanted to cry with the joy of it.

A voice whispered in her ear, 'You should see it when there is a full moon. That is the most romantic sight, when the moon lays a path across the water.' Mrs Carleton, standing behind her, was resplendent in a deep mauve gown and a feathered hat. 'If you believe in magic,' she said softly, 'and you're with someone you love, Neptune's Path is a wonderful thing to behold.'

Polly gazed at her with her lips parted. 'Yes,' she breathed. 'I'm sure it is. I hope – I hope that I find somebody who believes in magic.'

The elderly lady smiled benignly and patted her arm. 'I'm quite sure that you will, my dear. Come along, let's gather the others together and we'll visit the castle before we go home.'

The horse and carriage toiled up the hill past the old church of St Mary's and arrived at the castle gateway.

'You young people go and explore,' said Mrs Carleton, 'and I'll wait here. The hill is too steep for my old legs. But don't be long, as it's getting dark. I don't want you tumbling over the edge. Holmes,' she called to the driver. 'You'd better go with them.'

The young women piled out and walked up towards the ruined castle. They went through the gate and then Clementina said, 'It's cold. I'm going back. Are you coming, Rosalie?'

'No,' Rosalie said. 'I want to see it.'

Holmes turned to escort Clementina back to the carriage and Rosalie and Polly walked on, the grass damp beneath their feet. The towers and turrets were eerie in the fading light.

'Do you think there are ghosts?' Rosalie murmured.

'Oh yes,' Polly whispered. 'Bound to be. I hope so anyway. If I'd been here centuries ago, I'd have wanted to come back.'

They walked to the edge of the rocky promontory and looked down. They could see the red-roofed town laid out before them; the harbour, the lighthouse and the glinting silver sea, devoid of the gold which had recently transformed it.

'If I can't live on 'moors,' Polly murmured, 'then I'll live here. Oh,' she breathed, 'how lucky we are, Rosalie. I could die happy now.'

Rosalie tucked her arm into Polly's. 'So could I,' she said. 'But not yet, Polly. Not yet. This is just the beginning. Come on, here's Holmes coming for us. Let's go back.'

CHAPTER THIRTY

Howard came to collect them two days later. His grandmother smiled as she saw his arrival through the window and remarked, 'This is the second time this dear boy has come to see if you've returned. I've seen more of him lately than I normally see in a twelvemonth.'

She turned and raised an eyebrow at the three young women. 'It's clearly not my welfare he's interested in; I wonder whose it can be?'

Clementina sniffed and tossed her head. 'Well, not mine. Howard and I don't get on.'

Rosalie and Polly glanced at each other, and then Polly said impishly, 'Rosalie has many admirers, Mrs Carleton. Howard must be another.'

'What nonsense!' Rosalie retorted. 'Polly, do behave.'

Mrs Carleton looked enquiringly at them both. 'Mm,' she murmured. 'Well, well! I do

344

like intrigue, and it's about time Howard found romance.'

Howard opened the door as she was speaking and heard his name. 'What? Grandmother! Are you plotting behind my back?'

'I might be,' she said, and sighed. 'But I'm not going to tell you what about.'

They stayed to have the midday meal and Howard then said they must be off, as he had work to do. 'It's the shooting season,' he said. 'We've to prepare the butts, make ready for the Guns that are coming.'

His grandmother asked why he hadn't asked Amos to come for the girls, or even Luke and Anna, who might have enjoyed the visit.

'Oh, it's no bother,' he flustered. 'And I enjoy seeing you, Grandmama. I don't come often enough.'

'That you don't,' she agreed. 'So if these delightful young ladies come again, perhaps you'll come too?'

'Of course I will.' He bent to kiss her cheek. 'It's always a pleasure.'

'And perhaps Edwin will come with you? He never visits.'

'I can't speak for Edwin,' Howard said flatly. 'He sets his own plans.'

They arrived back at Nab Farm as the sun was descending behind the high ridges, setting the moor ablaze with the purple and gold of heather and gorse.

'I've missed it so much,' Polly murmured. 'I feel as if I'm coming home.'

She had taken the area to her heart. The view of the high moors from her bedroom window; the rushing gushing waterfalls as they cascaded over shiny rocks into silver pools. The sight of the sheep as they grazed the heather; the sturdy stone cottages nestling into the hillside and the grouse and pheasant which she could now recognize since Howard had described them to her. Even a glimpse of a fox or a roe deer filled her with absolute delight.

'Perhaps you have,' Howard said softly. 'Perhaps this is where you were meant to be.'

She looked up; his voice was quiet and husky, not jovial as usual. His eyes met hers and she suddenly felt vulnerable and unsure of herself. She glanced round for Rosalie, but she had already gone inside the house.

'It's – it's onny – only – because of Rosalie,' she stammered. 'I wouldn't be here but for her, and her uncle of course,' she added. 'If he hadn't wanted me I would have been on 'next train home.'

He gave a sudden grin and she felt instant relief at seeing the easy-to-be-with Howard again.

'Somebody would have rescued you and

brought you back,' he assured her. 'We wouldn't have let such a treasure escape.'

'Silly,' she said and gave him a tap on his arm. 'You're a jester.'

'Of course I am,' he agreed.

She and Rosalie settled into a routine again, walking the dogs or riding out on to the moor and coming home exhilarated at the end of each day. Just before supper one evening, Anna called Polly into the room she had claimed as her own. It was a sunny room, lined with books and littered with sewing materials on every available surface. Despite her elegant appearance she was quite untidy and wouldn't allow the servants to tidy away her 'things', as she called them.

'I want to ask if you'll do something for me, Polly,' she said. 'I'm a little worried about one of the servants and wonder if you could shed light on the matter. I'm still new to them and I don't think I yet have their confidence.'

So she knows, Polly thought. She knows I'm servant class, or else why didn't she ask Rosalie? Or even Clementina when she comes home; she's the daughter of the house after all. I'm onny a guest.

'It's Dora,' Anna said. 'She's only a bit younger than you, I would think, and might confide in you.' She smiled at her. 'You're so very easy to talk to.'

I suppose it doesn't matter if she does know, Polly pondered. If she does know and didn't like me being here, she would have sent me packing before.

'So would you talk to her?' Anna asked, tilting her head to one side. 'If you'd rather not I'd understand.'

'I don't mind,' Polly murmured. 'If you think it would help. I'd noticed that Dora was a bit quiet lately.'

'I would be very grateful,' Anna told her. 'I thought at first that Mrs Moody might have scolded her about her work, but now I know that's not the case because Mrs Moody herself came to me to say that she thought the girl was worried about something. I know,' she commented, seeing Polly's look of disbelief. 'Mrs Moody is a bit of a tartar, isn't she? But that's because her commitment to the family is paramount.'

'I see,' Polly said, and wondered if she had misjudged the housekeeper, who was always dowly and offhand towards her. 'All right, I'll talk to Dora and try to find out if summat's wrong. *Something*, I mean.'

'I know what you mean, Polly,' Anna said softly. 'And you don't have to pretend to be anyone you're not. You're open and honest and a joy to be with, just as you are.'

Polly was so taken aback by this show of

affection that tears spouted to her eyes. 'Oh!' Her mouth trembled. 'You're very kind, Mrs Kingston. Thank you.'

She sought out Dora the next morning and ran her to ground in the yard, where the maid was leaning against a wall. She was crying.

'Dora!' Polly said. 'What's up? What's wrong?'

'I'm sorry, Miss Polly,' Dora snuffled. 'I just had to come out for a minute. Mrs Moody keeps on at me, saying I'm slow and I have to buck my ideas up.' She lifted a corner of her apron and wiped her eyes. 'I'll go back in in a minute afore anybody misses me.'

'No. Wait,' Polly said. 'Why are you crying? Is it because of Mrs Moody? Because if it is, I'll have a word with Mrs Kingston. She's noticed that you're unhappy.'

'Oh, no, please don't.' Dora seemed horrified at the idea and not a little hysterical. 'It's not Mrs Moody. At least,' her tears started again, 'not really.'

'Can't you tell me?' Polly was at her most persuasive. 'I've been through some hard times, Dora, believe me, and the worst is having nobody to turn to.'

Dora shook her head and was consumed by tears. 'No, miss,' she blubbered and lifted her apron to cover her face. Then Polly observed her thickened waist.

'Oh! Dora!' Polly breathed. 'Are you in 'pudding club?'

'Yes, miss.' Dora showed her red tearful face. 'I am. I think I am. I don't know for sure, cos I've nobody to ask.'

'Well if you're not, then you've put on a bit o' weight. But you must know,' Polly said. 'There are other signs. Have you had a flux lately?'

'No.' Dora shook her head again. 'Oh, Miss Polly, what am I going to do? I'll lose my job; my ma won't have me, and where will I go with a bairn to look after?' She burst into another onslaught of crying.

'But,' Polly scratched her head in bewilderment, 'what about its father? Is it Sam?'

Dora put her fingers to her mouth and nibbled her nails. 'Not Sam,' she whispered. 'I wish it was. Sam's always behaved properly towards me and I hoped – I'd hoped that we'd walk out together. But not now we won't. He won't want me now.'

'Some other lad then?' Polly said. 'I'll come wi' you to see him if you like. If you're scared o' telling him or his family. But he must know it's happened. He can't deny it.'

Dora sniffed and took a breath. 'Oh, he will,' she said in a matter of fact tone. 'He'll deny it. He'll say it wasn't him.'

'Who?' Polly asked anxiously. 'Who is it,

then? You must say, Dora. It's 'onny way we can help you.'

Dora looked down at the ground. Her eyes were red-rimmed and swollen. She looked most unattractive with her red nose and her mouth turned down plaintively. 'You'll not believe me,' she said. 'Nobody will.'

'Try me,' Polly said. She was getting worried about the time this conversation was taking. At any minute Mrs Moody was likely to appear looking for Dora and then there would be trouble, for the housekeeper would be sure to winkle out the problem.

Dora gave a gulp. 'Mr Edwin, miss. He forced me.' She began to cry again, great racking sobs which shook her body.

Polly stared at her. 'Edwin?' she breathed. 'No!'

'There! Didn't I say you wouldn't believe me?'

'I didn't say I didn't believe you,' Polly murmured, knowing full well that it could have been Edwin. 'When was this?'

'Weeks ago,' Dora snuffled. 'And not just once. He made me meet him time and again. I didn't want to. But he said he would tell Mrs Moody and he'd tell Sam how I egged him on if I didn't. He hurt me, Miss Polly,' she blurted out. 'He wasn't nice. He was horrible and I was scared of him.'

Polly was silent. She was shaken by the revelation, but believed after her own experience with Edwin that he could be capable of violence. Poor Dora. How could she possibly make a stand against someone like him, the son of her employer?

'Go inside,' she said, 'and tell Mrs Moody or whoever's in 'kitchen that you feel ill and are going to bed. Then stay there while I think on what's to be done.'

Dora nodded, screwing up her apron with her fingers, but she seemed relieved that she had at last confided in someone.

'You'll not tell of me, Miss Polly? I don't want anybody to find out.'

'Dora,' Polly said patiently, 'this isn't summat you can hide. You're pregnant,' she said bluntly. 'There'll be a bairn at 'end of it.'

She had to tell, of course, and then it would be out of her hands. There was only one person she could confide in and that was Anna Kingston.

CHAPTER THIRTY-ONE

Anna sat quietly as Polly explained the situation. She appeared serene, her face impassive, but Polly could tell that she was upset by the way in which she clasped and unclasped her hands as they lay on her lap.

Not a good start to a marriage, Polly thought, when you're given the responsibility of telling your new husband that his son has raped a servant girl.

'Do you believe her, Polly?' she asked quietly. 'Do you believe that Edwin could do such a terrible thing?'

Polly swallowed. How to coat such a bitter pill and say that I know for certain that he could?

'I don't believe that Dora is lying, ma'am,' she hedged. 'I don't think she's capable of making up such a story.'

Anna looked up at her. 'I'm inclined to agree with you. She seems an inoffensive simple kind of girl – and I mean that in the kindest way

– who couldn't possibly calculate or devise such an appalling tale.'

She patted the sofa next to her. 'Please sit down, Polly. The thing is, how to tell my husband, for he must be told; and,' she sighed, 'what to do about Dora?'

'Could I suggest,' Polly said hesitantly, 'that you speak to Dora first? She's in a terrible state and afraid of being found out. She's scared of losing her job, says that she can't go home cos her ma won't have her, and, well, to be honest, she's at her wits' end.'

'Poor girl,' Anna murmured. 'Where is she now?'

'I told her to say that she was ill and go up to her room. 'Kitchen staff'll be sure to put two and two together afore long.'

'Yes, you're right, Polly, but I think I'll still speak to Luke first and we'll see Dora together.'

Polly was dubious about this, but it was out of her hands now and at Mrs Kingston's request she went in search of Luke. She found him in the stable yard talking to Rosalie and Sam. Sam was brushing down Hero, whose coat was gleaming.

'Ah, Polly. There you are.' Rosalie was dressed in a dark green riding coat and divided skirt. 'Shall we go out?'

'Yes, all right.' Polly licked her lips. 'Mr

Kingston. Mrs Kingston wants to see you most urgently!'

'Does she?' Luke seemed startled. 'What's going on that my dear wife can't manage?'

Polly shook her head. 'Can't say, sir. But she needs to see you now.'

'Oh, well.' He put on a hangdog expression. 'Better go then or I shall worry over what I might have done wrong,' he joked.

Polly walked back to the house with him, telling Rosalie that she would change her skirt and be only a few minutes.

'What's this all about, Polly?' Luke murmured as they mounted the steps to the house. 'Someone in trouble?'

'Yes, sir, but I'm not at liberty to say.' She looked up at him and wondered if he'd be angry or sad or if he would blame Dora for leading his son on.

'Not you?' he queried. 'I hope not.'

'No, sir.' She smiled. 'Not me. Mrs Kingston will tell you.'

She left him at his wife's sitting room door and started to hurry upstairs to change, but Anna came out and called softly to her.

'Polly! Will you go up to Dora's room and say that we wish to speak to her in half an hour? I want her to compose herself. Tell her not to be afraid,' she added compassionately. 'We'll do what we can.'

Polly continued up to the top floor and the maids' dormitory. She tapped on the door and entered. It was a long room with six beds, chests of drawers and washstands in it. The windows were narrow but there were several of them along one wall, making the room quite light and airy.

Dora was sitting on one of the beds. She looked up fearfully as Polly came in.

'It's all right,' she assured her. 'I've told Mrs Kingston. Don't worry,' she added as Dora gasped. 'She said you mustn't be afraid.'

'It's not her it's happening to, is it?' Dora wailed. 'I am afraid. And what will Mr Edwin say? He'll say I'm lying, that's what, and they'll believe him. Course they will.' Tears flooded down her cheeks. 'Why would they believe me? I'm nobody.'

'Dora, you have to trust us. Somebody has to take charge of 'situation. Go down in half an hour to see Mrs Kingston. It'll just give her 'chance to speak to Mr Kingston and—'

Dora thrust her hands to her mouth to stifle her sobs. 'Not Mr Kingston!' she begged. 'What'll he think?'

'I hope he'll think that Edwin is a villain,' Polly murmured as she left. 'But who knows?'

She changed into a riding skirt and hurried downstairs and out to where Rosalie was impatiently waiting.

'Where've you been?' she scolded. 'We're wasting the morning.'

How eager Rosalie was nowadays, Polly thought. She loved to be out on horseback and was becoming very proficient.

Sam helped them both to mount and they moved off out of the yard and up towards the top moor behind the farm. It was a beautiful day with barely a cloud in the sky.

'I'll tell you what delayed me in a minute,' Polly murmured. 'There's going to be such a cat among 'pigeons this morning it's as well that we're out of 'house.'

Rosalie turned an enquiring glance towards her but Polly wouldn't be drawn until they were well up the hillside and heading towards the summit where Polly had first met Luke Kingston, and they could look down at the farm below.

'Mrs Kingston asked me if I'd have a word with Dora,' she explained. 'Mrs Moody's been concerned about her work and thought that there was something wrong. And there is. She thinks she's pregnant.'

Rosalie gasped. 'Oh! How dreadful! Is it Sam's? I've seen her near the stables once or twice. Oh, no!' She put her hand to her mouth. 'Don't tell me! It isn't something we should gossip about.'

'It isn't,' Polly agreed and urged Hero

onwards to continue up the hill. 'But we're going to hear about it anyway. It isn't Sam's child,' she added. 'He's not to blame.'

'Not Sam?' Rosalie drew alongside her. 'Then – who?'

'You said you didn't want to know,' Polly said quizzically, thinking that the reason Mrs Kingston had asked her to find out about Dora was because she suspected it might be something unsavoury, and thought that she, Polly, wouldn't shy away from hearing about it. A woman of the world, I am, she reflected.

'Well . . .' Rosalie hesitated. 'I – I don't really, but I confess I'm curious. There's no one else. It must be Sam. Is he denying it?'

Polly reined in at the summit and looked about her; which way should they ride today? 'No,' she said. 'Sam doesn't know about it yet and Dora said he's never touched her.'

'Then who? There are no other young men at Nab Farm who—' Rosalie stopped. 'Oh,' she said softly. 'Of course there are, but – they wouldn't! Not Howard or Edwin!'

'Don't even *think* of Howard,' Polly said sharply, forgetting completely who she was speaking to. 'Howard would *never*—' She swallowed. 'Sorry,' she apologized. 'But he wouldn't. He's – such a gentleman, in spite of his jokes and being merry and easy-going and

– and everything.' Her words tailed away and Rosalie stared at her in bewilderment.

'I didn't mean to suggest it was Howard,' she murmured. 'I was only – not Edwin? Surely not?'

Polly nodded. Her own spontaneous outburst had startled her. Why did I do that, she thought. For all we know it could have been anyone, including Howard. The idea of it sickened her even though it was beyond reason.

'Yes. Edwin,' she responded quietly. 'That's who Dora said. And I believe her, because he'd tried to shame me.'

'No!' Rosalie said. 'Why didn't you say something?'

Polly shrugged. 'Because you'd have treated him differently had you known, so it was better that you didn't. But Howard knows,' she added.

'Howard!' Rosalie was aghast. 'How could you discuss such a thing with another man?'

'I didn't,' Polly said reluctantly. 'He just happened to come along at 'right time. Anyway, I don't want to talk about it. I just want to forget it.'

The whole incident had come back to her, when she thought it had gone away. She avoided Edwin whenever possible, but whenever they did meet she felt his eyes upon her and was sure he was gloating.

'Let's ride over to Ramsdale,' she suggested, 'and take a look at 'standing stones. Howard told me about them and said we could see 'coast from up there.' Polly was intrigued by the ancient monoliths and stones which could be found all over the moors.

'It's a long way,' Rosalie demurred. 'But still, we've plenty of time and no need to rush back.'

They broke into a trot and the ponies responded, their ears pricking up as they moved across the vast moor where the sheep cropped amongst the heather and skittered away as they drew near. High in the blue sky a buzzard wheeled and they could hear the defensive repeated warning of red grouse hidden deep in the old heather, the cocks noisy and aggressive as their territory was approached.

They rode for almost an hour without speaking much, both busy with their thoughts and enjoying the scenery. Polly was thinking she was in heaven, and yet her musings drifted constantly to Dora. I'm so lucky, she thought. If Sonny hadn't insisted that I apply for work at Rosalie's house, what would I be doing now?

Rosalie was looking far ahead across Kirk Moor, which was more open here and turning from green to a rich purple. The gorse, in contrast, was a deep yellow. To think that my uncle has always lived here and yet we never visited, she thought. Why did my father not bring me before? Did he never consider that I might like to know our relatives?

Her meandering thoughts also turned to Dora and the quandary she was in. Who will help her if she loses her job? How will she survive with a child to bring up? If she keeps it, that is. But she's young and healthy; and then she remembered that her mother had been healthy too and yet had died in childbirth.

They rode through a wooded area and within it they could hear the sound of rushing water.

'We must be near Ramsdale Beck,' Rosalie said. 'And I think there's a waterfall somewhere near.' They came through the wood on to open moorland again and now they could see the sea in the distance.

'Look.' Polly pointed. 'You can see a stone from here. Howard told me that they're prehistoric. And some of 'em have strange markings. He said that some of 'smaller stones on 'moor are hidden amongst 'heather and you can't see 'em unless you trip over them, and they've been there, oh, just about for ever!'

They rode a little further and then dismounted to take it in turns to hold the reins and scramble through the prickly heather and bracken to reach the standing stone.

Polly walked round it. 'Why are they here?'

she said. 'Do you think that ancient people lived here and practised magic?'

'If you believe in magic, yes. But as I don't then no.' Rosalie laughed. 'I think they were part of something else. They're medieval; perhaps part of a stone circle.'

She and Polly then swapped places so that she could take a look at the megalith. The heather pulled at her skirt and she bent and tore off a piece. 'For luck,' she said, holding it up and then putting it in a buttonhole in her lapel.

'I thought you didn't believe in magic,' Polly observed, and then looked up at the sky where dark clouds were driving in from Robin Hood's Bay in the east. 'It's looking like rain,' she called. 'We'd best get straight back rather than going on to 'beck.'

'Perhaps you're right.' Rosalie stumbled back through the scrub that surrounded the stone. 'I'm quite hungry, too. Why didn't we think of bringing an apple or cake or something?'

They mounted, both finding it much easier now than formerly, particularly when there was no one to watch their awkwardness. They moved off, both glancing up at the sky. It had been blue when they had set out, but now there were ominous black clouds overhead, dramatically lit by the sun behind them.

'Castles and mountains in the air,' Rosalie

remarked. 'How quickly the weather can change. And not a waterproof between us!'

'Won't hurt us,' Polly said cheerfully. 'I've been wet many a time and never a fire to dry me out. Come on, we can at least look forward to changing our clothes and getting dry when we get back.'

Rosalie nodded. She needed Polly to remind her how fortunate she had always been.

They had ridden only for half an hour and left the wood behind when the rain started. To begin with it was only a drizzle but within minutes it changed to needle-sharp sleet which wetted them instantly.

'There's nowhere to shelter,' Rosalie called out plaintively. 'We should have waited in the wood.'

The moor here was wide and without boulders or overhanging ridges to shelter under, and their vision was obscured by grey mist which had suddenly descended to blanket the landscape.

'Are we going 'right way?' Polly asked. 'There aren't any landmarks.'

'I don't know.' Rosalie drew in beside her and they both sat with their shoulders hunched, trying to work out their position. 'We've left the coast behind. Will the horses know if we give them their heads?'

Polly was dubious. 'They're new to this bit

o' moor. They might tek us back to where they come from. We could finish up at Egton Bridge.'

'Well, we can't just sit here,' Rosalie said. 'I shall order a compass on our return and in future always bring it with me.'

They moved on, but slowly as the path through the heather was often obscured and there were many stones and boulders. They were both now soaked to the skin and very uncomfortable.

Polly peered ahead. Was the mist lifting? She thought the view of the moor was clearing and that she could see further than previously.

'There's a building of some sort down there,' she said. 'Can you remember it from when we came up? And that broken wall, see, where 'stones are heaped up beside it. We're on 'right track, I'm sure of it.'

Rosalie narrowed her eyes. 'Yes, I see it,' she said. 'And look! There's someone climbing over it.'

'So there is,' Polly said. 'Whatever are they doing out in this weather, and where would they be going? Not looking for shelter, anyway.'

The figure was a good distance away and heading across the moor. There were no cottages or other buildings in the direction the figure was travelling.

'It's a woman,' Polly exclaimed. Her sight was sharper than Rosalie's. 'Shall we ride over and ask if we're on 'right track? Where can she be going?'

'Shall we call to her? Do you think she needs help?'

'She's running,' Polly said. 'Or trying to. Yes, let's go to her.'

They gathered up their reins and urged on the ponies, who swiftly responded. Rosalie thought they must be as eager as they were to be home and dry.

'Rosalie,' Polly said, 'there's no shelter and she's on foot . . .' Polly took a breath. The figure was familiar. 'It's Dora!'

CHAPTER THIRTY-TWO

'Dora. Come here.' Anna beckoned to Dora when she came hesitantly into her sitting room. 'Don't be afraid. We're here to help you.'

Dora glanced at Mr Kingston, who was standing with his back to her staring out of the window, and then with her head lowered she came towards Mrs Kingston.

'Dora,' Anna began quietly, 'we need to hear from your own lips what you have told Miss Polly. You have made a very serious charge against Mr Edwin and before we send for him we need the facts.'

'I said nobody'd believe me.' Dora began to weep. 'But it's true. I never wanted to go with him, but he made me. He said he would tell Mrs Moody I'd led him on if I didn't.'

Luke turned from the window. His face was pale and his mouth tight. 'Did he promise you anything? A present, or money?'

Dora stared at him from brimming eyes.

'No, sir, and I wouldn't have taken it if he had.'

'Why didn't you tell someone?' he bellowed suddenly, making her jump, and Anna shook her head at him, putting her finger to her lips.

'I didn't know who to tell, sir,' Dora mumbled. 'Not Mrs Moody, cos Mr Edwin's her favourite, and I thought she'd dismiss me.'

Luke gave a deep sigh and turned away again.

'Have you told Mr Edwin that you're pregnant?' Anna asked her.

'No, ma'am.' Dora bent her head. 'I daren't.'

'Then I will,' Luke said and marched to the door. 'Edwin!' He stood at the foot of the stairs and his bellow echoed throughout the house.

'He'll surely be out on the farm!' Anna said when Luke came back into the room. 'He won't be in the house.'

Luke grimaced and was about to say something, but then seemed to think better of it.

'Can you go home to your parents, Dora?' Anna asked. 'I realize that they'll be upset and angry, but if we send someone with you – and of course there will be help in bringing up the child—'

'We need to hear Edwin's side of the story first,' her husband interrupted before she could finish.

'Of course, dear,' Anna soothed. 'We must listen to what he has to say.'

The door opened and Edwin came in. 'Did somebody call me? I'd just slipped up to my room for something—' He stopped speaking when he saw Dora, and glanced at his father.

'You haven't been out,' his father accused him. 'You've been in your room all morning.'

Edwin flushed. 'No I haven't. I, erm, I came back in for a hat. I thought I'd ride over to . . .' His words tailed away. 'What?'

'You've been charged with raping a servant girl and making her pregnant,' his father said bluntly. 'That's why I called you. What do you have to say for yourself?'

'What?' Edwin blustered. 'Which girl? Not me.' He cast a furtive glance at Dora, who kept her eyes on the floor. 'I've never touched her.'

Dora gave a gasp. 'I said he'd say that. I told Miss Polly he would.'

'Miss Polly!' Edwin sneered. 'Why bring her into this? And who'd believe either of them, anyway?'

'Well I would for a start,' Anna said quietly. 'I can see no reason to think they would lie.'

'There's every reason,' Edwin said arrogantly. 'I've seen Polly and Dora hanging round the stables waiting for Sam.' He smirked. 'He's one for the ladies.' His lips turned down as he looked at Dora. 'Or even those who are not ladies,' he added.

'Why are you mentioning Polly?' His father's eyes narrowed. 'Have you reason to think she's accused you of something?'

Edwin shrugged, but he seemed uncomfortable, as if he'd spoken hastily. 'No,' he floundered. 'I thought – you know; kick a man when he's down. Anyway, I've not touched either of them.'

Anna looked alarmed. 'Polly has not blamed you for any indiscretion. Should she have done?'

'If I thought for one minute that you'd offended a guest in our house, let alone a trusted servant,' Luke was furious, 'I'd take a horsewhip to you.'

'Not me, Father,' Edwin mocked. 'You'll have to look elsewhere. Try Sam, he's the obvious one.'

'Not Sam,' Dora wailed. 'We're not even walking out, and he wouldn't.' She began to sob, her breath catching in her throat. 'It was Mr Edwin. And not just once. Since Christmas – and 'worst time was after the wedding, when he made me meet him; he said nobody'd notice we were missing.'

'Stop. I've heard enough.' Luke was red in the face with anger. 'I'll find the odious culprit. Edwin, you'll come with me and I'll talk to

Sam. Anna,' he commanded, 'do what you can for Dora.'

He strode purposefully across the room, beckoning his son to follow him, and as he passed her Edwin gave Dora a look of pure loathing, which Anna saw.

'Try not to worry,' she murmured to her. 'I believe you.'

'Sam! Sam! Where are you, boy?' Luke hurried across the yard.

'Here, sir.' Sam came out of one of the stables carrying a hay fork. 'I'm mucking out, sir, while the two young ladies are out.'

'There's trouble, Sam, and I need to know if you're involved in it.'

Sam looked startled, his fresh face flushing. 'What sort o' trouble, Mr Kingston? What 'ave I done?'

'Have you had knowledge of Dora?'

Sam frowned. 'I know her, sir, if that's what you mean.'

'I mean . . .' Luke hesitated. How to put the case without seeming to apportion blame. 'I mean that Dora is expecting a child and the act took place without her consent.'

Sam's jaw appeared to drop and he gave an involuntary gasp. 'Not Dora!' His voice was strangled. 'But,' he groped for words, 'I was going to—'

'What? You were going to what?' Luke took a step towards the stable lad.

'I was going to ask her to walk out wi' me. When she had her next day off, and now you're saying she's – she's got somebody else!' He looked the picture of misery. He shook his head. 'I didn't think she – who else is there?' He appeared to consider. 'But what do you mean, sir, without her consent?'

He's not very bright, Luke thought, but perhaps I didn't make myself clear. 'I mean that she was forced, and she's accusing my son, who in turn is accusing you!'

Sam shook his head in bewilderment. 'I wouldn't do that. Anyway, I hardly ever see Dora on her own. Onny sometimes if she brings me a bit o' pie from Cook.' He looked up at Edwin as if suddenly all was clear. 'Is it you? Have you done this?'

Edwin shrugged and lifted his hands. He wore a scornful expression. 'She says I have. It's her word against mine. You know what these young girls are like; they'll blame anybody as soon as their teasing goes wrong.'

'Dora's not a tease,' Sam shouted as if he'd suddenly found his voice. 'She wouldn't know how. We're not like that, her and me. We're different from you lot!' He lifted the hay fork threateningly. 'Are you telling me that you forced yourself on her and now she's carrying

371

your bairn? And you've spoiled her for any-body else!'

'Sam,' Luke broke in. 'Wait. Could it be any-body else? Was Dora seeing anyone else?'

'How?' Sam said belligerently. 'How could she wi' hours she works, and anyway who else is there? There's onny owd Amos, or it could be you or Mr Howard if it isn't Mr Edwin!' Even in his fury Sam gave everyone their title. 'It's him all right. I've seen him hanging about as if he was waiting for somebody. I never thought as it'd be Dora!'

He lifted the fork again and lunged at Edwin, who jumped back. 'You deserve a hiding for what you've done. Nobody'll want her now.'

'Come now, Sam.' Luke tried to intervene. 'Steady on. Dora's been wronged, but—'

Sam brushed his remark aside. 'My fight's not wi' you, sir. It's wi' that arrogant dog. He never does a hand's work; he lords it over everybody and doesn't know how we despise him.'

He threw down the hayfork and hurled him-self on to Edwin, jostling him to the ground and raining blows on him. He threw a punch under Edwin's chin, shouting, 'That's for Dora,' and then again in his ribs, muttering, 'and that's for me.'

Edwin pushed him off and hit out, but he was no match for the young stable lad, who hit back even more violently.

Luke, who was bigger and stronger than either of them, forced himself between them and yanked them apart. Edwin was battered and bloody but Sam was not yet finished with him and raised his fist again. Luke grabbed Sam's collar and pulled him off.

'That's enough,' he yelled. 'Stop it.'

Edwin rolled over and rubbed his hand over his face and saw the blood. 'Look what he's done! I'll have the constable here and charge him with assault.'

'On your feet, both of you,' Luke ordered. 'There'll be no police here. This is a private matter. Get inside,' he told Edwin. 'I'll deal with you shortly.'

As Edwin slunk off, Luke turned to Sam. 'I want the truth. If what Dora says is true then I'll disown him. Think carefully before you speak and condemn me to losing my only son.'

'I'm sorry, sir, but it's not my child.' Sam wiped his hand over his chin. 'I'm eighteen and never yet been wi' a lass. Whether it's Mr Edwin's I don't know, but if Dora says it is then I'd stake my life on it. Why would she lie?' He took a grubby rag from his pocket and blew his nose. 'He's ruined my life as well as yours and Dora's, for I'll not want her now. She's spoiled.'

'Then you are blaming her for a sin she's not guilty of,' Luke told him. 'This girl has been cruelly used.'

Sam frowned. 'But not by me. And why should I bring up another man's child?' he said bitterly. 'I'd see its father's face every time I looked at it. And,' he jabbed his finger in the direction of the house, 'he'd continue to deny it was his bairn if I married Dora to save her face. He'd walk off scot free!'

'No. He will not.' Luke turned away to go back to the house. 'He'll be punished.'

'What about me?' Sam called after him. 'Do I get fired now for giving the maister's son a beating?'

His employer turned to face him. 'You'll keep a civil tongue in your head, Sam Little.' His voice was tight and full of tension. 'Remember who you are speaking to. I've not blamed you, I simply asked you a question and you have answered it. Now go back to work.'

Luke felt low as never before. He gave a deep sigh. The happiness he had enjoyed since marrying Anna was melting away. He had always had a difficult relationship with his son; Edwin was a shirker, he knew that, but he would never have thought that he was dishonourable.

He went in search of Anna. He must talk it over with her and decide on the best course of action. She was a sensible woman as well as a beautiful one.

Edwin was waiting in the corner by the

servants' stairs. He hoped he might catch Dora and persuade her to change her story, but he saw his father go towards Anna's sitting room. He grimaced disdainfully. He'll be going to ask her advice. He can no longer make his own decisions. He'll let a pretty face decide for him.

Stealthily he stole out from his hiding place, unlocked the gun cupboard, took out his gun and moved hastily towards the door.

'I'll teach Sam Little a lesson he'll not forget,' he muttered. 'I'll show him for speaking to me the way he did.' He closed the door softly behind him and headed down the steps and round the house towards the stable yard.

Dora stood by the attic window. Mrs Kingston had suggested she go upstairs whilst Mr Kingston spoke to Sam. From her vantage point she'd seen Edwin come back to the house, holding a bloody handkerchief to his nose, and then Mr Kingston. Tears flooded her face. They'll have told Sam now, she thought. What will he think? Will he blame me? He'll not want me, anyway. Nobody will, not now. She stifled a sob. How ever will I manage? Where will I live? And even if Mr Kingston gives me money for the bairn everybody will know it for a bastard.

She leaned her forehead against the glass for

a better view. Mr Edwin was heading towards the stable block again. Was he going back to confront Sam on his own? Then she saw he was carrying a field gun like the ones they used for grouse shooting, and she drew a breath.

The crack of the shot was heard in the house and Dora up by the window saw Edwin run back across the yard.

'He's killed him,' she wailed. 'He's killed Sam.' She clutched her hands to her face. 'Will he be coming for me next?' She began to shake. 'What can I do?'

In her fear there was only one thing she could do, she decided, for no one could save her from the shame of her condition or being involved in a murder, and nobody would help her now that Sam was dead. Not Mr or Mrs Kingston. Nobody! She picked up her shawl and threw it round her shoulders and scuttled down the stairs towards the side door, which was hardly ever used. She rattled the rusty bolt with trembling fingers and it yielded, nicking her thumb and drawing blood. She pulled open the door and fled.

CHAPTER THIRTY-THREE

'Dora!' Polly and Rosalie raised their voices in unison. They saw Dora look up, hesitate and then hurry on.

'Where's she going?' Polly said.

They urged on their ponies and caught up with Dora, but she was reluctant to talk to them.

'Dora! What are you doing out here so far from Nab Farm?' Rosalie asked her. 'You'll catch a chill without a coat.'

'I don't care,' she moaned. 'I don't care even if I die. There's nowt left for me to live for.'

'You'll have a child to live for,' Rosalie said unwisely, which made Dora howl even more.

'I don't want it,' she wailed. 'I'm too young to be a mother. It was forced on me.'

True, Polly thought. But there's nothing to be done about it now.

Dora stopped her stumbling run and they

reined in. 'Besides,' Dora gasped and held her side. 'There's summat else and I don't want to be blamed for it.' She began to weep and then to run again.

'Wait! Wait!' Polly jumped down, handed the reins to Rosalie and ran after her. 'What? What's worse? Has Edwin denied it?'

'Yes. And he blamed Sam.' She opened her mouth and howled. 'And now Sam's dead!'

'Dead!' Polly breathed. 'How? Rosalie,' she called. 'Come here. She says that Sam's dead. She's hysterical.'

'We must get her to some shelter.' Rosalie dismounted and put her arm round Dora's shoulder. 'Will you come up on one of the ponies and we'll find a place to keep dry?'

Dora shook her head. 'No. I want to go home,' she mumbled. 'I want my ma.'

'Is that where you were going?' Polly asked her. 'You said your ma wouldn't have you.'

'She'll not begrudge me a night's shelter.' Dora wiped her eyes. 'But I'll have to be gone by morning. Especially when they hear about Mr Edwin and Sam. They'll not want owt to do wi' that.'

'With what?' Rosalie said.

'Did they fight?' Polly asked.

'I don't know,' Dora snivelled. 'I didn't see. But I saw Mr Edwin carrying a gun and going towards the stables, and then I heard a shot. I ran,' she said. 'Cos I didn't want to hear what had happened.'

'So – you don't know that Sam is dead,' Rosalie said slowly and calmly. 'You only think he is?'

'Why else would Mr Edwin take a gun?' Dora said. 'If it wasn't to kill him with it?'

'To scare him,' Polly said, 'but 'boot should be on 'other foot. Sam should be 'one with a grudge.'

'Where do your parents live, Dora?' Rosalie asked. 'We'll take you home.'

Dora agreed to go up behind Rosalie and they rode towards the stone cottage between Littlebeck and Grosmont. The rain had almost stopped, but now and again they heard the distant crash of thunder.

'It's onny a summer storm,' Dora muttered, when Rosalie remarked that she hoped the rain wouldn't start again. 'The weather changes quickly up here. One minute it's sunny and the next you can't see a hand in front of you.'

She seemed to have got over her crying fit, though every now and again Rosalie could feel a sudden sob shake her body.

Only Dora's mother was at home when they arrived at the cottage about an hour later. There was a bright fire burning and a pan of soup simmering on it. Dora burst into tears when she saw her mother and it was

379

left to Rosalie and Polly to explain what had happened.

'Dora's feared that you'll disown her,' Polly said. 'But it wasn't her fault.'

'We hope that you'll treat her kindly,' Rosalie added.

'What a showing up,' Dora's mother said, tight-lipped. 'I don't know what her da will say. He's allus held Mr Kingston in such high esteem.'

Rosalie and Polly glanced at one another. Such repercussions. The shame of it would reflect on everybody, not just Dora and Edwin.

'Will you allow Dora to stay for a few days?' Rosalie asked. 'Whilst the family decide what is to be done about supporting her and the child?'

'Aye, I reckon so,' the mother said. 'We'll not be able to afford to keep her, 'n' that's a fact. It's hard enough to mek ends meet without bringing up a bairn as well.'

Rosalie and Polly then left, saying they must get back before dark as everyone would worry about them. Had the weather been favourable it would have stayed light for much longer, but the sky was heavy with rain clouds and they had a considerable distance to travel.

'I'm so cold,' Rosalie said as she mounted Damon.

'Me too,' Polly agreed. 'And wet right through to my shift. Come on then, let's be off. Can we find our way back, do you think, or will we get lost?'

Luke and Amos carried Sam into the house. 'This is a fine kettle o' fish,' Amos muttered. Everyone had rushed outside when they heard the shot: Luke, followed by Anna, though she had made Elizabeth stay indoors; Mrs Moody and Amos, who were having a cup of tea in the kitchen. Sam was trying to stand but clutching his leg, which was bleeding profusely.

'Just as well Mr Edwin's a bad shot, sir, or we might have had a murder on our hands,' Amos continued. 'He never did manage to bag as much as a couple o' brace o' fowl.'

Luke nodded. And thank God for it, he thought. But where is he now and will Sam Little press charges?

They lowered Sam down on the hall floor and Anna and Mrs Moody brought a bowl of hot water, scissors and bandages. Luke cut through Sam's breeches to expose the wound, and said, 'Thank heavens. It's only a flesh wound, but we might have to get the doctor to look at it.'

Sam grimaced and said, 'Never had a doctor in my life, sir, but I don't want it to go septic. I need my legs for work.'

Anna gently bathed his leg. The shot had

grazed his calf, leaving a small hole, which was why there was so much blood, but she said she thought it would heal over.

'We'll get the doctor,' she said, 'in case he needs to put in a suture. I'm so sorry, Sam. So very sorry.'

The front door suddenly opened and Howard came in. 'Where is everybody?' he said. 'We have a visitor and no stable lad – oh!' He took a startled breath when he saw them all clustered round Sam. 'What's happened?'

'An accident,' Luke said. 'Sam has sustained a wound.'

'Cartridge!' Howard said, looking down at the injury. 'What was Sam doing with a loaded shotgun?'

'I'll tell you later.' Luke straightened up. 'Thank you, Amos. We can manage now.' There was no need to ask for Amos's discretion. Luke knew him well enough to know he would not discuss the incident. 'Who is the visitor?' he asked Howard anxiously. 'Someone we know?'

'Yes.' Howard rubbed his hand over his stubble. 'It's Sonny Blake. He's in the yard stabling the horses. I met him up on the moor. We got home just in time; there's a storm heading this way.'

'I'll give him a hand, Mr Howard,' Amos said. 'If I'm not needed here. Do you want me to fetch the doctor, sir?' he asked Luke.

'Yes, I think so,' Luke said. 'Just tell him there's been an accident and would he come and take a look.'

Luke was very anxious. If Sam made a complaint and told the doctor what had happened, the medical man was duty bound to inform the constable and that would mean very big trouble for Edwin.

Howard and Luke helped Sam into a chair by the hall fire and Mrs Moody brought a foot stool for him to put his leg up.

'I think a pot of strong tea is called for, Mrs Moody,' Anna said. 'And plenty of sugar in it for Sam.'

Sonny came in a few minutes later. 'Amos told me there's been an accident,' he said. 'Is there anything I can do?'

There wasn't and so they all sat about looking at Sam and drinking their tea. Presently Sonny said casually, 'And are the young ladies at home?'

'Clemmie's still in Scarborough,' Howard told him. 'I expect Polly and Rosalie are around somewhere.'

'Beg pardon, sir,' Sam said, clutching his cup. 'Miss Polly and Miss Rosalie have gone out.'

Anna glanced towards the window. 'I hope they haven't gone far. The sky looks very threatening.'

'Towards Kirk Moor, ma'am,' Sam said. 'Heading north, anyway.'

Howard bit on his lip. 'That's where the storm is coming from. I hope they've got waterproofs with them.'

'It wasn't raining when they set out,' Sam said. 'The sun was shining. It was about half hour afore – afore Mr Kingston and Mr Edwin came to the yard.'

Mrs Moody came up the back stairs. 'Excuse me, Mrs Kingston, but I've just been told that Dora isn't in her room and has hardly been seen in the kitchen since first thing.'

'Mm,' Anna murmured anxiously. 'I've been meaning to speak to you about her.'

The housekeeper folded her arms over her chest and said grimly, 'Young scullery maid said she saw her talking to Miss Polly earlier, and just after we heard the commotion from the yard she saw Dora running down the track.'

Clearly, from her tone of voice, she was blaming Polly for the maid's absence.

'I'd asked Polly to speak to Dora,' Anna said. 'And I'm afraid she was very upset when I spoke to her.'

'Who was upset?' Howard interrupted. 'Polly?'

'No.' Anna glanced at him, noting his instant reaction. 'Though she was concerned about

Dora. My dear,' she said to Luke, 'I'm afraid you'll have to explain this situation; distasteful as it might be there is nothing else for it. And by the way, where is Edwin?'

Sam didn't want to stay whilst the revelations of the day were being discussed, and asked if he might be taken to his room above the stable. Howard and Sonny piggybacked him across the yard and saw him safely up the wooden steps to the loft above.

'Very cosy,' Sonny said. 'Almost as comfortable as mine.'

Sam nodded. 'I expect I shall have to move out now. I can't work here any more. It'd never do.'

'So what's happened, Sam?' Howard asked. 'Let's hear it from your own lips.'

When they arrived back at the house, Sam had told them everything, and Anna had explained to Mrs Moody, who flatly refused to believe that Mr Edwin would ever do such a thing.

'The girl must have led him on,' she declared. 'You can't blame him. It's man's nature to – to . . .'

'It is not to be tolerated, Mrs Moody,' Luke bellowed. 'I will not have such conduct condoned. Now, please leave us. I expect you to be discreet about the whole affair.'

'Well, of course, sir,' she sniffed. 'That goes

without saying, but I know Mr Edwin as well as anybody in this household—'

'Enough!' Luke said curtly, his eyes cold. 'I don't wish to discuss it.'

Howard and Sonny came in to find that Anna and Luke had adjourned to her sitting room.

'Sam has told us,' Howard began. 'I'm so sorry, Luke, and sorry for the girl.' But I'm not sorry for that blackguard Edwin, he thought. And I hope that his father drums him out of the house.

'I'm getting concerned about Polly and Rosalie,' he said aloud. 'If you don't mind I'd like to go and look for them.'

'We,' Sonny interrupted. 'I'll come with you. The rain's heavy now and if they haven't gone prepared for bad weather we'd be as well to take waterproofs with us.'

'Yes, of course,' Luke muttered. 'They don't know the moors; they could easily take a wrong path. But what about the servant girl? Where do you think she's gone?'

'Perhaps she's gone home to her parents,' Howard said. 'They live somewhere between Grosmont and Littlebeck. We'll keep an eye open for her.'

There was a sudden crack of thunder overhead as the storm reached them.

'Oh, dear.' Anna was concerned. 'Yes, please

do go, Howard. I'd hate it if they got lost. But who knows where they went?'

'I think I might have an idea,' Howard said. 'Sam said they'd gone north and Polly mentioned the other day that she wanted to see the standing stones up at Ramsdale. She's intrigued by them. I reckon that's where they've gone.'

CHAPTER THIRTY-FOUR

The two men reined in and looked into the distance. They'd ridden almost as far as Ramsdale, but Howard had called a halt.

'They'd be on their way back by now,' he said. 'And there's no sign of them so they must be returning by a different route. They could be anywhere.'

'Do they have a favourite ride?' Sonny asked. 'Somewhere they've been before?'

Howard shrugged. 'They were becoming quite adventurous. They've been to Old Wife's Neck but that's not so far and they'd have been back by now.'

'Suppose they've been to Ramsdale and decided to cut across the top end of Fylingdale towards May Beck. That's a nice ride when it's fine.'

'Yes, you're right,' Howard agreed. 'Or they might have gone on to Littlebeck; I took them there one day.'

They swung about and set off at a canter. They both sat well in the saddle although Howard had a more confident seat. He rode every day when he was checking on the sheep. Sonny only rode when he came to the moors or when he was abroad. Both were wearing heavy waterproofs and hats and carrying blankets and waterproofs in case Polly and Rosalie needed them.

Another half-hour and no sign of anyone. The sky was overcast with dark and ominous clouds and there was an occasional rumble of thunder. Howard reined in again.

'I'm getting very bothered,' he said. 'I think we might have to go back to Nab Farm and raise some help.'

'Wait a minute.' Sonny pointed. 'Over there. Towards the ridge. Can you see? Two riders.' He put his hand to his forehead and narrowed his eyes. 'I think it's them!'

Howard exhaled. 'Thank God! This is no time to be out on the moor. Come on.' He dug his heels into his horse's flanks. 'Let's go and give them both a piece of our mind.'

They hollered as they drew nearer and waved their hats, and saw the girls wave back.

'Where in heaven's name have you been?' Howard shouted when they were near enough. 'Everybody's worried sick.'

Sonny glanced at him and gave a wry grin.

It was Howard who was more worried than anybody. 'We were about to send out a search party,' he added, knowing full well that he was anxious too.

'We wish you had,' Polly called in return, and as they met she blurted out, 'We found Dora; she was running away so we took her home. She gave us some story about Sam being shot by Edwin. Is it true?'

They said that it was but that it was only a flesh wound and Sam was going to be all right.

Polly sneezed. 'Good,' she sniffed. 'We got lost coming back from Dora's. I think we took the long way home.'

There was another crack of thunder, nearer this time, and as Howard glanced east towards the coast he could see flashes of lightning lighting up the sky.

'We'll have to find shelter,' he urged the others. 'We can't stay out here.'

'High Ridge House then?' Sonny said. 'It can't be far.'

'It's not,' Howard said. 'Thirty minutes if we get a move on, fifty if we dawdle. Are you ready, ladies? Have you the energy to canter?'

They had, they both agreed. Anything to get out of the constant rain. Urging on their mounts, within thirty-five minutes they arrived at the house on the hill. The horses were brought inside for shelter too and soon their flanks began to steam.

'I wish I could build up heat like that,' Polly said. She shivered; she was so cold that her teeth were chattering.

Rosalie too was shaking so much that she could barely speak.

'Here,' Sonny said. 'Take your jackets off; they're soaked through.'

Their fingers shook as they unbuttoned their jackets, while Howard took the blankets and waterproofs from the horses' backs. He and Sonny wrapped the girls snugly into them, and then without a moment's hesitation each enclosed a girl within his arms, Sonny holding Rosalie and Howard hugging Polly.

They stood by a cracked window and looked out at the storm, which was unleashing all the violence of strong wind and sleeting rain; heavy bursts of thunder and streaks of forked lightning lit up the sky and the moor.

Howard rested his chin on top of Polly's head. 'Magnificent,' he murmured. 'I know you're cold, Polly, but isn't that a wonderful sight?'

Polly nodded. It was; and she felt she was beginning to thaw now that she had the warmth of Howard's arms round her. It was very comforting, she thought; and safe.

'You think this is magnificent,' Sonny said,

'and it is. But I've been out in summer storms by the Italian lakes and that is a sight worth seeing. Simply fantastical.'

'I'd like to see that,' Rosalie's voice trembled. She was unnerved by being so close to Sonny. He was much taller than she was and had his arms about her shoulders, encircling her completely. It was not at all unpleasant, she thought, just unexpected. *It is as well that there is no one to see us, for I don't know what anyone might think.* She swallowed hard. *He is being kind, protecting me from the cold, but is he taking advantage of me? Will he speak of this incident to anyone else?*

She glanced at Polly, who was in the same situation yet didn't seem at all perturbed. *There are different rules,* Rosalie thought. *Polly hasn't had to follow the same path of convention, nor has she been taught to keep her emotions and feelings under control; and although I'm sure she is virtuous, she hasn't had to consider the moral path as I have.*

She gave a sudden start as she thought of her father, and what he would have to say if he should hear that she had been alone with a man, a man who had held her tight within his arms.

'Are you all right, Rosalie?' Sonny eased away from her and loosened his arms. He had felt her flinch as if she had been burned or scorched, and with a sudden awareness he knew that he shouldn't have stood so near. He had felt her hair on his face, seen her slender neck as he'd placed the blanket round her. It will not do, he thought. I've embarrassed her. Perhaps she thinks I've dishonoured her, and that was not my intention. He stood back. 'Are you warmer now?'

She looked away from him. 'Yes, thank you,' she murmured.

'Please don't be distressed.' His voice was low so that the others couldn't hear. 'I only wanted to keep you from catching a chill. See how the horses stand so close. That is what animals do to keep warm. The heat from their bodies . . .'

His words trailed away. What was the use, he thought impatiently. She has been ruined by pious dignity, never been allowed self-expression; will never be permitted to make her own decisions. She will fit into the slot which her father and her mother chose for her the moment she was born.

'Are you angry with me?' she said quietly.

'What?' he muttered. 'Angry? Why would I be angry?' But he was.

'I don't know,' she said. 'I just felt that you were.'

She gazed at him. A shiver ran down her spine, but it was something other than the cold.

Something she had never experienced before; she was unsure what it meant.

She took hold of his hand. 'I find that I am still very cold after all,' she murmured. 'Would you . . .'

She placed his hand on her waist and, though he frowned, instinctively he drew her closer.

'Are you sure?' he whispered in her ear.

'Oh, yes,' she breathed. 'I am. I'm very cold indeed.'

Howard was puzzled. Sonny was standing very close to Rosalie and they were murmuring something, but he couldn't hear what. It seems very odd, he thought. They seem so intimate, and yet I assumed that he and Polly . . . Sonny told me that he had promised her mother he would look after Polly. Always, he said. And he said he had met a lovely woman to die for. Didn't he mean—

He stood still, barely breathing. Did he not mean Polly after all? He gave an intake of breath. He meant *Rosalie*! Not Polly. Not my Polly, whom I adore!

'Howard,' Polly said. 'What'll happen to Edwin? Did he intend to hurt Sam, or was it an accident?'

She's still so young, so immature, he thought affectionately. Not ready for a commitment. But I can wait.

'An accident, I think,' he hedged. 'Look, the

sky's brightening. Another half-hour or so and we'll be able to move off.'

Polly turned within his arms and lifted her face to his. 'Thank you for rescuing us,' she said and reached up to kiss his cheek. She smiled. 'However would we have got home without you?'

He grinned down at her and patted her cheek. 'Always at your service, madam. Always ready to rescue you.'

When they reached Nab Farm, hot baths were prepared and Rosalie and Polly were sent upstairs to bathe before having supper brought up to them in bed.

'What bliss.' Polly pulled her white cotton nightgown over her head and climbed between the sheets. 'Do you feel all right?' she called to Rosalie. 'Are you warm now?'

'Oh, yes!' Rosalie called back. 'I feel absolutely fine.'

A few minutes later Polly's door opened and Rosalie came in. 'Can I get in with you?' Without waiting for an answer, she took off her dressing robe and climbed in beside her. 'I want to ask you something.'

She took a breath. 'Have you ever been in love, Polly? You've lived a different life from me and I don't know how it would feel to fall in love with someone. I've always lived such a sheltered existence.'

Polly gazed at her with wide open eyes. 'I'm not sure,' she said. 'Not when I was young, I didn't,' she said.

'But you're only young now,' Rosalie laughed.

'Yes, but now I'm a bit older I've got different feelings from when I was a child. It's to do with 'flux, I think,' she said seriously. 'You start to feel different about everything once that's started, and sometimes I feel all churned up inside as if I'm waiting for something to happen. Something nice, I mean.'

'Yes,' Rosalie said slowly. 'So do you think it's something physical? That churning? And it's got nothing to do with meeting someone whom you think you might fall in love with? It's a hypothetical question, of course,' she added hastily. 'I'm not speaking of real people.'

Polly gave a wide grin. She'd seen how close Sonny had been standing to Rosalie. Seen how they'd whispered together. And she knew, too, Sonny's secret.

'*Hi-pathetical!*' she teased. 'I'm not sure what that means; but I think if you meet somebody and you get that churning feeling when he's there, then,' she paused, 'I think 'chances are that you probably do love him.'

The front door slammed and they heard Luke shout something and then another door slammed. They looked at each other.

'Do you think Luke and Edwin are having a set-to?' Polly said. 'Edwin wasn't in when we arrived back, at least not unless he was in his room.'

'Perhaps he's been sent off in disgrace,' Rosalie whispered. 'How will he ever be able to face society again after getting a servant girl into trouble?'

'Never mind him,' Polly said fiercely. 'How will Dora ever face anybody again?'

After breakfast the next day, Anna asked Mrs Moody to ask Mrs Browning, the cook, to come upstairs as she wanted to speak to her. Mrs Moody looked askance at this as she generally passed on any messages to Cook.

'Please stay,' Anna said to Rosalie and Polly. 'I'd like your opinion after I've spoken to Mrs Browning.'

Cook was tall and thin as a stick. She hardly ever ate, not even at the servants' mealtimes, being always too busy dishing up and making sure everyone else was well fed.

'Mrs Browning,' Anna said, 'I want to ask your opinion of Dora. Is she, do you think, a reliable sort of girl? I'm not speaking of her present difficulties, but of how she is around the house and kitchen.'

'Aye, she is, ma'am. Well, when Mrs Moody's not about she is. If the housekeeper's there she gets into a bit of a pickle. I think the lass is scared of her sharp tongue, just like all the maids are,' she added.

'That's exactly what I thought,' Anna said when Cook had gone. 'Dora works well except under Mrs Moody's rule.'

'What are you planning, Aunt Anna?' Rosalie asked. 'Have you something in mind for Dora?'

'I have if my husband agrees and if Dora is willing. I'd like her to go to my farm. There are only two men living in and they need very little attention. There's a cook who comes in daily to prepare their dinner and supper, and a general maid who sleeps in. Dora could live in too and look after the place. And she could keep the baby there.' She sighed. 'But it depends on what's to be done about Edwin. Luke has to make a big decision.' She sighed again and then gave a sudden start. 'Rosalie! I quite forgot with all the fuss yesterday. A letter came for you by the second post. I think it might be from your father.'

The letter was lying on a plate on the hall table. Rosalie picked it up and, recognizing her father's handwriting, took it back into Anna's sitting room.

'It is from Papa,' she smiled. 'I was beginning to think he'd forgotten me.'

Anna handed her a paper knife to open the

envelope and she withdrew two sheets of note-
paper. She put them to her nose and sniffed.
Mm! Rose water, she thought.

My dear Rosalie [the letter began],

I apologize for the length of time
which has elapsed since the promise of
a letter. I regret also that a soldier's life
is so consumed with activities that I was
hindered in my duty of writing to you, my
dearest daughter.

I trust that your life at Nab Farm
continues satisfactorily and that you afford
your uncle and aunt every consideration
and gratitude which is their due for giving
you a home. I hope too that you have now
come to terms with your mother's untimely
death. She had a satisfactory though
relatively short life and we, that is you and
I, must continue with ours as she would
surely have wished.

I have decided therefore that when my
mourning period is over I shall marry
again. There is a widow of a fellow officer, a
Mrs Sherwood, to whom I have formed an
attachment; her mourning seclusion is over
and I have asked her if she will do me the
honour of becoming my wife in the near
future. I understand that she cannot take
the place of your own mother, but, caring

and charming as she is and mother to her own delightful children, she will, I am sure, find a place in your affections once you know her. To this end I wish you to prepare yourself to come to Aldershot before the winter to take up residence with her and her family. I am shortly leaving for abroad and when I return in the spring, when propriety concedes it appropriate, we shall be married.

There was more but Rosalie put down the letter. Her eyes roamed the room without seeing the contents or inhabitants of it. Marry again! So soon! How could he? She shook her head. And he wants me to live with her!

'I won't,' she said, and Anna and Polly gazed curiously at her. 'I won't!'

CHAPTER THIRTY-FIVE

'What?' Polly asked curiously. 'You won't what?'

'Papa is going to marry again and he wants me to go and live with this Mrs Sherwood until it's proper for them to marry! I won't go to Aldershot and live with this woman.' Rosalie's voice rose. 'I won't.'

'If your father says you must go, then go you must,' Anna said quietly. 'You're too young to make the decision to stay.' Her voice dropped. 'But for him to marry again so soon after your mother's death . . .' She was visibly shocked by the revelation. 'And this woman he is to marry – how long has she been widowed?'

'I don't know, but I can't go, Aunt Anna,' Rosalie said tearfully. 'How can I live with a woman I don't know?'

'But you didn't know Luke,' Anna reminded her, 'and yet you came here; and perhaps that is why your father wants you to live with her, so that you can get to know her.'

'But Uncle Luke was a relative,' Rosalie wailed. 'And besides, I had Polly with me. Mrs Sherwood is a complete stranger who's going to marry my father and I shall probably have to play nursemaid to her children! I must speak to Uncle Luke and ask him if I can stay here.'

'I don't know where he is, my dear,' Anna said. 'He's gone looking for Edwin. They had harsh words last night and Luke told him they must resolve the dilemma today.' She pressed her lips together. 'But this morning Luke discovered that Edwin had gone out. He's taken his horse and according to Amos he went off before dawn. I'm very worried about both of them. I just hope that Luke doesn't lose his temper when he finds him. He threatened to horsewhip him, but I don't think . . . no, of course he won't.'

'Oh.' Rosalie's hopes of getting Luke on her side were dashed. 'I don't want to trouble him when he has so much on his mind.'

Polly wore a sceptical expression. She said nothing, rather hoping that Edwin might get what he deserved, but she was unnerved by Rosalie's news. What would she do if Rosalie's father insisted that her friend went to live in Aldershot? Mark Kingston wouldn't include her, she was sure; she had seen it in his eyes when she had met him at the wedding. He knew she wasn't a suitable companion for his daughter.

Howard came into the dining room, followed by Sonny. 'Hello!' Howard said. 'I wondered where everybody was. Late breakfast?'

Howard and Sonny had risen early and the two of them had been repairing fences.

'I'm looking for Luke,' Howard went on. 'I need to ask him what we're doing about the shoot at the weekend. I've heard the guns already over at Goathland. We'll need to move the sheep if we're having folks up here.'

'Oh, heavens,' Anna said. 'I'd forgotten! Haven't you seen Luke?' she asked in concern. 'He went to find Edwin. He's been gone some time.'

Howard blew out his cheeks. 'No. And we've been out since six. Would you like me to look for him – them?'

'I'm sure they'll be all right,' Anna said nervously. 'It's just that he was rather angry when he went out. He and Edwin had words last night over the Sam and Dora incident. There's fresh coffee, Sonny, if you'd like it,' she added, always the gracious hostess. 'We're lingering. We're having a strange morning what with one thing and another. I'm bothered about Luke, and Rosalie – well.' She stopped, as if realizing that Rosalie might not want to discuss her father's ultimatum.

Sonny poured himself a cup of coffee and came to sit near Rosalie at the table.

'Has something upset you?' he asked quietly.

Rosalie nodded. 'Yes. I've just realized that I am not mistress of my own life but still a child,' she said rather bitterly. 'Even though I consider myself to be grown up.'

'Indeed,' Sonny agreed. 'Putting up one's hair does not a grown woman make.' He smiled at her. 'Circumstances can give liberation, and childhood is but fleeting.'

'At what age would you consider childhood to be passed?' she asked him in a low voice. 'Apart from the obvious, of course, when a child is dependent upon its mother for food and shelter.'

Sonny pursed his lips. 'That's a difficult question. For instance, I know that Polly has been grown up since she was twelve or thirteen, when she started work and began to earn her own living. For someone like you, bearing in mind that you could marry with consent, childhood would be behind you at sixteen, and the advantage of an education would hasten the onset of adulthood. If you'd attended to your lessons, that is,' he added teasingly. 'Is there a reason for the question?' he asked when she didn't smile at his joke.

'Oh, yes,' she said. 'There is.' She began to tell him of the contents of her father's letter, whilst Polly watched them solemnly from across the table.

Perhaps I could be a lady's maid, Polly told herself silently. Though I don't think I'd like that. Not to some toffee-nosed woman who only cared about her clothes and her looks. I've been spoiled now with 'freedom that I've enjoyed here at Nab Farm. Would Anna keep me on? I'd be happy to work for her, though she doesn't seem to require a personal maid; she's perfectly capable of looking after herself.

Sonny closed his eyes as he deliberated on what to say to Rosalie. It was too soon to declare his intentions, and in his present precarious financial position he was in no doubt that Rosalie's father would dismiss him out of hand. He had been offered a chance of a commission in Italy, which might lead to other work, but it could take years to become established. He felt totally despondent. Rosalie was too young to know her own mind and he wouldn't want her to consider marrying him only to escape the pressure of her father's demands.

'Could you, erm – could you forestall him?' he said in an undertone. 'Tell him that you have made other arrangements?'

He saw the puzzlement in her eyes and attempted to clarify his vague suggestion.

'Perhaps say that you're needed here for some reason or other?'

'Like what?' she said in frustration. 'I'm never needed! I'm not like Polly who is so practical and sensible. I'm totally dispensable!'

'Oh, my dear.' Anna had heard her outburst. 'That is just not true.' She glanced at the three of them sitting glumly at the table and at Howard, who was helping himself to a second breakfast at the sideboard, totally unaware of this other dilemma.

She huffed out a breath. 'We were not going to tell anyone just yet; Luke and I agreed that we'd wait a little longer. Elizabeth knows, but Clementina doesn't and nor does Edwin. We were not sure how they would take the news.'

Polly's face lit up. Brilliant! She'll need a nursemaid!

'What, Aunt?' Rosalie asked. 'Is it good news?'

Anna smiled. 'It's excellent news. I'm expecting a child.'

Howard put down his plate and Sonny pushed back his chair and stood up; both went towards her.

'I'm delighted,' Howard said and kissed her hand. Sonny too, bent over her.

'It's wonderful news,' he smiled.

Rosalie and Polly looked at each other. Their eyes gleamed, but for different reasons.

'We must take great care of you, Mrs Kingston,' Polly said, and tears came unbidden to her eyes as she thought of her own mother. 'Great care.'

'I'm thrilled, Aunt Anna,' Rosalie murmured, finding herself unexpectedly embarrassed. 'Are you pleased?'

'Oh, yes.' Anna laughed. 'I always wanted lots of children, but after my first husband's death I never thought my wish would be granted.'

'So . . .' Rosalie heaved a breath and dared, 'So may we stay and look after you? Polly and I?'

'I was hoping that you would,' Anna said softly. 'For a little while anyway. At least until the birth, which will be early spring, and then, well, who knows what you might like to do afterwards? You will no doubt have dreams of your own to fulfil, but you are always welcome here.'

The room seemed now to be filled with happiness when just a few moments before there had been anxiety and gloom.

'I'll go and look for Luke,' Howard said. 'And I'll ask Amos to come with me and we'll look for Edwin too,' he added. 'But not a word of this, I promise,' he said as Anna cast him a glance. 'That news is for you and his father to tell.'

And he will not be pleased, he thought as

he ran down the steps and made his way to the stable block. *If there is another son, Edwin will have his nose well and truly pushed out of joint.*

'Amos,' he called. 'Come on, we're on a mission!'

After an early breakfast Luke had sent Mrs Moody up to Edwin's room to tell him that he was waiting to see him. The housekeeper had returned to say that he was not there. Exasperated, he went to the stables and found Amos mucking out and not happy about it.

'We'll need another lad if Sam's not coming back, sir,' he said. 'I can't look after half a dozen hosses on my own, not as well as all my other jobs.'

'I know, Amos,' Luke said, 'and I don't expect you to. I'm going to fetch Mrs Kingston's lad up from Lower Farm until I've decided what to do about Sam.'

Amos leaned on the hay fork. 'There'll allus be trouble if you keep Sam on here after what's happened, sir. Mr Edwin won't tolerate him an' that's a fact.'

Luke nodded. He'd known Amos for so long that he trusted his judgement. Amos had worked for Luke's uncle when he was a boy and had stayed on when Luke took over.

'Sam's borrowed Miss Polly's hoss, by the by,'

Amos said. 'I told him it would be all right just this once.'

Luke was startled. 'Is he fit enough to ride?'

'He said he was, though the lad can hardly walk,' Amos commented. 'I had to help him up. But he said he wanted to go and see Dora; tell her he's not dead as she thought. Word got back to him from one of the maids that Dora had told the young ladies he'd been shot dead.'

'Have you seen Edwin this morning?' Luke asked.

'Aye, he went out afore fost light. In a mighty hurry he was.'

Mm. Avoiding me, I shouldn't wonder, Luke thought. He'll know I'm going to issue an ultimatum.

'I'll go and look for him,' he told Amos. 'If he should get back before me, tell him I want to speak to him.'

Amos touched his forehead and went to fetch Luke's mount. 'I'll tell him,' he growled. As if he'd listen, he reflected. Good-for-nothing cur.

'Which direction did he take?' Luke called as he mounted.

'Top moor,' Amos replied. 'As if he might be going towards Grosmont.'

Why would he be going over there, Luke wondered. To catch a train? Is he leaving home?

No, he decided. He wouldn't just leave his inheritance behind. But there was something niggling away in his subconscious. Grosmont? Someone had spoken about Grosmont recently. Who was it?

He rode to the top of what he called *his* moor. It was a beautiful morning. The storm of the day before had given a fresh look to the land and a distinctive aroma to the heather, and he took in a deep breath. He loved it here; had done from the moment he had first come as a boy, after which he couldn't wait to return on every holiday from school, unlike his brother Mark who longed to get away and join the military for adventure and excitement.

His thoughts snapped back to the present as he remembered when he had last heard mention of Grosmont. Howard – or was it Sonny? He wasn't sure – anyway, one of them had mentioned Grosmont and said that Dora's parents lived between it and Littlebeck. And of course they did. Dora's father sometimes came as a beater on the shoots. Was that why Edwin was heading that way? His heart gave a lurch. Surely he wasn't going to persuade the girl to say that it wasn't his child. What was he going to offer? Money? An incentive to lie?

'Oh, no,' he said aloud and urged his horse to a canter. 'Oh, no you don't, my boy! You'll face up to your responsibilities or leave the district. You have my word on that.'

Edwin sat astride his horse and looked about him. He hadn't been able to find Dora. When he heard that she had run away, he'd asked Mrs Moody where Dora's parents lived. Running home seemed the obvious thing for such an idiot of a girl to do. He was going to offer her money to get rid of the child and go and live somewhere else. Whitby or Scarborough, perhaps, where he wasn't known.

Mrs Moody had been reluctant to tell him at first, but he had persuaded her. 'Come on,' he'd said. 'I want to find out who really is the father. Why should I get the blame?' And she'd believed him.

'Somewhere near Grosmont,' she'd said. 'Top of Black Brow, I think, but I don't know where.'

There had been no one about to ask and he'd been out for hours. There was little habitation on the moors and he didn't want to ride into Grosmont in case anyone recognized him. The only person he saw was an old shepherd and he was as deaf as a stone and couldn't understand a word he was saying. But he must have read Edwin's disdainful expression for he shook his fist at him and indicated that he should clear off back to where he came from. Edwin gestured back rudely and turned about and headed back down the moor, seeing no alternative to going home to face his father's wrath.

He heard the guns blaring across the moor and remembered that his father would be holding a shoot fairly soon. I might get another shot at Sam Little, he thought. If he's able to walk! He gave a smirk of satisfaction at the thought of the stable lad having a limp for the rest of his life. That'll teach him to mess with me.

He lifted his gun as he saw rabbits in the heather. He carried a breechloader which his father had bought him when he had told him he was interested in grouse shooting. But he knew he wasn't a good shot. He was too impatient and hadn't a good eye, but the rattling fire gave him a thrill. He always blamed the gun for his misfiring, said that the lead escaped from the barrel so that he missed his shot, or that the cartridges were poor quality.

He fired, hit one rabbit but missed another. He didn't stop to pick up the game. He wasn't keen to carry home a bloody corpse; the target and the kill was the thing.

In this area there were many standing stones but he wasn't greatly interested in them, unlike his cousin Howard who had delved into their history. Howard had said, when they were just boys, that they might have been used for astronomical sightings, to which Edwin had replied 'Poppycock', which was his stock answer to anything he didn't understand or wasn't interested in.

To Edwin, the High Bride Stones, Old Wife's Neck and any of the dozens of monoliths on the moor were just rocks to climb on or kick at; he never gave a thought to what their original purpose might have been. From a distance some of them looked like people, some huddling together as if in conversation, others standing apart like strangers not speaking to each other.

He cantered back through them, the hooves of his horse kicking up the heather. He was feeling reckless, and though the horse was sure-footed he knew that some smaller stones were half hidden within the grass and heather and could make him stumble. He slowed a little and narrowed his eyes as he looked into the distance.

But something was moving ahead; was it a horse? Not a sheep, but yes, definitely a horse and rider. He debated whether to ride over and enquire as to the whereabouts of Dora's family home, or to head home; he'd been out since early morning and knew that he would already be in trouble with his father, who had said he wanted to discuss the situation in the cold light of day.

He rode towards the rider anyway, as he was on his track, and then he took a breath and grinned. Well, well, well! He was fit enough to ride, then! He slowed his mount to a walk and, gripping with his knees, raised his gun again. This time he'd make a better job of it. Aim for the shoulder – not to kill him, of course not, just to disable him a little more.

'Sam!' he called. 'Sam Little!'

The rider looked up, and as he did so Edwin took aim.

CHAPTER THIRTY-SIX

'They could be anywhere,' Amos said to Howard. 'Mr Edwin should be on his way back. He's been out since early dawn.'

'Unlike him,' Howard commented, knowing how Edwin liked his bed. 'And you say that Sam's gone out too? A bit unwise, I would have thought.'

'That's what I said to him. His bandage was bloody so the wound hasn't healed.' Amos looked keenly ahead. 'But he was intent on going.'

'Did he know that Edwin was out?' Howard said uneasily.

Amos pursed his lips. 'Not unless he saw him. I didn't tell him, at any rate.' He glanced at Howard. 'You don't think – lad wouldn't hold a grudge!'

'No, I don't think he would,' Howard agreed. 'I was thinking more of the other way round.

But what about Luke? Which way was he heading?'

'Towards Grosmont, I think, to look for Mr Edwin. That's probably where they're all heading.'

'It's a lot of moorland,' Howard said. 'Doesn't mean they'd be on the same patch.'

'No, it doesn't,' Amos muttered. 'They might have gone west across the top of Fylingdale on to Sleights Moor and then up to Grosmont, or north to Littlebeck and then back across Black Brow, but there's no saying that any of them will come back on the same route. So which way shall we go?'

'My instinct would be to head towards Sleights Moor,' Howard said. 'And I've absolutely no reason for saying that.'

'Best to go by gut feeling then.' Amos dug in his heels to urge on his mount. 'And get a move on if we're going to catch up.'

Howard cantered alongside him. He didn't know why he felt uneasy, but he did, especially since Amos had told him that Sam had ridden out. Could they catch up with him? If they did Howard would insist on his returning to Nab Farm. And Luke? Well, he'd been not far behind Sam, apparently. But it was Edwin he was bothered about and he felt that Anna was too. He was sure that she didn't like the thought of her husband and her stepson being

416

out on the moor at the same time when they were at odds with each other.

But why had Edwin gone out so early? Was he avoiding a showdown with his father, or could he not face the family? Was he ashamed of his conduct after all? Howard didn't think so.

They rode in silence, neither of them inclined to small talk. Howard admired Amos for his taciturnity and stability. He liked being out on the shoots with him. He was the most reliable man he had ever come across; he was also the best shot of anyone he knew out on the moor.

After about an hour's hard riding, Howard looked ahead and pointed. 'Is that somebody? Or is it a megalith?'

'Both,' Amos said. 'Looks like one of the stones and somebody – two riders!' He urged his horse to a gallop. 'One of them is Sam,' he yelled. 'I'm sure of it; he's bent over the saddle. I knew he shouldn't have gone out.'

Edwin lowered his gun. What was Sam Little doing? He was hanging over the saddle, one hand clutching his wounded leg. Edwin gave a grunt. He couldn't wing him if he wasn't sitting up straight, not if he hadn't seen him; Edwin wanted Sam to be looking straight at him and terrified of being shot at. I'll make sure that he disappears off the moor in fear of his life, he thought. I'll teach him to attack me; to speak to me the way he did.

'Sam!' He raised his voice again. 'Sam Little!'

He saw the boy look up and then straighten himself, lifting a hand as if imploring him for help, then lowering it again as he saw who was hailing him.

Edwin raised the gun again and took steady aim. 'I'll get you this time,' he muttered. He crooked his trigger finger, narrowed his eyes – and a sudden sharp pain shot through both his hands and arms. His face was peppered with hot lead as the barrel of his gun exploded in his hands. His horse, startled by the blast, reared, unseating him, and took off, leaving Edwin sprawled on his backside on the ground.

'Mr Edwin, sir, are you all right?' Amos towered over him. 'By heavens, sir, you were lucky. I was after that grouse just above you. Didn't see you raise your gun!' He didn't offer to give Edwin a hand up. 'Good thing you didn't fire,' he said. 'You'd have winged young Sam. Didn't you see him coming towards you?' He turned to see Howard talking to Sam. 'He shouldn't be out, o' course. Not wi' that leg.'

Edwin staggered to his feet. 'You've ruined my gun,' he said heatedly. 'Shot clean through the barrel!'

Amos shook his head and gave a deep sigh. 'You couldn't do that again if you tried,' he said. 'I'd call it a lucky shot.'

'A lucky shot!' Edwin screeched. 'A lucky shot! How can you say that? You damned nearly killed me.'

'But I didn't, sir, did I?' Amos stared him out, his back straight and his head up. He wouldn't take any nonsense from this whippersnapper. 'But you might have killed young Sam,' he added in a low voice. 'And that would have taken some explaining.'

Howard had deliberately gone to Sam's aid rather than Edwin's. Amos would be able to clear up any difficulties with Edwin, whereas Howard would have added to his cousin's anger and embarrassment at being shot at and unseated.

He was astonished at Amos's aim and accuracy. How he had managed to shoot the gun out of Edwin's hands without hitting him he'd never know. Amos had seen Edwin's intentions and seized the opportunity, racing ahead as Edwin had raised the gun. His cousin wasn't hurt, he thought, at least not much; only his pride and probably a minor burn.

Howard rather grimly hoped that Edwin might have sustained a slight scar or two. He was carrying his mark from boyhood when

Edwin had attacked him with a knife. It was deliberate, Howard knew, even though Edwin had claimed it was an accident when he was fooling about, and had voiced abject apologies in front of everyone.

'Come on, Sam,' he said now. 'Let's get off home and have that wound seen to.'

Sam was shaking. There was pain etched on his face and bewilderment too. 'For a minute I thought that Mr Edwin was going to shoot me again,' he quavered. 'I couldn't believe it! Good thing that you and Amos were so close.'

'No,' Howard said heartily. 'You know that Edwin's no use with a gun; he was probably aiming at the same grouse Amos shot at.'

Howard could see that Sam wasn't totally convinced, but the lad nodded and they turned for home, leaving Amos and Edwin behind. They heard Amos give a sharp shrill whistle and looking back saw Edwin's horse trotting towards him.

Luke was home ahead of them. He'd ridden as far as Littlebeck and then decided to turn for home. He was not in a good temper. Normally a mild-mannered man, Edwin's attitude and conduct had angered him intensely.

'You must talk to him when he returns, Luke,' Anna said. 'He's no longer a child. He must accept his responsibilities. He knew that you wanted to speak to him today and yet he chose to go out.'

'I shall,' Luke said grumpily. 'When, or if, he comes back.' He was upset that Anna sounded so cross. She was the most amiable of women, which was what had attracted him to her in the first place; now Edwin was upsetting her too. He looked up at the clatter of horses outside the window. 'Who's this?'

He got to his feet and went to look out. 'Ah, Howard and Sam. Sam's got a bloody leg. I'd better go and have a look at him.'

Anna had told him that Howard and Amos had gone looking for him and Edwin and he was perturbed that Amos and Edwin hadn't returned.

'They're on their way back,' Howard told him. 'Edwin got thrown from his horse. He's all right,' he added. 'Not hurt. But I think we need the doc to look at Sam's leg. The wound's opened up again, and it looks rather nasty.'

'Will you fetch him?' Luke asked him. 'I need to have words with Edwin when he gets back.'

'Yes,' Howard said, pleased to be out of the way if there was going to be a family row. 'I'll just make Sam comfortable and then be off.'

He bedded the boy down in one of the stables and covered him with a horse blanket. 'You'll be all right till I get back with the doctor,' he said. 'And Amos won't be long.'

421

'I hope Mr Edwin doesn't find me first,' the lad said nervously. 'I don't trust him, not after seeing him with the gun.'

Howard looked at him. It was true that he was vulnerable, lying there on the stable floor, but surely Edwin wouldn't . . .

'He won't know you're here,' he assured him. 'And anyway, Amos is with him. But I'll have a word with Mr Kingston before I go if you like.'

He went back into the house to talk to Luke. He found him with Anna, Sonny, Rosalie and Polly in the drawing room.

'Sam's very nervous,' he said. 'Will you keep Edwin away from the stables?'

Luke frowned and waited for an explanation.

'There was an incident,' Howard told him. 'Probably not intentional.' Why am I lying for that reprobate, he thought.

'What kind of incident?' Luke barked. 'With Edwin?'

'It was resolved,' Howard parried. 'By Amos.'

To his intense relief, Amos and Edwin rode past the window at that moment, and he didn't have to say anything further. A few minutes later Edwin stormed into the house looking for his father.

'That damned idiot nearly killed me,' he shouted as he came into the room. 'Amos! He shot my gun clean out of my hands. Ruined it completely! And just about shot my face off.'

He scraped his finger down his cheek. 'Look! Red hot lead,' he spluttered. 'He should be sacked! He's not fit to be in charge of a fire-arm.'

'Amos?' his father roared. 'He's the best shot in the district. Why did he fire? What were you doing to lead him to do that?'

'He said he was after a grouse,' Edwin blustered, his face red with fury. 'There was no grouse. I didn't see any. You!' He jabbed a finger at Howard. 'You were with him. You saw what happened. Tell them. Tell them how he tried to kill me!'

Howard shook his head. He wasn't going to argue with him. Edwin was raving; whatever he said, Edwin would argue against it.

'It must have been an accident, Edwin,' Anna's conciliatory voice appealed. 'Amos would never—'

'Mind your own business, bitch,' Edwin snarled. 'It's got nothing to do with you.'

For a second no one said anything, there was just a fusion of intakes of breath, and then Luke found his voice.

'*What* did you say? What did you say to my *wife*?'

'Wife! Hah!' Edwin sneered and his face was contorted with anger. 'Wanton. Fornicator.

Never wife! My mother was your wife and you've defiled her memory by bringing that woman here.'

Anna put her hands to her mouth. Her face was deathly pale and she sat still as stone. Polly and Rosalie stood as if they had been struck, whilst Sonny by the window and Howard near the door looked as if they were poised to spring.

Luke launched himself towards his son with his fist raised, but in an instant Edwin brought out a knife and held it in front of him. He flicked the blade and thrust it towards his father.

'Keep away from me,' he snapped. 'Don't dare touch me.'

Luke backed off, his hands lifted high. 'I won't,' he said quietly, though his voice trembled with shock. 'Let's just talk, Edwin, and find out what's gone wrong. If Amos has fired at you then I want to know the reason why and he'll be punished.'

He was coaxing, appealing; everyone in the room knew that, but Edwin knew it too. He gave a sly grin.

'Think you can soft-soap me?' he mocked. 'I know your game.' He jumped as someone gave a brief knock on the door. 'Who's this?'

The door opened and Mrs Moody came in. Edwin sprang towards her, putting his arm round her neck and holding the blade at her throat.

'Oh, Mr Edwin!' The housekeeper gagged. 'What 'you doing? Please. You're hurting me. Don't! Don't! Help me, somebody.'

'Shut up, you old hag,' he muttered.

'I'm your friend, Mr Edwin,' she moaned. 'Your only one. What 'you doing? Haven't I allus looked after you? Ever since you were a little bairn; anything you wanted you could have.'

Edwin put the blade closer to her throat. 'Why do you think I tolerated you?' he murmured into her ear. 'Don't think it was because I liked you, because it wasn't. It was only because you gave me everything I asked for.'

He had his back to the window and hadn't seen Sonny take a tentative step towards him. But Howard had, and so had Luke, and Luke engaged Edwin in conversation again.

'Let Mrs Moody go, Edwin,' he said. 'This is nothing to do with her. This is between you and me.'

'And her.' Edwin shifted his head in Anna's direction.

'All right. And Anna too. But let's talk about it. Settle our differences.'

'Huh!' Edwin gave a guttural grunt. 'And will you send her packing, back down the valley where she belongs?'

Luke hesitated and as he and Edwin stared at each other, Sonny sprang and so did Howard. Sonny launched himself on to Edwin's knees, making them buckle, whilst Howard grabbed Edwin's arm, jerking it upwards and releasing the knife. They manhandled him on to the floor, Howard holding his wrists and Sonny his feet.

Mrs Moody screeched and squawked. 'I'm bleeding!' she shrieked. 'He's cut me!'

'Get a cord, Luke,' Howard said. 'We must restrain him.' They were wrestling to keep Edwin down while he struggled, kicked and swore, using such vile language that even Polly was shocked.

Luke dashed out of the room whilst Rosalie and Polly tried to calm Mrs Moody, who was still screaming.

'It's only a small cut, Mrs Moody,' Rosalie said. 'Come and sit down. You're upsetting Mrs Kingston.'

The housekeeper pushed her away and went on flailing her arms and bellowing. Polly gritted her teeth, took a deep breath and slapped her across the face.

The housekeeper inhaled and for a moment they thought she would have a fit, but then she started to cry, sobbing into her hand.

'Never did I think I'd see the day when Mr Edwin would say such things to me,' she wailed.

'Me, who's been like a mother to him since his own mother died.'

She looked down at Edwin writhing on the floor, and as Luke came back with a length of cord with which to restrain him she shook her head.

'It's your marrying again what's done it, Mr Kingston,' she declared. 'That and bringing strangers into the house. It's turned his mind sour. We were all right afore. Proper little family we were. You, me, Miss Clemmie and Mr Edwin.'

She pointedly omitted Howard. Luke got up from his knees and stared at her, his face expressionless.

'Get out,' he said quietly. 'Pack your bags and go!'

CHAPTER THIRTY-SEVEN

Polly and Rosalie took Anna up to her room to rest. Her daughter Elizabeth sat beside her and held her hand. Fortunately she had been in the schoolroom with her governess during the debacle; she had been told that Edwin was ill and the doctor had been sent for, and that her mother should rest.

Anna had persuaded Luke that Mrs Moody should be allowed to stay until the following day before leaving. 'She will need a reference and her wages,' she said softly. 'You must allow her those at least.'

Howard had cantered down the valley after Amos, who, finding Sam on the stable floor and hearing that no one had yet gone for the doctor, had set off to fetch him, unaware of what was happening inside the house. Howard caught up with him and told him briefly what had occurred.

'Police need to be informed then?' Amos

said bluntly. 'Even if Mrs Moody doesn't press charges, Mr Edwin's not fit to be left alone. It's asylum for him, Mr Howard. He's allus been a loose cannon. He needs locking up.'

He needs help, Howard meditated as he rode back to the house, and that was what he suggested to Luke. They could hear Edwin drumming his feet on the floor of his room; he had been locked in until the doctor arrived.

'You're right,' Luke sighed. 'You know . . .' He put his head in his hands. There were just the two of them in the room. Sonny had made himself scarce. 'After Edwin's mother died, I was so pleased that you were here and that you wanted to stay. You were a sensible lad with a sense of fun and I thought' – he gave another deep sigh – 'that you'd be a companion and friend to Edwin. He was always highly strung and constantly seeking attention and I thought you'd be a good influence on him. What I hadn't realized was that Edwin was jealous of you, probably always had been, first because his mother was fond of you and later, I believe, because he thought that you might steal my affection away from him. In fact I had enough love to share between you all.' He gazed into nothingness and then said, 'What am I to do, Howard? How can I make good my mistakes?'

'From where I'm standing, sir, you haven't

made any,' Howard said. 'You did your best to bring us all up without a mother.' He stood beside Luke's chair and put his hand on his shoulder. 'But Edwin needs urgent medical help, and,' he added emphatically, 'he can't live here. Anna would be in constant fear for herself and her children. He must go away for his own good and for the sake of others. He mustn't be allowed to ride roughshod over family and servants.'

Howard was thinking of Dora, who was unable to resist Edwin's advances, and Anna's daughter Elizabeth who was at a vulnerable age; but he was thinking most of all of Polly, who had spurned Edwin once but might not be so lucky another time.

'Yes,' Luke agreed. 'And if he finds out that Anna is expecting our child that might be sufficient to tip him right over the edge.'

Howard considered that Edwin had already gone over the edge, but he kept his counsel. Luke had had enough misery for one day.

'I'm desperate for something to drink,' Anna said from her bed. 'I'm parched. Polly, would you . . . ? I don't like to ring. Do you think there's chaos downstairs?'

'I'll go.' Polly smiled. 'I know how to make a pot o' tea. I'm an expert!'

She slipped down the back stairs. She could

hear a regular thudding coming from Edwin's room and hoped the doctor wouldn't be long. Mebbe he'll sedate him. Give him a strong dose o' loddy mebbe. She felt vaguely sorry for Edwin even though he had been so vile, but she hoped that he would soon be out of the house. Mrs Kingston was nervous after what he had said, and had asked that she shouldn't be left alone whilst Edwin was still there.

The kitchen wasn't in chaos; rather, it was quite relaxed. Cook was preparing a late lunch of cold beef and chicken and game pie and one of the maids was setting out a tray to take upstairs.

'We'll put this in the dining room, miss, and then everybody can help themselves,' Cook said. 'Them as want it. Nobody'll feel like sitting down to a cooked lunch after all that commotion, I'll be bound. Then I'll do an early supper.'

'I'll take a tray up to Mrs Kingston, if you don't mind,' Polly said. 'She's in need of a cup of strong tea, and' – she gazed over the table – 'perhaps a slice of chicken and some bread and butter.'

'Yes, miss. Come on, Lottie,' she said to the maid. 'Look sharp about it.'

Cook said nothing about the housekeeper, though she surely knew what had happened, but Polly noticed that she hummed to herself as she bustled about. She's pleased, Polly decided as she waited for the kettle to boil. Mrs Moody will not be missed, even by those downstairs.

The maid took the luncheon tray upstairs and as Polly poured the water on to the tea leaves she asked the cook, 'Where will Mrs Moody go, do you think?'

'To her sister's, miss,' Cook said, without even looking up from the job in hand. 'And she's welcome to her. Good riddance is what I say.'

All the ladies were upstairs in Anna's room when they heard the doctor's carriage approach, immediately followed by another crunching of wheels on the gravel. Rosalie looked out of the window. She took a breath and licked her lips and glanced at Polly.

Polly sauntered over and casually looked out. Black Maria, she breathed. It was a cause of both dread and excitement whenever they were seen appearing at a scene of trouble in Hull. But out here in this quiet and lovely countryside it seemed an intrusion.

'Who is it?' Anna asked. 'Is it the doctor?'

'Yes.' Polly nodded. 'He'll soon put everybody right,' she said cheerfully. 'Do you want to see him, Mrs Kingston?'

'I don't think so,' she said. 'I'm perfectly all right. Just upset over what's happened, so I'll stay in bed for the rest of the day and keep out of everyone's way.'

'After the doctor's gone,' Rosalie said, 'shall we have a picnic? Here, in your room, I mean? We could bring our lunch upstairs. Or would you rather be quiet?'

'That would be lovely,' Anna said. 'It will take my mind off what will happen to poor Edwin. What do you think will? Will the doctor take him with him?'

'We're not even going to think about it,' Polly said. 'Not now. Don't worry.' Glancing out of the window she saw two police officers and a man in a white coat helping a comatose Edwin into the police carriage. 'Somebody'll look after him.'

The next day saw the housekeeper's departure. Luke called her into his study. 'I'm sorry it has to end like this, Mrs Moody,' he said as he handed her a letter of reference and her wages. 'But I can't have you speaking in such a manner about my personal life. I know you've cared for my son and daughter and I appreciate that, but they are mine and not yours, and soon we will have another child in the family, so it is best if we start afresh. I'm sorry too that Edwin was so rude to you, but he's sick and I hope you'll take account of that.'

Mrs Moody huffed into her coat. 'Well,

nobody has seen fit to ask if I'm all right. Nearly had my throat cut, I did. I was in fear of my life.'

'The doctor said it was only a scratch and barely broke the skin. And I don't believe that Edwin would have hurt you, of all people.' Luke held her gaze and hoped that she wouldn't spread the news abroad. 'He was angry, but not with you; you just happened to come in at the wrong moment.'

Mrs Moody huffed again and muttered something, but Luke got to his feet. 'Thank you for your past service, Mrs Moody. I hope you'll remember us kindly. Good day to you.'

She stalked out to where Amos was waiting for her with the trap. She got in and folded her arms across her chest. 'I could take them to court,' she said sullenly. 'I was in danger of my life, you know. Within an inch of having my life blood drained away.'

'Oh aye?' Amos said dispassionately. 'If he was as handy with a knife as he was with a gun then you'd nowt to worry about. Anyway,' he said as he shook the reins, 'would you bite the hand that's fed you for all these years?'

CHAPTER THIRTY-EIGHT

Luke had wanted to cancel the shoot that had been arranged for the end of the following week, but Howard pointed out it would be difficult to let people know that it had been called off.

'They'd also want to know why,' he said. 'They'd ask questions; and don't forget we have people coming from outside the district and we couldn't let them know in time.'

Howard and Amos and a local lad had been busy over the last few weeks building up stone butts across the moor where the men would wait for their prey.

Reluctantly Luke agreed. Grouse shooting was a sport he enjoyed and his household always put on luncheon and dinner for the many gentlemen, businessmen, farmers and sportsmen who gathered on the moor.

'I don't want to see any of it,' Rosalie declared. 'It's wholesale slaughter.'

'No, it's not,' Luke said reprovingly. 'Not on my land.' Luke was not in favour of mindless killing and so banned those who were only there for a record bag. He invited the sportsmen who came with their dogs, their beaters and their keepers.

Polly raised her eyebrows. She had no real opinion on the morals of it, but, she thought, it's food, just like having chicken or beef for dinner, and the game birds she considered had a pretty good life living wild out on the moor. Besides, she thought they had a chance. She was fairly sure that not all the gentlemen would be marksmen.

'Have you ever been to a shoot, m'dear?' Luke asked Rosalie. 'Your father never came to ours though he was often invited, but then he's always been busy shooting people!'

'No, I haven't. And Papa only shoots at the enemy!' Rosalie said in her father's defence. 'He's a soldier, so that's entirely different.'

'Yes, there's the difference between us,' Luke said. 'I for one couldn't fire at another human being, but I do enjoy a good game pie.'

Rosalie was silenced. That was what they'd had for dinner. A game pie of rabbit, grouse and teal. She had enjoyed it too. Perhaps she hadn't thought the subject through.

'You still have town in you,' Luke said mildly. 'You're not yet a country girl. Unlike Miss Polly

436

here,' he wagged a finger in Polly's direction, 'who I think is becoming one. And what about you, Sonny? Will you take up a gun this time?'

'No, sir, I won't. I'll try to catch the birds and their hunters on canvas.' He glanced at Rosalie. 'But I'll still enjoy a game pie. Like Rosalie, I have mixed feelings about the sport. Then I must take leave of your hospitality and prepare for my travels abroad.'

Luke sighed. 'I'm sorry that on this occasion you have become embroiled in our family troubles.' He was still hurt and smarting about what had gone before. 'But I hope we'll see you again soon under happier circumstances.'

'I shall look forward to that, sir, and in the spring when I return I hope to hear some good news.'

He meant Anna, of course. Luke had insisted that she see the doctor after he had attended to Sam, and now she was keeping to her bed on his orders. She was quite well but he said that she should stay quiet and rest and not come down whilst there were extra visitors arriving for the shoot.

Polly had volunteered herself and Rosalie to look after the shooting party, for now that Mrs Moody had gone there was no one to organize Cook or the servants. It'll be good practice for me, she thought. I could perhaps be a housekeeper if Rosalie goes away. She was constantly thinking of the jobs she could do, for in her heart she was sure that Rosalie would give in to her father's demands and leave for Aldershot, no matter how vehemently she insisted that she wouldn't.

She'd been brought up to be obedient, Polly knew. To do always what was expected of her. I can't think that Rosalie's uncle has laid down so many rules for Clementina. She seems to have complete freedom and leaves for Scarborough on a whim. Clemmie was still away and as yet didn't know about Edwin.

On the first morning of the shoot, Polly rose at six o'clock and went down to the kitchen to find Cook already baking bread and pastry. A shoulder of mutton was sizzling over the fire and a large cauldron of soup was simmering at the side. From the oven came the tantalizing smell of roasting beef.

'There are some gentlemen expected for breakfast, Cook,' Polly told her. 'What do you normally give them?'

'I thought I'd best do the same as last year,' Cook said. 'I sent up to Mrs Kingston to ask if that was all right and she said that it was. There's ham and sausage and plenty of eggs, and I'll prepare dinner for three o'clock for them as is going out to shoot in the afternoon.'

As this was Polly's first experience with

a shooting party, she decided that the best thing she could do was make sure there was a plentiful supply of food coming up from the kitchen and that the maids didn't dally with it.

At nine she took a breakfast tray up to Anna. She placed the tray on a side table and opened the curtains.

'Here we are, m'lady,' she said. 'It's a bright and beautiful morning.'

'Polly!' Anna sat up. 'There's no need for you to do this. You're a guest in our house.'

'I like to be useful, Mrs Kingston. I'm not used to sitting about doing nothing, and besides,' she said, placing the tray on the bed, "maids are busy helping Cook get things ready for when 'gentlemen arrive.'

'I'm not used to sitting around either,' Anna said. 'I don't take kindly to it.'

'But you have good reason for resting,' Polly said. 'I wish that my ma had been able to rest. If she had – well,' her face was wistful, 'perhaps she'd still be here. But then I wouldn't have known any of this.'

Her glance took in the view from the window: the blue sky and the glowing heather, the call of the birds and the bleating of sheep.

'And we wouldn't have known you, Polly,' Anna said softly. 'And that would have been our loss.'

'Good thing we don't know what's in front of us,' Polly said brightly. 'We'd never survive, would we?'

'Indeed we wouldn't,' Anna said. 'And thank you, Polly.'

'No need to thank me, Mrs Kingston.' Polly laughed. 'It's onny a breakfast tray.'

Anna shook her head. 'I didn't mean the breakfast. I just meant – thank you for being you. You're such an asset. I don't know what we'd do without you.'

Polly felt a lump in her throat. Perhaps I could stay here after all, she thought. Mebbe Mrs Kingston will have me as her housekeeper instead of hiring someone else. I'll ask Rosalie what she thinks about that.

But Rosalie had already gone out. She had overheard Sonny telling Howard the day before that he would go out early to look at the moor before there was too much sun on it.

'There might still be mist about,' Howard had said. 'But try not to disturb the grouse. They'll still be feeding and we want them well rested before the shooting begins.'

Sonny agreed and Rosalie was intrigued. Why did he particularly want to look at the moor then when it was there every day? She caught up with him at early breakfast and asked if she could go with him.

'I promise I'll be very quiet,' she said. 'And not talk.'

He smiled and said it would give him the greatest of pleasure if she came with him. 'I want to look at the heather with the bloom of mist still on it,' he said. 'Before the sun dries it off.'

When she raised her eyebrows questioningly he said, 'I'll make sketches and do some water colour and then go out later and roughly paint the hunters and the red grouse, and keep the colour of the moor in my head.'

'And finish it in your studio?'

'Yes.' He gazed at her and wondered how else he might paint her. 'As long as I have the general outline of the subject, I can use my imagination and memory of what I've seen.'

'How clever you are,' she murmured. 'I have no talent for anything.'

'You're still young. There's time yet to discover a flair for something.'

She gave a shrug. 'You're being kind,' she said.

'No,' he replied. 'I'm being truthful. You've not yet had the chance to make your mark.'

'Make my mark?'

'Yes. We all have the opportunity to do that, but not everyone takes it.'

They arranged to meet in the hall. He said he was walking and not riding so she changed into stout shoes and put on a comfortable skirt, taking with her a shawl in case it was cold. Sonny was wearing an ancient jacket and carried a rucksack on his back.

There was a soft breeze blowing as they began their climb up the moor and Sonny said the mist would soon be gone. It lay in hollows and Rosalie saw that it was lifting above the heather.

Sonny pointed. 'See how it appears to steam,' he said. 'And see how the light touches beneath the ridges, dispersing the dark shadows.'

Rosalie looked and saw. She saw as she hadn't seen before.

'How unobservant I've been,' she murmured, glancing up at him. 'But then I've never had anyone to teach me before.'

The heather was as thick as a carpet beneath their feet and they trod carefully, avoiding the thicker clumps of ling and rocky outcrops where the grouse might be sheltering. They had walked for about half an hour when Sonny called a halt.

A heap of rocks would be their resting place and Sonny took off his coat for Rosalie to sit on. He unpacked his bag and took out pencils, paints, brushes, a container for water and a pad of paper.

Rosalie sat quietly, determined not to disturb him as he began to sketch. He drew the horizon, etched in a stone wall reaching down into the valley, a thin sparse line of bent trees and a jagged heap of rock, and then marked with crosses where he would put the red grouse.

'I'll put in some water colour,' he murmured, 'and then later I'll paint in oils. Oils are my preference; the colour is deeper and richer.'

Rosalie nodded. She was fascinated. She had had drawing lessons with her governess but they had simply been copying exercises and she had always suspected that it wasn't a talent at which her teacher excelled.

'I'm leaving on Monday,' he said suddenly, 'and travel to Italy at the end of the week.'

She took in a breath. Why was he telling her? She knew he was going soon, but it was as if he wanted to remind her once more.

'So soon?' she murmured. 'Is it important that you leave now?'

'Afraid so.' He added a few more lines to the sketch. 'I have the chance of an important commission.' He turned to look at her. 'One which might make my reputation and my fortune.'

'I see.' She thought steadily for a moment. 'I'm considering travelling into Hull to, erm, to see my lawyer.' She swallowed. 'Perhaps – that is, I could also travel on Monday. Would you be so kind as to – it would save my uncle from sending the carriage twice . . .'

'If we travelled together?' he finished for her.

'Yes,' she said breathlessly.

'And Polly?'

'N-no! Not Polly. She'll be otherwise occupied.'

'And will you return alone?' His eyes held hers. 'Without a companion?'

'It's time that I did.' She lowered her eyes. 'I'm not a child, after all.'

He gave a little smile and turned back to his drawing. 'Indeed you are not.'

She felt that strange churning surge of elation that she had felt before when they had sheltered from the rain. She gazed at the back of his neck as he bent over his sketch; his dark hair curled on to his shirt collar and she wanted to reach out and touch it. What was the texture? Was it smooth to the touch or was it wiry and strong as it appeared to be?

He turned suddenly as if about to speak again and caught her gaze. His eyes searched her face and his lips parted. Then he pressed them together, took a breath and looked away.

'I feel that I must be getting back,' Rosalie said shortly after. 'I should have remembered that I might be needed back at the house.'

'There'll be plenty of people there,' he commented. 'There's Polly.'

'Yes,' she agreed. 'Polly is so useful. But I was thinking of Anna. She's confined to bed.'

'Her daughter?' Sonny turned his head. 'Elizabeth will sit with her.'

'Ah! So she will. So I'm superfluous.' Rosalie couldn't help but hear the sting in her own voice but she looked away from him as she spoke.

'So am I not worthy of your attention?' he bantered. 'Am I not important enough to warrant your presence?'

'I – I didn't mean that. You know that I didn't,' she protested. 'But you don't need me here. I asked if I could come.'

'And now you are bored with me!' He sighed. 'It was ever thus.'

'No,' she said, and he turned right round to face her as he heard the rebuke. 'I'm not. You know I am not. And – and you are simply patronizing me by allowing me to come.'

He seized her hand. 'Never!' he exclaimed. 'How can you say such a thing? I was – overjoyed when you asked. Rosalie!' He dropped his paintbrush and placed his other hand over hers. 'You don't know what you say, and cannot know how I feel. And I'm not at liberty to tell you.'

'Why?' she whispered. 'Why are you not?'

He shook his head. 'Because, like you, I'm bound by custom and honour, and I'm a guest

445

in your uncle's house. This is not the time or the place.'

'For what?'

Sonny briefly closed his eyes. 'I can't say,' he breathed. 'When I return in the spring, perhaps then, if your circumstances haven't changed . . . if you are still here . . .'

'Oh, I will be!' she exclaimed with a sudden surge of happiness. 'I will be.'

CHAPTER THIRTY-NINE

A company of men were already at breakfast when Rosalie arrived back. She had left Sonny behind and walked across the moor alone. She was pleased to be on her own to think about the implications of what he had said, and also to plan.

I shall write to Papa and tell him that I can't possibly leave here until the spring as Aunt Anna needs me until after her confinement; and I will intimate that it would be cruel to leave her at such a difficult time. I won't mention Polly so he will perhaps assume that she is no longer here.

She felt joyous and could barely keep a smile from her face as she considered what her future might hold. Then she pondered on what her father might have to say, which sobered her. But I shall be eighteen by then, she thought, and surely can make my own decisions.

Her attention was required as soon as she

arrived at the house. Polly suggested that she should act as hostess to the gentlemen whilst Polly herself concentrated on making sure that everything ran smoothly between the kitchen and the dining room.

'You look like 'cat that's got 'cream,' Polly said, gazing at Rosalie with her head on one side. 'What 'you been up to?'

'Absolutely nothing,' Rosalie beamed. 'Nothing at all!'

Luke was delighted with them both. He had been very sombre since the incident with Edwin, but with Howard taking over the arrangements for the shooting party and Rosalie and Polly so efficiently attending to the guests' needs, he seemed more relaxed.

'I wish that Clemmie could have been here,' he said to Rosalie. 'Usually she comes back for this event, although I must admit that she doesn't have your flair for conversation.'

'I'm pleased to have been useful, Uncle Luke,' she said. 'I wonder if I might speak to you later about something? I need your advice.'

'Of course you may, m'dear. I shall be pleased to help in any way I can.'

She thought how approachable he was and how easy-going compared with her father, with whom she felt restrained.

She and Polly ate a second breakfast after

the men had gone and then went to sit with Anna. Anna said she felt a fraud being in bed and was adamant that she would get up the next day.

'Would you mind if I went to Hull on Monday?' Rosalie asked her. 'Sonny is going then and I could travel with him. I'll only be away a few days.'

She felt her cheeks getting hot and out of the corner of her eye could see Polly's amused expression; Anna didn't seem to notice and she didn't enquire how she would come back, but simply said that she must do whatever was necessary, and added that the weather was good for travelling.

'I wish that Clementina would come home,' she added. 'I think that her father would like her here. I must persuade him to write and tell her about Edwin.'

Howard asked Rosalie when she planned to come back and whether she would like to arrange a day so that he or Amos could collect her.

'I really don't know,' she prevaricated. 'I have to see the lawyer and ask his advice on one or two things.'

'But that'll only take a day or two at the most,' he said. 'Suppose I arrange for say – Thursday? That will give you two full days to attend to whatever business you need.'

'She doesn't want to tie herself down to a timetable,' Sonny interrupted. 'I'm not leaving Hull until the end of the week. Rosalie can send Polly a postcard with details of her arrival and I'll see her on to the Scarborough train before I depart.'

'Yes,' Rosalie agreed. 'That will be perfect.'

Howard was uneasy about it. 'Be careful,' he murmured to Sonny later, when they were alone. 'She's a vulnerable young woman. Don't compromise her.'

'As if I would!' Sonny said sharply. 'It wasn't my idea that Rosalie should travel with me. It was hers.'

'I realize that,' Howard said. 'And that's what worries me. She's unskilled in the ways of men. She's been overprotected. She probably doesn't even know the facts of life.'

'Well it's not my intention to teach her,' Sonny declared. 'But I think you're wrong. She is not as aware as Polly, I grant you, but she's discerning and enlightened.'

Howard scrutinized him. Then he laughed. 'And you are going away!'

Sonny grinned. 'Yes. But I'm coming back!'

'You'll be all right with Sonny,' Polly said.

Rosalie turned to her. 'I know that,' she asserted. 'I wouldn't have asked him otherwise.'

450

'Oh ho!' Polly grinned. 'So it was you. I thought as much!'

'It seemed the sensible thing as he was travelling into Hull.' Rosalie shrugged as if it was of no account. 'I could have gone on my own, but—'

'I'll come with you if you like,' Polly ventured. 'I'm sure Mrs Kingston wouldn't—'

'I won't hear of it,' Rosalie interrupted. 'I wouldn't go if I thought you were not here to look after her. I'll tell you why I'm really going, Polly,' she said softly and Polly came closer. 'I was going to discuss it with Uncle Luke but now I've decided that I'll speak to our lawyer instead. I want to ask Mr Benjamin about an inheritance from my mother. I feel sure that she mentioned something when I was about fourteen. At the time I didn't really take much notice, but I'm almost sure that Mama said I would come into some money on my eighteenth birthday.'

'Oh!' Polly was round-eyed. 'And what will you do with it if you do?'

Rosalie smiled. 'I have not yet formulated my plans,' she said mysteriously. 'But you'll be the first to know, Polly.'

For the next few days the moor echoed with the sound of gunfire and the air was filled with the smell of smoke, both acrid gunsmoke and sweet tobacco smoke from the pipes which it seemed were an essential item for most of the men as they waited for the red grouse to appear.

Rosalie went towards the stables. She hadn't ridden for a few days and wanted to make sure that Damon and Hero were all right. Luke had taken on another stable lad who had been exercising the two ponies away from the area where the guns were employed. Sam had gone home to his parents to convalesce and no decision had yet been made about his future, but Dora had gone to work at Anna's house where she seemed to be content and accepting the fact that she was going to be a mother.

Rosalie walked across the cobbled courtyard and came to a full stop. The bodies of red grouse were laid in neat rows, their glorious colours bedraggled, their bodies limp. She counted the rows and stopped at one hundred birds, gazing at them, and as she did so Sonny followed her into the yard.

He saw her with his artist's eye: her face in profile, her downcast head as she sorrowfully surveyed the dead birds. In his mind he dressed her in servant's clothing: a dark skirt muddied at the hem, black stockings and worn boots, a white apron and cap and a basket over her arm.

Rosalie turned and saw him. There were tears in her eyes.

'They've had a good life,' he said softly. 'They are wild free creatures and have not been bred for the pot. They have a sporting chance.'

'Yes,' she murmured. 'I understand what you say, what you all say. But it is still so very sad.'

Anna was up and dressed on the Monday morning and said she felt quite refreshed and able to attend to her duties. She had always been a busy woman and didn't take kindly to being confined to bed.

'Bearing children is a perfectly natural occurrence,' she said to Polly and Rosalie. 'And although I realize that both your mothers died in childbirth, I don't intend that to happen to me. I'm a fit strong woman and you mustn't worry about me.'

Howard had volunteered to drive Rosalie and Sonny to Scarborough as he felt that Amos's presence would be more useful on the moor than his own.

'I'm sorry,' Sonny said as they stood by the pony and trap. 'I've chosen a bad time.'

Howard ran his hand over his chin. 'I was just thinking; suppose . . . no, maybe not, but on the other hand . . .'

'What?' Sonny questioned.

Howard looked at Rosalie and bit his lip, and then back at Sonny. 'Suppose you drive the trap to Scarborough and leave it with my grandmother, and then when Rosalie returns from Hull she could come back with Clemmie. She's due back any time now and maybe Luke would write and tell her.'

Sonny nodded. 'That sounds all right. And then you needn't make any unnecessary journeys. What do you think, Rosalie?'

'Yes, that sounds agreeable.' She was elated to be journeying with Sonny, but less so at the thought of returning with Clemmie.

So Howard, with some considerable relief, shook hands with Sonny and the two men said they looked forward to meeting again in the spring. Then he urged Rosalie to be careful when travelling alone by train.

She gave him a wide open smile and said that she would. 'I'm quite capable, you know,' she told him.

Rosalie vowed to herself that she would remember for ever that ride across the moor with Sonny as they made their way towards Scarborough. It was a glorious day, the sun warm though not too hot and the heather glowing in rich shades of purple. The landscape changed as they descended into valleys of varying hues of lush green and wandering sheep cropped the grass. They skirted rushing becks and sparkling waterfalls, splashed through shallow streams and led the horse as they walked on foot over narrow stone bridges.

Sonny from time to time turned his head to look at her but didn't speak, simply giving her a tender smile. She gazed at his long brown fingers as he lightly held the reins and saw the dark hair at his wrist escaping from his sleeve and she wanted to reach out and put her hand on his. They stopped at an inn and bought bread and ham. Sonny had a glass of ale and she had lemonade and they sat on the grass outside and spoke only in snatches of conversation which later she couldn't recall.

When they reached Scarborough and Mrs Carleton's house there was no one at home. Her housekeeper called for a boy to take the pony and trap to the mews down the road, and assured Rosalie that she would tell her employer as soon as she returned and that someone would take care of the animal. She shook her head when asked about Clementina and replied that the young lady was hardly ever in.

The train into Hull was on time, and as Sonny had more baggage than Rosalie he suggested that they take a hansom cab to her house and he would see her safely inside before going home himself.

'Perhaps I could take you for supper,' he said. 'Neither of us will have food in the house.'

She agreed and they arranged that he would call for her at eight o'clock, it being already seven. They were both hungry, not having eaten since their picnic outside the inn.

Rosalie unlocked the door and stepped inside. The hallway was cold and smelled damp even though the day had been warm. Sonny came inside with her and checked the downstairs rooms.

'Would you like me to look upstairs?' he asked.

She said it wouldn't be necessary; everything seemed to be all right. 'Perhaps,' she said, 'I could unpack my bag and walk across to Charlotte Street and meet you at your lodgings, rather than wait here for you.'

He hesitated for a second and then said, 'Yes. I'll drop my bags off and unpack later.' He smiled. 'Then we'll have supper.'

Rosalie looked in the kitchen and the drawing room. The furniture was covered with sheets and the curtains were closed. Then she went upstairs. The house was gloomy and dark, she thought, but had it always been like that? Did she only notice it now because she was used to the light and space that she had been enjoying at her uncle's house?

Tentatively she opened the door to her mother's bedroom, the room her father had shared with her mother on the few occasions he was at home; the room in which her mother had died.

She wrinkled her nose. A faint spicy aroma hung in the air. But it was not one that she recognized. It was heavier than the floral scents her mother preferred.

Martha had stripped the bed before she left and had been about to put a fustian sheet over it, but Rosalie had asked her to put the satin bedspread over the mattress and the sheet on top. It had been a whim and not one she could explain. The sheet was still there, but looked as if it had been only casually thrown over. She pulled it off and saw that the bedspread was crumpled. She lifted a corner and there were blankets beneath it. How odd, she thought. I'm sure they were taken off for washing.

She turned and glanced round the room. Everything else appeared to be as she had left it except – except for a silk scarf draped over the back of the chair by the dressing table. Rosalie put her hand to her mouth. What did it mean? She picked it up and ran it through her fingers. It was very pretty but not one she had seen before. Certainly not her mother's. Her mother never wore blue.

Someone has been here. Did Mr Benjamin hire a housekeeper to check on the house and light fires as had been suggested? But it was an expensive scarf, not one which a housekeeper would possess, and if she did, then why hadn't she returned for it?

Rosalie gave herself a shake and set her thoughts to one side, put her bag in her own room, washed her hands, changed her coat and, locking the front door behind her, set off for Charlotte Street.

Sonny was running down the wooden steps as she approached the mews building and she was a little disappointed as she was hoping to see his studio. But perhaps tonight is not a good time, she decided. Maybe during the day.

He greeted her, and tucking her arm into his led her off to an inn in the High Street which had a separate room for dining.

Rosalie told him about the silk scarf and he considered for a while and then said, 'I think you're probably right about the housekeeper. It might have been given to her as a gift or she might have bought it second hand. And perhaps she hasn't yet missed it.'

'I expect you're right,' she agreed. 'I'm being fanciful.'

He gave her a quizzical look. 'You? Is that possible? Is that within your character?'

She laughed, whereas once she would have been cross or offended. Now she knew him better. 'Oh, yes,' she said. 'I can be very fanciful indeed. Bordering on the ridiculous at times.'

'And what forms do these ridiculous fancies take?' he asked, leaning towards her across the table.

Rosalie shook her head. 'I couldn't possibly say.' A blush came to her cheeks and his eyes creased as he smiled. 'If I revealed some of my imaginary whimsies they would be considered far-fetched and preposterous.'

'And does that apply when thinking of the scarf found in your mother's bedroom?'

She swallowed and looked away. 'No,' she said quietly. 'That is something quite different. That is fact. Someone has been there.' She looked across at him with wide eyes. 'When I spoke of my imaginary whimsies I was speaking of an extravagant desire for the impossible.'

Sonny reached for her hand and held it. 'Nothing is impossible,' he said softly. 'Not if you want it badly enough.'

CHAPTER FORTY

Sonny walked Rosalie back home, and although she had felt a little uneasy about sleeping alone in the house she slept quite well. The following morning she made a pot of coffee which she drank without milk or sugar, and opened a tin of pears which she found in a store cupboard and ate those for breakfast.

She had a half-hour wait before she could see Mr Benjamin as he was with a client, so she went back into the street and found a café just opening its doors. She ordered tea and muffins and sat at a table in the window looking out at passers-by until the time came for her appointment.

'Miss Kingston! How very nice to see you.' Mr Benjamin was effusive in his greeting. 'I was about to write to you.'

'Were you?' she said. 'Have you news for me?'

'Well, only confirmation of what your father

has decided. He will have told you about the house?'

Rosalie shook her head. 'I'm afraid my father is very lax about letter writing. I'm sure he intends to write but there is always something more pressing to be done first.'

She smiled as she spoke; she felt more benevolent towards her father than she sometimes did. He was remiss, she realized, in his attitude towards her, but today, as she was feeling happy and more confident, she was prepared to forgive him.

'Mr Benjamin,' she continued. 'Did you arrange for a housekeeper as you suggested? Or has someone been to check on the house?' She was thinking of course of the silk scarf and she was taken aback by his answer.

'Only your father himself.' The lawyer frowned. 'He said there was no need for a housekeeper as the house is to be sold.'

'My father? Oh, so not recently – that must have been in the spring?' He was going to visit the house after Uncle Luke's wedding, she remembered. But I have been since and the scarf wasn't there then.

'No no,' he exclaimed. 'This time. The week that's just gone. He came to see me on . . . erm, let me see.' He glanced at his diary and flicked back a couple of pages. 'Wednesday, it was. I assumed he would visit you at his brother's house. Although I do recall his saying that they didn't have a great deal of time.'

'I see.' She felt grieved and disappointed. How could he come all this way and not come a little further to see her?

'So yes,' he went on, 'I was about to dictate a letter to confirm his instructions. The house is to be sold and I understand that you will be going to live in Aldershot. A busy military town, I believe, although I have never been.' He smiled broadly. 'Plenty for a young lady to do, I imagine. Parties and balls and suchlike!'

'I expect so,' she said vaguely, and almost forgot why she had come to see him. 'I wanted to ask you something, Mr Benjamin.'

'Well, ask away, Miss Kingston; what can I do for you?'

Rosalie took a deep breath. There was something not quite right. She felt uneasy. 'I seem to recall,' she began, 'that some years ago my mother said something to me about an inheritance when I reached my eighteenth birthday. I think it was from her family estate and nothing to do with my father.'

'Mm,' he said. 'Well, I'd have to look that up. When is your birthday, Miss Kingston? Is it soon?'

'January the fifteenth,' she said. She hesitated. 'And I want to make plans. Which do not include going to Aldershot,' she added firmly.

Mr Benjamin suggested that she come back the next day and in the meantime he would seek out the details she required.

Rosalie rose from her chair. 'Thank you,' she said. 'Until tomorrow, then.'

It was as she left his office and stepped outside the door on to the footpath that she realized what it was that had made her uneasy. She stood stock still as pedestrians pushed past her.

'They didn't have a great deal of time,' she muttered, her lips barely moving. That's what he said. Was it a slip of the tongue? She frowned as she concentrated on his exact words. Mr Benjamin had said, 'I do recall his saying that *they* didn't have a great deal of time.'

He was at the house with a woman! Mrs Sherwood. The widow he wants to marry. The person who will introduce me to society! What kind of society is that, she thought, horrified, which allows a woman to gallivant alone with a newly widowed man?

'You might be mistaken,' Sonny said to her, when he called on her at midday with a view to going out for a hot dinner and she blurted out the sorry tale. 'There might be a perfectly rational reason.'

But she didn't tell him about the blankets in the bed. That would be so very embarrassing and she hardly dared think about it. I might tell Polly, she thought. She would have a view on the matter and wouldn't in the least mind discussing it.

Sonny took her to a café on Savile Street not far from her house and they both ordered steak pie. They sat in silence for a time and then he said, 'You know, Rosalie, there are different rules for different people. And you ought not to make a judgement on what your father does or doesn't do. He might have had this Mrs Sherwood staying with him, but I'm sure that if he did they would have considered carefully whether or not there would be speculation or gossip.' He gave a little shrug. 'And if indeed it was she, then she might have had good reasons for travelling with him.'

Rosalie scowled. 'So are you saying,' she said in a tense whisper, 'that it's all right for a man and woman to stay alone in the same house if neither of them is married to anyone else?'

'No.' Sonny waited for the waitress to finish serving them. 'I'm not saying that it's all right, but your father is a widower. Would you condemn him to be celibate for the rest of his life?'

He looked at her, waiting for her to express shock at his words or to stand up and leave the table. But she did neither of those things.

'So when do proper rules apply?' Her voice was restrained.

'When it's a very young woman or a woman who has never been married,' he said. 'It's especially important for a young woman to be chaste, if she and her family want her to marry well.'

She stared at him and toyed with her fork. 'Does that not apply to young men?'

He shook his head and cut into the pie crust. Then he grinned. 'I'm afraid not.'

She grimaced, and they both continued eating. Then Sonny remarked, 'Of course, you are behaving quite out of character by being here with me in a public place. What would your mother have thought – or what will your father think if you should tell him?'

Rosalie wiped her mouth with her napkin. She sighed. 'If Mama had still been alive, then I wouldn't be here with you, would I?' She gave a pensive smile. 'I wouldn't even have met you, or Polly. I would be living a different life altogether.' She looked at him. 'I suppose we have to accept the life we're given. There's no point in railing against it.'

'But on the other hand,' he said softly, 'we are at liberty to make changes.'

'Is that what you are going to do? Is that why you're travelling abroad?'

He nodded. 'My aunt, who brought me up, said that it was entirely up to me what I did with my life, and because I want to paint

I'd like to go abroad to gain experience and study the truly great artists. If this commission proves successful I might earn enough money to do just that.'

Rosalie had a sinking feeling in the pit of her stomach. 'So you might not come back for a long time? Or ever?'

'I shall come back in the spring,' he said. 'And come to see you.'

'Will you?' she said softly, and didn't draw her hand away when he clasped it.

'And depending on what you have done with your life – whether you have gone away to live with your father or have decided to make your own plans . . .' He paused.

'Yes?' she breathed, her lips apart. 'What then?'

'I have no money, Rosalie,' he said quietly. 'Only enough for myself to live on.'

She swallowed. 'I went to see the lawyer about a possible inheritance,' she whispered. 'When I'm eighteen. In January.'

He smiled and gave a little shake of his head. 'An heiress!'

'No. No, not really. I don't suppose it will be much.' She hesitated. 'But it might be enough to allow me to be independent.'

'Good! Wonderful! That's what I like to hear, Rosalie. You are making up your own mind about your future.'

It wasn't quite what she meant. She was trying to say that if he declared himself she would say yes, and they could live off her inheritance, if there was one. It would be his in law anyway if they should marry. But he didn't appear to understand what she was saying. He just looked and sounded delighted that she was making decisions about her life.

When they had finished their meal, she asked him if she could see his studio and his work.

He was reluctant at first. If any of his friends heard that he had been entertaining a young woman in his room, there would be some jibes and speculation as to who she was. And then he thought, what of it? He would be leaving at the end of the week and by the time he came back the matter would be forgotten. And no one in his circle knew Rosalie in any case. If ever it was mentioned I could always say that it was only Polly, and then they would know it was harmless.

'All right,' he agreed and wondered what she would say when she saw her portrait leaning on the wall, about to be packed to show his prospective client.

But her eye was immediately caught by a sketch on the easel. It was of a servant girl, but with her own sorrowful face, gazing down at a heap of dead grouse. How is it possible to create such expression, she thought, with just a few pencil lines?

'When did you do this?' she murmured.

'Last night. It was so vivid in my head that I had to put it down on paper. It's only a rough sketch,' he said. 'It needs a lot of work.'

She glanced round the room at the canvases leaning against the walls, the chairs, the cupboards, as if in an exhibition. And then she saw her portrait and took in a breath. She put her hand to her chest. 'That's me!' She was astonished. 'When did you do that?'

'Just after we first met,' he said sheepishly. 'In Albion Street, when I asked you if you'd let Polly work for you.'

'I gave that dress to Polly,' she murmured.

'I know.' He gazed at her. 'But the colour was so vibrant I thought it was probably once one of your favourites.'

She nodded. It was, but how did he know? 'What are you going to do with it?' she asked, her eyes on the portrait. She thought it was like looking in a mirror.

'It's going with me.' He reached for her hand and held it. 'Not just to show the countess who I hope will want me to paint her,' he said quietly, 'but also because I can't bear to be without you and this will remind me of how you are.'

Rosalie moistened her lips with her tongue.

'Take me with you,' she whispered. 'I want to come.'

He drew her towards him and gently kissed her cheek. 'No,' he answered. 'I can't do that. I don't want you to risk making a terrible mistake and then regretting it for the rest of your life.'

She shook her head. 'I won't.'

He kissed her again, this time on her mouth. 'I'll come back in the spring, and if you're still here waiting for me I'll paint you in sunlight with a smile on your lips, and not looking sad as you were when I saw you for the first time.'

CHAPTER FORTY-ONE

On Monday evening all the guests had left, and Howard and Luke were relaxing in Luke's study with a glass of whisky after supper.

'A good shoot,' Luke said. 'I think everybody was satisfied. Even old Burnham, and he's a hopeless Gun.'

Howard laughed. 'Amos takes him to a low butt to give him an easy shot.'

'Ah, yes.' Luke smiled. 'Flatter the Gun!'

'Or else he fires beside him but doesn't claim the bag,' Howard went on. 'He sends his dog off to retrieve the birds and tells Burnham that they're his.'

Luke was silent for a moment, sipping his whisky. 'Rather like with Edwin,' he said. 'Except that Edwin knew they weren't his and that made him angry. He's going to be away for a long time, you know.'

'Yes,' Howard said quietly. 'I know.'

'I've written to Clemmie and explained what happened.'

They both sat gazing at the fire flickering in the grate. It wasn't cold, but Luke always liked the comfort of a fire even in the summer.

'It's a pity we missed the twelfth,' Luke said after a while. 'I understand there was good sport at Goathland.'

'But it was wet that week,' Howard said. 'We've had glorious weather. Just perfect, and next week promises the same. Sir, I'd like to discuss something.'

Luke turned to him with mild eyes. 'Whenever you said *sir* like that when you were a boy I always knew there was some serious intent. You're not going to leave me, are you?' he said suddenly. 'Not going to set up on your own land somewhere?'

'No,' Howard said. 'Why would I do that?'

'I don't know. But you're a young man; you must have ambition.'

'I do have ambition,' Howard agreed. 'But it's to keep this farm successful. To carry on with the tradition that you've followed since you came here.'

Luke nodded in satisfaction. He had taken over from his uncle, and he was touched to think that Howard wanted to do the same.

'I'm pleased to hear it.' There was a suggestion of a break in his voice. 'And even if Edwin hadn't . . . gone away, had these incidents not occurred, I realize that he didn't feel the same about the farm as you do.'

'No.' Howard was careful not to insinuate that Edwin hated getting his hands dirty, which was nevertheless true. 'You're probably right.'

'So what is it? What do you wish to discuss?'

Howard put down his glass and clasped his hands together. 'It's something I've been thinking about for some time, especially since you married Anna and are now expecting another child to add to your family. Between you, you'll have five children, not including me, and then there's Rosalie and Polly living here as well. That's eight of us, and the two of you makes ten. I know,' he added as Luke started to say something. 'Edwin isn't here, but he might be in the future.'

He didn't really believe that Edwin would return, but he wouldn't hurt Luke by voicing his opinion on that subject.

'I think too that Anna might like to have a little more space in the house, and so what I was wondering is . . .' He took a breath. 'Would you let me have High Ridge House to live in? I can work from there just as well as I can from here, and I'd still be here every day.'

'It's a virtual ruin,' Luke said. 'Though I agree it's in a splendid position.' He frowned a little and looked quizzically at his nephew.

472

'Alone? Would you live there alone? Or is there something you're not telling me?' He laughed when he saw Howard raise his eyebrows. 'There is! Are you contemplating marriage?'

'I might be.' Howard grinned. 'More than possibly, in fact. But not yet, not until I have a home to offer.'

'Which you haven't at the moment. I see. Well, in that case I can't stand between a man and his heart's desire. Do we know the lady?'

'Mm, yes. But I can't reveal her name as she doesn't know yet. And she might not have me,' Howard said wryly.

'She doesn't know? You mean you haven't asked her?'

'I haven't. I rather think that she regards me as the joker in the pack. I'm quite sure she doesn't take me seriously at all.'

The following day, after they had finished their midday meal, Howard announced that he was going to ride over to High Ridge House.

'That's nice,' Polly said, and asked eagerly, 'would you like any company?'

'Don't mind.' Howard caught Luke's quizzical glance, which he chose to ignore. 'Would you like to come?'

'Yes, please.' Polly looked at Anna for approval. 'Unless . . .'

'I'm going to have a lie down, Polly,' Anna

said. 'You go. You've worked so hard these last few days you deserve some time to relax. I wondered if later you'd perhaps help me draw up a list of requirements for when we advertise for a new housekeeper.'

Polly's face fell. 'Yes,' she said in a small voice. 'Of course. I think I know just 'sort of person you need.'

She hasn't thought of me for the post, Polly thought as she ran upstairs to change. And yet she won't expect me to stay here if Rosalie goes to her father's. I'm nothing to them, even though they are always so nice to me.

She gave a deep sigh. Just when I think that life is grand and I'm enjoying myself. I've got a horse and a dog and a little lamb, except that I don't know where Louis is now he's out on the moor; and I've got Rosalie and Howard, almost a family. Suddenly, it struck her with such force that if she had to leave she might never see them again.

'Come on, then. What's up?' Howard had already saddled up Hero when she joined him at the stables. 'Lost a tanner?'

She shook her head and kept her mouth buttoned up. She was almost afraid to speak in case she blubbered.

Howard glanced at her but didn't ask any further questions as they rode up on to the moor. There was the sound of sporadic shooting

474

from Sleights Moor, the cackle of grouse and the call of golden plover, but even the occasional whistle of a train over at Grosmont barely disturbed the peace of the day.

They rode on towards High Ridge House and Polly sighed deeply.

'So are you going to tell me?' Howard asked.

'What?' she mumbled. 'What's there to tell?'

'Why you're so miserable. Where's our merry Poll?' Howard frowned. 'You were all right this morning. What's changed?'

They slowed to a walk. 'It was just when—'

'When what?' he asked, leaning forward to see her face.

Polly took a breath. 'When Mrs Kingston asked me if I'd help her advertise for a house-keeper.'

'I'd have thought you'd be good at that. You're so practical.'

'Well, that's just it.' She turned an anguished face towards him. 'I was going to ask if I could be her housekeeper if Rosalie goes away, cos if she does – go away, I mean – I'd have to leave and I might never see any of you ever again.'

Polly began to cry, and Howard reined in. Dismounting, he turned to her and put out his arms to help her down.

'I'm sorry.' She wept against his rough

jacket. 'But I've been so happy here and I can't bear to go back to the life I once had. I just can't!'

Her hair was so soft, he thought as he rested his chin on her head, and it was lighter in colour, bleached by the sun, than it had been when she first came to live here. He recalled meeting her and Rosalie for the first time, at the inn near Hackness. Polly had had a red nose and looked completely bedraggled, and Amos had told him later how she'd fallen in a snow-filled ditch and thought it hilarious. In Amos's opinion she was way above the usual run of young women.

'She's a good 'un, that one, Mr Howard,' he had said. 'That she is.'

'I think you're wrong, Polly,' Howard said now, kissing her wet cheek. 'On two counts. First of all I don't think that Rosalie will go to live with her father.'

She looked up at him and sniffed, blinking away the tears which clung to her lashes. He dug in his breeches pocket, brought out a clean handkerchief and handed it to her. Polly blew her nose, loudly, and he smiled.

'And what was the other?' she said, darting a glance at him.

Still holding her, he looked down into her eyes. 'The other what?' he said vaguely, kissing her forehead.

Polly licked her lips. 'You said there were two counts.'

'Two counts?'

Polly laughed and hiccuped at the same time. She blew her nose again. 'You are an idiot,' she gulped. 'You said there were two counts why I shouldn't—' Tears filled her eyes again and she laughed and cried together. 'I can't remember now. Something about Mrs Kingston, and me leaving.'

'Oh yes,' he said, releasing her. 'Tell you what, let's go on up to the house and we'll both try to remember what it is that we've forgotten!'

He helped her mount, lifting her up by her waist, and then he sprang easily into his saddle.

'I'd like to learn to do that,' Polly said. 'Can you teach me?'

'Yes,' he said. 'Anything. Anything at all.'

They rode in silence the rest of the way, Polly giving the occasional sniff or taking a deep breath as if she'd been running. When they arrived, the descending sun was hitting the sandstone of the building, giving it a rosy glow.

'This place is so lovely,' Polly murmured. 'It ought to be lived in. It's surely a sin that it stands empty.'

'Rabbits and ravens,' he said. 'That's what I used to find here when I was a boy.'

They sat on the ground and looked down the valley. 'If I could have a wish . . .' Polly began.

'Yes? What would it be?' Howard looked at her. The sun was casting a glow over her and he wished that he was a painter like Sonny, so that he could capture this moment.

'Oh.' She shrugged and sighed. 'I don't think I should say. An old woman I once knew used to say be careful what you wish for.'

'You have to have wishes,' he protested. 'And dreams. What is life without them?'

'I never used to wish for anything but food in my belly and that Ma and me would allus have work so that we'd keep a roof over our heads.' Polly was pensive, her face sad. 'And these last six months I've had more food than I'd ever imagined I could eat, and good friends and a comfortable bed, and now,' she paused and her voice cracked, 'now there's a chance I might lose them.'

'It must have been hard for you, Polly,' he said softly.

'Harder than you think.' She kept her eyes on the panorama before her, etching it on to her mind. 'And although I don't want to forget that time, neither do I want to go back to it.'

'You won't have to, Polly,' he said, taking hold of her hand. He turned it over to look at her palm. Such a small hand, he thought, and no sign now in the softness of her skin to show the hardship she had endured.

Without thinking, he kissed her fingers, letting his lips linger, and she turned and gazed at him, a look of bewilderment on her face.

'Kissing it better.' He smiled at her, and then, with a sigh, he stretched out on the heather and put his hands behind his head and closed his eyes. Polly continued to gaze at him and wondered why she should feel so strange: so filled with hope and yet confused and somehow bewitched.

When she was in bed that night she pondered on Howard's reason for going to High Ridge House. He did nothing whilst he was there except look up at the walls and roof, noting the tiles that had broken away and then spread his gaze round the outside.

She drew her knees up high and hugged her arms round them, feeling comforted. 'You won't have to, Polly,' he'd said when she'd told him that she didn't want to go back to the life she had had. What did he mean? He hadn't enlarged on it. But she'd believed him, and then he'd kissed her fingers, and – and before that he kissed me when I cried.

She touched her cheek and ran her fingers down to her lips, and remembered that she had felt that she would have liked him to kiss her mouth too. Which was ridiculous, because he was her good friend Howard who wouldn't dream of doing such a thing.

Polly smiled and pulled the blanket over her head and hunched into herself. But, she thought, I wish that he had.

CHAPTER FORTY-TWO

Rosalie travelled back to Scarborough with mixed emotions. Sonny had taken her to the railway station and seen her on to the train. He hadn't said much as she stepped on, except that he wouldn't promise to write.

'May I write to you?' she'd asked.

He'd shaken his head. 'I don't know where I'll be, but I'll come back in the spring. I might be a rich man or still a poor one.' He'd smiled as he said it.

'It won't matter,' she said wistfully.

'It might.' He'd tapped his finger to his lips. 'Don't make any promises, Rosalie. Not yet.'

Did he know, she thought as the train steamed away from the platform. Did he know that I was going to say that I would be waiting for him?

She felt both happy and sad. Happy because she knew that she had claimed his heart, but sad that she wouldn't see him over the long winter. She was worried, too. What if her father insisted that she go to Aldershot?

Arriving in Scarborough, she took a hansom to Mrs Carleton's house. Holiday visitors were strolling the streets or walking on the sands. Children and adults were paddling at the water's edge, and she thought that she would like to do that. She felt curiously uninhibited and decided that she would buy a bathing costume and swim in the sea. Polly would like to do that, she thought as the cab drew up at the house. She would think it great fun.

Mrs Carleton's maid took her through to the sitting room where Mrs Carleton was enjoying a glass of sherry as she sat in the window which overlooked the gardens in the square and watched people pass by.

'This is one of my favourite occupations,' she told Rosalie, inviting her to join her whilst her maid prepared tea. 'I sit here and wonder where all these people have come from. I can tell the residents from the visitors: the visitors saunter along as if they've all the time in the world, whilst the residents always walk very purposefully. Now, my dear, there seems to have been a misunderstanding. Not on my part, I hasten to say, but on Clementina's. She has already gone home, taking the pony and trap. My housekeeper told her that you would be returning, but' – she lifted her hands in mock despair – 'she is such an impulsive young woman.'

'Oh!' Rosalie exclaimed. 'So what am I to do?'

'You must stay with me, of course! I should love to have your company. Perhaps you'd like to write to Howard and he will come for you when you're ready to leave.' She gave her an endearing smile. 'But there's no hurry. No hurry at all.'

'Why do you think Clementina made such a hasty decision?' Rosalie asked. 'I thought she usually stayed for the whole summer.'

'So she does.' Mrs Carleton looked thoughtful. 'But a letter came for her on the day after you called and she was packed within the hour. She said she couldn't wait for you but must go home immediately.'

'A letter from her father, perhaps?' Rosalie suggested.

'Possibly,' Mrs Carleton agreed. 'I have never known her receive correspondence from anyone else.'

Rosalie hesitated. It wasn't her business to talk about Edwin, but she thought that if the letter was from Luke it must have been to tell Clemmie of Edwin's behaviour. That would certainly explain her hasty departure.

'I think he misses her,' Rosalie said, recalling that he had said that he wished Clemmie could have been at home for the shoot. She was sure he would not want his son's actions to become common knowledge, even though Mrs Carleton was family.

After an early supper, Mrs Carleton suggested a walk. It was still warm and sunny and she told Rosalie that there were great plans for Scarborough.

'It's already a lovely town, but we now have a wonderful Spa building. I can recall the old wells where people queued to drink the water, which I must add tastes quite disgusting, and though I am ready to concede that it might have health-giving properties, in my opinion listening to the music which is played in the new concert hall is far more beneficial to the health of body and soul than the waters ever were.'

As they promenaded, Mrs Carleton, who was dressed in dark brown figured silk and a brown and gold straw hat with a veil, nodded to some acquaintances and greeted several others. Occasionally she stopped to talk for a few minutes, introducing Rosalie as a friend of her granddaughter. When they reached the seats overlooking the sea they sat down to rest, and Rosalie admired the Italian style terraces and stone balustraded staircases of the Spa, the new bandstand and the floral beds.

'It's no wonder that Clementina likes to

come to Scarborough so often,' she remarked as she sipped lemonade. 'It's quite lovely, and although of course she loves being with you she must enjoy the company of other young people.'

She had noticed the young women lagging behind their chaperons in small groups and intentionally or not attracting the attention of young men, who tipped their hats or gave exaggerated bows as they passed them, causing the young ladies to giggle into their handkerchiefs.

Mrs Carleton agreed. 'I believe she thinks that she might find her own true love here in this romantic setting, but Clementina will find someone more suitable at home. She doesn't realize it now, but eventually she'll be happier in the country with her dogs and her horses.'

She turned to Rosalie. 'And what of you, my dear? Have you any plans for your future?'

Rosalie found herself confiding in Mrs Carleton. Had Polly been there she would have opened her heart to her, but in her absence this warm and friendly grandmother, who was open and logical and wise to a fault, didn't talk down to her as another older woman might have done, but listened quietly and seemed to remember what it was like to be young.

'So I shall have my legacy at eighteen,'

Rosalie concluded. 'It will mean an income of fifty pounds a year until I'm twenty-one, and then I shall receive the capital. It will be enough to give me some freedom, but not so much that I will be considered a good catch. Not that I think,' she added hastily, 'that Mr Blake would be so mercenary.'

'Has this admirable fellow given you any cause to think he wishes to marry you?'

Rosalie hesitated. Sonny had not said it in so many words. 'I believe he thinks I'm too young to know my mind.' She swallowed and thought how bereft she had felt as the train pulled away and he hadn't given her any reason to think he would ask her father for her hand. 'At our last meeting he said that I mustn't make any promises. He believes that women should be allowed the freedom to express themselves and make their own decisions regarding their lives. He is,' she added, 'a most unconventional man.'

'I hope, then, that Mr Blake has considered that this year has been full of changes for you,' Mrs Carleton said. 'You lost your mother, I understand, and then almost immediately went to live on the moors with an uncle you didn't know. You have been living a life totally unlike anything you had known before. He must have realized that you were very vulnerable and,' she paused and looked over the rolling, crashing waves below them, 'therefore could have become attached to anyone who seemed to be sympathetic, supportive or affectionate. Any man worth his salt who has thought of these things *would* wait. He's giving you time to consider and reflect, and also giving you a chance to meet other young men.' She patted Rosalie's arm. 'That's my opinion,' she said. 'I might be totally wrong. And,' she sighed, 'I'm probably not the right person to give advice to anyone.'

Rosalie looked at her; she seemed so content within herself. 'Why?' she asked. 'You seem to be so wise.'

'Because, my dear,' Mrs Carleton raised her head, and gazing through the veil of her hat seemed to be contemplating neither sea nor sky but some other place which only she knew, 'I am a complete Romantic. When I was seventeen I ran away with the man I loved. Whom I have always loved, even though he has now gone from me. Were I to advise you, I would say what others would regard as totally unwise. I would say that when your Mr Blake returns, if you feel the same as you do now, you should follow your heart.'

Two days later, as Rosalie and Mrs Carleton were sitting in the window drinking coffee, they saw Howard and Polly arrive in the trap.

'Oh, my dears.' Mrs Carleton put out her hand to greet them. 'I'm not ready to relinquish my companion just yet.'

Howard bent to kiss her cheek and Polly dipped her knee. 'We haven't come to take her back,' Howard said. 'We've come to stay, if that's all right?'

'Oh, yes! How lovely,' his grandmother exclaimed. 'What a treat! You are usually too busy to come.'

'Clemmie rushed home because her father had written to tell her about Edwin.' He glanced at Rosalie, who gave a little shake of her head, and then back at his grandmother. 'I'll explain that in a moment,' he added. 'And then Polly received Rosalie's letter to say she had arrived in Scarborough.'

'And Mr Kingston said that Howard deserved a holiday and so did I,' Polly volunteered, 'and we should come to Scarborough to visit you. He said that you wouldn't mind,' she added as an afterthought.

'So you're both going to stay?' Mrs Carleton asked. 'How lovely,' she said again, when they both nodded. She rang for another pot of coffee.

'I hope it's not a bother to you, Mrs Carleton?' Polly said.

Mrs Carleton's eyes gleamed. 'Not a bother at all,' she said. 'And I can make such plans.'

'Grandmother!' Howard said in a warning voice.

She raised her eyebrows at him and assumed a haughty manner. 'Yes, Howard? I was going to say that we could go to a concert at the Spa, or perhaps these young ladies might like to take a walk on the sands? Or,' she continued, 'there are of course two bays at Scarborough, but to see the North Bay you must take a carriage ride and walk or else go up to the castle cliffs and look down at it.'

'Goodness,' Polly said. 'So much to do! How long may we stay?'

'Only until the day after tomorrow,' Howard interrupted. 'I have to get back. The sheep won't wait, but Clemmie needed time to be with her father, and he needed to be with her.'

That evening Mrs Carleton ordered a carriage to take them to the Spa to listen to a concert in the Gothic Saloon. Polly was enthralled once again. The wonderful music, and behind the music she could hear the sound of the sea, a gentle sighing as the waves kissed the sands.

I'm so happy, she thought. If there's nothing else in my life I shall always remember this.

After the concert was over they stood outside on the terrace and Howard ordered sherry for his grandmother and coffee for himself, Rosalie and Polly.

'Won't you join me in a glass of sherry, Howard?' his grandmother asked.

He said no, not just now, perhaps later when they were back at the house. 'Would anyone like a walk on the sands?' he asked. 'Look how white they are, bleached by the moon.'

'Silver,' Polly said. 'Silver sand.' She was filled with a strange excitement. 'And a silver sea; look how it glistens. I'd like to go down, please. Wouldn't you, Rosalie? Mrs Carleton?'

'Not for me, my dear. I'll sit here and watch you.'

'I won't,' Rosalie said. 'I'll stay here too, but tomorrow I shall buy a bathing costume and go in the water. But you go with Howard.'

Howard looked down at Polly, who was hurriedly finishing her coffee. 'Don't rush,' he said, amused. 'It won't go away. The sea is here for ever.'

There was a path down the cliff side and Howard took Polly's arm to guide her; she was perfectly capable of walking down herself, even though it was steep, but she didn't say so as she thought it was very noble of Howard to assist her as if she were a lady and not just a ragamuffin urchin used to doing everything for herself.

She took a deep breath when they reached the sands and then turned back to look up and wave to the dark figure she guessed to be Rosalie standing on the terrace looking down at them.

'This is so lovely,' she exclaimed. She linked her arm in Howard's as they walked across the damp sand. 'Do you know, I was just thinking back there, as I listened to 'music, that even if nothing else nice happened in my life, I'd have had enough already to last me for ever.'

Howard put his other hand over hers. 'I'm sure lots of other nice things will happen to you, Polly. All the good things will gravitate towards you, like bees to a flower.'

She looked sideways at him. 'I'd miss you if I had to go away,' she said. 'You know – if—'

'I know,' he interrupted. 'If Rosalie leaves. But you mustn't live your life round Rosalie. You've a life of your own to lead.'

'But I've so much to thank her for. I wouldn't be here having such a lovely time if it wasn't for her.'

'I realize that,' he said. 'But I'm talking about the future. Your future.' His fingers stroked her hand and she looked questioningly at him. 'Your future without Rosalie, I mean,' he said.

She stopped walking and gazed out at the sea. A huge moon had risen and was casting its light on the waves.

'Harvest moon,' he said vaguely, as if she had asked him a question about it. 'She won't

491

always be here. One day she'll go away and live her life without you.'

'The moon?' she asked softly.

'No! Rosalie!'

'If she does go away,' Polly murmured, 'then 'sensible thing would be for me to go back to Hull.'

'Why?' he asked sharply.

'Because I'd be with my own kind.' She paused. 'When I'm on 'moor I feel that I don't ever want to leave it, and yet I don't really belong there. I'm just a street lass. I should go back to 'town where I was born; to people who know me so I don't have to pretend to myself that I'm summat I'm not.'

He turned her round to face him. 'Polly, have you heard a word of what I've been saying?'

She looked up at him. The light from the moon was bleaching his fair hair so that it looked almost white, and she gazed at him with parted lips. He looks like a picture of an angel I once saw, she thought. But an angel he's not.

'Yes,' she whispered. 'I heard you.'

I know what you're saying, she thought. That I must live my life without Rosalie. Suddenly, without warning, she felt weepy and emotional. That I can do, but what I can't do, or at least don't want to do, is live my life without you.

*   *   *

Clemmie had sobbed in her father's arms when she arrived after a breakneck drive home. 'I always knew there was something wrong with Edwin,' she said. 'He was often unkind to me. He used to say I was ugly, and he was horrid to Howard. He used to encourage me to be nasty to him too, because he was jealous of him.'

'I didn't know,' Luke said. 'How blind I was.'

'Mama knew,' Clemmie said. 'She was fond of Howard, and tried to protect him, and that made Edwin even worse.'

'There's something else I want to tell you,' her father said. 'But it's good news; at least I hope you'll think it is. Come along.' He took her arm. 'Come and say hello to Anna and Elizabeth. They're waiting for you.'

Anna and her daughter were in the sitting room. Anna was sewing something small and white and Elizabeth had a book on her knee. Elizabeth got up from her chair when they entered the room and came to greet Clementina. She kissed her cheek and said shyly, 'I'm so pleased you've come home. You've been away such a long time.'

Clemmie blinked at this show of affection, and when Anna patted the seat beside her and asked her to come and sit down she did so, leaning over to kiss Anna's upturned cheek.

'We're so glad to see you back again, Clementina,' Anna said softly. 'We've missed you, and we want to hear all that you've been doing in Scarborough. And *we've* something to tell you.' She lifted up the garment she was sewing. 'Can you see what this is?'

Clemmie took it from her. 'It's so sweet. It's – it looks like a tiny nightgown.' She gazed at Anna, and then turned to Elizabeth, who was smiling gleefully. 'Is it?'

'It is,' Anna said. 'You and Elizabeth are going to have a sister or brother in the spring.'

'And Jonathan,' Elizabeth reminded her.

'Yes,' her mother said. 'And Edwin too.' Her gaze was concentrated on Clementina. 'Are you pleased?' she asked anxiously.

Clemmie let out a breath. 'Yes,' she said huskily, and a tear ran down her cheek. 'I am.' She took hold of Elizabeth's hand and gently squeezed it. 'Very pleased.'

CHAPTER FORTY-THREE

The winter began in November and was raw and cold. In December the snow began and soon lay thick on the ground. The road to the farm became almost impassable except on horseback or by the most intrepid of travellers.

"Difference for me,' Polly tramped down the moor after offering to help Howard and Amos look for sheep lost in the snow – they'd rescued one and found a dead one beside it – 'between here and town is that there's a blazing fire to come home to. Listen. I can hear . . . there.' She held up a finger. 'There's one.'

A plaintive bleat came from against a stone wall.

'Aye, you're right,' Amos said, and strode across the snow towards the wall with his spade across his shoulder. 'There's another over here.'

They rescued two more and shepherded

them closer to the house, then decided that they could do no more as darkness was drawing in. Most of the flock seemed to know when bad weather was coming and brought themselves down near the farm, but there were always some who became separated.

In another week it would be Christmas. The postman, who had battled through blizzard conditions to bring their letters, gave them the news that the queen's husband, Prince Albert, had died just a few days before, on the fourteenth of December. The postie sat in the kitchen warming his toes by the range and sipping hot tea and told them that the whole country would be in mourning and that the funeral would be on the twenty-third; that church bells would be muffled and ships' flags would be flown at half mast.

Polly and Rosalie had been dreading the anniversary of their mothers' deaths and this news gave the date an extra poignancy. All the ladies in the house wore dark clothing and Luke, Howard and Jonathan wore black arm-bands.

Rosalie received a short letter from her father, sending Christmas greetings and condolences in her mother's memory. She also received a letter from Sonny.

She opened it eagerly in the privacy of her room, but she could just as easily have opened it in company, for it told her merely that he had completed his commission for the countess, who in turn had recommended him to someone else, and he was now in Verona. *Such a romantic place*, he had written, *with beautiful buildings and architecture. There are splendid palaces and squares* – 'piazzas' he had put in brackets – *and it is a rich and prosperous town, which is why I cannot stay long and will return very soon to Florence, where I have rented a studio.*

'Verona,' she breathed. 'Home of Romeo and Juliet.' She chided herself for being starry-eyed and fanciful; but she was heartened by his last few words on a separate page. *Italy is a wonderful country, but it would be even lovelier if there were someone else here to share its beauty with me.*

She carefully folded that page and put it in a drawer, and then took the rest of the letter downstairs to read to Polly.

Since Edwin's departure, the atmosphere in the house had lightened; he was now undergoing medical treatment in a private institution near York. Luke had been to visit him and had found him much calmer. Clementina was friendlier than she had been and seemed excited about the new baby, due in March; she and Elizabeth had vied with each other in their sewing to add to the baby's layette. Rosalie too had done some embroidery and smocking, though she wisely drew back from contributing

497

unless she was asked, for as she confided to Polly it wasn't going to be her brother or sister to fuss over, but only a cousin.

They both spent Christmas Eve quietly, each of them mourning in her own way. 'It'll be hard when this babby comes,' Polly said. 'We're bound to be thinking on what might have been.' She gave a deep sigh. 'Except I know that if Ma – if my ma had given birth to a living bairn, we'd have been in dire straits. How would we have managed? We'd have finished up in 'workhouse, more'n likely.'

'I can't imagine what that would have been like,' Rosalie confessed. 'What a sheltered life I've lived, Polly. How could I have not known what was happening in my own town? It was meant to be that we met each other, and it was to each of us an advantage.'

Polly had agreed. Her former life and poverty were slowly fading in her memory, but she knew that she should always remember in order to savour the life she was living now.

On Christmas Day, after a huge dinner, Anna rested on the sofa, Clemmie, Elizabeth, Jonathan and Luke played cards, and Rosalie took out a book to read. Polly sat by the fire feeling restless. She needed something to do.

Howard was watching her. 'Would you like some fresh air, Polly? We could take the horses and ride. They need some exercise.'

'Yes, please. Rosalie?'

'Mm? What? Oh, no thank you. Too cold.'

Polly ran up to change and put on warm stockings and a woollen hat and scarf, then ran down again and took a thick padded coat from a downstairs cupboard.

Howard laughed when he saw her struggling into it. 'I'm pleased you're not bothered about the latest fashion, Polly.'

'I'm not,' she said, her voice muffled beneath the scarf. 'I don't know who this coat belongs to but it suits me fine.'

He turned up the collar so that it covered her ears. 'It was once mine. I hadn't the heart to get rid of it even when I outgrew it.'

'When you were a boy, you mean?'

'Yes. Luke bought it for me because I was always outside even when it was cold. It suits you.' He grinned. 'You can call it yours.'

The dogs were waiting eagerly by the door with their tails wagging, and raced down the steps as soon as they were let out.

They saddled up Polly's pony and Howard's mount, put Damon on a leading rein and set off across the moor, the dogs keeping pace with them. The sun was low but brilliant and they had to shield their eyes from the brightness of the snow, which was melting and showing rock and greenery beneath.

'Where shall we go?' Polly asked. 'We can't

be too long as it gets dark so early now.'

'As far as High Ridge House, then?' Howard said. 'That's about the right distance for us to be home before sunset.'

'Lovely,' Polly said. 'I really like 'view from up there.'

'So do I,' he agreed. 'My favourite.'

'Mine too,' Polly said as they trotted, the horses' hooves kicking up a flurry of snow. 'I often think – well, I wonder anyway – what it would be like to live up there. 'View would be different every day depending on 'season and 'weather.'

Howard nodded, but didn't say anything. He was concentrating on what he would say, exactly, when they reached the house.

They were warm by the time they got there, though the air through their nostrils felt sharp. The dogs sniffed about for rabbits and dug in the snow whilst they went inside with the three horses, who stamped and snorted vaporous breath and pushed against their shoulders.

'All right. All right,' Howard said, patting their necks. 'We'll be off in a minute. Polly, look over there.' He pointed towards a heap of boulders which the sun was causing to shine like glass. In front of the boulders a roe deer stood perfectly still, only its erect head slowly turning as it surveyed the scene, particularly the dogs, who it seemed hadn't seen it yet.

'Beautiful,' Polly breathed and gazed with her lips parted. 'Absolutely beautiful.'

She turned her head to speak to Howard and found him looking down at her.

'What?' she said, brushing her gloved hand across her nose. 'Have I got a red nose?'

He laughed. 'Yes, as a matter of fact.'

She sniffed. 'So have you,' she retorted, and lifted her fist to cuff him.

He caught hold of her wrist. 'I'm going to live here.'

'What?' Her forehead creased. 'When?'

'Soon. I'm going to start work on it in the spring. Fix the roof and then the walls. Get it ready for habitation.'

Polly swallowed and shook her head. 'Shan't see you so much then if you're going to live up here.' She bit her lip. 'Can I – erm – shall I be able to come and see you? Or . . . Will you be by yourself?' she added hurriedly, her cheeks pink, though not because of the cold.

'Depends.' He gave a shrug. 'Might be. Or not.'

'Oh,' she said in a small voice. 'Why are you coming here?'

'I think it's time to give Luke and Anna some breathing space to bring up their family, especially when they have a new addition.' He continued to look down at her as if he wanted her to say something.

501

'Do you think there are too many of us living there? Mebbe I should move out. I'm 'onny one that's not family.'

The thought of not being wanted made her feel cold with dread.

'But also,' he continued, avoiding her question, and still holding her hand, 'I've long wanted to have this place for my own. It was a boyhood dream, even though I was happy living at Nab Farm. But now,' he looked down the valley at the long shadows as the sun began its descent, 'now more than ever I want to set up here. I'll still work for Luke – this is his property and land – but he says I can have it to live in. To treat as mine.'

Polly looked away from him. The deer had gone, disappeared without her noticing. That's what happens, she thought. You just catch sight of something special and then suddenly it's gone. She gently nodded her head as she contemplated. But there we are. She sighed inwardly. I've seen it, which is better than not having seen it. Known something, which is better than not ever knowing.

'Polly. I'm speaking to you.' Howard put his other hand on her shoulder and turned her round. 'Look at me when I'm talking to you.'

'I didn't hear what you said.' She looked up at him and felt her mouth tremble. She'd still see him, of course. They'd still be pals, but, well, it wouldn't be enough. She'd got used to him being around. She'd miss their banter, the fun they had together, that was for certain.

'I said that I didn't have to be alone.' He cupped the palms of his hands on either side of her face. 'I would in fact rather have someone living with me. Someone who could make me laugh, who'd light up my life by being there.'

Polly blinked. She could feel tears gathering. 'Do you know somebody like that?' she asked huskily.

'I do,' he said, and bent his head to kiss her mouth. 'But whether she'd want somebody like me is a different matter, though perhaps it might make a difference if I told her I loved her; that I've loved her for nearly a twelve-month.'

Her eyes opened wide. 'And you've never said?'

Howard grinned and said, 'I thought she might have thought I was joking. So I waited.'

Polly gave herself a mental shake. 'So who is this idiot girl who doesn't know when a man loves her, whether he tells her or not? And does this man want to marry her, or – or what?'

Howard picked her up and swung her round and she put her arms round his waist and held on tight.

'Well, definitely not *or what*!' Howard

503

laughed. 'What ever would the neighbours think? So what do you say, Polly?'

She planted a kiss on his cheek. 'Yes. Please.'

They decided that they would wait until after the birth of Anna's baby before marrying. Luke had asked Polly if there was anyone she should ask for consent as she was still under twenty-one.

'Of course marriage is allowed at sixteen with a parent or guardian's permission,' he said, 'but—'

Polly shook her head. 'There's nobody,' she said. 'Nobody to say what I can or can't do. If we can find a parson to marry us,' she grinned happily, 'then it's all right.'

Rosalie was thrilled for them both, but in the privacy of her own room she was churning with anxiety. I won't lose Polly as a friend, I know that, but I'll be lonely without her. And, she thought wistfully, if Sonny doesn't return, what will I do? I do so want him to, and if he does and Papa objects then I'd run away with him if he asked me, just like Mrs Carleton said she did when she was young. But she was unsure of Sonny for he hadn't made any promises, except to say that he would come back.

In January Rosalie and Polly celebrated their eighteenth birthdays together and marvelled at how their lives had changed during the last year.

'I'm so *lucky*!' Polly said time and again and Rosalie agreed that they both were, but occasionally she saddled up Damon and went off on her own and Polly would come looking for her and find her gone.

'Why didn't you wait for me?' Polly asked once. 'I would have come too.' Seeing Rosalie's hesitation, she said, 'Just because I'm going to marry Howard doesn't mean that you're not my best friend ever.'

Rosalie looked wistful and said, 'I know, but I just needed to be on my own for a while.'

And then Polly chastised her for riding alone when the snow was still thick and the winds were icy, and reminded her of the time when they had become lost on the moor, even in the summer, after taking Dora to her parents' home.

In February they were beset by blizzards and thick snow which froze overnight. Icicles hung from gutters and water pipes and the men were kept busy bringing in logs for the fires and tending the animals. Jonathan was back at school and a new housekeeper had come to the farm to replace Mrs Moody. Anna was satisfied.

'I don't feel like an intruder,' she said, 'not as I did with Mrs Moody.'

She was blooming with health. Her skin was clear and her eyes were bright, and she said she felt as happy as she had ever been. She was a woman who thrived on being in the midst of a large family and was looking forward to being a mother again, despite the fact that it was fifteen years since the birth of her last child.

In March the thaw began. Lambing time was hectic but once more the moor was greening over and there was a constant bleat of sheep and the cackle of grouse and pheasant; primroses and cowslips were appearing in ditches and trees were throwing out fresh buds. After finishing his work on the farm Howard went up to High Ridge House to make plans. Polly went with him and sometimes Rosalie came too, though often she declined.

'I'm worried about her,' Polly confided to Howard one evening when they were alone. 'She isn't happy and I don't know what to do about it. I think that she thinks that Sonny won't come back.'

Howard smiled. 'And I think – in fact I *know* – that she's wrong. He will come. He always does.' He bent to kiss Polly's cheek. 'And he'll come for her, because he's besotted with her. But,' he warned her, 'he's not the sort of man who'll stay in one place. Not for him hearth and home and slippers by the fire. If Rosalie wants him she'll have to accept him for what he is.'

It was a few days later, when Luke had gone over to Grosmont and Amos was out on the moor with Howard, and Polly had ridden off to High Ridge House on her own because Rosalie hadn't wanted to go, that Anna began in labour.

'I'm sure it's not due yet,' she said weakly. 'But then perhaps it is; it's not exactly science, is it? There is no true way of telling, and it's such a long time since Elizabeth that I can't remember if I was early or late.'

Rosalie tried to recall what she had read in the book she had found in her father's study so long ago, but even that, she thought, hadn't made it exactly clear.

'We should send for the midwife, Aunt Anna,' she said firmly. 'Just in case.'

'Whom might we send? Howard, perhaps?' Anna grimaced. 'Yes, someone should go, please.'

'Howard's not here,' Rosalie whispered to Clemmie out in the hall. 'Nor is Amos. Shall I go? You can tell me where. Or would you rather fetch her?'

Clementina shook her head. 'I'd rather stay. Elizabeth is very nervous and I can help Anna upstairs to her room.'

It was true, she could, Rosalie thought. She

was a strong young woman, born and bred in the country, and being used to the births of puppies, kittens, lambs and calves she would be better able to cope than Rosalie was.

She gave Rosalie directions to the midwife's cottage on Howdale Moor. Rosalie wrapped a shawl round her shoulders, not stopping to put on a coat, and ran to the stable yard to ask the stable lad to bring out the trap and harness the pony.

'Hurry, please,' she said to him. 'And then go up on the moor and see if you can find Mr Howard or Amos and ask them to come back to the house immediately.'

Clementina had said it was a half-hour drive down to Howdale Moor and then another half-hour back again. 'Plenty of time,' Rosalie murmured as she gathered up the reins. 'Babies take ages to come.'

But as she set off on the narrow road she thought of her own mother who, although she hadn't thought of it before, she now surmised would have been about the same age as Anna.

She cracked the whip above the pony's head. '*Come on*,' she shrieked with a break in her voice. '*Come on!*'

CHAPTER FORTY-FOUR

The midwife must have been looking out of her window, for as Rosalie drove up to her door she came out with her shawl on and a basket over her arm.

'Is it for Mrs Kingston?' she called. 'She'll be due any time.'

'Yes,' Rosalie said. 'We think she's begun in labour.'

'Don't you know?' The woman climbed in the trap.

'Her pains are spasmodic,' Rosalie told her. 'Not regular.'

The woman, Mrs Shoesmith, pursed her lips and turned to look at Rosalie. 'Spasmodic! Well! Do you know much about it, miss?'

'No,' she said. 'Not really. Only from books.'

'Books!' Mrs Shoesmith snorted. 'Books is no good when you're giving birth.' She laughed heartily. ''Cept for propping up the bed!'

Rosalie urged on the pony. 'I'm sure

you're right,' she agreed. 'Nothing quite like experience.'

Mrs Shoesmith folded her arms across her bosom. 'I've got plenty o' that. Been delivering babbies for twenty years; what I don't know about it isn't worth knowing. Delivered both of Mrs Kingston's children when she was Mrs Radcliffe. Nivver thought she'd have any more. Let's pray that it'll be delivered safely.'

'Amen to that,' Rosalie murmured fervently.

'So who are you?' Mrs Shoesmith asked, holding on to her bonnet as they picked up speed on the bumpy road. 'Are you one of them nieces of Mr Kingston's? Like twins, I heard, though you're not.'

Rosalie nodded. 'Yes,' she said. 'We are alike.'

'And one of you's getting married to Mr Howard? That'll be a fine occasion. He's well liked, is Mr Howard.'

'Yes,' she murmured. 'But it's not me.'

'Nivver mind,' Mrs Shoesmith consoled her. 'Bonny lass like you; it won't be long afore some young farmer snaps you up.'

Rosalie sighed. But I don't want to be snapped up, she thought. I know who I want and he's not here.

They drove up the track to the house and Elizabeth, her skirts flying, came running down the steps towards them as they reached the entrance.

'Oh, be quick. Be quick!' she shrieked. 'The baby's coming!'

'What?' Mrs Shoesmith exclaimed. 'Already? Can't it wait?'

Elizabeth grabbed the midwife's arm and hauled her up the steps to the door. 'Please hurry,' she urged. 'It's almost here. I've been watching out for you from the window.'

She rushed them upstairs to her mother's room and as they reached the threshold they heard the wail of a newborn child. Mrs Shoesmith opened the door and they saw Clementina bent over the bed, her face flushed with pride and excitement, with a slippery squalling child in her arms. Anna lay in the bed looking exhausted.

'It's a boy!' Clemmie's voice was shrill as she proclaimed the news. 'We need scissors! To cut the cord! It was the one single thing I forgot to bring up.'

Rosalie stared open-mouthed. 'You delivered him, Clemmie? On your own?'

'Come now; let's take a look at him.' Mrs Shoesmith took charge, cut the cord in seconds, wiped the baby's eyes and mouth with a clean flannel and wrapped him in a cotton sheet taken from her basket. Then she handed him to Anna.

'A fine boy,' she confirmed. 'Well done, Mrs Kingston, and you too, Miss Clementina. Now,' she said. 'If you'll all disappear for ten minutes while I make the mother comfortable, and mebbe somebody will make a good pot o' tea, then mother and baby'll be ready to receive visitors, or even Mr Kingston if he's about?'

'Mrs Shoesmith!' Anna's face creased. She pressed her free hand against her belly. 'Help me!'

The midwife shooed them all out, and then turned to Clementina. 'You can stay, Miss Clemmie.'

As Rosalie closed the door behind her, she saw Mrs Shoesmith hand the newborn to Clemmie. Then the midwife turned to the bed and drew back the covers. Rosalie sat abruptly on the top stair and put her hand over her eyes.

'Please don't let her die,' she muttered. '*Please* don't let her die.'

Elizabeth sat next to her. 'What is it?' she pleaded. 'Mama's going to be all right, isn't she?' She prised Rosalie's fingers from her face, which was flooded with tears. 'Rosalie! She is, isn't she?'

Rosalie nodded and swallowed. 'Yes, of course—' She was interrupted by a triumphant shout from Anna, followed by the mewling cry of a baby. She stood up, her hand pressed to her mouth and Elizabeth clutching her arm.

The door opened and Clemmie stood there, still holding the baby, with a huge smile on her face.

'There's another,' she cried. 'A little girl! Twins!'

Rosalie stood on the steps of the house looking towards a ridge in the far distance where she could see a line of four riders. She gave a sigh of relief and satisfaction. Luke must have met Howard and Amos on the way back. She narrowed her eyes, which were still swollen from her tears. One of the riders was smaller than the others so that must be Polly on Hero.

I'll go and meet them, she thought, dashing down the steps. I'll tell Luke that he's a father again, but I won't say to how many!

There was no sign of the stable lad so she led Damon out to the mounting block. He was already wearing a bridle but no saddle, but as she was in a hurry and because she was now so much more confident with him, she sprang on to his back and gripping hard with her knees trotted out of the yard and down the track. As she crossed the moor she urged Damon on to a canter and waved her arm to the riders in the distance. Her hair came out of its coil and streamed free over her shoulders and she lost her shawl but didn't stop for it.

A sense of exhilaration came over her as she felt the wind in her face and hair and the pounding of the animal beneath her as they raced on, and then she slowed the horse as the riders came nearer and their figures became recognizable. Luke and Polly, side by side with Howard. But not Amos! Amos was heavily built and rode a powerful muscular Cleveland Bay. This rider was tall but slimmer and rode a cob which looked to be too small for him. A hired hack, perhaps? Sonny!

She waited, and then wheeled round to join them. 'Uncle Luke!' she called, and only he saw her radiant but tremulous smile. 'Hurry home!'

He gazed at her for a second, saying nothing, and then digging his heels into his mount's flanks set off at a gallop.

'Sonny!' she greeted him. 'Hello.' Then she turned to Polly and Howard, who were looking at her expectantly. She started to speak but as she did so the emotion of the morning and the moment was too much for her. She put her hands over her face and began to sob.

They all dismounted. Howard and Sonny lifted her down and Polly pulled at her sleeve.

'What?' Polly said in a choked voice. 'Rosalie! What? Tell us, for God's sake!'

Rosalie's shoulders shook but she took her

hands away from her face and they saw that she was both weeping and laughing.

'Twins,' she cried. 'A boy and a girl.' She began to cry again and could hardly speak. 'And mother and babies are doing well.'

When they arrived back at the house they'd paired off, Howard and Polly leading the way and Rosalie and Sonny following behind. Luke was upstairs but they heard the boom of his laugh and a few minutes later he came to the top of the stairs. He put out his arms as if to embrace them all.

'Twins!' he bellowed. 'A boy and a girl! And my clever darling Clemmie delivered one of them before the midwife got here.'

Polly looked at Rosalie who nodded. 'She did,' she whispered. 'She was incredible.'

No one had eaten dinner that day and Luke ordered as much food as it was possible to bring to the table. He brought wine from the cellar and insisted that they all hurry to wash their hands and faces, but not to change. They would celebrate the safe arrival and deliverance just as they were.

The babies were inspected after the meal had been eaten, and then Anna was left to rest with the twins in a cradle by her side. Luke went up to sit with her and Clemmie and Elizabeth sat in a corner of the sitting room with pencils and notepads writing down names that they thought would be suitable for the new arrivals.

'I need to stretch my legs.' Sonny glanced at Rosalie. 'Anyone like to walk?'

Polly shook her head. 'No, thanks. I've been out all day.'

Howard was already asleep in a chair by the hearth.

'Yes, I'll come,' Rosalie said. 'I'm so wound up after the excitement of the day that I can't settle.'

She went to fetch a shawl to replace the one that was lost on the moor. Her hair was still loose on her shoulders, for although she had brushed it she hadn't coiled it in her neck in her usual manner.

'I came back, you see.' Sonny held her hand as they walked up the hill at the back of the house. 'A little bird told me that you had some doubts.'

'Polly,' she said.

He shook his head. 'Howard. I'm going back,' he added softly. 'The portraits have led to another commission.'

He drew her near to him and stroking her hair he wound a strand round his finger. 'There's more work for me in Italy than there will ever be in England. I can earn some kind of living there.'

Rosalie shivered. A wind was getting up and the sun was slowly sinking, casting a deep red flush over the moor. The end of the day, she sighed. A day which has brought new life, but what does it mean for me? I feel as if time is suspended, as if it's waiting for something else to happen; which is ridiculous, she chided herself, because time is abstract and unsubstantial until we use it or fill it or waste it. And what am I waiting for?

'I asked you once before.' She bent her head and spoke in a low voice. 'And I'm asking you again. Take me with you.'

A flicker of a smile crossed his face. 'And I believe I said then that I'm just a poor painter and only earn enough for myself to live on.'

Rosalie looked up at him. 'Do I have to beg? If you don't love me, then say so and I'll never see you again!'

He put his arms round her waist and kissed the top of her head. 'Never seeing you again would be too much to bear. And I do love you.'

'Well then?' Tears gathered and spilled. 'Take me with you.'

'And live on your allowance?'

'Yes,' she said. 'Yes. It isn't much, but it's yours.'

'I'll be a kept man!' he joked. Then he stroked her face. 'I've written to your father.'

'What?'

He nodded. 'I wrote asking for his permission to call on you, pay court to you and marry you.'

She started to laugh, and then to weep. 'You brute! Making me beg!'

'I needed to be sure,' he whispered in her ear.

'And what did Papa say? Not that it matters, because I've already decided that I'll run away if he objects.'

'Run away? From me?'

'*With* you!' She wiped her eyes. 'But what did he say?'

They started to walk on again up towards the summit. 'A rather strange short letter, but he said that I could call on you. He said he was re-evaluating his circumstances and that he'd write to you shortly with his answer.'

She shook her head. 'He hasn't. When did he write to you?'

'Oh,' he said vaguely, 'two weeks ago?'

'He was always negligent over writing letters,' she said, 'but I wonder what he meant by re-evaluating his circumstances?'

Sonny didn't reply, but turned her round so that they were looking over Nab Farm, nestling halfway down the hill. It seemed so calm and peaceful, no one could have guessed at the dramatic, critical, happy and significant

518

scenes that had been played behind those
sturdy, resilient walls.

They kept their secret to themselves although
Polly kept probing and Rosalie kept deflecting,
until two days later a letter came from Rosalie's
father. She and Sonny went outside in the
sunshine and sat on a seat under a window.

My dearest daughter [she read],

Forgive me for not having written
to you for a considerable time, but my
circumstances have been such that my
thoughts I regret to say have been with my
own problems, and I was unaware that you
were contemplating a suitor.

I will tell you first of the decisions I
have made for my own life and then of my
thoughts on the proposal regarding yours.

To my dismay, Mrs Sherwood has
declared that she will not marry me after
all; that being the wife of another soldier is
not something she wishes to embark upon
and she has now left Aldershot to live with
her mother. I have therefore decided that
I will concentrate all my energy into my
military life, and accordingly will travel
abroad to wherever I am needed to fight for
my country.

There will therefore, alas, be no
permanent home for you here. Which

brings me to the proposal I have received from Mr Sebastian Blake, who says he met me at Luke's wedding, although I cannot recall him, and that he wishes to pay court to you with a view to marriage.

In view of my changed circumstances I can only say that if you feel fondly towards him, and if he can offer you more affection as a husband than I, regrettably, have done as a father, you should accept him.

I understand that he is a man of independent means and that you will be comfortably established, which is what I wish for you more than anything, although his chosen career is not one that I can comprehend.

I shall shortly be leaving the country with my regiment, but you know that you can always rely on your uncle to give you sound advice. He was always wiser in matters of the heart than I ever was.

I remain always, my dear Rosalie, your affectionate father,

Mark Kingston.

He had put in a postscript:

I called to see Benjamin on a brief visit to Hull. My intention was to call on you at Nab Farm and bring Mrs Sherwood to meet you; regrettably it was during our visit that she had a change of heart and I therefore escorted her back to Aldershot. I stayed one night at the house and left behind a small gift I had bought for you. In my haste I forgot to pack it or post it. If you should return to the house before it is sold, you will find it there. Just a small token of my affection. I recall that you once were fond of blue.

Papa.

Rosalie put down the letter. She felt full of remorse. 'I misjudged him,' she said bleakly. 'How could I have done so? He means well. Poor Papa!'

She turned to Sonny and smiled. She had her father's blessing, at least. 'I wonder why he thought you were a man of independent means.'

'Erm, well, perhaps because of what I told him.'

Rosalie frowned. 'Which was?'

'Because of a legacy—'

She gasped. 'But it's only fifty pounds a year.'

'What is?' Polly and Howard came down the steps towards them. 'What's onny fifty pounds?' Polly repeated.

'My legacy,' Rosalie explained.

'Sounds like a lot o' money to me,' Polly said sagely.

'No,' Sonny said. 'Not your legacy, Rosalie. Mine.'

They all turned to look at him and he shrugged his shoulders. 'I, erm, I forgot to tell you, Rosalie,' he said. 'Well, I didn't forget. I would have told you eventually. My aunt, who has been more than a mother to me throughout most of my life, died suddenly whilst I was in Italy. I came back earlier than planned to attend her funeral.'

'I'm so sorry,' Howard murmured. 'I know how fond you were of her.'

Sonny nodded. 'I'd been to see her before I left and she seemed to be very well.' His voice broke slightly as he spoke. 'She approved of what I was doing, and I told her about Rosalie. After the funeral I was summoned by her lawyer for the reading of the will.' He gave a wry smile. 'My mother was there – my birth mother. She didn't know me, nor did she acknowledge me, and she'd come not to mourn her sister but in the hope that there'd be an inheritance for her. There wasn't.' He grinned. 'It was left to me.' He put his arm round Rosalie's shoulder. 'So I'm sorry, Rosalie, but if you marry me – and I hope that you will – you won't be a poor girl after all, but a moderately rich one.'

'Oh, no,' Rosalie said in mock despair, but

with mounting happiness. 'I was hoping to struggle. I thought that I could take advice from Polly.'

Polly came and gave her a hug. 'Not me,' she said, and going back to Howard stood on tiptoes and planted a loving kiss on his cheek. 'I'm as rich as Midas. I know nowt about poverty.'

'And will you still be able to paint, Sonny?' Howard asked his friend. 'I thought artists couldn't create unless they were living hand to mouth surrounded by the aura of penury!'

Sonny laughed and his gaze swept from Howard and Polly to Rosalie, who was sitting so close. 'Of course I will. I'll be the greatest painter ever! Didn't I say that I'd be taking my inspiration, my Muse, with me? If she will come?' he added softly, and bent to kiss her as she murmured, 'I will.'

THE LONG WALK HOME
by Valerie Wood

Young Mikey Quinn, scavenging on the
streets of Hull, is thrown into prison for
stealing a rabbit from the butcher. His chief
accuser, a well-to-do lawyer, has a daughter,
Eleanor, whom he badly mistreats. When
Mikey is released he finds that his mother
has died and his brothers taken into the
workhouse. Determined to find a better life
for his family, he walks all the way to
London to seek his fortune.

There he finds that the grim realities of
city life are even worse than they were in Hull,
and comes under the evil patronage of the
sinister Tully, first encountered when he was
in prison. But he also meets Eleanor again,
and between them they face the dangers
of London and gradually make a
new life for themselves. Together they
have to face journeying back to Hull – the
long walk home.

9780552156790

FALLEN ANGELS
by Valerie Wood

Lily Fowler, shunned by society, is alone,
frightened and heavily pregnant on the
streets of Hull. When her attempts to find
work prove futile, her only option is to work
as a madam in a brothel, where she finds
unexpected solace in the company of the
other women working there. Together they
strive to leave these miserable times behind.
Bound together by bonds far stronger than
normal friendship, these fallen angels bid
farewell to the slums, and to their very great
surprise, doors swing open, lost loves are
recovered and the happy endings that
none of them dared to dream of
begin to materialise.

9780552156592

NOBODY'S CHILD
by Valerie Wood

When Laura Page goes to the remote
Holderness village of Welwick, it is to try
to discover the mystery of her mother
Susannah's early life. Now a successful
businesswoman in Hull, Susannah never
speaks of her childhood, when she was
brought up with the terrible stigma of
bastardy – of being nobody's child.

Born into poverty, living in a tiny labourer's
cottage with her father, Susannah's mother
had caught the eye of the local landowner's
son. She was his one and only great love, but
when their daughter Susannah was born he
was unable to acknowledge Susannah as his
child. Instead he had to watch her growing up
in hardship. As the years passed and Laura in
her turn became curious about her mother's
past, would she ever discover the truth about
that far off family tragedy?

9780552152211

THE SONGBIRD
by Valerie Wood

Poppy Mazzini, born in Hull over her father's
grocery shop, lives up to the promise of her
fiery red hair and Italian ancestry. Her lovely
singing voice and good looks lead her to her
great ambition – to go on the stage and see
her name top of the bill. She becomes a music
hall star both in her native town and in the
south, after an appearance in the theatre at
Brighton – she even performs in Paris,
to tremendous acclaim.

But when her first love, an ambitious
shoemaker in her home town, becomes
engaged to someone else Poppy is devastated.
She disappears, believing that she will never
return to her life of stardom. But her fame
cannot be kept a secret . . .

9780552152204

THE KITCHEN MAID
by Valerie Wood

Jenny is determined to make her own way in the world, and she secures a job as the kitchen maid in a grand house in Beverley. She gradually gains the attention of Christy, the young master of the house, and they fall in love. But slowly their hopes and dreams turn to nightmares and culminate in a scandal which will force Jenny to leave Beverley and everything she knows.

Cast aside by her own family, and all alone in the world, Jenny has to rely on her ailing aunt Agnes, who was banished from the family many years before. Living with Agnes and her husband Stephen St John Laslett, she learns that Stephen's wealthy family have disowned him and they have to eke out a meagre living on their small farm.

Times are hard, and as Agnes grows weaker, she asks Stephen to make her an unusual promise, one that will affect the rest of Jenny's life. Jenny the kitchen maid becomes the mistress of Laslett Hall, and although she tries to fit in with the world that she now inhabits, she never forgets the words that the gypsy told her that one day she will return to where she was once happy – and there Jenny will find her true love.

9780552152174